MORE PRAISE FOR VICKI STIEFEL!

BODY PARTS

"Drawing inspiration from the likes of Mary Higgins Clark and Sue Grafton, Stiefel creates a tenacious but vulnerable heroine in Massachusetts homicide counselor Tally Whyte."

—Publishers Weekly

"An interesting read that concludes in an unexpected, dramatic fashion."
—RT BOOKreviews

"Stiefel has the psychological thriller down so well you might think she invented it. An original, brilliant novel of the human experience worthy of anything James M. Cain could have done."
—Crimestalker Casebook

"Tally Whyte is full of warmth and wit—and she'll keep you turning pages through this engrossing mystery thriller."
—Jan Brogan, author of A Confidential Source

ROAD RAGE

I pushed on my turn signal, so I could pull over until the storm passed. The rain sheeted across my windshield. The car felt hot and musky from my sweat and Penny's fur and overuse. The copper scent of congealed blood on the clothes I'd tossed in back grew stronger.

An explosion! Glass shattered, and I pulled to the right, anything to get away from the flying bullets. I punched the gas, just as another explosion hit. A spray of glass coated me from the backseat.

I pulled hard to the right, then forward, and—*smack!*—right into a metal guardrail. My whole body shook as the truck's frame shuddered.

I ducked down, peered all around. The rain was coming too fast for me to see much of anything.

Then I got hit from behind.

The truck slammed into the guardrail that was inches from coming apart. I stood on the brake and pushed the 4Runner into park. My arm was killing me. My side, too.

Another hit and the shriek of metal ripping.

Other *Leisure* books by Vicki Stiefel:

THE DEAD STONE
BODY PARTS

THE
GRIEF SHOP

VICKI STIEFEL

LEISURE BOOKS NEW YORK CITY

To Melissa, Mike, Sarah, and Summer.
For the great joy you have brought to my life.

A LEISURE BOOK®

September 2006

Published by

Dorchester Publishing Co., Inc.
200 Madison Avenue
New York, NY 10016

ISBN 0-8439-5743-3

The name "Leisure Books" and the stylized "L" with design are trademarks of Dorchester Publishing Co., Inc.

Printed in the United States of America.

Visit us on the web at www.dorchesterpub.com.

ACKNOWLEDGMENTS

Without the following people, I could never have written this book. Blame me for any errors, not them.

To my darling husband, Bill Tapply, for his invaluable critiques and even more invaluable love; to my beloved family—I could never, ever write these books without you: Blake and Ben and Sarah and Mike and Melissa; Mum T; Peter, Kathleen, and Summer.

To my dear friend, Donna Cautilli, whose spirit and homicide counseling experience continue to inspire me; Dr. Rick Cautilli, for sharing his exceptional medical expertise; Massachusetts State Police Detective Lieutenant Richard D. Lauria, for his invaluable insight and assistance; Massachusetts State Police Detective Lieutenant Paul Litalien for his amazing Crime Scene Services aid; the members of the Massachusetts State Police Canine Corps, both human and canine, who enable Penny to continue her work in my books; the MEs, Crime Scene Services teams and support staff of the Office of the Massachusetts Chief Medical Examiner; Dave Badger of the Badger Funeral Home, who keeps me a truth-teller; Wanda Henry-Jenkins and Paul T. Clements, Ph.D. RN, whose work with Philadelphia's Grief Assistance Program is legend; Dr. Barbara Schildkrout, for her psychiatric expertise; Andrea Urban for keeping me shipshape.

To my fabulous vet, Dr. Tom Dowling, his assistants

Joby G., Sharon D., and his outstanding staff.

To the Bradys, John and Kim, for their crucial help with translations; to Karin Lorenz of Berlin, Germany, and Albert Fischer of The Netherlands for translating my dialogue into German that actually sounds like real German; to Danielle and Henry Pedreira for having Carmen's Spanish be real Spanish; to Andrew D. Zboray, Manager, Monadnock State Park, and Tara Mayo, Asst. Manager, Monadnock State Park, for answering myriad questions about the park and Grand Monadnock; to New Hampshire's exceptional state and municipal police officers for keeping Tally's NH adventures on track; to Jane Eklund for her assistance with newspaper speak.

To Kate Mattes of Kate's Mystery Books, Willard Williams of the Toadstool Bookshops, The Paper Store, John Garp of Epilog Select Books, and Debbie Tomes: A profound thanks to you and your staff for your support and enthusiasm for my work.

To Lisa Souza and Maggie Roe and Susan Gray because without their encouragement I couldn't write these novels.

To all the fabulous Hancockites who create a writing environment beyond compare; to Julie Warner, Carolyn Boiarsky, Saundra Pool, Dorothea Ham, Barbara Fitzgerald, and the five original Wannabes (D., Linda W., CJ, Pat and Suzanne), all of whom support my writing in myriad ways.

To my tireless critiquers—Barbara Shapiro, Bunny Frey, Tamar Hosansky, Pat Sparling, Jan Brogan; my amazing editor, Don D'Auria; and Dorchester's terrific public relations gal, Brianna Yamashita; and my agent, Peter Rubie.

I thank each and every one of you for helping me make this book a reality.

AUTHOR'S NOTE

No Massachusetts Grief Assistance Program exists within Boston's Office of the Chief Medical Examiner, whereas Philadelphia's Grief Assistance Program continues to work out of the Philadelphia Medical Examiner's Office. There are many grief assistance programs throughout the U.S., and they continue to do amazing work with the families of victims of violent death. I applaud them all. Please remember that Tally and her gang at MGAP exist in a world of fiction.

*In the depth of winter I finally learned
that within me there lay an invincible summer.*
—Albert Camus, 1913–1960

*When someone makes you angry,
walk a mile in his shoes. That way, you are a
mile away. And, you have his shoes.*
—Source Unknown

Chapter One

I hate going to the vet and Penny hates it worse than I do. I practically have to drag my three-legged former Canine Corps dog, leash taut, coaxing her all the way with doggie treats through the infirmary door. Then I feel guilty when I tug too hard and ...

But this time was different. This time, I was scared. Penny had a lump, a giant one that seemed to have sprung up overnight. The thing was round and hard and the size of a golf ball. It sat right on the knee joint of her front leg.

What if ...? No. My three-legged pooch had been through enough. This had to be nothing, a cyst, or from a cat scratch or an abscess.

My Penny couldn't live with two legs.

"C'mon, Pens," I said.

I turned the cold knob that led to Dr. Joby's waiting room. The large room smelled of piney woods, and the linoleum floor gleamed from the sun streaming through the high clerestory windows. Screw that. I wanted the day as gloomy as I felt.

I moved forward. Penny dug in her nails and didn't budge. Her chocolate eyes regarded me with profound sadness, a touch of guilt, and grim resolution.

"You like Dr. Joby, Pens. You do. She's associated with Angell Animal Medical Center right here in Boston. You know, the people who took care of you when your leg was …"

My voice trailed off to a whisper. Why was I saying these stupid things? *"Ke mne,"* I said in Czech. "Come."

She raised her head proudly and walked forward on her three legs.

Inside, we shared the room with two pugs and a Boston terrier whose rear end wagged like crazy at the sight of my huge German shepherd.

When I sat, the terrier stretched on his leash toward Penny. Oh, my—Pens and the terrier began sniffing and licking and bouncing in the typical doggie mating dance. I laughed out loud, as did the terrier's owner, a Waspy-looking fella in a tweed jacket. We shared a smile, and he beamed a come-on. He really was a good-looking guy.

Didn't matter. My curmudgeonly Maine sheriff, with his faint Buddha belly and bristly mustache, had it all over Mr. Terrier. Mr. Terrier's smile widened. Good God, he winked!

"Tally?" said the vet's assistant. "We're ready for Penny."

I inhaled deep and exhaled long and slow. *Please let her be okay.* Then we followed.

Dr. Beth Joby scooched in front of my shivering dog.

"Hush." The doctor smiled at Penny. She brushed a wing of gray hair away from her face. "Good girl."

"How does she look, Beth?" I said.

Beth Joby nodded as she ran her hands down each of Penny's strong thighs. She pressed a gnarled hand to Penny's belly and lifted paws and examined teeth and shined a light on each eye. She scratched Penny behind the ears.

I couldn't stand it anymore. "The lump?" I sounded desperate.

"In time." The doctor closed her eyes and gently felt Penny's front stump, then her good leg, home of the lump. She twitched a frown. A tech entered with a tray of syringes. She held Penny, cooing at her, while the doctor drew a vial of blood. She took a second syringe and pulled a vial of fluid from the lump.

"Beth, I …" I'd run out of things to say.

Beth Joby raised a hand to the tech, who leaned down, and the doctor whispered into the tech's ear. The tech nodded.

I swallowed, but my parched throat caught, and I coughed. "Beth?" I croaked out.

The doctor massaged Penny between her shoulder blades, slapped her thighs, and stood. "She seems to be fine, Tally. We're just going to do an X-ray of that leg."

"Where the lump is."

The doctor nodded.

"Why?"

"Just makes sense."

"That's not saying why."

"No." She slipped Penny a treat. "I'm not sure I like what I'm feeling there."

"No?"

She shrugged. "It's most likely nothing, but you know what a cautious person I am."

I knew, but all I could think was that Beth Joby was lying to me, that Penny had a death sentence, that she would leave me—way too young—and I would … "How long will the X-ray take?"

"Maybe a half hour, forty-five minutes."

I whooshed out a breath. "I'll go in with her."

"You're too invested," she said. "We'll take care of her. You know we will."

I nodded. I'd said the same words to countless grieving parents of homicide victims as they viewed their loved one's body at The Grief Shop, aka the Office of the Chief Medical Examiner for Massachusetts and the place where I worked.

I knew all about grief. I *got* it. But I still wanted to go with Penny anyway. "Okay," I said. "The waiting room."

I crouched down and explained it all to Penny. Her eyes said she wished I'd stay with her. I hugged her hard. "I'll just be outside."

The doctor hitched on Penny's leash and began to lead her out. Except Penny didn't budge.

"Come!" the doctor said.

Penny remained an oak planted on the linoleum.

Beth Joby twitched an exasperated smile. "I thought Penny knew English commands by now."

"She does," I said. "But she prefers her native Czech. That's what they used with her in the Canine Corps." I turned to Penny. *"Volno!"* I said. "Go ahead."

Penny looked back at me. I gave her another swift hug. She licked my ear, my cheek, my nose. "I love you, Pens," I whispered. *"Volno."*

Penny walked forward, and the tech closed the door behind her.

I flipped pages in some dog magazine, pretending I was interested, terrified for my beloved dog. Stupid. I was acting stupid. Overreacting, in fact.

Mr. Terrier was gone, thank heavens. The sun blazed in, and I slipped off my jacket. Of all April days for the weather to pretend it was June, I wished it wasn't this one.

They should be done with the X-rays by now. I checked my watch. Five minutes. It had only been five minutes.

I pulled out my cell phone to call Hank, tell him …

My phone chimed and the screen read "Office of the Chief Medical Examiner." The Grief Shop's call wasn't unexpected. The extension read "Massachusetts Grief Assistance Program," my bailiwick.

I'm MGAP's director, with a staff that's second to none.

Although we rent space at OCME, we are a private, non-profit organization. Our job is to aid the bereaved when their loved one is the victim of a homicide. We walk with them during the aftermath of their devastating loss, we counsel them—often for many, many years—and we also help them deal with more practical stuff, such as legal matters, the courts, the press and the cops.

Fewer than sixty professional homicide counselors exist in the United States. I'm proud to be one of them.

The phone chimed again. Gert, my assistant director, could handle it. So could Donna or any other staff member. I looked up and caught the receptionist staring. She knew what I did for a living, and her expression said she wondered if the call was another corpse.

Pretty much everyone found my career choice weird.

Another chime. Damn, the office again. I flipped open the phone. "Tally Whyte here."

"S'me," Gert said.

"Wassup? I'm with Penny at the vet's and—"

"Ya gotta come back. Now."

"You can handle it, Gertie. You can handle anything that I—"

"What's wrong with Penny?" she said, her voice an octave higher.

"Nothing. Not really. Just … procedure."

"You're lyin'," she said, her Brooklynese thickening. "You still gotta get your butt over here. We got a real problem."

"Believe me, Gert, you're up to any challenge."

"Mostly, I guess. But it's not MGAP. Something Twilight Zone's going on with OCME."

I started pacing. "I don't get it. What do you mean, Gert?"

"I dunno what I mean," she said. "We're in lockdown, like some prison. Nobody'll talk ta me. We got crime scene tape over the doors. Nobody's allowed to come in or leave. And the lobby's fillin' up like a cop convention."

"Where's Veda?"

"I dunno. Dr. Barrow isn't here. Nobody'll say squat. It's creepy. And we got some poor couple whose kid got knifed trapped here like sardines."

I looked at the receptionist, who held my eyes. "I will call you," she said. "The minute Penny is out of X-ray."

"Okay, Gert, I'm on my way."

The Grief Shop houses the administrative offices and operations for Massachusetts's medical examiner system.

We're on Albany Street in a bland, three-story brick building dwarfed by the campuses of Boston City Hospital, Boston University Medical Center, and Boston University Schools of Medicine, Dentistry, and Public Health. We're also smack at the crossroads of Boston's South End and Roxbury neighborhoods.

Medical pathologists, a forensic anthropologist, administrative staff, and an elite State Police Crime Scene Services unit work out of The Grief Shop, as does Chief Medical Examiner Dr. Veda Barrow, who also happens to be my foster mother.

The ME's office includes a forensic pathology center, a large and a small autopsy theater, the large cooler and a small decomp cooler, a trace evidence room, and MGAP's suite of rooms for family counseling and identifying human remains.

The Grief Shop sounds scientific and unemotional. That's only part of the story.

When I blew through OCME's doors, I met chaos. The lobby's pervasive calm was percolating with people milling about—some detectives and a bunch of Crime Scene Services guys. One of the MEs was racing around, white coat flapping. I didn't see Veda, who had to be out back where the real action of the ME's office took place.

In the twelve years I'd worked out of that office, I'd never seen anything like it.

I made it down to the hall to MGAP's offices, found the tearful couple with Gert, and offered them my office to make any calls they wished or arrangements for their deceased son. I left them in Gert's excellent hands.

I then skirted the lobby crowd and coded my way through the touch-pad-locked door into the recesses of the building.

The back corridor was bizarrely crowded, too. I spotted a hulk of a man in a rumpled blue suit—Sergeant Rob Kranak, the CSS officer in charge at OCME. He waved me over.

"What the hell is going on, Rob?" I said.

"We got a corpse."

"Gee, that's odd for the medical examiner's office."

"Yeah, well it is." He cocked his head, and I followed him to a bend in the corridor. He turned his back on the chaos and leaned toward me. "It's bad shit, Tal."

"So where's Veda?" I said. "She'll handle it."

"Who the fuck knows where our esteemed chief medical examiner is?" Kranak brushed a hand across his flattop. "She isn't here."

That bothered me. "She's always here. Whatever. What's with the odd body?"

"Nothing odd about her. She's in the cooler. What's odd is how she got here. One of the techs discovered her this morning."

"Discovered her?"

He rocked back on his heels. "Yup. She's an extra. We never logged her in, never saw her before. No toe tag. No record. No nothin'. Looks like something bad. From the signs, we're seeing suffocation, maybe drugs. Too early to tell."

"So you're saying a homicide, one who just appeared in our morgue?"

He nodded. "That's what I'm saying."

"Holy moly."

"It gets worse. The corpse is a kid."

Kranak's words goosebumped my arms. A murdered child was bad enough, but one who'd materialized at OCME by magic felt infinitely worse.

He shoved his hands deep into his pockets. "The damnedest thing. A little girl ... a kid ... someone just fuckin' noticed her this morning. I can't tell ya how much this sucks.... I've been in there for a couple hours, taking snaps and all sorts of samples, everything and anything. Never thought I'd see the day when I treated the cooler as a crime scene."

"I'd like to go in and see her," I said.

"Yup. Once Fogarty's outta there."

"What's El Creepo up to?"

Kranak's bloodhound eyes slid to the stainless steel door, behind which lay a nameless child on a gurney. "We couldn't reach Veda this morning. Fogarty's second in command, Tal. Accept it."

I snorted. "Never. Veda may be my foster mother, but I will never understand what quality she sees in him. How long's he been in there?"

"Ten minutes maybe." He grinned. "Get this. Fogarty's at some frou-frou brunch or other. He had a fit when I called. See, I didn't tell him exactly what was what. So he comes in all pissed off and the cameras got him with a puss on his face. He almost crapped his pants."

"Not nice, Rob."

He shrugged. "Yeah, well now he's lovin' it. Big smiles for the press, then looking all solemn about this little one that he could give a shit about. Look, soon as he's done, I'm gonna wrap it up in there. I'll get ya inside then. As soon as I'm set, they're gonna wheel her into the suite. So lemme tell ya about her."

I rested a hand on his arm. "Don't. You know I'd like to see her with fresh eyes. That's the best way."

What did she look like? White or black? Brown hair or blonde or red? Short or tall or in-between? Was she a child with a sense of humor or a serious soul? Did she want to be an astronaut or an artist? Was she … God, who would murder a child and stick her in the morgue? And *how* did he get her there?

Just then, the cooler door opened and Fogarty stormed out, pausing to give me a disapproving look. In his wake, another white-jacketed ME followed. Dr. Judy Ethridge, Fogarty's sycophant, who banked on his being the next Chief Medical Examiner for Massachusetts. I hoped not in my lifetime.

Kranak mouthed "come on," and we threaded our way through the dozen people crowding the door.

Fogarty turned. "Not her. Not now."

I started to spew words, but Kranak touched my shoulder and said "Yes, her. Tally has different eyes than we do, Fogarty."

And in we went.

Chapter Two

A faded pink blanket with satin trim wrapped the child's body like some sad birthday present. The small bundle on the steel gurney looked lonely. She was slightly askew, as if left in haste. I wanted to rest my hand on the blanket, to comfort her, but didn't dare. Not yet.

Crime scene tape formed a little cubicle around her space, so that no careless tech or ME would blunder into her.

The room was cold and lined with wrapped bodies on gurneys waiting for autopsies, and others—Jane and John Does—waiting for names. Each was cocooned in a body bag, maybe black, maybe white, or perhaps a blanket or sheet like our newest arrival.

I still wore my barn coat from my visit to the vet's, so the cold didn't bother me much. But what about her, that little girl, all tucked up in her pink blanket? Kranak handed me gloves, but before I put them on, I ran my fingers across the blanket's softness. A little scratchy. "I'd guess wool."

"We think so," he replied.

"Not that common anymore."

"No. I wrapped her back up so you could see."

And what was I seeing? A small form, swaddled like an infant in a blanket that appeared faded with time and many washings. I nodded, trying to understand. Kranak began to unwrap her.

I sucked in a breath. My heart squeezed as our mystery child's face emerged. Deep brown, straight hair. Bangs. Livid staining one side of what appeared to be a fair complexion. Blue lips. Asian eyes, lids closed. Prepubescent. Between nine and eleven years old, I judged.

"Oh, Rob. Who would kill this child? Who would abandon her here?"

He continued to unwrap her. "Dunno. Can't imagine."

"Neither can I." Her upper chest was livid, too. Odd. She was leggy, coltish, with no breasts or body hair. She was nude.

I found the child deeply upsetting. I almost turned away. I didn't view most victims anymore. Not like I used to do. Not while they were in the refrigerator. I found them naked and bereft and unbearably alone. My armor of detachment seemed to be crumbling year by year.

Yet for those homicide victims whose families I counseled, I forced myself to see and to understand what had been done to them. No surprise, a child was always the worst.

I peered up at Kranak. Like my Hank, Kranak wore a bushy mustache that half-covered his upper lip. He chewed the end, his eyes distant.

"Hey, Rob?" I said.

"Here. I'm here, Tal."

"I need all of you here for this." I returned to the little girl. "She looks well fed. Healthy."

Her mouth was open, and Kranak pulled her lips back from her teeth. "Braces."

"Someone cared for her," I said. "She certainly doesn't present like an abused child. No visible old bruises."

"They're good at hiding stuff," he said. "Once she's X-rayed, we'll know if she's got a history of broken bones."

"I'm not feeling any of that," I said.

"Me neither, which is why I wanted you to see her. Fogarty's sure she's been knocked around."

"Is he the one doing the post?" I asked.

"Insists on it."

"Damn. When he gets these ideas in his head, he fits his autopsy results to what's in his mind."

Kranak shook his head. "Somethin' tells me he won't. Not this time."

"I hope you're right."

I touched the child's hand with my gloved one. She'd passed beyond the full rigor stage. I rolled her as gently as possible toward me. Lividity stained her posterior, the backs of her calves, and the heels of her feet.

I tried picturing her position at death. I squeezed my eyes tight. All I saw was the child, alive, animated. *I'm so sorry, hon. God, I'm sorry.*

"Okay, Rob. I'm ready."

"One more thing." He leaned in close and uncurled her left hand.

Someone had written on her palm in black marker.

Sins of the Father, it said.

Back in my office, I hung my coat on the rack and slumped onto the couch. I closed my eyes and tried to go where that little girl had gone. I saw her smile, lips closed, embarrassed because of the braces. And hugged. Yes, hugged by her ... mom. I rubbed my fingers across my eyes. I saw a man hugging the mom, and the little girl hugging them both around their waists. A happy family.

Sins of the Father.

Was her death some sort of martyrdom? Was she paying for someone's sins? For her own? No. She was pure. Maybe that was the point. What sins was she paying for? Whose sins? Her biological father? A symbolic one?

Or perhaps the note was scribbled to divert the police.

Set them on the wrong track. Lead them down an illusory trail.

A knock at the door popped me from my reverie. I inhaled a deep breath, slapped my knees. "Come in."

Fogarty startled me when he breezed info my office. "Any idea where she is?"

I shook my head. He meant Veda. "I haven't talked to her today. A meeting, maybe?"

His brow furrowed. "No. Not that I'm aware of." He compressed his lips.

"You're worried?" I said, disturbed by Fogarty's atypical behavior. "What about her secretary? She must—"

"I checked. She has no idea."

His beeper blipped, and he removed it from his lab coat pocket and read the message. His frown deepened. "Find her."

I bristled, but before I could rip out a scathing retort, he was gone.

I sat back on the sofa, reached for Penny, found emptiness.

I dialed the vet, got a busy signal.

The disturbing thing about Fogarty's command wasn't the order, but the plea I'd seen in his eyes.

Where could Veda be?

I walked across the hall and into MGAP's central office. Gert raised a finger in hello even as she spoke in soothing tones on the phone. Donna was also on the phone, taking notes. I beelined to the coffee machine, poured a mug, and mouthed for Gert to come see me when she was through.

Again I dialed the vet, and this time the receptionist answered. Penny was resting comfortably after the X-rays. They'd had to give her some anesthesia to calm her down, and it would be at least two hours before it wore off. I could pick Penny up then. She had no word on the lump.

I inhaled a jittery breath. At least the news wasn't bad-bad. I couldn't bear losing Penny. She was only four, not old at all. She meant more to me than most humans.

I took another sip of Jazzy Joe as I slid behind my computer. I tapped out my impressions of the dead child, as well as my imaginings of her as a happy girl from a caring family.

I ran to the bathroom and returned to the computer. As I clicked "Save," I spotted the phone's red blinking light. Wouldn't you know someone had called while I'd been mere minutes out of the office. Mr. Murphy, hard at work. I pressed the button for my voice mail.

"This message is for Ms. Tally Whyte. You are listed as next of kin for Dr. Veda Barrow. Please come to Hawthorne Medical Center in Acton as soon as possible. Dr. Barrow is here."

Dear God, what could have happened to Veda?

I raced for my car.

I squeezed onto Storrow Drive and into the left lane. I cranked it, zoomed past Fresh Pond and jammed on the brakes at the Arlington light. The day had finally turned gray, and a giant raindrop splatted on my windshield. The light flashed green, and I again I revved the 4Runner as I drove madly toward Veda. What an awful message. Why hadn't they said what was wrong?

I called the hospital on my cell, but they would give me no information.

Cars jammed Route 2, but I was still able to weave through traffic to make headway toward Acton. The hospital wasn't far, but it wasn't near enough, either. Not nearly.

I punched out numbers for Gert, asked her to call the vet and to pick up Penny. I told her I had something I had to attend to, and I disconnected before she could grill me. I'd hear about that later, for sure, but I couldn't tell Gert, couldn't tell anybody I was on my way to a hospitalized Veda. At least not until I knew what the deal was.

I squeezed the steering wheel. Veda might be the Chief Medical Examiner for Massachusetts, but to me she was foster mother and best friend rolled into one beloved package. She was one of a handful of humans who trumped Penny.

I floored it past a lumbering Volvo. I couldn't think now; I just had to get there.

Thirty minutes later, I peeled off Route 2 in Acton and screeched into the hospital parking lot, scaring a flock of pigeons and a guy carrying a medical bag. I trotted across the tarmac and through the sliding doors of the emergency room. The lobby was empty except for a couple watching a game show on the high-perched TV. I panned my eyes across the room ... waiting area, cubicles for paperwork ... ahh ... I raced to the desk with an INFORMATION sign above it.

"I got a call about my mom, Dr. Veda Barrow. Can you find out where she is, please."

The woman put down her nail file. "She was admitted for ...?"

"I don't know." I ran my fingers across the smooth stone hanging from my neck and tried to bank the fire in my gut.

The woman pressed numbers, talked softly into the phone, smiled, nodded.

If she took one minute longer ...

"She's on the third floor," the woman said. "Around that corner, through the doors, then down the hall. The elevators will be on your right."

As the last words left her mouth, I flew.

I stared down at Veda, a diminutive woman with the life force of a titan. She was sleeping, a faint smile on her lips, the black hair she always wore up pinned atop her head. In a vinyl chair beside the bed, Veda's sister and the woman I called Aunt Bertha, slept.

Bertha was night to Veda's day, yet watching them both sleep, I saw more similarities than differences.

On the wheeled tray positioned across the bed, Veda's ever-present laptop hummed while a screensaver of morphing *Buffy the Vampire Slayer* images played. Her half-glasses, her Palm, a pen and paper, and a tube of lipstick—red, I'd bet—lay beside the computer. I smiled. That was the Veda I knew and loved.

A tall nurse in a Snoopy tunic leaned into the room and waved me over.

"I guess she was on a case, and had a fainting spell," the nurse said. "The flu, we think."

"Does she have a temperature?"

The Snoopy nurse checked the chart and nodded. "Not too bad. One hundred and one. We're giving her IV fluids to rehydrate her. Her potassium count was a little low, so we're giving her supplemental potassium, too. She should be fine in a day or so if we can get her to stop working like a crazy woman."

My pent-up fear broke, and for a minute all I could do was stand there fighting the dam of tears that wanted to burst. I loathed crying.

Thankyouthankyouthankyou, I said silently to the gods I wished I believed in. I thanked the nurse, too, who answered me with a warm smile. I sank into a vinyl chair. My eyes drifted shut.

"So this is the greeting I get?"

I opened my eyes. Veda was smiling at me as she polished her lips red. "Veda!" I smothered her in a huge hug. "You scared the hell out of me."

"You?" she said. "You? What is this? I haven't been in a hospital in forty years. And look where I wake up. Did you bring fresh clothes?"

I saw where she was heading and laughed. "No way are you leaving with a temperature. Hell, you're contagious!"

She shrugged. "I can recuperate at home."

"Not today you can't. Just stay here for another day. If you're better tomorrow, I'll come get you."

"Ach!"

"If not for yourself, for Bertha. Look at her."

Veda eyed her sister with a combination of humor and

concern. "She looks fragile, but she has the constitution of a goat."

"Goat?" Bertha straightened her housecoat and smoothed her gray hair. "Sister, you try my patience."

"You're not the only one, Bertha," I said.

Veda narrowed her eyes. "Tally, we must talk. Tom Fogarty phoned. He told me about that poor child they found in our refrigeration room. Our sanctum invaded. The *Sins of the Father*. What a foolish, showy allusion. Any news?"

I shook my head. "Nothing new that I'm aware of, Vede. It's pretty awful."

She sighed, nodded. "I loathe not being there. Now, I must ask—did you get that gun we have been discussing?"

"*Gun? We* haven't discussed any gun. You and Bertha talked, while I politely listened."

Bertha smiled and began to knit, and I knew she was paying absolutely no attention to my point of view. "Aunt Bertha, I am not getting a gun, no matter how much you two push me to do so."

Bertha wagged a finger at me. "Your job. You are not safe. Look what happened in Maine."

"Absolutely," Veda chimed in. "You have a predilection for getting into messes."

"Nice," I said. "Very nice. Not."

"Papa taught us," Bertha said. "We will teach you. No one will have to know."

"No. Nada. No way. End of discussion."

"For now," Veda said.

"I'm going to get some lunch," Bertha said. "I won't be gone long, sister."

After she left, Veda said, "She's driving me crazy. Fussing. It's enough to give me hives. So start packing me up, Tally."

"No way," I said. "You are not, dear Vede, coming home today."

"Yes," she said. "Today."

"At least let me talk to the doctor," I said.

She pushed herself up in bed. Her lips thinned, and I suspected she was in pain. "No need."

"Yes, need."

I scooted from the room, retuning in minutes to see Veda throwing up into a pan held by a nurse.

"Can I help?" I asked.

"By leaving!" she sputtered.

I did a U-turn, waited five, and then back I went.

Veda lay back, head on pillow, cheeks sunken, eyes closed. Her horrible frailty slammed my solar plexus. I couldn't remember seeing her so helpless, not for years and years.

"Vede? *Veda?*"

"What did the dammed doctor say?" she barked.

"Two days. You'll be much better and fit for travel."

A knock on the door, and in glided gallery owner Nick Wirth. He and Veda were both of an age and German-born. They'd been friends forever.

"Nick!" Veda said. "You devil!"

She beamed in a way I hadn't ever seen. Oh, *my.*

Nick went to kiss her, but she shooed him away. "Infectious," she said.

I could only stare. Good Lord, Veda was blushing like a schoolgirl, and it wasn't the fever.

"Tally," Veda said. "Look who's here, Nick!"

"Good to see you," I said.

Nick smiled. He was tall and handsome, and white wings highlighted his gorgeous brown hair. He wore his sixty-something years lightly, and his bow tie and wire rims and tweed jacket gave him a debonair professorial look. Easy to see what attracted Veda. But this blushing thing was definitely new.

"Tally Ho, my dear," he said in a voice smoky and rough from years of smoking Gauloises and drinking Scotch. "You look lovely as always."

"How's the gallery?"

"Marvelous. Even better than usual."

"Nick," Veda said. "Did you bring the art book I wanted to borrow?"

He slapped his thigh. "Darn, I forgot."

Veda's most saucy grin peeked out. "Maybe because it weighs so much?"

He smiled back. "Perhaps. Or maybe because I wish to share it with you in my lair."

Good God. *I* was about to blush. Fortunately for me, the talk turned chit-chatty, and when Nick left, I had to ask. "Vede, um, do you and Nick have a thing going?"

Her black eyes filled with stars. "Thing? Oh, Tal, I don't kiss and tell."

"No, really, Vede."

She began to cough, spitting up gobs of nastiness from her lungs.

I handed her the tissues. "I'll call the nurse." I went to press the buzzer, but her hand clamped around my wrist.

"No! Get an ambulance. Take me to Mass General."

I saw where she was going with that one. "No way. That's just because your buddies are mucky-mucks there, and you think they'll turn you loose. They won't. At least here, no one really gets that you're a big cheese. Anonymity is good. It'll give you time to rest, to recuperate. In town, you'll be swarmed by press and people from the office and the state house. Anybody and everybody who needs you."

Her coughing eased, and her black eyes flared, then softened. "*Ach.* I hate to admit it, but you, my dear Tally, are right."

"What do you mean you hate to admit it?" I grinned.

She chuckled. "As long as you come and visit. Just two days."

"Yup. If you're not better by then, I'll bring you home myself. Deal?"

"Deal." Her eyes sparked fire. "If not, Tally, I'll walk out of here on my own."

She waved me off as I reached to hug her good-bye. "Contagious," she barked.

"I don't give a hoot." I hugged her fiercely.

As I turned to leave, she awakened her computer and began tapping keys. On my way out the door, the lieutenant governor of the Commonwealth of Massachusetts brushed by me. "Veda, my dear!" he said.

Veda tossed me a wink before offering him a handshake.

Outside the hospital, I called the vet. The line took me to voice mail, and I hung up. The April day had again warmed, and although patches of dirty snow flecked the ground this far west of Boston, I tasted spring on my lips. My step lightened. Even with all that had gone wrong that day, my heart couldn't help lifting at the prospect of greening trees and light the color of saffron and the emergence of crocuses and forsythia.

But I was bothered. Veda looked lousy. I wasn't used to that. She was the one who always took care of me when I was sick. And, yes, I was a grown-up, and, no, we never see our mothers using grown-up eyes.

I tried the vet again, got voice mail again, and I left a message asking if the X-rays had been read.

I stepped into my 4Runner and pointed it toward OCME. I'd retrieve Penny from Gert, finish some paperwork, and head home.

I pushed Gert's extension on my cell. "Did you get her?" I asked. "How's she doing? She hates going to the vet."

A Bazooka bubble popped, then, "I don't have her."

Molecules stilled. "How come?"

"I was gonna go over and then the vet called. She wants to keep Penny overnight and do a biopsy."

I slipped into the left lane, took the Arlington turnoff, and drove to the vet's.

Chapter Three

Penny's large head lay on my lap. Her nose was cold, a good sign. She wasn't sick. I didn't sense it at all.

Dr. Joby's brow furrowed. "We're just being cautious, Tally. The X-ray was inconclusive. We need to gather more information."

"I understand the need for a biopsy. But that means more anesthesia, which is never good."

Dr. Joby folded her arms. "Penny's strong. She'll be fine."

"I know." I nuzzled my face close to Penny's and received a tongue bath in exchange. "And I can't bring her home tonight?"

"We'd rather you didn't. Better for her. Better for us. Safer."

Safer. Yes. I nodded. "You'll know more tomorrow."

The vet's assistant entered. She hunkered down and scratched Penny's head. I sighed. *"Volno,"* I said in Czech. "Go ahead." I gave her a final hug, repeated the command, and watched until the door closed behind her.

Dr. Beth Joby's eyes, a leafy green much like my own, darkened with concern. She was a round woman with a big heart. "It'll be seven to ten days, at least, until the biopsy results are back."

The waiting ... "When can I take her home."

The doctor smiled. "If all goes well, tomorrow afternoon, after she's slept off the anesthetic." She held out her sturdy hand, and I took it. "Me comforting you. Quite a role reversal, isn't it, Tal?"

Beth Joby's father was the victim of an unsolved hit-and-run. For several years, she'd been a member of one of my counseling groups for the families of homicide victims. "Yes, it is."

It was late, maybe four, when I walked through the doors of The Grief Shop. All I wanted was to crash at home, but I had paperwork to clear off my desk. Plus I wanted to see if they'd learned anything about the little girl who'd "appeared" in the refrigeration room.

OCME's usual tomblike silence had replaced that morning's earlier chaos. I coded myself into the back. Janey Doe wasn't in the large cooler.

I peered through the autopsy suites' windows, but saw only adults on the tables. Fogarty must have finished with her.

An ME rounded a corner, and I asked where they'd put Janey.

"The decomp room," he said.

I donned scrubs and a mask and scrunched my Medusa hair beneath the sterile cap. I tugged on latex gloves, then pulled open the smaller cooler's heavy door. The smell slapped me, and even with the loud whirring of the blowers meant to cleanse the air, my stomach flip-flopped.

The smell belonged to the floater who'd been hauled from the Charles minus half of his head. He lay on the table near the wall. Janey Doe lay to his right. She took up less than half the gurney on which she rested, and some gentle soul had covered her. I stepped toward her when I heard the door behind me whoosh open. I started to turn, and a blast of pain cracked my skull.

The floor reached up for me.

My shivering awakened me. Or maybe it was the screech of pain in my head, or the sweet, earthy smell of purification that slipped into my consciousness. I retched, stopped the bile. Sweat dotted my upper lip. I pushed myself up to one knee, hands pressed against the icy tile, staggered, scanned the room. Where was I? Why was I so cold? Had I fallen asleep with the heat turned down?

I rubbed my temples, trying to erase the throb in my head. The pain came from further back, and as I wove my fingers through my hair, I felt warmth and stickiness and an increasing tenderness. I pulled my fingers away. Red smeared the tips. Blood. Mine.

Cripes. What the …

I remembered it all. I flattened my back against the chilly wall, peered around the steel and tile room.

I saw no one. At least no one breathing.

My eyes jumped to the floater. The smell, of course. And the gurney with the little girl was …

There. There she was. I'd half expected it to be empty, but her petite form still rested beneath that comforting pink blanket.

I floundered to my knees. A rocket of pain blazed through my head. I wrapped my hands around the icy steel door lever and managed to pull myself up. My hands were half numb, my fingers spastic and stiff. I leaned on the door for support until I found my balance.

My body convulsed in a shiver. God, it was cold.

I again looked around, then walked to the inner refrigeration door and peered through the window. It was dark inside. I saw nothing.

What if he was still here, waiting for me to turn to leave? He'd open the door and ...

I blinked fast, trying to fight the throb in my head.

I had to open the door, push on the light. I wished the damned thing was outside the door, but it wasn't. It was inside.

I lifted the handle on the massive inner cooler door, the one inside the decomp room. The inner cubicle was like a meat locker and reserved for the most dangerous, toxic, or decomposed cases. A corpse that was long past its human form would wait there for an autopsy.

The room was empty.

I closed the door and turned to go, but I wanted to see the child again.

Why would someone hit me in the decomp room, if not for her?

I leaned on a gurney as I walked the few steps to little Janey Doe. I drew back the wool blanket and reached out to touch her. I stopped.

A lamb. Someone had laid a fuzzy beige lamb in the crook of little Janey's arm, so it looked like she was hugging it.

The sacrificial lamb, which represented Janey. *The sins of the father.* Who or what was the father?

I looked closer. The lamb was worn around the ears and feet and one ear was repaired with pink thread.

The child had something to hug.

I bent closer. The stitching and the worn ears and feet made the lamb appear old. Yet it looked immaculate. Perhaps recently cleaned.

I covered Janey and her lamb with the blanket. "Poor child. Who loved you so, but left you like this?"

"Ya gotta get stitches," Gert said as she dabbed some vile liquid on my head.

"Not a chance," I said. "Ouch! Dammit! Are you trying to kill me all over again?"

"You are being a baby," she said. "It's just antiseptic."

"It hurts like hell." The clock in my office read 6:30. "I've got to get going."

"Yeah? Really? Ya lucky I didn't have you patched up by one of the MEs."

"Oh, that would've been just peachy."

"Yeah, it woulda been." She scooched her rear end onto the corner of my desk and pulled the scissors from the pen mug.

"What are you going to do with those?" I said.

"You'll see."

"Dammit, Gert."

Her snip, snip boded ill for my hair.

"I'm gonna butterfly it with this Band-Aid," she said. "I've gotta hold it together with something. I was thinking superglue."

"You're a laugh riot, Gertie. What was it you just said about sarcasm?"

She blew a pink Bazooka bubble and I heard the pop as she slammed the Band-Aid down on my scalp.

"Ow! Shit!"

"It'll hurt like hell if you take it off, so don't!" she said. "Hey, looka who's here."

Kranak plowed into the office, his face a furious red, his unibrow a black caterpillar above angry eyes.

"You called him," I said to Gert.

"Yup." She waved from the doorway. "See ya later."

Kranak settled his large frame into my desk chair. He tented his fingers, resting his pursed lips on the tips, and made tsking sounds.

I downed four ibuprofen.

"Well?" was all he said.

"I'll write it all up and e-mail you," I said.

His expression told me that wouldn't cut it.

"You're just ticked because I got knocked on the head. I'm fine."

"Ticked?" His eyes darkened. "I'd like to wring your neck."

I gave up and recounted my misadventure in the cold room.

He phoned his CSS office down the hall, shotgunning orders to his men to seal off the room and do a thorough forensic shakedown, but to do it on the q.t. and keep a low profile.

He poured us both coffee and laced it with some bourbon from his pocket flask. It went down easy and softened the throbbing from the bowling ball atop my shoulders.

"You see the guy at all?" he asked.

"No," I said. "I don't even know if it was a guy or a woman. I smelled nothing. The floater's decomp odor obscured anything else. All I may have seen was a flash of blue."

"Scrubs?"

"I'm guessing." I took a sip from my mug, and the coffee-bourbon warmth infused my body. "You shouldn't drink, you know," I said. "Not with the diabetes."

He loosened his tie, unbuttoned his shirt collar's top button. "I can't give up everything, Tal."

"I know." I paused. Kranak's diabetes might kill him. Some days, when he took terrible risks, I tried to pretend his illness didn't exist.

"Our killer's a strange one, Rob," I continued. "He's feeding off remorse. Weighted down with it, in fact." I leaned back on the sofa. "He kills this child. Someone he knew? Maybe. And he can't stand burying her, say in the woods, or even leaving her body exposed. No. He's got to put her where he feels she'll be safe and found and cared for."

"Safe?" Kranak set down his coffee and took a straight shot from the flask of bourbon.

I closed my eyes. "Yes. Even with the autopsy, she's watched and protected here. In his mind, that's safety, I suspect."

"If we're lucky, the guy didn't clean the stuffed lamb so good."

I reached to scratch Penny, didn't find her, and looked around the room. Then I remembered where she was. Worry squeezed my heart.

"Tal?" Kranak said. "Something wrong?"

"No, um.... Nothing. I suspect you'll find that lamb to be especially clean. Let's not forget to return it to the little girl after CSS is done with it."

"Can't do that. You know it's evidence."

I did. "I wish we could comfort her."

"Me, too," he said. "Nobody's saying it, but this thing with the kid sure looks like an inside job."

"I know. Disturbing to think that someone who works in this building is a killer."

I brought home the file with notes about little Janey Doe that had been collected by Crime Scene Service. Kranak had asked me to process it so he could put my intuitive ideas into his forensic mix.

Kranak was unusual for CSS, in that he often said how the combination of forensics and intuition produced better results than one or the other alone. On my way home, I stopped to pick up a squishy white lamb. I brushed its fleece against my cheek. It was silky soft and had a sweet mouth and funny little nose. Janey Doe needed that lamb.

As I unlocked my apartment door, I realized I was crying.

Thoughts scattered as two immense, hairy paws slammed me on my shoulders. I laughed as I hugged Peanut like mad, not only thrilled to see the giant Irish wolfhound, but even happier to see that her owner and my lover had come down from Winsworth, Maine for a visit.

"Well if it isn't Sheriff Hank Cunningham!" I said. "Damn, but you're a good sight."

Our eyes met, and we both grinned.

"My turn." Hank slid the giant wolfhound off me and enfolded me in one of his marvelous grizzly hugs.

I hugged him back.

"Why were you crying?" he whispered in my ear, his voice rough with concern. "Can't remember when I've seen you cry."

"It's nothing. Just a case at work."

His hands roamed my shoulders and breasts, and I cupped his butt. His hardness pressed against me and he deepened our kiss.

God, he felt good.

His fingers threaded my hair, and I yelped "Shit!"

He cradled my face. "Now what?"

His tone of resignation was all too familiar. I laughed. He and Kranak were spiritual brothers, cops first and last, but they both worried about me—a grace I tried not to abuse.

I took his hand. "C'mon, I'll tell you all about it. After."

He nibbled my neck, then my cheek, then my lips. I explored his mouth with my tongue. My nipples tingled, and I grew wet and full.

"I've missed you," he whispered.

"Me, too."

We dozed for a bit, and when I awakened I licked his belly button and smiled. "It's good to have you here." We talked for a while about Penny and Veda. I'd swear he had more sympathy for my dog, but given his somewhat "lively" relationship with my foster mother, I understood.

"How long can you stay?" I asked.

He kissed my temple. "The usual. Three days."

I wished it were longer. "You're about the only person who could make me smile today."

"You mean me and my dog."

Peanut filled the foot of my bed, belly up, legs stretched in a blissfully ridiculous position.

"Oh, Peanut's a big part of the equation!" I sat up and scratched her behind the ears. "She misses Penny."

"Yeah," he said. "She'll be back tomorrow?"

"She'd better be, or I'm gonna go batso."

"Hard to believe those bugs dared attack Madame Veda." He kissed my throat. "You going to call her now?"

"Right now."

When I hung up, Hank crooked his finger for me to follow him.

"She sounds good," I said. "Recovering."

He nodded. "Her sister Bertha?"

"She's doing okay," I said. "When Bertha's Rock of Gibraltar sister gets shaky, she tends to fall apart. They both started harping on me about the gun thing again."

"You know my feelings on the subject. Don't. Period."

"I know. And I agree."

I rounded the corner and found Hank unloading an array of Chinese takeout boxes from the fridge. "Oh, yes!"

"I'd have gotten sushi, too, but I didn't know when you'd appear."

"That's cool. This looks scrumptious."

We dined on dim sum. I let Hank have the chicken feet, a taste I'd never acquired. I watched him eat. I loved his bushy red mustache and auburn hair and his face creased with wear. I never grew tired of his kind eyes or broad shoulders or crooked nose. I found his gentleness fascinating. I'd seen his ferocity in action and was amazed by his dual nature. He was so contained. Where had that come from? What had changed the outgoing boy I'd known as a kid?

"Hey, Tal, where'd you go?" he said.

"Nowhere, hon. Nowhere at all. This killer's scary, Hank. Your numbers are smaller in Maine, thank heavens, but after fifteen years with NYPD, you must have seen everything."

"Enough." He gathered up the dinner remains and brought them into the kitchen. On his return, he said. "More than enough."

"So think about this. The killer seems to come and go at will, which leads Kranak to believe he's a member of the ME's office."

He sat back down and pulled my back against his chest. "Why be so sure the person who left her there is the killer?"

"I'm not *sure*-sure. But I'm thinking they're one in the same."

"Sounds like he's playing with a sandwich short of a picnic."

"Probably. I believe he … she … is lugging a sackful of burdens." I told him about Janey Doe, and the "Sins of the Father" written on her hand.

"Whose father?" he said. "God? The killer's father? Or, maybe Janey Doe's father?"

"Or it could be subjective, rather than a more literal meaning. It *is* complex, and so much depends on us understanding the killer."

He leafed through the CSS report pages, often going back and rereading pieces of the documents.

"You're methodical," I said.

"I am." He didn't look up.

"You weren't like that as a kid."

"People change."

"Why?" I said.

"Not now, Tally." He scanned the final report page, and then closed the folder.

"I'm leaning toward a man," I said.

"Looking these over … not me," he said. "It feels like a woman's handiwork. Suffocation. The positioning. The care. The lamb. I read girl."

"I don't agree, but interesting. Back in a sec." In the kitchen, I dumped the empty boxes in the trash and washed the rosewood chopsticks Veda had given me one birthday.

Damn, I hated that she was in the hospital. She'd be out tomorrow, at the latest the next day. That was a good …

A surge of dizziness weakened my knees. I gripped the edge of the counter and waited for it to pass.

"Tal?" Hank called.

"Nothing. I, um, I think you'd better do the rest of the cleanup."

After cleaning the dishes, he took care of my wound and changed my bandage. The bump throbbed like hell. We finally lay in bed holding hands and watching a rerun of *Friends*. I smiled at what an unhip couple we were.

My eyes drifted closed, and I heard him don the earphones I'd gotten him so he could watch late-night TV while I slept.

As I began to doze, I raised his hand and brushed my lips across his fingers.

I wished he could stay forever.

Chapter Four

The following morning, I called first thing about Penny. Dr. Joby said she'd had a good night and their receptionist would call when they'd completed the biopsy. I hated this, just hated it.

Work amplified my feelings of malaise. I walked into our daily OCME staff meeting with dread. The place felt empty without Veda and her warmth and energy. Fogarty gave me a dirty look when I took my seat at the conference table. He'd already started, and was droning on about Janey Doe's killer and publicity, a theme we'd heard too often and loathed.

His voice became a bee buzzing in the background. I'd thought about the killer a lot last night, when I'd awakened at four A.M. with the TV still on and Hank snoring beside me. It had taken two hours to fall back asleep, and in that time I'd moved away from Janey Doe's killer belonging to the ME's office. Something was off. I couldn't place it yet, but I was confident it would emerge as I processed the chorus of facts gleaned by CSS.

I'd also created different scenarios for Janey's parents, and how MGAP would go about helping them through such a debilitating time.

And I'd worried about Penny, who ran through my dreams as well as my waking thoughts.

Fogarty slapped the table. "This should make you all perk up!" He paused, ever the drama queen. "You. All of you. Your DNA is being tested against DNA found on Janey Doe's gurney."

"Christ," muttered Kranak under his breath.

He'd told me earlier that he'd ordered the testing, except it was to be kept low key until the results were in.

Fogarty's smile slowly emerged from his salon-tanned face. "You are all suspects until then."

"What the fuck!" Kranak barked.

I could never figure the workings of Fogarty's mind, today less than ever. If a killer lurked inside OCME, why alert him?

"Do you have a problem, Sergeant Kranak?" Fogarty said.

"Yes, I have a problem, you dickhead." Kranak pushed himself to his feet, leaning forward, aggressive, chin thrust out.

Fogarty jerked back. "How dare you?"

"I dare, you preening pimp. Tell 'em to get lost."

Fogarty straightened his tie. "I agree. We've accomplished all that we needed to at this meeting. You're dismissed."

The staff filtered out slowly, some lingering in hopes of catching the upcoming confrontation.

I stayed behind, and remained silent and unnoticed by either man in hopes that I could stave off Kranak from throttling Fogarty.

Kranak shut the door behind the last staff member with such intense gentleness, I shivered. A river of testosterone flooded the room.

Fogarty bared his teeth. "You have balls, saying such a thing to me in front of my staff."

"They're not your fuckin' staff, and you're an asshole for telling 'em about the DNA. If it's one of them, we're fucked."

"Of course it's not one of them," Fogarty said. He looked away from Kranak, and I was pinned. "What are you still doing here, Tally Whyte?"

"Staying."

"Get out."

I shrugged. "Make me."

Fogarty snorted, and turned back to Kranak. He rubbed his forehead, and I glimpsed the weary man beneath the self-important exterior. "It's highly unlikely a member of our staff brought the child's body into OCME. Our people need to know we're on this. The whole incident has shaken them badly."

"They're not the only ones, Tom," I said to Fogarty. I looked at Kranak, who nodded. "My people are unnerved, too."

"The perp left her a cuddly lamb," Kranak said.

Fogarty lifted from his seat. "What!"

Kranak frowned. "He bonked Tally on the head—"

Fogarty's head snapped around. He narrowed his eyes. "You have nerve, going into the decomp cooler without my permiss—"

"Now isn't the time for tantrums, Tom," I said. "It's simple. I went into the room to see the child. He came at me from behind. When I woke up, he'd left a fuzzy lamb, a well-used one, tucked in her arm."

Fogarty's face flushed red. "I forbid—"

"Chill, man," Kranak said. "No one's forbidding anything. Tal's just helping out, like usual. We got the lamb."

"Her 'help' is useless." Fogarty stood. "She'll be written up for this. One more misadventure, Madame, and you can hightail it back to Maine and that juicy offer."

I sauntered from the room, making a point not to seem hurried. I wondered how Fogarty had found out about my job offer from Maine's chief medical examiner.

Fogarty was such a nasty man. He knew every button of mine to push. All my MGAP people had been at the meeting earlier, and I stopped at our central office to hear the buzz. No surprise, everyone was up in arms about Fogarty's DNA announcement, and Gert's Bazooka bubbles were being blown and popped machine-gun fast.

When I did a U-turn, my staff hollered at me to get back there. "In a sec," I said.

I grabbed the toy store bag from my office and headed down to see Janey Doe. If Fogarty spotted me, I'd just breeze on by looking purposeful.

I peered down at little Janey, who now seemed utterly alone without her lamb. I slipped the one I'd bought into the crook of her arm. Yes. Better. I took my time with her, doing what I'd hoped to do the previous day.

I held her hand. Someone had polished her nails a pretty violet. One nail was scraped of polish, I presumed by CSS so they could match the make. She appeared remarkably healthy, with full cheeks and shiny black hair. She had few scars and her ears were unpierced. Her lips had grayed. Her essence, gone.

Speak to me, little girl.

She remained silent. I saw only her open arms, begging for help.

I lifted the clipboard at the end of the gurney and read Fogarty's autopsy report. As of yet, he'd drawn no conclusion. And so we would wait and hope the lab tests would point the way.

After having my mouth swabbed for the DNA test, I returned to my office in hopes of a phone message from Veda or the vet. Nada. I slid behind my desk. My skull pulsed. Not that much fun getting bashed on the head.

I didn't know whom to call first—Veda or Hank. The vet said they'd call about Penny, and I was trying to be patient. Things were definitely not shaping up. The paperwork on my desk had begun resembling Mount Fuji. I read my to-do list and shuddered. The intercom bleeped.

"Yes?"

"Got us a live one, Tal," the desk sergeant said. "Guy ripped in half by a train. Suicide? Homicide? Accident? Don't know. But the parents are on their way in."

"I'm on my way, too."

An hour later, I was rubbing Mrs. Hulbert's ice-cold hands. "Do you think you are ready for the ID?" I said.

She nodded, tried to smile, started to cry. Fresh tears drizzled down her white, wrinkled face. She was in her sixties. Brad had been her only child. Her husband was hospitalized with chest pains.

"Why don't we wait a sec, huh?" I said.

"No," she said through a sob. "Now. Get it over."

"As I mentioned earlier," I said. "We can do this with a digital photo." The detective handling the case nodded.

"Oh, no." She dabbed a handkerchief to her lips. "I want to see Brad, not some photograph."

"Yes. I understand." I hugged her, and we stood. She leaned on me, and I wrapped an arm around her waist as we walked. The detective hung back.

"He was a troubled boy," she said. "Troubled. But this? I didn't see this coming."

I flicked my finger, signaling Gert to tell the tech backstage that we were on our way. We walked through the lobby and through the door into the family viewing area. The detective closed the door behind us. Mrs. Hulbert sank into one of the too-soft chairs.

"I don't know if I can do this," she said.

"You have time. You can wait."

She sighed. "I'd better do it now."

She stood, and we approached the viewing window. It was large and framed like a picture, with beige curtains hanging in soft folds to hide the mystery behind.

I tightened my grip on Mrs. Hulbert's waist. She nodded. I pressed a button, and the curtains slowly parted to reveal a handsome young man, maybe thirty-two, with curly brown hair and a chin dimple.

Mrs. Hulbert moved forward. She lifted one hand to the glass. She looked and looked, as if examining every pore on the young man's face. Then she rested her cheek on the glass and closed her eyes.

"Oh, yes. That's my Bradley."

She slipped her hand into the pocket of her wool jacket. I expected her to fish out a tissue, but that wasn't right. Her hand was fisted, and when she uncurled it, what looked like bath salts rested in her palm. She raised her hand to her mouth.

I screeched "No!" and I reached for her arm.

Mrs. Hulbert screamed and pulled away, her hand nearing her mouth.

I tackled her, the salts went flying, and she and I thumped to the ground.

I gasped for breath and prayed I hadn't broken the poor woman's bones. "This isn't the way," I gasped. "It's not."

"Yes." She sobbed. "Yes, it is. Please. I want to be with Bradley."

"I understand. I do. But, no." I hugged her to me and rocked her while sobs wracked her body.

"That was a first, Hank." He made a left turn toward the vet's. I was on pins and needles to pick up Penny. "A first. Cyanide. The cyanide salts would have killed her instantly. I've worked with hundreds, but I've never had a woman, a mourner, try to commit suicide on me like that."

He nodded, scratched his mustache. "Can't figure 'em, can we? Not ever."

"I can, though. Most times, but not today. Up to the moment when she tried to kill herself, her behavior appeared within the normal emotional spectrum for her son's passing. You know? Thank heavens I smelled almonds. This is a strange day."

His hand brushed my cheek. "Sorry, babe."

I held his hand. "Tell me again when you have to go back to Maine."

"Two more days."

"It seems like it's never enough," I said.

"I know. Your choice."

"Don't," I said. "Not with Veda sick and all. It's been almost nine months since I was up in Winsworth."

"And you haven't made any progress on whether you're going to accept the job in Maine or not."

"It looks easy. I want to come, but ... nothing's clear right now."

He snorted and looked away. Hank was tired of my putting off the Maine ME's generous job offer. If I took the job, I could move to Maine, be close to Hank, move things along in the way we both wanted them moved.

But if I took the job, I'd leave everything I knew and much that I loved behind. I couldn't blame him for being annoyed with me. Nor could I decide. Not just yet.

"Turn right here," I said.

He pulled into the vet's parking lot, and I got out. I didn't want to think about what the vet would have to say. I was too scared.

I stroked Penny's soft fur while she rested her head in my lap.

"We've sent her biopsy out," Dr. Joby said. "It should take ten days to two weeks. I'd hoped it would be sooner, but they're jammed way up. I'm sorry."

"What do you think it is, Beth?" I sucked in a breath, terrified.

She snuggled her hands into her pockets. "It could be several conditions. How about we wait to see the results."

I shook my head, peered into Penny's chocolate eyes. "I need to know what we might be facing."

She pressed a hand to my shoulder. "It could be a soft tissue carcinoma."

I patted her hand. "I understand. Cancer."

She nodded. "Normally, we could isolate it, destroy it, and amputate the leg. In Penny's case ..." She scratched Penny behind the ears. "There are appliances with wheels for dogs whose—"

"I wouldn't do that to her." Penny. Missing one front leg to cancer and one to a bomb. That would be worse than hobbled for life.

I hugged Pens. "Death would be preferable." I stood, a numb feeling making movement awkward. "I'll wait for your call about the biopsy."

"As soon as I hear ..."

My face was tight with pain, my eyes blurry as I walked beside Hank and Penny to the truck. "It could be a lot of things," I said to him. "Cancer's one, but I'm betting ..."

His eyes drifted to the ugly lump on her foreleg. "A lot of things," he repeated.

Penny hopped up into the front seat as if nothing were wrong.

If I lost her ...

I called Veda, who sounded absolutely chipper. I suspected she was faking it, as she was desperate to get out of the hospital. I made a note to call the doctor to make certain she didn't scoot out of there too soon. I didn't mention Penny or the knock on my head. Instead, I yammered on about the little mystery girl. Veda was fascinated. She hated not being at OCME.

"I'll stop by tonight, after work," I said.

"I expect nothing less, my dear. Be sure you have a *full* report. A full report."

That night, I only partially filled Veda in on the goings-on. She looked greatly improved, and her temperature was close to normal. All good stuff. She again insisted on leaving that night, and I, again, refused.

"This place is wearing me out, Tally," she said.

"I know what you mean." I scooched beside her on the bed. "I hate hospitals, too. You'll be out in a day, and soon back to raising hell at work."

I spotted the huge art history book on the bedside table. "I see Nick Wirth's been by."

A smile popped out. "Yes."

"Is it serious?" I asked.

She shrugged. "You know what really scares me?"

Fear flip-flopped my stomach. "What?"

She laughed. "*Ach,* you worry so. Relax. I'm talking about all the paperwork that Tom Fogarty will have ignored."

Intense relief flooded my body. "Let's hope paperwork is the only thing Fogarty's left undone."

Even after such a good visit with Veda, my sleep that night was fitful. I tossed and rolled and scrunched, seeking that perfect position for sleep.

But while my body begged for rest, my mind went gerbil-fast. I worried about Veda and Penny and poor little Janey Doe. I imagined Mrs. Hulbert's grief, and frustrated myself trying to remember if Mr. Hulbert had been contacted. I dozed, burst awake with some revelation that I never could remember, and then fell back into an exhausted sleep after wandering the maze of my mind for another half hour or so.

And so it went, while Peanut and Penny snored at the foot of the bed, and Hank slept motionless beside me.

Four A.M. The blue moon peeked into the bedroom window. I slipped Hank's flannel shirt over my T-shirt and tiptoed into the living room. Penny followed me. Moonlight poured into the room. I opened the French doors and stepped onto the balcony. The night was chilly, like most spring nights in Boston, but I found the blaze of moonlight utterly magical. I sat on the old green bench and rubbed my temples, exhaustion a heavy blanket on my body.

I peered at Penny, curled at my feet, instantly asleep in the comfort of her world. I loved her so. The thought of losing her pushed tears down my cheeks. *We don't know yet.* I slipped to the deck floor and hugged her tight. Like all dogs, she was only eighty percent asleep. She licked my cheek.

"What a slob," I said.

She kept licking, and I chuckled and hugged her tighter, her fur warming me.

I started awake. So did Penny. Grey light streaked the French doors and across the yellow pine floor.

"Tal?" bellowed Hank. "Where the hell are you?"

"Out here," I yelled. Penny got up and trotted toward the towering man standing there, hair porcupine wild, belly heaving, foot tapping, hands on hips.

"Well, what the hell," he said.

"Um, could you help me up? My left leg's gone numb." I held out my hand, but instead he wrapped an arm around my waist and lifted me from the deck.

His lips were taut and white, his face frozen into one of his scary-mad faces that usually made me laugh. That morning was no exception.

"What the hell is so funny, woman?"

"You gotta work on that face, Hank."

He took a deep breath. "I ... couldn't find you." He helped me to the couch, and I pulled the afghan over me. I shivered beneath its cozy folds. He sat at the end of the couch and rubbed my feet.

"That's heaven." I smiled. "Did you think I'd been abducted by aliens?"

"Knowing you, the possibilities are endless."

"Of course they are. What time is it?"

"After eight."

"Shit! I've got a hair appointment at eight-thirty. They're doing my nails and ... That's it!"

"Your hair is it?"

"Come on. We've got to go into the office." I stood, my numb leg collapsed, and I promptly fell on my face.

Chapter Five

I walked down the corridor at OCME with an air of non-chalance I was far from feeling. Hank and Gert walked beside me and pretended to check a chart. The ME techs had moved Janey Doe to the large cooler, and we planned to look in on her. We had to appear casual. If Fogarty got wind of my excitement, he'd surely join us.

Hank heaved open the cooler door and we slipped inside. I peered around, looking for a smallish body bag. We circled the room filled with bodies on gurneys lined up against the walls.

"Here," Gert said. She waved us over.

I unzipped Janey. She was smaller, somehow shrunken and diminished. Fogarty had sewn her Y incision with his usual meticulous stitches. I gloved my hands, and then reached for one of hers.

"Do you see?" I asked.

Hank shook his head.

Gert's eyes narrowed, and she popped a grape Bazooka bubble. "Yeah. I see. I sure do."

"How about clueing me in, ladies," Hank said.

"Look at her polished nails, Hank." I pointed to them. "See how the polish is so sloppily applied? True, Janey was only about ten or eleven, but she still would have loudly complained at the crummy polish job."

"So what if she got together with some pal and did it? You know, girly stuff."

Gert chewed like mad. "Naw. The kid's got no earring piercing. Her hair's cut like a child's. I'm thinking these parents wanted to keep the kid a kid. Maybe momma would have painted her nails, but ... I don't see the kid doing it herself."

"Either way, once we know who she is, we can find out." I peeled off shots of Janey's hands on my digicam.

"Now I get it," Gert said. "You think she was dead. Yeah. She was all dead when this creepo polished her nails."

"And it was a guy, don't you think?" I said.

"Sure was," Gert said. "No woman would apply nail polish that way and leave it, even if it was for a little dead girl." Gert sniffled. "Sorry. This little girl makes me so sad."

"I know." I tucked Janey's arm back around her new lamb and zipped her up.

Thirty minutes later, Hank's hand on my shoulder stopped my forward momentum as we walked to tell Kranak about Janey's nail polish.

I turned. "Hank, what—"

"Ssshhh." His eyes were closed and he chewed the end of his mustache.

Something had clicked with him, something about Janey. Hank couldn't be rushed.

"Was her hair washed, Tal?" he asked.

"I think so. Yes. Shiny clean."

"And the nails. Huh. Had she been washed?"

I thought back to the first time I saw the child's body on the gurney. "Now that you say that, I think she may have been."

He nodded, still working his mustache, when Fogarty walked by. He rolled his eyes heavenward. I almost stuck out my tongue at him.

"Do you have a problem, Tom?" I said.

"None at all." Fogarty coded the door and whisked through.

"Come." Hank slipped a hand through my arm. "We need your pal Kranak. As the CSS in charge, we should talk to him first."

Kranak was on the phone, nodding and sighing. He waved us into his cubical.

I tugged Hank's shirt. "Would you please—"

"Sshhhh." He held a finger to his lips, then pointed to Kranak.

I threw up my hands. Why the big stall by Hank?

Something bleeped. Hank, Kranak, and I all reached for our beepers.

Mine was silent, and so, apparently, was Kranak's.

Hank peered at his, and then shook his head.

"Hank?"

"I need a phone. A land line. Be right back."

He left just as Kranak hung up. "So where's loverboy going?"

"Not funny, Rob. He got beeped. We found something with Janey Doe."

"Me, too. That was a cop up in Temple, New Hampshire. We've located Janey's parents. That child's name was Rose, Rose Noguchi."

When Hank didn't reappear, I headed back to my office to pull some paperwork for Rose's parents, who were on their way into OCME. I opened the door and there was Hank pacing my carpet, phone to his ear, face taut, nodding, and barking commands. Not good. Not good at all.

Peanut lay sprawled on the couch and Penny was curled

on her dog bed. I wished I could do the same. It was only eleven A.M., and I was pooped.

I closed the door so Hank would have some privacy, and made a U-turn for MGAP's small central office. "Anything up?" I said to Gert.

She shook her head as she typed. I told her about Rose Noguchi and her parents in Temple, New Hampshire.

"You tell Kranak about the polish?" she asked.

"Not yet. Things started happening pretty fast." I took a seat at one of the empty computer stations and plucked out the commands for the paperwork the family needed to complete before they could take possession of the remains.

No one wants to do paperwork when their spouse or child or brother is lying dead on some gurney. So we in MGAP would assist them, most often accompanied by the detective who'd caught the case. Almost always, someone in law enforcement would be present.

But first, of course, I'd accompany the parents for the ID.

A murdered child trumps just about anything else at OCME and MGAP.

How had Rose happened across the path of a killer? No matter what's portrayed on TV, most child homicides are committed by someone who knows or is friends with the child or their family.

I sighed and stretched my shoulder muscles.

Hank poked his head into the room and waved me to come along. His vibe was urgent, which was unusual for my laconic fella. He waved, and then made a beeline for Kranak's office.

"Wait up," I said.

"I've got to run home." He tossed the words over his shoulder.

"To the apartment?"

"No. Home. To Maine."

I sped up. "What's happened?"

"An old woman who lives down the street from Carmen

was getting the soil ready for spring planting. Guess she decided put in a new patch this year. Was all excited 'bout it. Yup-suh. Trouble is, she dug up a bunch of bones. Human ones."

"Cripes."

"Wish you were around up there to help out."

"Me, too." To act as the state of Maine's official homicide counselor was intensely appealing. I'd get out of the city's hustle and bustle, have more time, more air to breath. But it was so hard to leave MGAP, my baby.

Kranak sat slumped at the computer, two-finger typing some report or other. He swiveled around in his chair when he heard us.

"Now you wanna tell me what's up?" Kranak said.

Hank squeezed himself into a too-small, too-delicate chair, scratched his mustache, his blue eyes lasering from me to Kranak.

"Hank?" I said.

"Kinda funny," he said. "Tally showed us little Janey Doe's nails, and she and Gert came to the same conclusion. Tal?"

I leaned forward. "We believe Janey's nails were polished *after* he'd killed her. It was a lousy polish job, one done by a man, we suspect. They were a mess. Streaky, polish on her cuticles. Just not something a woman would do."

Kranak snorted. "This is the big news? You kiddin' me?"

"Wait," Hank said. "I got to thinking about that and the way she was killed. I looked at the kid's tox report just now. She had marijuana, a lot, in her system. That, the fact that she was asphyxiated, had painted nails and clean hair and possibly a bathed body. How she was arranged. It all points to a sacrificial killing for me."

"Some kind of ritual," Kranak said.

Hank nodded.

Kranak leaned back, eyes closed.

The idea snapped in place for me, too. "Yes," I said. "A

cult killing. God, I hate to think of it as that. But it's possible. Very much so. Bad stuff. These ritual killings, they usually don't stop at one."

Alone again in my office, I cupped Hank's face in my hands, kissed him long and hard. "I'll miss you."

He hugged my waist. "Me, too."

"Tell Carmen I send my love."

"Yup. Tal—"

I shushed him with my finger to his lips. He kissed it. "I can't, Hank. Not now. Not yet."

He bent down for another kiss, and he pressed himself against me, enveloping me. I bowed back with the pressure, his hardness finding that soft, aching spot of mine that wanted him so much. His tongue teased my mouth, his mustache tickling my upper lip. We rubbed and squeezed and tried to devour each other, knowing too well the brevity of the moment.

Still, I sank into the passion, drowning in his embrace, absorbing his love.

The screech of the phone jerked me into the present. Hank and I parted, our eyes signaling our regret.

Sill mesmerized, I said, "I hate this."

"Yeah," he replied.

My eyes locked on his, I groped behind me for the phone. "Hello."

"Rose Noguchi's father is here."

Outside, I waved Hank and Peanut off. I wished they could stay. I knew they couldn't. I breathed deep and then returned to the lobby, where I approached the handsome, Asian-looking man wearing a leather bomber jacket. His distraught eyes pinned me as I approached him. A plainclothes detective stood beside him with his hands behind his back.

I introduced myself. The father wiped his hands on his jeans, and we shook. His hands were moist, clammy. He said he was John Noguchi, that his daughter, Rose, was ten, and that she'd been missing for only a day.

"It's a small thing, you see," he said. He sounded rational, clear, as if he were explaining the obvious to a somewhat slow student.

"I do see," I said.

"Such a small thing, one day. A single day. So you see, she can't be dead. It's impossible. Do you understand?"

I understood, all right, that finite, yet radical slice of time—the distance between life and death, hope and despair, a future and the possibility of none. I'd been there with my murdered father, when life had left the body, when the soul fled, when that final shuddering exhale signaled the passing of the beloved. And all you wanted to do was scream, "Come back, please!"

"I understand," I said. "I do. And I'm so sorry."

We entered my office. "Come. Sit, please." I left the two men to fetch them drinks, something cool for Mr. Noguchi and warm for the officer.

"She was playing out back after school," Mr. Noguchi said when I returned. He began shivering.

I sat across from him. "May I hold your hands?" They rested on his jeaned legs, curled into fists.

He hesitated, and then nodded.

I reached for his hands and uncurled them. They shook. I wrapped my sturdy hands around his long, thin ones. I wanted to warm him. "Go on, Mr. Noguchi."

"With a friend," he said. "Rose was playing. I was at work. My wife was home. She is in a wheelchair, but she gets around just fine. Very well." He took his hands from mine and wiped them up and down his jeans. His knee jiggled. "She, my wife, she went out on the deck to call the girls. They were gone. We have acres of woods out back. The girls know not to go there, but sometimes—you know how children are—they disobey." He sucked in a sob, his face tight and impossibly lean.

The detective started to speak, and I held up a finger. We waited for Mr. Noguchi to compose himself.

A minute later, he began again. "So she, my wife, called Bella's house, to see if the girls were there. We live in the country, but our houses are actually quite close. Bella lives right next door. But they were not there. They were not playing there."

I turned to the detective. "Where is Bella?"

"Hell, I don't know," the detective said. "This is the first I've heard of her. I'm here for Rose."

With frightening clarity, I saw what had happened. The detective was a Massachusetts state detective investigating Rose Noguchi's homicide, since Rose was found here, at OCME. Mr. Noguchi, of Temple, New Hampshire, had learned of his daughter's death, and that was all he had thought about. He'd forgotten all about the other little girl. It was entirely possible that Rose's friend, Bella, was still missing. Or worse.

I sounded the alarm.

I had Gert accompany Mr. Noguchi through the painful steps of filling out the necessary paperwork and then identifying Rose. A beautiful name for a beautiful girl. My mind twirled as I punched out the number of a friend, Special Agent Kathleen Lauria with the FBI.

"Hey, Kath."

"Tally Whyte! How are you?"

"Not so hot."

"Ouch. What's the problem this time?"

"A big one." I filled Lauria in on Rose Noguchi, how we'd found her body in the refrigerator room, and what I knew about Bella. "Little Bella could still be missing. Her last name is Marsh, according to Mr. Noguchi."

"We would have heard if a little girl was missing. Remember the Amber Alert."

"Not if no one alerted the authorities. Maybe she's fine, but ... I have a nasty feeling about this."

"I hate your feelings, Tally Whyte."

"Me, too."

I joined Gert, Mr. Noguchi, and the detective while I waited for Lauria's return call. I played it calm, while my nerves shrieked imagining the lost Bella.

Mr. Noguchi pressed against the viewing glass, although the curtains had long been closed.

Gert stepped away and whispered, "He wants to touch her. The post's been done. I don't see why not."

"I don't, either. I'll go tell them to fix her up, while you—"

"I'll do it," Gert said. "The dad's ... I think he'll do better with you."

Gert disappeared out back. I approached Mr. Noguchi, who remained pressed against the glass, as if he were worshipping it. He sobbed silently.

"Mr. Noguchi." He didn't react, and I rested my hand on his shoulder. "I'll take you to see Rose, if you'd like me to do so."

His sobbing quieted. "You'll let me touch her?"

"Yes. Would you like to hug her?"

He nodded. "Very much. Yes. Very much."

"Come." I nodded to the detective, who would remain behind. I wrapped an arm around Mr. Noguchi's waist. He was tall, nearly six feet, but in my two-inch heels, I matched him. "This will be hard."

Rose's body had lost its rigor. She was limp, boneless, like a doll. Mr. Noguchi lifted her from the gurney and sat with her on his lap. He rocked, and Rose's long black hair swayed as they moved together. What he whispered to her, I couldn't hear. Things, I presumed, a father would speak to a child who had been brutally taken from him.

I turned away, giving them privacy. A fog of pain consumed the room's air.

Bella Marsh. Would this scene be repeated in a day or two?

"I am finished," Mr. Noguchi said. He raised his daughter's body toward me. I took her and peered down at that sweet innocent face. Man's brutality sometimes overwhelmed me. Mr. Noguchi kissed his child's brow, then turned and left the room.

I slid Rose back on the gurney, pressed my cheek to hers, and smoothed her hair with my hand. "Good-bye, little girl. Safe journey to that mysterious place beyond now."

CSS had taken the pink blanket, and I pulled a sheet over her gray face.

Gert finished up with Mr. Noguchi, and I checked for messages. Kathleen Lauria hadn't called.

By the time I gave Penny a quick walk around the block, my message light blinked red. I was to meet Lauria at the Marsh home in Temple, New Hampshire.

Chapter Six

On my drive to Temple, I got Kranak on speakerphone. He told me that Rose Noguchi's father worked with Bella Marsh's mother in Merrimack, New Hampshire, as air traffic controllers. They were old friends and workmates, and lived next door to each other in Temple, a semi-rural town in New Hampshire's Monadnock region.

Bella's father was an academic and literary writer. He was usually home when Bella returned from the school day. Bella had no siblings. Her father was the last one to see her.

I pressed the gas pedal, feeling an accustomed urgency. Penny rested her head on my lap. She knew my moods.

Bella Marsh had been missing for over twenty-four hours. A horror for any parent. The irony was, her parents hadn't known she was even missing until Lauria had called and peppered them with questions.

The afternoon of the disappearances, Bella had called and asked if she could spend the night at Rose Noguchi's house. Rose had gotten on the phone to beg, and the father had said yes.

So Rose had gone missing, and the Marshes had assumed Bella was sleeping over at Rose's.

All the while, both girls were in the hands of a killer.

I passed Hawthorne Hospital in Acton, and almost stopped to see Veda. But I'd be taking her home later that day. At least, I hoped so. She'd shoot me if I didn't.

I'd been told the Route 2 way up to Temple wasn't the fastest, but I was familiar with the drive, which is why I took it.

I imagined Rose's killer. Had he meandered, driven back roads, coveted his time with the dead Rose? Or had he sped down Route 3, over superhighways jammed with construction and traffic, eager to leave her corpse at the medical examiner's office?

We still didn't know how he'd gotten into OCME at night. The card-swipe system should be infallible. It wasn't.

Why take Rose from Temple, New Hampshire, all the way to Boston? Made no sense. At least not yet.

I drove past malls and houses and that wonderful swamp in Acton where the herons roosted.

I turned north onto 495, then west on 119, a two-lane road never intended for the crowds of cars that jostled over its well-worn pavement on a daily basis. I'd forgotten how cars crowded the roads nowadays.

As I plodded along 119, I reexamined the discovery of Rose Noguchi. *Why* had the killer left her body at OCME? The obvious answer was that he wanted her to be found. The gift of the stuffed lamb. Another hint of his caring? The original lamb was old, used, loved. It bore repair stitches and wear—apparently a beloved toy, which the killer believed would comfort Rose in some way.

Why? Because he was ashamed and saddened by what he'd done? But he was still resolute. Suffocation takes time, more time than a bullet. A victim, even a small one, would struggle. Would she if I factored in the marijuana? I'd have to check if the marijuana was potent enough to keep her unconscious while he went about stealing her breath, her life.

A caring killer. A loving killer? A killer expiating the sins of the father?

Or was it all part of the killer's ritual, and his need to show off?

He was certainly bidding for attention. Where he'd left her body would do that, for sure. He must have known that the gift of the lamb would send off forensic alarm bells. Yet the act held powerful emotional resonance.

Something nagged at me, a familiar feeling that, whenever I got it, bugged the hell out of me. Now what? Of course!

I punched out Kranak's number at work. "Rob!"

"What's up? You there yet?"

"No, Mr. Pissass, I'm not. I just remembered something. The cameras. What about the cameras in the decomp cooler? The guy who bonked me on the head would be on video!"

Kranak snorted. "Yeah. Great idea, Tal. I thought of that, too. Only one problemo. They don't work."

"They have to work," I said.

He barked a sour laugh. "Not when Fogarty's in charge. He's been responsible for the physical plant forever. They broke. Couple months back. Said he didn't have enough money for them and for the new brochures. So he chose the brochures. I wormed all this outta him. He never told Veda. Figured he'd get the camera fixed before she found out."

I disconnected with such fury I knocked my phone on the floor. I left it there. Fogarty would destroy the place if Veda didn't get back soon.

The killer had to have known about the cameras. Had to.

He was one crafty fox, and he was trying to tell us something. Just *what* was eluding me.

I sped up Route 13 from Townsend and then turned west onto Route 101. I spotted Mount Monadnock in the distance. My heart always thrilled at the sight of her.

All told, it took me eighty minutes to reach Temple Mountain. I turned left, still climbing as I headed toward the village of Temple.

Rustic and sparsely populated, the Monadnock region was far enough north of Boston for spring's leaves to still be in their bud cocoons.

I cracked open my window. The gray day had turned sparkly, and the air felt crisp and clean. I drove over gentle hills dotted with homes built in earlier centuries and passed farms where horses and cows grazed. The road narrowed as I neared the village. I passed a quintessential New England town hall, and on the left of a pretty little green stood an old rambling brick inn with a sign that proclaimed: ESTABLISHED 1775. Gorgeous.

I slowed and checked my map. The road split, and I bore right. I drove past a white antique colonial shrouded in darkness—the Noguchi home—and pulled into the driveway of an antique, yellow-painted colonial, complete with mullioned windows and an onion lamp out front. I spotted Kathleen Lauria. She leaned against the bumper of her black SUV. I waved. She'd poured herself into a stylish navy suit that barely fit the FBI's apparel requirements. Rather than heels, she wore her ubiquitous Merrells, better suited to chasing evildoers.

A curtain moved in the front window. There it was, the hope. Maybe it was their Bella, returned home. That kernel of hope would be with them until Bella appeared or her remains were found.

I said a prayer that it was the former.

I parked parallel to the house, on the still-brown grass behind a New Hampshire State Police car. Lauria appeared at the car door, and I stepped out. We hugged.

" 'Bout time," she said, pushing me back and giving me her Clarice Starling stare. "You're okay?"

"Yup," I said. "Good to see you, too, kiddo."

"Another crappy one," she said.

"Yeah."

"Funny, you don't look any different after your Maine adventure."

"Ayuh," I said.

She chuckled as she scooched down to scratch Penny's chin. We had a history—Kathleen Lauria and I—that went back to my near death from a crazed serial killer. When Lauria was around, people were always safer.

As she stood she waved a finger, and we walked behind her SUV so we wouldn't be observed.

"Where are we at?" I asked.

"Nothing much more than you know. The dogs are on their way, but I'm glad you've brought Penny. With each passing minute …"

"I know," I said.

"It's just as you said. They thought the kid was staying at her friend's overnight, so they didn't sound the alarm. They're still in the disbelief stage."

I nodded.

Lauria placed a hand lightly on my back. "Let's go. I'm glad you're here."

We walked the path to the house.

I heard the screech of tires and trucks varooming in the distance, and over the crest of the small hill came a caravan of media trucks followed by two Temple cop cars. Lauria hustled me into the house.

Marlene and Andrew Marsh were tall and stately and blond.

Bella must be a beautiful-looking child. I wanted to know what she was like on the inside, so I could attempt to judge how she'd react to being kidnapped.

The house was a classic center-hall colonial, and we took a left into a living room filled with damask couches and oil portraits and a silver tea service set on a graceful Hepplewhite sideboard. We exchanged introductions while Lauria closed the room's drapes.

The place was swarming with FBI forensics and special

agents, but when they tried to mob our space, Lauria told them to hold off while we talked to the Marshes.

Andrew Marsh poured us all tea with a deliberateness that only served to reinforce his terrible state of panic. His hand twitched as he placed porcelain cups steaming with pungent orange tea in front of his wife, Kathleen, and myself.

Marlene Marsh glanced at her husband with a look that spoke equally of disdain and sympathy. Beside her was a silver tray piled with plump johnnycakes, and alongside the tray was a stack of what looked like photo books.

Here was a couple desperately trying to act normal while their eyes revealed a sense of urgency and terror I'd sadly seen before.

"Here's our Bella." Marlene Marsh opened the topmost book, revealing an eight-by-ten of her daughter. "Isn't she perfect?" Her voice caught on a sob, and she looked away.

Bella was lovely, with a sweet, shy smile, and mischievous eyes that dared the viewer to join her for a romp. She wore a saucy hat and a sleeveless dress as she sat on a huge boulder. I quickly leafed through the album. All photos of Bella, all perfectly composed and beautifully photographed. Not a snapshot in the bunch.

I swiveled, so only Kathleen could see my face. "Shouldn't we get going with the interview?"

Kathleen leaned forward. "You've got ten minutes, then we take Penny out back for the search." Lauria held up ten fingers as she left the room.

I turned to Andrew Marsh. His red, swollen eyes asked me questions I couldn't answer.

"As Special Agent Lauria has told you, I'm here to help you, and also because I have been involved in the aftermath of Rose Noguchi's death."

"We didn't know Bella was missing!" Andrew said.

"We didn't know!" Marlene echoed. Her voice rasped with fear.

I explained to the Marshes what I knew of Rose's death.

I omitted any mention of the lamb, which was being kept from the public and everyone involved, even the Marshes.

"I'd like to hear about the phone call from Bella," I said.

"I took it," Andrew said. "I was home. Marlene was at work. The phone rang."

"Around what time?" Lauria asked.

Andrew gnawed his bottom lip. "I think around four. The girls were home. They had been out playing. Yes, it must have been around then."

"What did Bella say exactly?" I asked.

Andrew pressed his hands to his knees and looked away. His whole body trembled.

He was probably thinking about how that call might turn out to be the last time he ever heard his daughter's voice, how he hadn't recognized her distress, how he could have done things differently, how if he'd handled it differently she'd be safe. I'd played that game myself when my father was murdered more than twenty years earlier.

I groped for one of his hands. "Andrew, I'm so sorry. But we need to move so we can find Bella. We must."

"Oh, Andrew, come on!" spat Marlene. Tears cascaded down her porcelain cheeks, but she looked at me dead on. No hiding for Marlene Marsh.

A huge sigh, then Andrew began again. "It was four, four-fifteen, perhaps. Bella called and asked if she could spend the night at Rose's. They do that a lot. Those sleepovers. The Noguchis live right next door. What harm?" He turned to Marlene. "What harm?"

"None, dear." Marlene kissed his temple. "And so you said yes."

"I did. And … and Bella … she said 'love you, *Papa*,' and I said 'love you, Pumpkin,' back. And that … that was it. All done." Then he mumbled "Excuse me," and rushed from the room.

"Mrs. Marsh," I said. "Marlene. Can you think of anything unusual or different about Bella's sleepover?"

She snapped a nod. "I can. I remember when I got home … I get home very late on nights when I'm working. Last night was no different. I got in at three A.M." Her face had frozen into glacial stiffness. "Andrew was up. He often waits up for me." She stood and began to pace, her high heels clacking on the wide pine boards. "I went into Bella's room. I always kiss her good night. That's when Andrew told me she was on a sleepover at the Noguchis's."

She stopped pacing and faced me. "I remember lifting her pillow and inhaling her scent." She sighed. "I whispered good night to her anyway, then went to sleep. I was exhausted. I always am after a shift."

"Forgive me," I said. "But I'm not clear on what was unusual."

"I didn't notice last night, either. If I had … Her blanket. Her Pooh blanket. It's one of those things she has to drag to bed with her every night. I hated the filthy thing and wanted to get rid of it when she turned ten, but Andrew wouldn't hear of it. He said it would break her heart. I let him have his way, but I certainly didn't approve. In any event, her Pooh blanket was there, in her bed. But I didn't notice, not until this morning."

I clenched my hands in my lap. "In other words, Bella would not have gone on the sleepover without her Pooh blanket. And you're telling us this for the first time now?"

"Yes, now!" She waved her hands. "What do you expect? What?"

I excused myself, and went in search of Lauria. *Christmas!* Had the Marshes noticed the blanket last night, the odds would have been much more favorable for Bella's recovery. Things that small changed the course of a life.

I raced through the family room to the open kitchen, then upstairs to the bedrooms, poking my head into rooms looking for Lauria.

A noise. "Kath?" Inside a large front-to-back room, Andrew Marsh sat head in hands, rocking back and forth on the master bedroom bed. My heart ached, but I moved on to Bella's room down the hall. Her room was all violet and pink and green and filled with stuffed animals and toys. Pictures of animals were everywhere and books were stacked beside Bella's canopied bed. Equestrian trophies and ribbons lined two bookshelves. A furry guinea pig slept in his large wire cage. He had lots of toys, too.

A princess's room.

But no ratty blanket lay on the bed. I scooched to my knees and peered under the bed. Not even a dust bunny.

"You lookin' for me?"

I jumped, banging my head on the bed rail. "Geesh, Kath. You don't need to scare a delicate soul like me." I rubbed my head.

She snorted. "Pretty grim." She held out a diminutive hand. I took it as she helped me to my feet.

"Grim, it is," I said. "What I'm looking for … Did your guys find a Pooh blanket. It was Bella's. Her special one. She wouldn't sleep without it."

"Well why the fuck is this the first time I'm hearing about the damned blanket?"

Lauria checked with the FBI's forensics team, as well as the New Hampshire State Police crime lab in Concord. No Pooh blanket. Not anywhere.

"Let's get Penny," Lauria said.

On the way back to the house, leading Penny, a breeze ruffled my hair. It was warm and caressing, a new spring breeze. I felt like crap.

"I can't help but wonder if little Bella will see full spring," I said.

Lauria nodded. She was a woman of few words, but furrows of worry ran between her brows.

"It's the same perpetrator who killed the Noguchi child," I said.

"Of course," Lauria said. "You almost sound emphatic."

"The fuzzy lamb. Now Bella's blanket is gone. I bet he

stole it to give to her. I fervently hope because she was crying for it and not—"

"No."

Penny nudged me, and I felt her sense of urgency. We picked up the pace. "Kidnappings are tough on you, aren't they?"

"Yes," Lauria said. "Each day I wonder if I can do another one. Somehow I do. Murderers I can handle. Graft, corruption. Sure. Even serial killers, as you know. But this? This is hard."

I nodded. "Let's go find Bella."

Chapter Seven

The woods were deep and chill and silent. New Hampshire woods. Endless forest pricked by huge granite boulders and tumbles of stones. The woods stared at me as I changed from pumps into my sturdy Merrells. The Marshes had turned out the lights. The house was dark, quiet. Fingers of terror crept from the house. What might we find moldering in the forest?

Penny yipped and bounced with excitement. For an instant, a twinge of worry about Penny ousted the child from my thoughts.

I slipped my hand through the leash's well worn loop. We'd done this before. If she got a scent, she was so fast I couldn't catch her.

State cops and FBI and the Marshes and Noguchis clustered around us.

Andrew Marsh offered me a purple shirt with bright flowers for Penny to smell. "Is this okay?"

"Did she wear it recently?" I asked him.

"Of course," replied Marlene Marsh.

I took the shirt and offered it to Penny. She buried her nose in its soft folds and drank in Bella's scent.

"*Stopa!*" I commanded. "Find! *Stopa!*"

Penny grew still. She sniffed the air, head up, nose pointed. I gripped the leash even more tightly.

Penny tilted her head. I'd swear she was listening to something humans could never hear. One final sniff, and she exploded toward the woods.

We ran through the dense wood in silence. Penny stopped by a large oak, sniffing the ground. I caught my breath, while Lauria removed a small red flag from her jacket and poked the metal end into the ground. Penny wasn't even breathing hard.

A hard pull, and Kathleen and I were again on the move. A root snagged my foot, but I recovered. As time passed, I lost awareness of anyone but Penny and myself, and I sank into a near meditative state. We traveled deeper into the woods, and the silence reminded me of Maine. No whooshing cars or chattering people. My panting became my mantra.

While a member of the Mass. Canine Corps, Penny was a highly talented, multipurpose dog. She was trained to guard, to protect, to attack, and as a search and rescue, or SAR, dog. She did all of these fairly well. In fact, she was an excellent cadaver dog. Dogs trained in only one specialty could often outdo her, but as an all-around talent, she excelled.

Part of Penny's training was as an air-scenting SAR, meaning she smelled the air currents rather than ground smells, although she might also pick up a ground scent of a missing person. If that happened, she'd run with it.

A specially trained SAR dog and her partner can often produce the results of twenty-five or more human ground searchers.

The forest floor was spongy. Furry mosses grew, and layers of old leaves clumped where only recently the snows of winter had retreated. The air was musty and heavy with a presence of old forest unwilling to give up ground to civilization. Odd to think that much of this land was once cleared and farmed by settlers determined to get crops from the rocky soil.

We came upon an ancient stone wall, beautifully laid and lichen covered, and just beyond it, an old cellar hole. Penny sniffed with great interest, and Lauria placed another red flag. We trotted on, Penny smelling well beyond our senses.

A clearing opened up onto a dirt lane, well tended and with only one approaching car. Penny knew enough to wait for the pickup truck lumbering way too fast down the small road.

As we waited for the truck, Lauria muttered something into her walkie-talkie. "Thank God Penny's giving us a breather," she said between pants.

"I know. My girl can motor. What's with the red flags? New?"

"Something I'm trying out," she said. "I've radioed forensics. They'll find and comb the spots where we leave the flags, since they hold so much interest for Penny."

A tug and we were off. Penny broke into a lope.

"Slow down, Pens!" I commanded. We hadn't tracked for a while, and she'd forgotten that I wasn't as swift as she, even on her three legs.

Penny slowed, but her tail was raised, and her excitement electrified me.

She stopped so abruptly that Lauria bumped into me.

"Ouch," I said. "Oh, God, I hope not."

Again and again, round and round, Penny paced over a spot of seemingly undisturbed leaves. I would swear I smelled death.

Penny leaned on her front paw, while her back paws dug the earth. A shower of leaves and dirt and small stones flew into the air. I tugged the leash, but she kept at it.

"*Ke mne!* Here! *Ke mne!*"

Penny stopped. Her whole body shook with her reluctance to leave off her digging.

I couldn't pull my eyes from the place where she'd dug. I pulled a treat from my pocket, leaned down and handed it to her. She refused it. A bad sign. A very bad sign. "*Hodny!* Good girl!"

Her ribs bellowed, and for the first time I realized how winded she'd become. But she wouldn't relax. Not yet. Not until we unearthed the *something* that she believed rested beneath that earth.

We stood just outside the circle of yellow tape rigged by the FBI and watched them dig. I'd gotten Penny some water, and she was eagerly lapping. Slowly, carefully, they peeled away layers of leaves and earth and rocks. The sun pierced the budded trees as they dug. I sat on the perimeter. At some point someone handed me an apple and coffee.

As they dug, I pictured Bella's lifeless body beneath that layer of rock. I wished I didn't, but I couldn't help myself.

"Got something!" shouted a digger.

A patch of dirty pink poked up from the mulchy soil. CSS cameras snapped, and then with great care, a burly gloved digger hefted a bowling ball-sized rock. Then another. Someone brushed off dirt with what looked like a large paint brush, then more photos, and then an opening where the blue over-alled diggers stepped back.

The group's collective gasp was broken by "It's just clothes!"

"Don't be so quick!" someone else said.

"She could still be under there!" chimed a third.

Andrew Marsh winced. I walked over and whispered that maybe hollering play-by-play about their child wasn't what the Marshes needed to hear right now.

The digging resumed, and in the distance I heard the barks of the official SAR dogs. I massaged my neck. With the other dogs here, Penny and I could leave if the current spot revealed no remains.

I checked my watch. I still had plenty of time to pick up Veda and drive her home.

A golden retriever appeared leading a New Hampshire police officer in overalls. The cadaver dog. They led her under the police tape to where the men were digging. The retriever sniffed the ground.

All eyes were glued to the sweet-faced dog.

"She's interested," her human partner finally said. "But I doubt there's a corpse here."

He was right. There wasn't.

Penny had found Bella's pink PJs. That was it. No Bella and no blanket.

Penny and I piled into the police car with the Marshes and Lauria, and we were driven back to the Marsh house. Friends of the Marshes met us in the driveway bearing casseroles and comfort.

"I'll talk with you tomorrow," I said to the couple, whose red eyes and sagging bodies spoke of their grief and exhaustion.

"Tomorrow," Marlene Marsh said.

"We're leaving a team of agents with you," Lauria said. "If the kidnapper makes any demands, we'll be the first to know. We'll do everything that's necessary to get Bella back."

What was left unsaid was that Bella's taking was no typical kidnapping, given Rose Noguchi's homicide. I calculated Bella had maybe twenty-four hours. Not much time at all before the rescue became a retrieval.

"If you need me for any reason ...," I said to the Marshes. I gave them my card and my myriad phone numbers, and then I loaded Penny into the 4Runner and off we went to get Veda. A nurse was standing by at Veda's house to help my foster mother finish her recovery at home.

For now, Bella Marsh was alive. I believed it. But where? With whom? And why?

Why?

That puzzle occupied me on my drive to the hospital. Twenty minutes out, my cell phone chimed.

"Tally Whyte here."

"Ms. Whyte, this is Hawthorne Medical Center. Dr. Barrow's had a development."

"What do you mean 'a development'?"

"I'm sorry, but we can't explain on the telephone."

I pressed down on the gas, hard.

I stood beside Veda's hospital bed, hands gripping the metal bed rails. Bertha wasn't there. Sun poured through the windows, and I was glad I'd made sure to park in the shade, the windows half-down, and plenty of water in Penny's portable bowl.

Veda was asleep, her breathing normal, not labored. They'd hooked her up to a heart monitor, and the blips and beeps registered typical activity from the plastic clamp on her finger. Her complexion looked good.

But things were strange.

When I'd arrived, I searched for the phone caller. I hadn't gotten her name. Why would I? Yet now, I wished I had. None of the nurses on duty were aware of any "developments" with Veda's case. They were busy—nurses always were—bustling about, talking on phones, checking with doctors, retrieving meds.

I smoothed a hand across Veda's brow. She felt warm, but not overly so, and she wasn't greasy with sweat. I took her hand in mine, lightly, so I wouldn't wake her. The back of her hand was softer than silk, her skin warm and velvety, like a child's.

Why hadn't I ever noticed that before?

I sat beside her for a long time. I should wake her, given her eagerness to go home. But I let her sleep on. The room smelled of antiseptic and cloves. I picked up a *Time* magazine and began paging through the month-old copy. Every few minutes, I'd look up. Finally, her eyelids fluttered open. She beamed. I smiled back and my body relaxed. I hadn't realized I was so tense.

"Tally," she finally said. Her voice was rusty from disuse.

"Hey, Vede."

"I had a bad night. A bad one."

Perhaps the call had been about that. "How come?"

Her brow furrowed. "A needle, poking and poking and poking into me. Oh, it hurt so much!"

I gently pushed up the sleeve of her nightgown. The soft flesh of her inner elbow was blue and magenta and swollen, as if she'd been punctured by dozens of needle pricks.

She began to cry.

"Vede?" Fear nibbled at my throat. Veda cried less often than I did.

I lifted her shoulders—she was so light, so small—wrapped my arms around her, and pressed my cheek to hers. The warm wetness of her tears soaked my cheeks. I tasted their bitter salt. I hugged her tighter.

I finally leaned her back against the pillows. Clouds scuttled across her usually bright eyes. I forced a smile. I plucked a tissue and wiped the wet from her lined face. When had all those wrinkles appeared? I couldn't remember. "I'm so sorry, Vede. What can I get you?"

She wagged a hand. "My Tums. They're in the bathroom. My belly hurts."

I pointed. "That bathroom?"

Veda nodded a yes.

It didn't make sense, but … I opened the bathroom door and flicked on the light. Glaring white. But no Tums. No anything.

My bewilderment increased, and I turned back to Veda. A nurse pushed a rolling cart into the room.

"No!" shouted Veda, her face a mask of fear. *"No!"*

"What is going on here?" I barked at the nurse.

She puffed her chest. "Nothing. Nothing at all. I'm just bringing Dr. Barrow something to drink."

"She's terrified of you." I lifted Veda's arm and showed the nurse the plentiful back and blues. "And look at these."

"Huh," she said. "I guess they had trouble finding a vein last night."

"A vein for what?"

The nurse checked Veda's chart, frowned. "Hmm. It looks like a fluid drip was ordered by the doctor."

"In the middle of the night? Which doctor? I'm not getting this."

"Pardon?"

"Something is wrong with Dr. Barrow."

"Wrong? She's recovering nicely. We've postponed her release until tomorrow, but she's really doing quite well."

Veda's face had slackened and she stared out the window. Her lips worked, silently at first, then she said, "Look at that plane landing, Tally. Over there, by the mountain."

Out the window, a field of tall brown grasses waved in the afternoon breeze. What was Veda talking about? "There's no plane, Vede. No mountain."

"Of course there is. Right there." She pointed to the meadow.

Dear God. "Veda, let me—"

She grabbed my hand, her stubby nails biting my flesh. "See the plane land. Bertha and I are getting off. Down the steps. See? See us? But we want to run back inside. Not get on the train. Do you see it now? There. The Wirth Gallery. You must go. Must. See? The doors are opening. Promise you'll go."

"Of course, I promise," I said. "I'll go. I will. Listen, I'll be right back."

Veda sighed and smiled. "That's nice."

I grabbed the nurse's arm and hauled her out of the room.

"What the hell is going on?" I asked. "Dr. Barrow is hallucinating. She thinks she's on some frigging plane. She's crying. She never cries. Never."

The nurse nodded sagely, and I wanted to shake her.

"This happens to some patients," she said. "Those who are hospitalized for a while. They become a bit confused. It will pass as soon as she's home."

"Dr. Barrow is not your typical patient." I sighed in frustration. "Where's her doctor?"

The nurse scooted inside the nurses' station and returned minutes later. "I paged him."

I went back inside Veda's room. She'd fallen asleep again. I waited, tapping my foot, pacing. The doctor was taking a helluva long time. Veda's eyes opened. She smiled. "I'm tired, Tally. You'd better go home. Bertha will be waiting."

"Bertha's not at my house, Vede."

"Of course she's at our house. She's making sauerbraten for our dinner. Your favorite." I hadn't lived with Bertha and Veda for over twelve years. What was happening to Veda?

Thirty minutes later, a man in tortoiseshell glasses and pleated pants breezed into the room.

"Doctor?" I said.

"So sorry," he said in warm tones that defined *patronizing*. "Emergency."

I explained how Veda was not only acting strangely, but was actively hallucinating.

In what seemed like a parody of the nurse's prior movements, he lifted the chart that hung at the foot of Veda's bed. "Hmm. Dr. Barrow's behavior is not uncommon. Particularly since she's been here for several days."

He turned to Veda. "Dr. Barrow?"

"Yes?" She smiled.

"And how are we feeling."

"Are you the doctor?"

He nodded. "I am."

"I'm feeling well, thank you."

He shrugged and hung the chart back up. "See?" he said to me.

"I'm afraid I don't," I said.

"Do you mind if I sleep now?" Veda asked.

"Not at all," replied the doctor.

She turned on her side, hands beneath her head, and closed her eyes.

"As soon as she's home," he said, "she'll be her old self."

"But what if you're wrong? What if she's—"

"We're not. We really do know what we're doing here at Hawthorne. We may not be one of your big Boston hospitals, but we're at the top of our game."

"But ..." It was like talking to a wall of foam.

"Must run," he said. "I'll see you tomorrow?"

"Sure. Of course. Tomorrow."

Chapter Eight

Once home, I called Bertha. "Are you making sauerbraten, auntie?"

"I haven't made that for years. It troubles my sister's stomach. And why ...?"

"Oh, I just got a bee in my head." I told her the hospital wanted to keep her sister for one more day.

After we rang off, I dialed the Wirth Gallery and asked for Nick or his brother, Stan.

"Tally Ho!" Nick said when he came on the line. "How is dear Veda?"

"Um, she's a little under the weather, and I know you two were working on something. She mentioned an opening you and Stan were having?"

"Yes. She plans to bring you as her date."

"I had no idea," I said. "I'm not sure she'll be able to come."

"The event's important to her, my dear Tal. She must come. So must you."

The last thing I wanted. "I'm not sure Veda can. And I sure can't, Nick. I'm on a disturbing case and—"

"The little girl?"

"Yes. And Penny has a lump on her leg that's—"

"I have a marvelous vet," he said. "Marvelous. He's at Angell and, well, he's a master. Put those troubling things aside and—"

"I'm so sorry, Nick, but I can't." My phone beeped. Hank calling from Maine. "I've got to run. Forgive me. I'll call if something changes. Again, many apologies."

I clicked over to Hank and poured out my guts. His resonant voice soothed me, until he started agreeing with the doctor and nurse. What Veda was experiencing was temporary. Sundowning, he called it. He was as glib as they'd been. Swear to God he sounded like Mary Poppins.

He brought up Bella Marsh, and there he sounded doom and gloom, going on about kidnapping statistics that I didn't want to hear.

"She could still be alive," I said.

"Doubt it," he said, and plunged into another soliloquy on statistics.

I was worn out by the time we said good-bye.

I scooped kibbles for Penny, and then took her for a run. She seemed fine, and if it weren't for that golf ball-sized lump, you'd never know something was wrong.

As my feet pounded the pavement, I kept replaying my visit with Veda, how disoriented she'd been, her dreadful look of bewilderment, of fear. Back home, I scooched on the couch, tried to read a book, watch some TV.

My body screamed exhaustion while my mind volleyed between Bella Marsh and Veda, the suicide and Penny and Hank and Rose and ...

Feeling much like a hamster racing pointlessly on its wheel, I loaded Penny into the car and returned to OCME. We had to be missing something that would help us find little Bella.

OCME was quiet. The dead slept soundly; too much so. Charley, the tech on duty, checked me into my office. Charley and I were the only breathing ones in the place.

Penny curled up on the sofa in my office and slept. I flipped open my PowerBook and did my usual creation of folders and such for Bella and Rose's cases. Writing stuff down always helped me connect the dots.

After I noted all I could remember about little Rose Noguchi and Bella Marsh, I checked OCME's database for the past two days' memos.

Since I couldn't sleep, I might as well catch up on paperwork.

Fogarty had peppered the place with announcements. Cripes. He was a power trip looking for a permanent berth. I filed a few memos of my own, but I remained restless.

I walked to the main cooler, where Rose rested. She was still there, and a note on her chart said she would be released to her family in the morning. I didn't lift the sheet covering her face. Time had passed. She was already being reclaimed. I didn't know if she was to be embalmed or not. I hoped not. I pressed my hand to the sheet, felt the lamb she clutched in the crook of her arm. A part of me noted how her flesh lacked any resiliency.

Rose was long gone. I'd never known her, and I regretted that.

When I got home I crashed, except I couldn't sleep. Since it was only around nine, I phoned the Noguchis to see how they were doing. Poorly, as expected. We made a date for the following day. I usually didn't make house calls, but for little Rose, I'd make an exception.

I passworded into CSS files and learned that Rose had not been raped, nor did it appear that she'd been molested in any sexual way. I didn't get that feel from the case, either. Hank, Kranak, and I had talked about a ritual killing of some sort. It made sense—the nail polish, the posing, the lamb. Yet I was feeling strange things about Rose Noguchi's death, things I couldn't identify.

Unusual for me, and troublesome.

I hoped to have more answers in the morning, about Rose and Bella and Veda and Penny. I stole a section of the couch from Penny and pulled the afghan up to my shoulders.

How many balls could I juggle before I dropped them all?

The following morning at the meeting in the conference room, Fogarty held forth. He harangued his staff, as well as the ancillary attendees, about the mess at the Medical Examiner's Office. As if they were the cause. Right. He berated all of us about what a hassle it had been collecting our DNA, and how evidence had gone missing from an old case, and how the door to the storage room had been left unlocked.

He never made eye contact with me. He knew I'd fire right back at him, and he sure didn't want to get burned by me. Not that morning. Yet without mentioning my name, he ignited over Mrs. Hulbert's suicide attempt and the resulting bad press. Lucky for me, my job didn't depend on the largesse of the chief medical examiner. But boy was I boiling when we all filed out of the meeting.

Fogarty had minions now. Dr. Blaine LeCase and Dr. Judy Ethridge followed him like sheep. I'd at least figured Ethridge for having more backbone than that. Wrong again.

A spiderweb of cracks had begun to form due to Fogarty's inept reins. The murmurs of resentment, the slacking of procedure, the sloppy paperwork, the focus on glitz and publicity. The staff was overworked and undermotivated. Veda couldn't get back quickly enough.

I twirled in Gert's crinkled leather chair as I reviewed that day's schedule. Donna pounded reports into the computer at Mach speed, and Ben gathered paperwork for his group counseling session for the families of homicide victims.

A bubble popped in my ear.

"Gert, dammit," I said. "Don't do that."

"So whacha think?" she asked.

"The schedule?" I rehung it on the wall. "Excellent. It's clear and efficient."

"Yeah. It came out pretty good."

I ran my finger down our copy of OCME's new arrivals. "No new ones today, at least not for us."

"Nope. We got enough ta do with Fogarty on the warpath. Hey, when's Veda getting out?"

"Any day, I expect."

She flipped me around to face her. "What's wrong?" Her sweet, pretty-girl face now scowled up at me. "So?" she said.

I sighed, looked away, didn't want to hold those corn-flower blue eyes to mine. "Things aren't great, Gertie. Not great."

A hand on my back steered me into my office. "How aren't they great?"

I shut the door behind us. "I don't know yet. Not really. I'm just worried about her."

She rubbed her fingers across the back of my hand. "You never knew your real mom, and now you're afraid for this one. It's hard."

"More than I would have thought."

"She'll be okay. She survived the Holocaust and the camps. She's one tough old bird." A smile peeked out, and I answered it with my own.

"That she is." I checked my watch. "Shit. I'm supposed to be out in Temple with the Noguchis in ninety minutes."

Zooming down Route Two, I flipped open my cell, slipped on my Bluetooth ear piece, and called the hospital.

Veda was sleeping comfortably, according to the nurse.

"How was her night?" I asked.

She checked her chart. "Good, as far as I can tell."

I hesitated, and then plunged. "And how did she seem this morning?"

"Fine. She ate a good breakfast. No temp. Her blood count is back to normal. Looks like she can go home, um, they're saying tomorrow."

"Did she seem ... normal?"

"I would guess. We chatted for a minute. Her sister is here now."

"Excellent. Call me if you need me for anything. I'll be out to see her later today."

I allowed myself a nanosecond of relief, and then the phone bleeped.

"How's Penny doing?" Dr. Joby asked.

"She seems fine." I glanced over at my sleeping dog. The lump hadn't changed, and Penny had worked hard the previous day. A good sign? I scratched behind her ears while I told Beth Joby about Penny's workout.

"That sounds good," she said. "I thought I'd just check in."

"You're wonderful, you know."

A bellow of a laugh. "That's me, the wonderful vet. And, no, we don't have the information from the biopsy back yet. Takes time."

I chuckled. "You read my mind."

" 'Course I did. You take it easy."

"Oh, 'easy' defines me. Yup suh." I ruffled Penny's fur. "Call me. Please."

I took Route 93 this time, the fastest way from Boston to Temple and the Noguchis. It occurred to me that the lab might be done with Rose's stuffed lamb. Just after I turned onto Route 3, I called the lab in Sudbury. I got my friend Billy and was told that they were so jammed up, he hadn't even looked at the lamb yet.

"*What?*" I said. "Don't you realize that time is of the essence."

"How come?" Billy said.

"Because we've got a little girl who's been kidnapped. We

could learn a hell of a lot about her kidnapper from that lamb."

"The kid's dead, Tally," he said. "Haven't you heard?"

My heart squeezed as I pictured the little blonde girl with the impish smile. I sighed. "They found Bella?"

"The kid's name is Rose."

A truck cut me off, and I cursed. "Sorry. Lousy drivers. You said 'Rose.' This is like a bad comedy routine, Billy. I know Rose Noguchi is dead. But her friend, Bella Marsh, is still missing. They were together. Hasn't anyone filled you in on this?"

"Well, fuck, no! All I heard was that this was found on the dead kid."

I filled Billy in on what I knew. The second I finished, he slammed down the phone without a good-bye. The laconic lab tech was ticked—a rarity—and it wasn't with me.

How could no one have told Billy about Bella Marsh? Again I felt things falling apart. With Veda out of the picture, the systems that she'd spent years putting in place at OCME were now crumbling.

The mystery of Rose Noguchi felt a part of it all. Kranak, Fogarty, and others believed that someone inside OCME had killed Rose and left her in the cooler. Made sense. Yet it didn't ring true with me. I couldn't explain why. All I knew was that I felt a sense of wrongness, much like when flesh begins to corrupt and you smell that first whiff of death.

Something was bothering me. A "whatever" that I hoped would float into my consciousness.

Until then, like everyone else in this crazy case, I'd wing it.

I turned off Route 101, and began my meander on narrow back roads peppered with old New England Capes, small farms, and the occasional trailer. I reviewed what I would talk about with the Noguchis, if, in fact, the heartbroken family had anything to say. They had a son, too. One I hoped to meet. He was older than Rose. Maybe a teen? Yes, fifteen.

In a blink I passed through the quaint New England village of Temple. I spotted the Noguchi's majestic white colonial, right next to the Marsh's yellow one. The Marshes hadn't called, and I saw no cars in their driveway.

I parked on the street beside an old maple that would dress in spectacular colors come fall. Now, it wasn't even budded out. A sigh caught in my throat. Rose would never see the bright green of spring.

I walked up the pretty brick path toward the white antique colonial's side door and pressed the bell way too hard.

Someone yelled "coming," and seconds later the red door opened. A large woman peered up at me from her wheelchair. Mrs. Noguchi's apple-red cheeks spoke of the outdoors, as did the calloused, square hands she held out for me to shake. She enfolded my hand in her much larger ones. She didn't smile, but waved me inside.

"Bob is still at work," she said. "He got held over. Come, have a seat."

She wheeled down the narrow center hall and into a combination kitchen/family room decorated in traditional New England style.

"Mrs. Noguchi—"

"Call me Teresa."

"Teresa, how are you holding up?"

"Just fine." She glided her wheelchair across the wide pine boards, stopping opposite the checked couch. She gestured for me to sit.

She bustled around the kitchen designed for her chair, and soon produced tea, two mugs, and all the fixings on a tray she placed on the coffee table in front of the couch.

"Help yourself," she said. "Anything to keep busy, to not think about Rosie."

I noted her misbuttoned shirt and the swollen flesh

around her eyes. "Nothing is harder than what you're experiencing," I said.

"No." She focused on the bay window and beyond, perhaps imagining her little Rose playing out back on the swing or digging in the garden.

Or maybe Teresa Noguchi was thinking how much she'd like twisting a knife into little Rose's killer's heart.

Even after twenty-some years, those feelings about my father's killer still ate at my soul. Survivors walked so many trails. I pictured Bella Marsh and shuddered.

"What can I do for you?" I asked.

Teresa Noguchi smiled with an irony and anger I'd seen hundreds of times. "Leave me alone with Rose's killer for five minutes. That would be enough. Just five minutes."

"No," I said. "That I unfortunately cannot do, although at this point, revenge does sound sweet, doesn't it?"

"Oh, yes. *Yes!*"

A huge yellow Labrador retriever galumphed in, followed by a tall boy with electroshock hair and a passive face peppered with acne. He hugged his mother and flicked his head my way.

"Who's this?" he said.

I introduced myself, accepted his derisive snort, and waited. Their lab was all over me, alternately licking and smelling.

"Where's Pop," he asked.

"On his way," said his mother. She held his fingertips in her hand.

"He's always late."

"It's his job," she said.

He flicked his chin at me. "You wanna give me a ride to baseball?"

"Sure."

He turned. "Let's go."

"Silas, wait," said his mother. "I can—"

"Forget it, Ma. Too much hassle. This lady here can do it. It'll only take five minutes."

"But, Silas ..."

He breezed out the door.

"You don't mind?" I said.

"I mind. He sometimes reacts to me the way Rosie's friend Bella does. Only Rosie dealt with my disability in a good way." She slapped the arms of her wheelchair. "But, sure, go ahead."

"Perhaps your husband will be here by the time I get back."

I walked toward the door.

Teresa snorted. "Don't count on it."

Chapter Nine

Silas waited for me by the car, a huge green baseball bag slung over his shoulder. His lips were compressed in annoyance.

"Your dog wouldn't let me in the car." He jerked his thumb toward Penny.

"Without my command, Penny lets no one in the car but me."

"Stupid."

"He's okay, Pens." I nodded to Silas.

He reached for the passenger-side door, and Penny's tail thumped a hello. He relaxed when she licked him. He tossed his bag on the floor and scrunched beside Penny, his arm around her, hugging and scratching her behind her ears.

"Buckle up, please." I said as I snapped on my seat belt.

"Naw," he said..

"Yeah."

He turned his head toward me. His flat, opaque stare prickled the hairs of my neck. Penny rumbled a growl. Silas smiled, and his black eyes washed with warmth as he fastened his seat belt.

Whew. What the hell was that?

Silas again scratched Penny's ears, and she wuffled a sigh and rested her huge head in his lap.

I did a U-turn on the street and headed toward Peterborough, where Silas said he attended high school, and where Bella Marsh and Rose Noguchi went to middle school.

"Penny likes you," I said.

"Most dogs do. How come she wouldn't let me in the car at first?"

"She's trained to protect and guard, among other things."

"Cool," he said. "She the one who was looking for Bella yesterday?"

"Yes, until the official SAR dogs arrived."

"SAR dogs?"

"Search and rescue."

"She's dead, y'know."

"You sound quite certain."

"I am. Why would he kill Rosie and not ..." He peered out the window, his arm tight around Penny's shoulder. She licked his cheek.

"I don't know."

"You should! Like why the fuck would some monster kill my little sis?"

Out of the corner of my eye, I saw tears river his cheeks.

"Turn left here," he mumbled. "When we get to Peterborough, take a right onto two-oh-two. You'll see the sign. You're a touchy-feely shrink, right?"

"I am. And the survivor of a homicide that took my dad."

He shook his head. "You're just saying that to shrinky-dink me."

"I wish I was," I said.

"People are dickheads."

"They can be."

"I'd like to cut off his balls and—"

"Hang on to that anger, Silas. It'll help get you through this. You're in for a tough, tough time."

"Yeah, right." He stifled a sob. "I wish Rose'd had someone with her. She wouldn't a been so scared."

"No. I understand. But her ending was soft, Silas. She was asleep. She felt no pain. And she had her fuzzy lamb."

"Here's where you go right. What lamb?"

"The lamb I assume she slept with. It was repaired and well used."

"She slept with Teddy Two Toes and that was it. Rose never had any fucking lamb."

On my way back to the Noguchis, I dialed Billy at the lab, got his voice mail, and asked him to put a rush on that lamb. It was a stretch that the killer had left his own beloved stuffed animal with Rose, but I could see no other explanation.

The sins of the father. The sacrificial lamb. Obvious. Maybe too obvious? Could the clever killer who'd somehow managed to hide Rose's body at the medical examiner's office be that clichéd? Or, rather, were all the signs and symbols merely a play he was producing for our benefit?

When I returned to the Noguchis's an hour later, John Noguchi still hadn't arrived home. I tried to chat with Teresa, but she begged off, saying she needed a nap. I didn't blame her. I felt like I needed one, too.

I'd give the father fifteen more minutes. I checked that Penny wasn't too warm in the car, gave her water, and returned to the house.

I walked up the thick carpeted stairs and down the hall toward Rose's room. I wanted to reconnect with the child I had seen at OCME.

I was surprised by the room's beauty and austerity. It offered none of the chaos that bubbled in most girls' rooms. A tiny self-contained fountain played a soft melody and a sweet American Girl doll that looked remarkably like Rose perched on a shelf. Another shelf held books, and in a corner was a small Buddha surrounded by unlit candles and silk flowers.

I sat on the sisal mat that covered the wooden floor. One

picture of the family, another of the lab, and one of two girls, arm-in-arm. Bella and Rose. The soothing smell of roses permeated the room.

Rose's room was neat and gracious, with a hint of the Buddhism she apparently practiced.

The bed was platform-style, with nothing underneath. Toys and books and clothes jammed the closet, and I was about to check out the top shelf when I saw Rose's purple hairbrush. I picked it up. Some strands of Rose's hair wove through the white bristles.

"What are you doing in here?"

I spun around.

John Noguchi's face was tight with anger, his teeth clenched.

"I'm trying to get a sense of Rose, John."

He deflated. "Yes, of course you are. Would you like to pray with me at Rose's shrine?"

We knelt and sat back on our heels. I folded my hands and bowed my head. I wouldn't pray—didn't know how anymore—but I repeated a mantra I'd learned years ago. It soothed me.

I saw little Rose playing with her friend, Bella. They were laughing and skipping rope. A figure loomed over them, a shadow that grew large. And they smiled up at the shadow, openly, warmly.

Rose turned away and looked at me straight on. *Go to her. Go to Veda.*

I shook my head. The voice, it had been all in my head, of course. But ...

A whisper ... *Go to Veda.*

I inhaled deeply, blinked with reluctance and opened my eyes. John Noguchi was staring at me.

"You spoke," he said.

"Did I?"

"You said the word 'Veda.' "

"Yes." I pushed myself off the floor. My legs, half-numb, tingled. "I must go, John."

He nodded, remained kneeling on the floor. "I know. Rose told me."

I'd had stranger things happen, but not many. Rose's voice had rung clear in my head.

I sped toward Hawthorne Medical Center, worry gnawing my gut. Just as I reached the heron rookery, my cell beeped. I pushed my earphone into my ear and flipped open my phone.

"Tally! Tally! *Ach,* you must come!"

"Bertha? I'm on my way. What's wrong?"

"Veda. She is bad. Very bad. I am frightened. Oh, do hurry."

"I am."

When I varoomed into Veda's hospital room, I found Veda asleep and Bertha dozing, her head resting on her hand.

I sighed deep and long. Veda was alive.

Dear Bertha. She was the excitable one, the antithesis of Veda. Her emotions were a well-worn suit she rarely put away. Nowadays, she'd be called a drama queen.

Yet as children, both had survived the Holocaust camps, which led me to believe dear Bertha had as much grit as Veda. She just revealed it in different ways.

"Hey, Bertha." I scooched down and hugged her.

"Thank God you've arrived, *Liebchen.*"

"What happened?"

"*Mein schweste! Sie ist nichet …*"

"English, Bertha."

"*Entschuldigungen.* Apologies. My sister is not herself. Not at all. She has been inhabited by another person. I am so frightened by it."

I kissed her forehead and walked to the bed. Veda looked normal. Better, in fact, than on my last visit. I took her hands in mine. They were warm, rather than chilled. Her chest rose and fell with regularity and seeming ease. Her skin was peachy, not flushed, nor sallow. I leaned closer. "Veda. Veda, can you wake up?"

Her eyelids fluttered. Lines creased her hawklike face. For a woman in her late sixties, she'd changed little in the twenty years I'd known her. I smoothed a hand over her ink-black hair.

"Vede?" I said.

Her eyes opened and her lips bent into a slow smile. "Emma, my sweet. How's college going? Did you pass that dreaded trig class?"

I jerked. Emma? Although my given name, she hadn't called me that since high school, sixteen years earlier. "College? You mean work?"

She pulled her hand away. "You hurt my hand." She pouted.

Veda pouting? Inconceivable. "I'm ... I'm sorry. How are you feeling today?"

"I ... I don't know." Her eyes crackled with fear. "Something's wrong, Tally. Very wrong. I can't seem to focus on where I am or ... Are you in college?"

I pulled a chair over. "No, Vede. I run the Massachusetts Grief Assistance Program."

"Oh. Oh, yes." Again, that vapid smile, the unfocused eyes, the vibe of confusion.

She terrified me, this new and strange Veda.

"Of course you run that ... program?" she continued. "Where is that?"

I forced my hands to relax around hers. "Your building. The Grief Shop. OCME."

"I see."

But she didn't see. Not at all.

"I'll be back in a sec, Vede." I kissed her cheek and then carefully walked from the room. Once through the door, I raced for the nurses' station. I entered a glassed room positioned between two hospital halls.

"I need to speak to Dr. Barrow's nurse."

No one looked up.

"I know you're busy, but I must speak to Dr. Barrow's nurse. Now."

Perhaps something in my tone attracted a nurse in a Garfield top. She reviewed a list, and then beeped an intercom buzzer. "Nurse Ledesma. To the station, please. Nurse Ledesma."

Then everyone went back to ignoring me.

Minutes passed. I tried to imagine what had happened to Veda. A stroke? A virus? Lack of oxygen to the brain?

I had no idea. None. I felt helpless and was getting angrier by the minute.

"Can I help you? I'm Nurse Ledesma."

The nurse came up to my shoulder. She wore a Spider-Man nursing top and her raven hair was done up in a ponytail.

"My foster mother, Veda Barrow. She's acting very strangely. Not herself. Not at all. Even stranger than yesterday."

The nurse nodded. "Let me get her chart." Minutes later, she was reviewing what I assumed were the previous night's notes on Veda.

The nurse nodded. "Yes. She had a bad night last night. First, we had trouble getting a line into her."

"A line? You mean an IV?"

"Yes. I guess several of her veins collapsed. The doctor ordered more fluids and ..." She shook her head. "It was tough. But after that she seems to have rested comfortably for several hours."

"And that's it?"

"I'm not done!" she snapped.

I wanted to shake her, I was so disturbed. "Sorry. I'm ... upset. So then what?"

"She began shouting. Something like 'elfie bitter.' That's what's written here. This was at four-twenty-three A.M. She was speaking in German, I guess. And no one here understood her. By the time a nurse got to her, she'd quieted. Her vitals were good at that time. It most likely was a bad dream."

"It wasn't a dream. Something was wrong." I read pity and resignation in the nurse's deep blue eyes.

"Life in a hospital can be different," she said. "Dr. Barrow has been with us for several days. As often happens, she may have become disoriented."

"You mean sundowning?"

"Some call it that. Yes."

"Well, we have a real problem here, because she is definitely not herself, and she keeps getting stranger by the minute."

"That happens."

Our conversation was smoke and mirrors. "I'd like to see her doctor, please."

She shrugged. "He's doing afternoon rounds. I'll put a call into him."

I returned to Bertha, and we waited and waited and waited. She whimpered, I grew more and more furious, and Veda slept.

"This is a load of crap," I said sixty minutes later. "I'll be back."

Out to the nurses' station I went. I was so pissed, I almost couldn't see. When I stomped into the room, this time everyone looked up.

"Excuse me. I know you are understaffed. Terribly busy. Have too many patients in your care. That said, we have been waiting for an hour to speak with Dr. Barrow's attending physician."

"Oh, sorry." Again, the nurse in the Garfield outfit, not the least bit ruffled. "I'm not sure where he is."

"She's awake, Tally," Bertha called from Veda's room.

"Then please send in the nurse who attended Dr. Barrow the day she was admitted. Please. Now."

I moved beside Veda's bed and clamped one hand around the cold rail. I smoothed the hair back from her forehead with the other. She was cool and soft. Vulnerable, like I'd never seen her. "Hi, Vede," I said. "You have a good snooze?"

She nodded, and I ached again as I watched that tentative smile form on her lips, the smile that said she had no idea what I was talking about or, possibly, even who I was.

The nurse I recognized from that first day entered the room with machine-gun steps.

"You were with her for two days," I said to the nurse.

"Yes." She gave Veda a warm smile. "She's an amazing woman. She regaled us with some of her adventures in medical school."

"Talk to her. You'll see how she's changed."

The nurse moved to the head of the bed and took Veda's hand. "How are you feeling, Dr. Barrow?"

Veda reach up and tweaked the end of the nurse's steel-gray braid. "Fine," Veda said.

"Is the food okay?" the nurse asked.

"Terrible!"

They laughed.

How could they laugh? This wasn't Veda, but some Stepford Doctor Barrow.

"Veda," I broke in. "When's my birthday?"

Her eyes slowly traveled to mine. She blinked rapidly, as if searching for some inner encyclopedia. She bit her lip, looked at the nurse, then back at me. "Why, I don't know. Should I?"

I hauled the nurse from the room. "What is wrong with her?" I said.

"Nothing that some bed rest won't cure. I've seen it a thousand times."

"Not this, you haven't."

"She's depressed, for one thing."

"Veda doesn't get depressed."

"She doesn't get hospitalized either, from what you've said."

I knocked my head back against the cement block wall. "Look, she is not depressed. What she is, is not normal."

"I'm sorry, but she seems fine to me." Her pager beeped, and after a pseudo-comforting pat on my arm, she bustled down the hall.

I wanted to scream.

I spotted Veda's doctor. He was about my height, with a slight comb-over and a twinkle in his eyes. He wore a tie but no jacket, as did many of the physicians doing rounds. He aimed for jolly, which that afternoon annoyed me intensely.

"Dr. Graham," I said. "Could I have a minute?"

"Sure, Ms. Whyte. But only a minute." He smiled, and there was that damned twinkle again.

"It's Veda. She's not … right."

He clutched his clipboard and nodded. "The nurses mentioned you've been saying that."

"It's not what I've 'been saying.' It's true. She's not herself. Not at all."

He waved a hand. The ring on his wedding finger was loose. "What does 'not at all' mean, really? She's out of sorts. A bit, um, drifty. But she's on a lot of meds, Ms. Whyte. A lot. That can affect a person."

"Not unless she was incorrectly medicated."

"Are you accusing someone of making an error?"

I turned away, trying to keep it together, feeling I was about to fail with that asshole. "Look. Dr. Veda Barrow is acting as if she's got Alzheimer's, which she hasn't. Something has happened to her to cause this change. I want a CAT scan and an MRI. I want her blood tested. I want every damn test in the book. Hear me?"

He jotted some notes on his Palm and nodded in a way that was supposed to be sage, which served to annoy me even further.

"No need to get so worked up, Ms. Whyte," he said.

"Worked up? Are you kidding me? Dr. Barrow is one of the bright lights in our state. A brilliant, award-winning doctor, and you're telling me not to get worked up when she's acting like a Fruit Loop?"

"Really, Ms. Whyte, please control—"

"For you, it's Dr. Whyte. And lemme tell you, you have yet to see me out of control. Something is damned wrong. And I want to know what the hell it is and what caused it. And pronto!"

He sneered. "Or what?"

"I'll have her moved to Mass General, where her dear friend is Chief of Surgery. And I'll make sure that the Chief gets the word out about you and this hospital's incompetence. Got it?"

"Oh, I've got it, Dr. Whyte. But my money's on nothing showing up in any tests we run. Not one damned thing."

I was terrified of that, too. "Just do it."

Chapter Ten

I drove Bertha home, and then called my old friend and former professor, Dr. Barbara Beliskowitz, a forensic psychiatrist. I might be decent at analyzing people with aberrant behaviors, but Barbara was the best of the best.

Her voice mail clicked on. My feelings of frustration and fear mingled into one nasty cocktail.

I left Barbara a message, then called Veda's primary care physician. His receptionist said he was away for two weeks and some Dr. Joe Blow was filling in for him. Someone who wouldn't know the real Veda Barrow. Swell.

I was frantic, acting out of panic. I zoomed into the OCME parking lot and squealed to a stop. I closed my eyes and hugged Penny. Her fur was soft and comforting. She licked my face. She smelled of doggie and the chamomile bath I'd recently given her.

I hugged her tighter. I was acting like a baby. Ridiculous. Geesh.

A knock on my car window. I jumped, hit my elbow. "Ouch! Dammit!"

No growl from Penny. Must be a friend. I didn't want to see a friend, didn't want to see anybody. "Go away."

Again, the knock.

I turned.

There stood Kranak, palms up, a frown pulling his mustache to his chin. "Wassup, Tal?" he mouthed.

"Nothing's up," I said. "I said go away."

"Tal, dammit, open the fucking window," he barked.

I slammed the truck into gear, ready to drive off. But I couldn't do it, not to Kranak. I sighed and powered down the window. "Want to go to the boat?" I said.

"Yeah, sure," he said. "I'll bring pizza. And no coppin' out on me or you're dead meat."

"Right. I'm terrified. Make mine Vidalia with bacon and goat cheese."

"Dis-gusting."

I wove through Boston's traffic and serpentine streets on the drive to Kranak's boat, which had a permanent berth in Charlestown Harbor's Constitution Marina. Although close in miles, it was a painful bumper-to-bumper trip. I called Billy at the lab in Sudbury.

"Hey fella," I said.

"Tal," Billy said. "How goes it?"

"Strangely, for sure. I'm calling about little Rose's lamb, the one that was tucked in her arm when she appeared at OCME. Would you get it for me?"

"Not a good time, Tal."

"It never is, Billy. But I really need for you to look at it."

"Okay. Two seconds."

I inched forward, waiting for the light to change. I peeked at the floor in the backseat and spotted the cans of Alpo I'd been hoping were there. I had some kibbles in the way back, too.

"Tal, um, you there?" Billy said.

"Yup." I adjusted my headset. "Is there any dried blood on the lamb, Billy?"

"Dried blood?"

"Yes. I can't remember, and although Rose wasn't bleeding, I thought I'd seen some. I'd like to confirm if it's there, and if the blood was ritualistic."

"You mean like an offering? A sacrifice?"

"Exactly. The sacrificial lamb, which is what I believe Rose represented. The lamb didn't belong to Rose. It may have been her killer's own lamb. Or maybe even a previous victim's toy. I'm desperate to find anything that might make sense and help us find Rose's friend, Bella."

Silence. Horns honking. I pressed my foot to the gas pedal.

"Billy? Are you there?"

"Yeah. Yeah, I'm here."

"Oh, crap. Something's wrong, isn't it."

Huge sigh. "I dunno. Maybe. I can't exactly find the lamb."

"Geesh, Billy. It has to be there."

"I mighta misplaced it. Or maybe I never got it. I'm not sure the ME's office delivered it. I'll look in the lockers next to where we put her stuff, Tal."

"Thanks. I absolutely saw that lamb. It was stitched in places, well worn."

"I'll start lookin' ASAP. But I'm jammed up like crazy. You know how many people are screamin' at me about cases? I can't promise soon."

"You've got to, Billy. For Bella."

At Constitution Marina, I let Penny out for a trot before we walked down the wharf to Kranak's boat. It was here in Boston Harbor where the sea met the Charles River. The smell of the ocean was overpowering and delicious. I inhaled deeply, and my lungs drew in the briny ocean air that always reminded me of sailing with my dad in Maine.

Across the water, downtown Boston spread before me, with the Pru and the Hancock jutting high in the sky.

Gulls cawed and whirled above us, and colored boats bobbed in their slips, while a few remained wrapped in their winter plastic. As always, I got a kick out of seeing the marina manager's sixty-foot sail boat that was permanently docked in front of the club house. He'd named her *Rocinante,* after Don Quixote's old and randy nag of a horse. Obviously a man with a sense of humor.

Although the days lurched toward summer solstice, April's twilight had begun to curtain the city. Dock lights glowed as Penny and I walked towards Kranak's reproduction Friendship sloop. The sloop was Kranak's home, and was as far as possible from death at The Grief Shop and yet still in town.

Penny must have spotted the *Far Away*, for she quickened her steps. A little farther down the dock, I saw the maroon boat bobbing in the wake of a passing tour boat. It almost felt like home.

Rose would never see her home again. How could the lamb be missing? But of course it could, given the bizarre nature of the whole case. Hadn't Rose first appeared on a gurney at The Grief Shop? My gut said Billy would never find that lamb.

I sat on a blue cushioned bench that ran along the stern, Penny at my feet, and gazed out into the harbor. A nearby sloop cast off and *put-put*ted out to open water. She was abuzz with activity. The crew furled the sails and raised the jib, and suddenly she took off, skimming the waves as the breeze pushed her toward infinite possibilities.

"Hey," Kranak said.

I raised my hand above my eyes to shield them from the sun. "You're here. I've been watching. Pretty, isn't she?"

"Not as pretty as my girl."

"Well, of course not. Mmmmm. The pizza smells yummy."

"Let's eat." He punched the key code into the lock, and then opened the cabin door. "You coulda gone in, Tal."

"I know. Why don't we eat out here, al fresco?"

"Sure." He brought drinks and a small plastic table from the cabin, and we dived into our food. We didn't talk at first. As day dimmed, the harbor came alive with lights.

"Your hair looks like ... well, it's scary-lookin', the way its sticking outta that pink Red Sox hat."

I could picture my Medusa hair and laughed. "Thanks, Rob. You look cute, too."

"That's what my mama always used ta say."

While I fed Penny, Kranak opened some Cabernet and poured it into NPR mugs.

"Don't get that gross pizza near mine," he said.

I took a long, slow bite into the soft goat cheese and crispy bacon and onion. I smiled. "Oh, yum."

He stuffed a half slice into his mouth, swiped it with a napkin. "So what's the matter?"

My next bite hid the trembling of my lips. I shrugged. "Just stuff."

"Goddammit, Tal. What the fuck's wrong?"

I had trouble swallowing, but finally got it down with a gulp of wine. "I ... Will you come see Veda with me tomorrow morning?"

"I thought she was getting out of the hospital."

"Not for a couple more days," I said.

"Sure, I'll come see her. What's up?" He topped off my mug with more Cabernet.

I took a swallow. "I'd like you to see for yourself."

That night, Penny lay heavy on my feet. I moved, hoping she'd reshift her position, but no such luck. I cranked open an eyelid. Watery sun filtered in from the French doors. I'd fallen asleep on the couch.

I blinked a couple of times to focus. I checked my watch. Five A.M. What the hell ...

The phone rang again. Ahhh.

I groped for the portable and clicked it on. "Tally Whyte here."

"She's back," Kathleen Lauria said. "Bella is back."

I tossed on my clothes, splashed water on my face, and piled Penny into the 4Runner. Boston was only beginning to stir as I raced through town, aiming for the New Hampshire countryside.

Lauria had said Bella Marsh had wandered into Peterborough, New Hampshire's Monadnock Community Hospital about two hours earlier. She'd been dirty—filthy, in fact—and they'd immediately examined her. They'd given her a room, as they had no idea of her identity, and called the Peterborough police. Within the hour, Bella was identified as the missing Amber Alert child from Temple. They'd called Lauria, which was when she called me.

Amazingly, Bella was apparently in decent shape, hadn't been sexually molested, and appeared not to be frightened. Lauria said the child wasn't in the mood to talk, either, and she hoped I could get Bella to open up. Once Lauria and I arrived at the hospital, Lauria would call Bella's parents. Lauria wanted me to interview her first.

I crossed the hospital's waiting room aiming for Lauria and Bella Marsh. With Lauria's permission, I'd brought Penny because she always managed to put victims at ease. Another special agent led us to a carpeted room off the lobby.

Bella sat poker-straight, hands folded in her lap. Lauria was talking, but the little ten-year-old wasn't listening. A flash of Rose hit me hard. Did Bella know her friend was dead—murdered?

I slowed my steps. She'd been cleaned up and dressed in pink jeans, a pink flowered turtleneck, and a pink sweater. All new, apparently, and all to cheer up a child who'd just returned from the dead. Bella's long blonde hair had been cleaned and combed, and a scrunchy held it in a ponytail.

Her only outward sign of trauma was a jagged scratch that lightninged across her left cheek.

She was pretty kid, for sure, but no stunner. Not so striking that a pedophile would spot her and feel compelled to take her. Then again, she could be one of those people whose animation makes them gorgeous.

As Penny and I neared Bella, I caught Lauria's eye. She rolled hers. Either Bella was uncooperative or the conversation's ebb and flow had stopped at ebb.

I scooched down in front of the child and held out my hand. "Hi, Bella, I'm Tally and this is Penny."

Serious blue eyes studied me for long minutes, turned to Penny, and then quickly back to me. She tucked her hands beneath her fanny. "When am I going to see my Mom and Dad?"

"They're on their way, hon. They'll be here very soon. Did you have some breakfast?"

She shrugged, hands still plastered beneath her.

"Want to get some cereal, eggs, Dunkin' Donuts?"

She avoided my eyes. "That stuff isn't cool. We have, like, granola and healthy food."

I glanced at Lauria, who fanned her hands with an "I don't know."

"Would you rather wait to eat with your parents?" I said.

She nodded, and I caught a gleam of excitement in her eyes. I pulled a chair over, so I faced Bella. "Agent Lauria tells me that you weren't afraid."

Bella twirled her ponytail. "I wasn't. Why should I be?"

Why indeed. "Can you tell me where you were for the past couple of days?"

"First, get rid of that thing."

"Pardon?" I said.

"That!" She pointed at Penny.

Thing? "Kathleen, um, would you mind taking Penny to my truck?"

Lauria raised her eyebrows. "Not at all. Be right back."

"So where were you?" I said. "For the past couple of days, I mean."

Bella nodded. "I was in stasis."

I scooched closer. This little girl was calm and collected, too much so. Posttraumatic stress disorder was a distinct possibility. "I'm not sure what you mean by stasis, Bella."

She rolled her eyes. "Like in *Star Trek*, where someone's asleep while the spaceship travels millions of light years away."

"Ah. I get it. Sure. While you were in stasis, could you see or hear anything?"

"Not really."

I smiled. "I understand." Lauria returned and sat beside Bella.

"Did you get rid of it?" Bella asked.

"Um, yes," Lauria said, her face betraying her surprise.

"So tell me," I said. "How did you get out of stasis, Bella?"

She pressed a finger to her front tooth, and then grinned. "I was very clever, as my dad would say. I stayed very quiet and at night, when I felt the stasis getting looser, I slipped my hands and feet from the machine and snuck out the front door of the spaceship."

"You snuck. Smart girl. Did you see any space aliens or humans?"

"You mean Klingons? I did. The Klingon was in shadow. This was before my stasis was loosened. He was tall, with a big head."

"How were you able to see him?"

"When I went to the bathroom."

"Oh, I get it."

"I'd like to see Rose now. She was in stasis, too. Is she coming with my mom and dad?"

"She won't be with them, hon," I said.

Her fingers fluttered across the jagged scratch that marred her cheek. "Wh-why not?"

She *knows* Rose is dead. "Can you tell me why not?"

She glanced at her lap. "No. *No!* Why should I?"

"Because I would like to help you. Because you're afraid."

"How do you know?"

I rested a hand on her knee. "I can feel it, Bella. And I'm so sorry."

Her delicate lips wobbled. "No."

"Let me help, Bella," I said.

"We need to know things to help other little girls," Lauria said.

"Other girls?" Bella leaned toward me, and one hand grazed my shoulder. "Other ones?"

"Maybe," I said. "Agent Lauria and I don't want any other girls put in stasis. We could make you sort of a deputy FBI agent. Right, Agent Lauria?"

"Absolutely," Lauria said.

"I ... I would like to help." Bella said. "Yes, I would like to help other girls." Bella's eyes suddenly glittered, and she opened her arms. "Mama! Papa! There was a deformed dog! You should have seen it!" She leapt off the chair and ran across the room.

The Marshes fell to their knees and clutched their child. My chest felt heavy. So lucky. Did they know how lucky? Oh, yes. And glad that their Bella wasn't the one lying on the slab at The Grief Shop. And guilty that they felt those feelings of relief. And so much more filled their hearts and minds.

I waited while Lauria greeted the Marshes and explained what we were working on with Bella. The family approached me as if one entity.

"This can wait," Mr. Marsh said. "Can it not?"

"I'm afraid not," I said. "Bella's memories are fresh and important. We believe he may take another child, and soon."

Mr. Marsh cupped Bella's chin. "But our child needs rest."

I realized that Bella was rubbing her cheek against an

aged blanket with Winnie the Pooh on it. I looked at the Marshes, and then Lauria. "She's got her Pooh blanket."

Lauria opened her mouth, but Marlene Marsh spoke first. "Yes! We brought it. I know we said it was missing, but I found it in the wash. Stupid. I'm so sorry."

"Well, good," I said. "Yes, that's good news."

"Mr. Marsh," Lauria said. "We really must insist on continuing our interview with Bella."

"And we must insist that you leave off until tomorrow," he said.

I felt Lauria's fury and rested a hand on her arm.

"All right, Mr. Marsh," Lauria said. "Tomorrow."

I scooched down in front of Bella. "We'll see you tomorrow, hon. We'll talk more about stasis and the Klingons. How's that sound?"

"Okay," Bella said. "As long as you leave the creepy dog home."

It hurt to hear Penny called that. Distaste made a frown of Mrs. Marsh's lips, and I saw the source of Bella's indoctrination. Sad. Mr. Marsh mouthed "sorry."

"I'll leave her home, little Bella. Will do."

Chapter Eleven

After the Marshes had left, Lauria walked me to my truck. I opened the door and Penny leapt out and pranced around. She trotted over to a small stand of pine trees and did her business.

Penny knew exactly what Bella had felt about her. She was an unerring barometer for human feelings. Mrs. Marsh's attitude disturbed me. Not healthy teaching a child that a missing leg was revolting. I wondered how else she'd indoctrinated Bella.

I handed Penny a treat, and then turned to Lauria. "He allowed Bella to escape, Kathleen."

She nodded. "Why? Why Bella and not Rose?"

"I know. Unusual. Very. I thought I got his motivation. Now, I'm not so sure. I wish they'd told us about the Pooh blanket."

"Yes," she said. "They're anything but helpful."

I checked the time. "I've got to run and see Veda."

"How's she feeling?" Laura asked.

"Better. Much better, really. She'll be out of the hospital in a couple days."

Lauria knew a lie when she heard one. She hugged me. "Tomorrow, then."

"Tomorrow." I sped from Peterborough to Acton, Massachusetts, anxiety my now-familiar companion.

Kranak met me at the door to the hospital's main entrance. He slid a hand around my waist and gave it a comforting squeeze. His brown eyes telegraphed compassion, and I almost laid my arms around his neck and sighed in fear and frustration.

Instead I sucked it in, gave his hand a "thank you" squeeze and marched toward the stairway door.

"They don't have elevators in this joint?" he said.

"I'm too pissed to wait."

"Christ, Tal, I'm an old man."

I pulled open the door and began to climb. "You're forty-two, which in my book says young."

"Yeah, but I feel about eighty-five."

"You're not even wheezing." I grabbed the rail and sped faster up the cement steps.

"But I feel like I'm wheezing."

"You're in fabulous shape."

"Compared to what? A stroke victim?"

"Not funny, Rob." Too close to the bone, that one.

Veda's black eyes tracked me as I walked into the room. Confusion creased her forehead at the sight of Kranak, a man she'd known for a ten years.

"Hey, Vede." I leaned over the bed and kissed her cheek.

She beamed back that vapid smile I'd come to loathe. It was as if the smile would mask the unknown and stop others from asking questions she couldn't begin to answer.

I hoped I was wrong. "How are you feeling today?"

More smiles. "Good. Good." This from a woman who

talked a blue streak before her first cup of coffee in the morning.

"Hey, Veda," Kranak said in his usual abrasive manner. "You comin' home soon? We need ya."

She wouldn't meet Kranak's eyes, but instead gazed out the window as if it held the promise of knowledge and salvation. The horror of her changed self tiptoed its way up my spine. I so wanted to be wrong.

"Vede?" I said.

"Soon." More smiling.

Damn the smiles. Stop! I wanted to shout. "Is this yours, Veda?" I handed her the Palm she used to schedule her life.

She opened it like a book, stared, tentatively pressed a button, then another. Shook her head, bit her lip. "No," she said. "I, um, here." She thrust it at me.

I slipped it back into my purse.

"Ya look good, Vede," Kranak said. "So when is soon? Tomorrow? Friday? We got Fogarty workin' his black magic. We need ya. Bad."

Veda's face crumbled, a tragedian's mask. She whimpered. "Something's wrong, Tally. Something's very wrong. I … know it. I …" She gnawed her lip and looked away from me, at the gnarled hands that lay in her lap.

"Back in a sec, Veda," I said, and I walked out.

I found a corner down the hall and hidden from view, and pressed my back, my palms, my "self" against the corridor's cinder block wall. I struggled to smooth my breathing. I sought a velvet cave inside my head where I could hide until I got a handle on my emotions.

Kranak's voice, pitched so low I couldn't hear, rumbled from Veda's room. The rhythm was soft and slow. He was such a damned softie.

I closed my eyes, but failed to dam the tears that slid hot and acidic down my cheeks.

Who was this woman who looked at me with such pleading eyes? Who was this stranger who overflowed with fear?

Where had my ballsy, witty Veda gone? Would she ever return? How could a person's self just disappear? I couldn't see my way.

But I had to for all the love that she'd given me over the years. For the courage that she'd handed me when life was darker than hell. For the sense of confidence she'd shared when I'd had none. I owed her, big time. I loved her, too. Madly. She must never know what she had lost.

"Excuse me," came the whisper.

My eyes flew open.

"Do you remember me, Ms. Whyte?"

She came into focus: tall, long brown hair in a braid, bright blue eyes. "I ..."

"I was Ms. Barrow's nurse for a few days, while she had the flu."

I didn't remember, but ... Of course. She'd worn that same faded Snoopy tunic she had on today. "Yes. Forgive my ... Please, call me Tally. I'm afraid I don't know your name."

"Brooke."

I held out my hand. "Nice to see you again, Brooke."

She held my hand extra long, cradling it with compassion. "Nothing nice about it, Tally. I think someone may have tried to kill Dr. Barrow."

"What the hell are you talking about?" I said.

Her eyes darted around the empty hall. She tugged me around another corner, into the alcove of a stairwell. "Several nights ago, around three A.M., while I was checking my patients, I saw a shadow, someone I didn't recognize, going into Dr. Barrow's room. I couldn't tell if it was a man or woman, but I heard them talking and then her yelling and—"

Voices from the staircase, getting louder.

She gripped my arm. "Dunkin' Donuts," she hissed. "Twenty minutes." Then she was gone.

The door flipped open, and two doctors deep in conversation breezed into the hall.

* * *

Kranak and I sat at a booth in Dunkin' Donuts. I sipped Diet Coke, while Kranak slurped a chai. The clock above the counter struck half-past ten, which was fifteen minutes after Brooke was supposed to appear.

"Ya think Ms. Snoopy Tunic'll show?" he said.

"Her name is Brooke, and, yes, I think she'll show."

He snorted.

"That's gross."

"So what. You should be used to me by now, Tal. She's not gonna show."

I checked my watch. Again. "Brooke said she'd be here by ten-fifteen. She said she couldn't talk at the hospital, which makes perfect sense to me." I craned my neck, hunting for a Snoopy tunic. No luck.

"Why wouldn't she show?" I said.

"Because she chickened out … or it's bullshit … or she got mugged."

"Stop it. She was sincere, Rob. Concerned. Deeply so."

He stared into his cup for a moment, and then reached for my hand. "Something's very bad with Veda, Tal."

"You saw it."

"Hard to miss, kiddo. Veda's not home, that's for sure."

"No, I know. She's not. All the medical professionals keep denying it. It's horrible. Terrible. But it's a relief that you see it. What happened to her? I have no idea. None."

"How the hell should I know? Some medical mumbo jumbo, maybe to cover their fuckup."

"Then why isn't anybody admitting she's different? How come everyone's just saying it's because she's been in the hospital for so long?"

He took a sip of his chai. "C'mon, Tal. You know. They're covering their asses. I'm bettin' that's what that Brookie girl had to tell ya."

I shook my head. "It was more. I felt the fear in her."

"For not wanting her ass in a sling."

"You drive me crazy," I said. "Brooke said someone went into Veda's room. Do you always have to play devil's advocate?"

"Do you?"

I tossed my balled up napkin into the trash and stomped out. Kranak lived to infuriate. I leaned against the 4Runner's fender, fuming.

Kranak sauntered out, one eyebrow raised. This was the man who'd saved my ass more than once. God, he was maddening.

"C'mon back in, Tal," he said. "Let's give her another thirty minutes."

"Yes, let's."

But Brooke never showed.

When I walked through The Grief Shop's door, I was startled to see no one behind the main desk. I beelined into CSS.

"Hey," I said to the officer. "Where's Dennis?"

His freckled baby face twisted into a scowl. "Dennis? Christ. He quit. Told Fogarty to fuck himself."

"Dennis? Sweet Dennis?"

The officer nodded. "We're going to hell damned fast. Charley almost quit, too. Said he'd hang on for a little longer, since business was good. That Charley has a sense of humor."

"I've noticed."

"You'd better get Doc Veda back here quick. You ain't heard the worst."

If he only knew. "Which is …?"

"Keyswipe's been messed with on the outer sanctum door. Been like that for at least two weeks. That's how we think the kid's body got in here. The guy musta disabled it. Fogarty's been covering."

"Geesh. Anything else?"

"You don't want to know." He stretched out in his chair, hands behind his head.

"What?"

"Amery. Last week he gave a John Doe to BU med."

I shuddered. There had been irregularities at plenty of other medical examiner's offices around the country, but not ours. Never ours. "Money?"

He shook his head. "An old buddy at the school needed one. Couldn't get a hold of one. So ... Fogarty never noticed. He's got his head up his ass. It's all about drama-rama with him. Now he'll get all that he ever wished for and more."

I wished I could be happy for Fogarty getting his just desserts. But the whole tale made me feel lousy. "Thanks." I gave him a two-fingered salute. "If you have any good news, come on down."

I entered my office hoping Nurse Brooke had left a message on my voice mail. No such luck.

"Ya hear?" Gert said when I poked my head into our central office.

"CSS filled me in. I assume that pile of do-do was all of it?"

She shook her head. "Fogarty sent some temp to access our records."

I bristled. "He has no right—"

"Anyway, she lost about fifty of 'em before I stopped her. Gonzo. Toast. They were old ones, but, y'know, they matter."

I hiked my fanny onto one of the vinyl stools. "Oh, I know all right." I filled her in on Bella Marsh and Veda. "You didn't get a call from some nurse named Brooke, did you?"

"Wish I had. You think she was for real?" Gert popped a purple Bazooka bubble.

"I do. What I don't know is if she meant someone intentionally hurt Veda or that a staff member at the hospital bungled badly. She was paranoid about talking to me. Anxious. I sensed great urgency. Hey, how about you call the hospital and ask for our Snoopy nurse?"

Gert donned her old Brooklyn accent and called. "You sure?" she said into the phone. "Yeah, yeah, yeah. Sorry."

"So?" I said.

"Whoever answered said she never heard of a nurse named Brooke, and that I should stop bugging her. I can try back or—"

"Let's wait," I said. "You know, Gertie, life's getting a little too weird."

I dragged my ass into my apartment around seven. I carried takeout pad Thai, and a list of "to dos" a mile long. I balanced dinner in one hand, shucked my jacket, and scooped up the mail from the front hall table. I rifled through it quickly. Only a note from Maine's chief medical examiner was worth opening.

I scanned Dr. Grace Whedon's note as I slid the pad Thai onto the kitchen counter.

The doc had sent an official offer from the State of Maine. Seventy thousand, autonomy, the ability to hire whomever I wanted, a state car. In other words, a sweet deal.

I sat on the sofa and reread the letter. I longed to say yes. I saw myself back where I began, sailing my little Blue Jay around some sweet ocean cove.

"Crap," I said to Penny. She perked her ears. Poor pup was hungry. I gave her a pat, and my hand slid over the soft, furry bump atop her front leg. "Double crap." Still no word from the vet. Maybe she'd e-mailed me.

I nuked the pad Thai, fixed Penny's chow, and clicked some keys for my e-mail. No news about Pens.

I called Hank, and we chatted for about fifteen minutes. He was embroiled in a murder case in Winsworth, and I could hear the distraction in his voice. In truth, I was distracted, too.

I felt tight. So tight. My heart ... my head. I flicked on the tube, channel surfed while I ate. Why the hell was there nothing good on my two hundred-some channels when all I wanted was to escape for an hour or so?

Penny. Veda. They needed me. So did Bertha. I'd better get my shit together, and fast.

Time to stop feeling and start using my brain.

The idea of Veda a homicide victim was plausible—too much so. She had plenty of enemies. And where would a person be more vulnerable than in a hospital?

I slipped back into my desk chair, put some Emmylou Harris on my Mac, and tapped out keys for Hawthorne Medical Center. I found lists of doctors, but no nurses on the site.

I chomped on a piece of shrimp. How to find Nurse Brooke without alerting the hospital? She probably worked on another floor than Veda's. Hmm. Maybe I could find her with flowers.

I blocked my outgoing caller ID and called the hospital. I laid on a thick Southern accent.

"Hey, ya'll," I said to the nurse who answered the phone. "I've got some flowers hea for someone named Nurse Brooke. You got a Nurse Brooke?"

I was transferred to the third floor. Veda's floor. Made no sense.

"Flowers, eh?" said the nurse who answered. "Whoo-eee. Cool. Brooke's not here. But she'll be in at eight."

"I'll leave them in the cooler then and bring them by in the morning."

So how come the staff member had lied to Gert about Brooke? Maybe she didn't know her? Either way, I didn't feel good about Hawthorne Medical Center.

Chapter Twelve

I called Veda's room. Bertha answered. "How's she doing tonight, Bertha?"

"Ach. I'm sure she's getting better. Yes. Very sure."

"Of course she is. I'll see you tomorrow. Is Jenny driving you home?"

"Yes. She's a good girl, that Jenny. Veda likes her, too. Veda …" A sob, and she disconnected.

Dear Bertha. She was so fluttery, like a butterfly. But she'd survived Auschwitz, too.

After dinner, I took a bourbon on the rocks out to my tiny deck. It overlooked one of the prettiest little gardens in Boston, where tulips and lupine and coneflowers and day lilies bloomed in spring and summer.

April in Boston was a mixed bag, and tonight hinted of chilly rain. I crossed my ankles on the balcony railing.

A soft sigh from Penny, who lay at my feet, added to my sense of contentment. It felt like the first minute I'd relaxed in forever. I swirled the cubes of ice, then took a sip of smoky bourbon.

What if the missing Nurse Brooke was really onto something? Would it be possible for a person intent on homicide to enter a hospital and do something to a patient that mimicked a typical hospital event? Maybe a stroke? An aneurysm? Someone had said "a bleed." Possible.

Before the flu, Veda had been in good health. And the flu gave whoever was after her a grand opportunity.

"Pretty mind boggling, isn't it, Pens?"

Penny perked her ears, and then decided she wanted a trot in the yard. Her nails clacked on her way down the stairs.

So motive, means, opportunity. Opportunity. Someone could masquerade as a doctor or a lab tech or a nurse easily enough. Hawthorne wasn't huge, but it wasn't tiny, either. It was almost simpler to kill someone than disable them. But maybe he'd bungled the job.

Means. He'd have to know about medicine, but killing someone was easier than curing them, particularly if that person knew illnesses and meds. I tried to remember if Veda was on oxygen before "the change." I thought she had been, but that wouldn't necessarily alter anything.

I was getting all tangled up in what-ifs.

A sharp breeze slapped my cheek. "Penny, come. *Ke mne!*" The sound of her familiar tripod gait warmed me. "Time to go in."

Comfortably ensconced before a roaring fire in my living room, I played the motive and opportunity game over and over in my head. Veda. The warm flames reflected off the facets of my glass. I slid behind my computer and pressed a couple of keys. The room filled with the moans of Scottish pipes. I hunkered beneath the afghan my birth mother had knit long before she'd met my father.

The elephant question on my mind in this rather elaborate hypothesis was why? Why try to kill Veda? Who would want her dead?

I came up with nothing. Penny, in stealth mode, crept onto the couch, pretending to be chihuahua-sized.

I cuddled and allowed my lids to drift closed.

The ring of the phone rocketed me awake.

"Dammit." I groped and found the phone. "Tally Whyte here."

"Get your ass outta bed," Kranak said. "We got a body. I'll pick ya up in ten."

For the second day in a row, Penny and I stood outside my townhouse apartment in the pre-dawn chill waiting for Kranak. I was *not* a morning person, dammit.

Moist air coated my face, and I'd swear I smelled the tang of the sea. My porch light cast an amber glow, a comforting one. Ever since I'd been stalked by a killer, my landlord and former lover Jake made sure the light always functioned. That frightening time felt like decades ago, rather than just a few years.

I brushed back my sleeve to look at my watch. Almost five. What was taking Kranak so long?

Screeching tires alerted me to his impending arrival.

Kranak drove through a silent city, foot on the gas heavy, his hand in a tea-mugged embrace. He chewed the end of his mustache, and I realized with a shock that Hank did the same thing. How odd that the two most prominent men in my life looked ... I jammed that thought to a halt.

Diffuse moonlight pulsed across the Charles River as we drove down Storrow Drive.

I waited the requisite ten minutes of silence, and then ventured, "So why call me about a corpse? And how come we're leaving the city? Who is it?"

He took a long swallow of his tea. "I got the call forty minutes ago. We're shorthanded tonight, and I'm on call. Couple doing the dirty out in some parking lot in Maynard."

"Maynard." A town I'd never forget.

"So they hear some catfight. A literal one. Interrupts the hot-and-heavy, since the guy's a bleeding heart animal lover. He decides to break up the fight. So over he goes to this Dumpster."

Kranak careened half way around the Arlington circle, zoomed over the bridge, and flew past Alewife. Teeth tight, I clung to the armrest.

"You can be such a wuss about my driving," he said.

"Are you kidding? None of the guys will ride with you. Go on. What happened next?"

"So this idiot kid leaps up to the Dumpster and is about to reach in for one of the cats, when he sees this naked lady, and, man, is she ever dead. According to the local cops, the kid pukes all over her, which didn't help the crime scene, lemme tell ya."

"Bad stuff, I agree. But why call me?"

He raised his right eyebrow. "'Cause they found a balled-up Snoopy tunic buried along with her in the Dumpster. She wasn't naked or anything, so how come she's got a nurse's tunic in there with her? Y'know?"

Twenty minutes later we were on Nason Street in Maynard, headed for the bright beams that CSS used to light crime scenes. Kranak hooked a right just before The Paper Store, and we drove down a small side street that spilled out onto a parking lot. I spotted one of the homicide detectives from the DA's office. Standing off to the left was the second detective, eyeballing two kids sitting on the curb looking downtrodden. Had to be the lovers who'd found the body.

Someone had rolled out the crime scene tape, and a bunch of local cops and some EMTs milled around. Kranak's Crime Scene Services compatriot was setting up another light. Cop car bubbles whirred, and radio chatter filled the night air of sleepy Maynard.

"You wait here," Kranak said. "Be right back."

Kranak conferred with his partner and one of the state cops. He came around to the back of the truck and hauled out his large CSS bag. He handed it off to his partner, and then pulled out a stepladder.

I slipped outside, the better to hear the talk, but left Penny in the car. She'd already caught the corpse's scent and was whining. Kranak donned a white jumpsuit, slung his cameras around his neck and climbed the ladder. When he reached the top of the Dumpster, he started snapping off digital images of the scene and the body.

"... raped her ..."

"... not a bruise."

"... who she is ..."

"... neck broken ..."

Kranak finally waved me over.

I shoved my hands in my pockets and walked toward the Dumpster. I thought of the victim's pain, and that of her husband's or child's or parents'. Sadly—too often—a loved one was the perpetrator of the homicide.

As I approached the Dumpster, a pair of uniformed cops waved. I just nodded, preoccupied with what I was about to see in that trash bin.

Kranak handed me down a pair of gloves. I put them on and climbed the ladder.

I'd just seen her the previous day—Brooke, a pretty girl who appeared to be trying to help Veda and myself. Who'd apparently risked her neck. Literally. I tried to prepare for the viewing and failed, as usual.

I reached the top of the ladder and carefully placed my hands on the sides of the Dumpster. A surreal brightness lit the scene.

I hesitated. Pretty long brown hair. Curly. High-beam smile. Warm eyes. Trying to help. Just trying to help.

"You okay, Tal?" Kranak, at his most compassionate.

"Okay." I peered down.

The young woman wore pants and shoes, but only a bra on top. She was smeared with refuse. She was long in limb and had brown hair and ... "I don't think its Brooke."

"What?"

I leaned forward, closer to the girl's face, which was round, with a dimpled chin. Definitely not the Brooke I'd met at the hospital.

I climbed down, shaken at seeing the unexpected.

Who was the girl in the Dumpster with the same Snoopy tunic as Brooke?

I approached Kranak's partner, a guy named Danny. I didn't know him well.

"Hey, Danny. Do you have the tunic they found?"

"What are you doing here?" Danny said.

"Kranak brought me. I thought I knew the dead girl."

"So what's with the tunic?" he asked.

"I don't know," I said. "I'd just like to see it."

"You don't belong here."

I crossed my arms. "Well, I am here. And I need to see that tunic."

"You can see it after we've processed it."

I looked toward the Dumpster. Kranak was still inside, and I didn't want to be a pain and ask him for help. "I would appreciate seeing it now. Two minutes, is all."

He rocked back on his cowboy-booted heels. "You don't even remember, do you?"

Crap. Now what had I done? "Sorry."

"You. I asked you for a date. And you, Miss High-and-Mighty, declined."

"I was seeing somebody, Danny."

He smirked. "You're fulla shit. Not then you—"

"Are you having a problem, Ms. Whyte?" One of the state detectives materialized beside me. He was tall, and peered down at Danny as if he were a bug.

"Not at all. Danny and I are old friends, and we were talking about the Red Sox's chances at the pennant this year."

The detective turned from me to Danny. He practically exhaled skepticism. "Sure you were."

He winked at Danny, and the look was the opposite of friendly.

"Prick," Danny said as the detective walked away.

"You're being a pain in the ass," I said. "I'll just ask Kranak." I turned, and Danny's hand wrapped around my arm.

"I'll get it," he said. "You leave Kranak outta this."

He returned carrying a bagged Snoopy tunic. He held the bag with both hands, as if it were a precious relic.

"I'll hold it," he said. "You look."

"Sure. Let's move into the light a bit more."

Through the plastic I saw the dark stains that smeared the back of the tunic, something no nurse would ever tolerate, were she alive. Were the stains dried blood or refuse? Hard to tell. The tunic looked just like Brooke's, but there was no reason two nurses couldn't have purchased identical tunics from the same medical supply house. "Would you flip it over for me, Danny."

He exhaled an elaborate sigh. "Here ya go."

"It's got a name tag."

He smirked. "Yeah. Nobody mentioned that?"

"No."

I ran my finger across the clear plastic above the name: BROOKE.

Hours later, after one of the MEs showed up and Kranak could finally process the woman, Kranak joined Penny and me in the cab of his crime scene truck. Salt-and-pepper stubble grazed his chin, and bags pouched beneath his bloodshot eyes.

I handed him his diabetes glucose test kit that he kept in the glove compartment. He raised a bushy eyebrow before he took the kit.

"*Fine,*" he said.

The anger threading his voice hurt. "Rob, I ..."

"Forget it. You're a pain, but this thing, well, I don't mean to take it out on you." He turned his back to me, and gave himself the test for blood sugar levels.

He shoved the kit back into the glove compartment and slammed the door. Minutes later, the ME's van with the victim inside left the scene.

Kranak put the truck into gear. "We're outta here. Danny's got all the bagged garbage, and we've finished processing."

"We've got to find her, Rob," I said.

"That Brooke woman."

"Yes. The woman at the hospital was wearing the same tunic with the name Brooke on it. She said she'd been Veda's nurse."

"And ...?"

"What do you mean, 'and'?"

He shrugged. "And so what? Maybe there's another nurse named Brooke."

"It's not that common a name."

He grinned. "So let's say we stop by the hospital. I got a picture."

My pulse did a flip-flop. Nothing I'd like better. "You mean it?"

"Sure."

"What aren't you telling me? This isn't like you, Rob."

"Say I've turned over a fresh leaf."

"Leaf, my ass. You're up to something."

The squeak of my sneakers sounded loud as I walked down the too-familiar hospital corridor. It felt like the crack of dawn, but it was after nine. I'd expected bustling, but what we got was silence.

"They've heard," I whispered in Kranak's ear.

"What's with the heavy breathing in my ear?" he said. "You tryin' to turn me on, or what?"

"Cut it out," I hissed. "They know one of their own is dead."

We approached the nurses' station in the middle of the hall. Women and men sat around looking grim and frightened. Even the doctor with the open chart spoke in hushed tones to the nurse beside him.

They knew, all right. And they hated it and were terrified by it.

One of their own was dead. A homicide.

Every eye turned to Kranak, who stood legs apart, arms akimbo, filling the doorway. No one seemed to notice his rumpled clothes and unshaven face.

Nor did anyone ask if they could help. They just looked. They knew who he was, and that frightened them more.

"I got some questions." He held up his badge.

A middle-aged nurse with red hair and a neon pink tunic nodded. She cleared her throat. "How can we help you, officer."

"Anybody missin' from the morning shift?" he asked.

Heads nodded like bobble toys, but no one said a word.

A throat cleared, and Kranak and I turned in unison.

"Sergeant. Ms. Whyte," said the plainclothes state detective I'd met at the crime scene. "Or should I say, Detective Whyte?"

"Funny," I said. "Not."

"Sergeant Kranak," he said. "Aren't you out of your purview, my friend?"

"No, Sergeant, I am not. I got a question for these people. You got a problem with that?"

A testosterone pissing contest. Just what we didn't need. "Stop it, both of you." I pulled the two men out into the hall. "It was getting damned crowded in there, with the oversized egos. Look, Sarge, Kranak just wants to show them a picture to ID the woman."

"My ass," the detective said. "This is my case."

Kranak's dimpled chin thrust forward. "Not if it involves Dr. Barrow, it's not."

The detective stepped back. "You mean the Chief ME?"

"That's who we mean, asshole. And if Tally here is right, we gotta post somebody at her door. She's a target."

"What?"

"I'll explain later. Now just let us get on with it."

The detective straightened his tie and nodded. But he didn't leave.

Chapter Thirteen

Kranak told one of the nurses to gather the third-floor staff to the nurses' station. While we waited, Kranak and the detective exchanged looks of annoyance. It was obvious that each wanted the other one out of there. All I cared about was identifying the body and finding Brooke. I feared for her, afraid that she was the killer's real target.

Minutes later, the nurses' station was abuzz with soft chatter. Kranak shoved a hand in his pocket.

"We've got sad news and a situation here," he said. "We hope you can help."

Much nodding of heads.

"I've got a photo of a woman found earlier this evening. She appears to be a victim of a homicide. She may or may not be on the staff of this hospital. We're hoping that you can identify her."

"Let's get it over with," said one of the doctors. "Stop playing games, eh?"

Kranak's eyes lit with fury.

"He's not playing games," I said. "This is complicated. We are trying not to prejudice you."

They quieted down, although the doctor muttered something under his breath.

Kranak took a seat at the desk in the corner. "One at a time, we'd like to hear if you can identify this person. Got it?" He tweaked a finger at the mouthy doctor.

A scowl planted on his face, he walked to the desk. Kranak raised the baggied image. "I might know her. I don't know."

"C'mon," Kranak said.

"What?" said the doctor. "She looks like all the other nurses."

The state detective smirked.

"Get lost," Kranak said.

I pulled a chair up beside Kranak. "Stop ticking these people off, Rob."

"Yes, your highness."

"Cut it out. This is about Veda, and you know it."

"Yeah. I do." He crooked his finger at a steel-haired nurse, who looked terrified.

"I got this," said the nurse in the pink tunic.

"Fine by me," Kranak said. He waited until she sat across the desk from him. He lifted his hand from the photo and slid it forward.

"Dear God!" the nurse said. "No."

"Ma'am?" Kranak said.

Her lips wobbled, but she didn't cry. "Is this for real? Not a joke?"

"No, ma'am," he said. "Not a joke at all."

She brushed her fingers across the face of the dead woman's picture. "She was the sweetest, kindest …" She turned away and rubbed her forehead. She held up a finger.

"I hate this shit," Kranak mouthed.

I nodded, waited a second, and then began. "Nurse Connor, we realize this is difficult for you. We're sorry. But it's

Sergeant Kranak's job to learn your friend's identity and to find out who did this to her. Now is when we need your help."

She nodded, hiccoughed.

"Could we get you some water?" I said. "Coffee? Anything?"

She shook her head. "No, I'm ready."

"Ma'am?" Kranak said.

She looked up, shoved a lock of red hair back from her face. "The girl is Brooke. Brooke Simmons. She works night shift usually. Nicest kid you'd ever want to—"

"But I met a Nurse Brooke," I said. "Are there two on this floor?"

She frowned. "Now what do you think? C'mon."

"Sorry," I said. "Twice I've met a nurse who wore a tag named Brooke. She told me her name. I first met her when Dr. Barrow was her patient. It wasn't this Brooke."

"I don't know what you're talking about. There's only one Brooke here at Hawthorne and ..." She broke off with a sob. "Oh, boy. How am I going to tell them?"

I leaned forward. "If you would like, we can—"

"No, no. It's my duty." Her eyes met mine as she excused herself.

"Whatever's going on here, Rob," I said, "I don't get it.

Kranak drove me to the State Police Crime Lab in Sudbury, where we met with a sketch artist. She worked on her computer, and we reviewed eyes and ears and noses and mouths until the facsimile of the woman I knew as Nurse Brooke appeared.

I left Kranak at OCME, and spent a busy day bonding with paperwork and other essential tasks I'd left fallow of late. I kept wondering about the identity of "my" Brooke, and her involvement in Veda's current state.

How hard was it to slip into a patient's room? To drug them into senility? To kill that patient with a lethal dose of a medicine that would dissipate by morning? To be a ghost in a setting where no one would notice a strange nurse or doctor who wore the uniform of invisibility.

When I finally turned the key in my apartment on Appleton that night, I was wiped. I'd been on high alert for more than four days, been awakened by phone calls at strange hours, and was emotionally stressed to the max. The bod was beat.

I dragged my ass inside, scooped the mail from the hall table, and dropped my briefcase and purse on the floor. I sank onto the couch, shucked my shoes, and lifted my protesting feet onto the redwood coffee table.

I exhaled slowly, deeply, until my lungs emptied of the day's turmoil and exhaustion. Relief flooded my body. Penny rested beside me, muzzle on my thigh. She sighed, too.

My eyes drifted shut, and I allowed the comforting pulse of my home to soothe my jangled nerves. Heaven.

A door slammed, and I levitated off the couch. "What the hell!"

"Let's go, Tal!" Jake said in that whiskey voice he used on women.

My landlord and former lover was all spiffy in a black turtleneck, charcoal pants, and black Frye boots. A lock of his black hair flopped over his forehead, just like Superman's. Damn, he was gorgeous.

"I'm not going anywhere, Jake. I'm beat."

He rested a booted foot on my coffee table. "C'mon, Tal. The Wirth Gallery opening. Nick Wirth called me. Said you had to be there. Figured I could do the job. So let's do it."

"Let's not." I pushed off from the couch and retrieved a bottle of Rebel Yell. "You?"

"Nope," he said.

While I poured, Jake walked into my bedroom. Just as the smoky bourbon was hitting my belly, he reappeared with a black dress and a pair of strappy heels.

He held out his arms. "Do it. Veda wants you there, kiddo."

I'd forgotten. Days ago Veda had talked about the opening. Said I should go. I'd even spoken with Nick Wirth, who'd said it mattered to her, too. But I'd declined, and Veda would never know that I hadn't attended. She was so ill, so out of it. Dear God, how had this happened? Fingers of exhaustion curled across my shoulders. My guilt gene kicked in. Crap. I scooped the shoes and dress from Jake's arms.

"I'll be ready in ten," I said. "Give Pens a walk out back, please."

He saluted me and whistled for Penny, who obediently followed him out the back door.

I flew into my large bedroom, which overlooked the street. I pulled the second layer of curtains, and then shucked my work clothes for the black turtlenecked sheath chosen by Jake. But I bagged the sandals, choosing instead my black cowboy boots and antique concha belt with Cerrillos turquoise. I grabbed my shawl, swiped some lipstick across my lips, tugged a brush through my hair, and took a look in the mirror. Acceptable.

I stopped to pick up the photo of Veda on my dresser. She should be going to this with me. God, how she loved the art scene. Would she ever go to a gallery opening again?

I straightened my shoulders. "Ready, Jake."

Our taxi idled in the line of cars. I fingered the invitation with Veda's name spelled out in gilt that Jake had handed me. *We request the honor of your presence ...*

"These Newbury Street openings suck," Jake said.

Jake showed his incredible sculptures in the more hip and cutting-edge SoWa section of Boston.

"Hey, this is your fault," I said. "Don't look at me. Let's just get out. We can walk from here."

"Your feet. Those boots."

"They're comfortable as slippers. Let's go."

Jake paid the driver and we stepped onto a street filled with crowds cued up for the several openings that were being held that night.

Down two cement steps, and we entered the Wirth Gallery. Wall-to-wall bodies jammed rooms filled with laughter and raised voices and the overpowering scent of hundred dollar-an-ounce perfumes fighting for dominance. I turned tail.

"Don't." Jake gently gripped my arm, stroking it with his thumb.

I pushed away memories of our long-ago lovemaking. "I'll come another day. See the exhibit. This is horrible."

"You know the deal. An opening without a crush is a disaster."

"Why couldn't this one be ... smaller?" We threaded our way through sequined women and turtlenecked men.

"You're a pain in the butt," I said.

He chuckled. "Sweet as always, babe."

"Sorry. I'm just pissy."

I let Jake lead me in the direction of the largest cluster of toned bodies. Nick Wirth stood in the center, holding forth—ever the dashing showman in his tweed jacket and bow tie. His expressive hands waved toward paintings and sculptures, and I admired how he treated everyone with equal distinction.

Beside him was Stan, Nick's less dashing, much older brother. Stan was a huggie bear next to Nick's elegant swan, but why he had to wear black turtlenecks and motorcycle boots I never knew. Maybe it was the height thing, since he shorter than Nick, or maybe the art gallery thing. Whatever. I still thought he was a dear man.

Stan gave me a warm smile.

Ouch. Too late to leave now. I smiled back. Stan elbowed Nick, who waved and plowed through his guests in our direction.

A miniskirted hottie blew Jake a kiss. He winked back, and I remembered why we were no longer a couple.

Nick Wirth scooped me up just as Jake said, "Be right back," and departed for the greener shores of Ms. Miniskirt.

As always, Nick smelled of Royall Lyme aftershave. Ever since I was a kid, it reminded me of key lime pie. I hugged him back.

"Come," he said. "Come. Say hi to Stan. Then I want you to meet someone. A surprise planned by dear Veda."

I had no clue what he meant, and I followed him docilely as he parted the waters. Stan and I hugged, and as I looked down at the small balding man in his funny "hip" costume, I felt an enormous wave of affection. Of the brothers, Stan was the gentle one.

"Good to see you, Stan."

"And you, Tally. We have a surprise. Go with Nick, and I'll hold the fort."

Nick and I walked beneath an arch into a quieter and obviously more exclusive area of the party.

On a tapestried sofa, a raven-haired woman wearing boots, turquoise bracelets, and a long, flowing skirt talked with balletic hand gestures to the couple that faced her. The woman turned and gestured toward a clay sculpture that had been hidden by a waiter.

"Oohhh my!" was all I could say.

A Nila Wendall sculpture in clay of a blanketed American Indian woman holding a scruffy dog, a small smile on her face, eyes alive with joy, sat on a pedestal directly in front of me. "Oh, wow."

"I know," Nick said. "When I told Veda that Nila was coming to the gallery, she swore me to secrecy."

He left my side and walked to the dark-haired woman. He bent down and whispered in her ear. She turned, a smile transforming her face, and I stared into the velvet eyes of Nila Wendall, my favorite artist on the planet.

I held out my hand and moved forward. "I'm ... um ..."

She took my hand in both of hers. "A pleasure, Tally."

"The pleasure truly is mine," I said.

"How do you like the piece?" she said.

"My ... ahhhh." I left her and walked toward the sculpture, caressed it softly, gently. The clay seemed to welcome my hand. Nila's eyes, curious, stayed with me.

"Your sculpture," I said. "Seeing it in the clay ... it's more than I could ever have imagined."

"We've made bronzes," she said.

I was sure they were well beyond my reach. "I know they'll be wonderful."

Her smile broadened. "But the clay is always best. I'm glad it will go to you."

I turned to Nick. The piece was many thousands of dollars I could never afford. "Nick?"

"From Veda," Nick said. "A gift for her Tally who so loves animals. She's been working on this for months."

"Oh, Nick. She ..." I turned away to hide my tears. They blinded me.

"Come," Nick said. "Let's go where it's quiet." He led me through a door with a sign that said KEEP OUT, into yet another room, one that looked more like a museum than a gallery. He brushed my face with his hand. "It's all right, Tally."

"No," I said. "It isn't." I leaned against a wall. "I can't believe I reacted like a wuss in front of Nila."

"She understands," he said. "You'll have time to talk to her later. We're all going out to dinner."

"Stan and Alex?"

"My son wouldn't miss it," he said. "Veda ... she was to be here."

I nodded. "Yes. Oh, Nick."

I shook my head, and his arms wrapped around me. It all felt alien, like my dad, but not. I smelled the oily tweed of his jacket. He patted me lightly on my shoulder, telegraphing his discomfort.

I drew away, stuttered a sigh. "Thank you." I rubbed my

temples, wishing my father were alive to help me through this "thing" with Veda. But of course, if he were, I would never have known her.

I told Nick about Veda's illness and her disturbing behavior.

Nick's face tightened with pain. "I know. I visited her yesterday. She ... You know we've been dating, and for quite a while, I might add. Yesterday she, um, she called me Papa. When I said I wasn't her father, she stopped talking altogether. It scares me. Just last week, we had dinner. She looked marvelous. I don't understand, Tally."

I'd suspected that Nick and Veda might be more than friends. Now it was out there. Made sense; they came from the same worlds, had similar histories. I'd be happy for them, except ... "I don't understand either," I said. "It's bad. Very bad."

I didn't mention nurse Brooke's allegation of murder.

I turned and the room came into focus. It was nothing like the rest of Nick's contemporary gallery. Old world and moody, with walnut wood trim and lush red Persian carpets. A dozen paintings lined softly lit walls. And what paintings. "Nick, these pieces are incredible." I walked past a Picasso sketch and an oil signed *Gauguin*.

Nick walked up behind me. "Yes, aren't they marvelous?" He pointed to another painting. "This is very old. Italian Renaissance. And that one is even older. I intended to show them to you this evening, just not quite like this."

I chuckled. "No, I'm sure you didn't plan on my overwrought emotions. I'm sorry."

"No need."

I walked the perimeter of the room. "All masterpieces. Where did you get them?"

"From the families of Holocaust victims. These have all been returned to their original owners or their families." He waved at a spectacular oil of what looked like Moses leading the Israelites from Egypt.

"They're for sale?" I said.

He nodded. "Most. The owners, most of who wish to be anonymous, need the money. Some just want to move on with their lives. These paintings are but a few of the hundreds of thousands classified by the Nazis as 'decadent' art and confiscated. They represent a dark, dark time in each family's life. Many are covered in loved ones' blood."

I saw Veda and Bertha as children in the camps. Auschwitz, Dachau, Buchenwald. So many more. "Has Veda seen these?"

"Of course! In fact, she helped us put the room together. It's almost complete now."

"Some of these are worth … God, I can't imagine how much. You could auction them for big dollars."

He nodded. "True. But the owners don't want them sold to just anybody, you see. They want us to vet the purchaser. My brother Stan has worked with families who wish to donate the returned art to American and Israeli museums. Some of those pieces are here, but most aren't. It's been a huge undertaking, and Veda has been a big help. It devastates me that she's not with us today."

"She'll be better soon. You'll see. You should be proud."

He shook his head. "I am humbled. We plan a large opening soon. Can we talk about Veda?"

A tap on the door. "Come," Nick said, and the door cracked.

"Ms. Whyte?" said a tall young man in a retro blue suit and bow tie just like Nick's. "I'm Alex, Nick's son. Remember me?"

"Of course. Hi." We shook hands. "It's great to see you again."

"What is it, son?" Nick said.

"Someone's here to see Ms. Whyte." Alex frowned in distaste. "She's a weird one, Pop. Maybe you should—"

"I'll take care of it," I said. "I'm sure it's a friend or something who—"

In barged a frowning Kathleen Lauria. "What the hell is taking so long?"

"See what I mean?" Alex said.

"Oh, stick it." Kathleen strode past the young man, her blue eyes ablaze.

"Something's happened to Bella?" I said.

"He's taken another one, Tally."

Chapter Fourteen

Lauria and I sat at a scarred circular table in Trip's, a bar on East Berkeley, named for the Triple Crown stallion, Secretariat. Trip's was home to off-duty cops, attorneys from the DA's office, and much of the OCME staff. I loved the privacy the place afforded me, and I felt comfortable bringing Kathleen there.

Lauria and I ordered burgers and sodas, and once the waiter dropped off our food, Lauria began.

"The little girl's name is Eva Lange," Lauria said. "She's the same age as Bella Marsh and Rose Noguchi. She's a foster child who …"

The smell of Brut wrinkled my nose. I spotted the predator, and waved him off. "Go on," I said to Lauria.

"She's a foster child who lives in Peterborough, New Hampshire."

"It's near Temple."

Lauria nodded. "Next town over the mountain. And it's where that hospital is where Bella appeared." She slipped a cigarette from her pocket and began to light up.

I rolled my eyes, but of course she didn't care. She was purposefully being provocative.

She inhaled long and slow, and then the smoke slipped out of her nose and mouth like nicotined fog. She beamed me her Cheshire Cat smile, aware of the illegality of what she was doing. Her blue eyes drifted out of focus, and I sensed how deeply this case was affecting her.

"Any idea why this latest child, Eva Lange?" I said.

"None."

"It's as if he's traded one child for another, Kathleen. Bella for Eva. Why? What was 'wrong' with Bella and 'right' with this new little girl."

"Nothing obvious," Lauria said. "That's for sure. Unless you count that both their names end with the letter 'a'."

"That could matter, except Rose's didn't." I waved the cloud of smoke away. "I hate this. Little kids in jeopardy. God, it's horrible."

"I want you to come with me right now," she said. "To talk with Bella. Maybe she'll give you something she didn't give us."

"We can't wake her up in the middle of the night." I checked my watch. "It's past twelve. She'll be groggy, her parents defensive. Kathleen, think. You don't really want to do this now."

"No, I don't," Lauria said. "But I am. Come with or don't." Laura's thin lips tightened. She took a hard drag on her cigarette and dropped it into her soda. It hissed as it went out. I wouldn't budge her. No way.

"Fine," I said. "We'll go see Bella now. It's your play."

We pulled into the Marsh driveway around two A.M. Lauria had called ahead, so at least the family was prepared for our arrival. Mr. Marsh said his wife was working at air traffic control and wouldn't be home until four A.M.

He hadn't bothered with a porch light, but a living room light was on. Lauria used her flashlight to make it to the front door, which opened just as she was about to press the buzzer.

"You've got some nerve," Marsh said as he waved us inside.

Lauria turned to me. "Tally?"

I took a deep breath. "Mr. Marsh, I'm sorry we have to wake Bella, but another child has been taken. A little girl named Eva Lange. Time is of the essence. We do not want Eva to die like Rose Noguchi."

He swiped a hand across his face and turned away.

I wished he looked more surprised with the taking of Eva.

We followed him into the house, and when he reached the living room, he rounded on us, arms crossed, foot tapping.

"We'd like to see Bella now," I said.

"Forget it," he said.

Lauria straightened. The smile that played her lips made me think of a mongoose I'd once seen toy with a snake. The outcome was never in doubt.

Marsh's puffed chest imploded. He chewed his lips. "I'll get her."

"Something's up," I said to Lauria after he'd left the room.

She nodded. "I don't like this guy."

"I don't much, either. One minute he plays the poor soul, the next … I don't trust him. Period. I wonder what he's hiding." I walked around the room, again struck by the minimalist decor.

"Any word on the missing lamb?" I asked.

"It's still MIA, far as I know. What's your buddy Kranak got to say about it? It went missing on his watch."

"He hasn't said much."

"Here's our girl," Marsh said as he emerged from the hall carrying Bella. Her arms and legs were wrapped around her dad, crablike, and her head rested on his shoulder, her eyes closed, her hand clutching a stuffed bear.

"Let's sit here, hon." He sat on the sofa with Bella still attached.

"I bet she'd like some water or warm milk," Lauria said.

Marsh scrunched his forehead. He seemed to make some sort of decision. His narrowed eyes shined fury at Lauria. He forcibly detached Bella, who whined and held out her arms to her father.

"Stay here, Bell." He stormed out of the room. "I'll get her the milk."

"I'll come, too," Lauria said.

I got on my knees, and smiled. "I'm sorry, Bella, to get you up like this in the middle of the night."

She clutched her bear to her chest and rubbed its ear back and forth across her cheek. "Where'd Daddy go?"

"Just to get you some milk to drink."

"I hate milk."

"Even with cake?" I said.

"Well ... no, not then."

They'd cut her fall of blonde hair to the tips of her ear-lobes and given her bangs. She looked like a different child. Perhaps that was the point.

"I need to talk to you, Bella, because another little girl needs your help."

She yawned. "How come?"

"Someone took her. We think it's the same person who took you."

Her eyes blinked rapidly and she scooched back into the couch. "I was in stasis. Nobody took me."

"I'm sorry, Bella, but someone did. And we need to learn more about that person. You are the only one who can tell us."

"I am not. Rosie can tell you."

"She can't, Bella. Rose is gone. She's dead."

Her eyes pooled with tears that dripped down her cheeks like reluctant raindrops. "I know," she whispered.

I felt evil and mean, battering this kid who'd been through

so much. "Can you remember any sounds when you were in stasis?"

She shook her head, her bear clutched tight, eyes wide and fearful.

I'd struck a reality that terrified her. I shelved the sounds—she'd heard something key—and changed direction. "How about smells? Think, Bella. How did it smell?"

She smoothed the bear's ear across her cheek. "Like Daddy's pipe, only, um, sweeter."

"Did you eat anything in stasis?"

"A brownie and soda. Soda's illegal, Mom says. But it was okay this one time."

"I see. That makes sense to me."

She grinned. "The brownies were really good."

Alice B. Toklas brownies? Possible. Rose had been medicated with marijuana. "Did you eat anything else?"

A door creaked. Bella snapped her head around.

Mrs. Marsh strode through the arch, tossing her coat and purse to the floor. She scooped up Bella, who rested her head on her mother's shoulder.

"How dare you?" Mrs. Marsh said. "Get out."

"Another little girl has been taken. Her name is Eva Lange. She's Bella's age. I've been told she likes to play softball and—"

"She does not!" Bella shouted. "She hates it! She hates it!"

"Get out! *Now!*" Mrs. Marsh stormed from the room cradling Bella like an infant.

"Bella knows Eva Lange," I said. We were on our way back to Boston. The night had deepened, the stars obscured by clouds. "I wonder if they go to the same school. It's possible, even though they don't live in the same town."

"I'll check when we get back."

"A lot's going on in that house. More than just the return of a kidnapped child. If only the parents were more cooperative."

"That's an understatement," Lauria said.

"So Bella, Rose, and Eva all knew each other. They're all around the same age, but what's the connector? Why these three girls?"

"Yeah." Lauria reached for the pack of gum on her dashboard. "You?"

"Sure." I slipped a stick of spearmint into my mouth. "Something's very off there. We should go back in the morning."

"I was thinking the same thing," Lauria said.

I rubbed the smooth leather of the seat. They were heated and felt great. I allowed my eyes to close. The calm, quiet of the night softened the world.

"What aren't you telling me, Tal?" she said.

"About the case?"

Kathleen chuckled. "You know I don't mean the case."

"I'm not up for talking."

"Tough. Kranak said they found a body in a Dumpster. That you thought you knew her. That she's a nurse where Dr. Barrow—"

"C'mon, Kathleen, I just don't feel like yapping about this."

Kathleen's quiet anger filled the SUV. I pressed my cheek against the chill of the closed window. Maybe I could sleep until we got back to Boston.

"I don't give a fuck," she said, "whether you want to talk or not. You *need* to tell me."

Relentless. "It's Veda. And the nurse who died. And the alleged nurse who wasn't really a nurse, but who tipped me to the fact that someone's trying to kill my foster mother. And I have no idea why. No motive."

Lauria nodded. A clump of hair slipped from her bun. It brushed her cheek, hiding her profile.

"Go on," she said.

I stuttered in a breath. "The person who tried to kill Veda

failed in that. But somehow he disabled her marvelous mind. She's changed."

"And?"

"And the Veda we knew is gone. Gone! Poof."

"She'll be back."

"I hope so. I pray so. I swear, I'd do anything. Every time I look at her, I expect her to be Veda. But she's not. She's a scared, fragile woman. A stranger. She was a young-looking sixty-eight. Now? She looks old and tired. So tired."

"What about the tipster?"

A car varoomed by us, then another. We were getting close to Boston and the cars and city lights turned the black sky gray. I wished the night would swallow me.

"The nurse who called herself Brooke has disappeared," I said. "She's involved in what happened to Veda. But I have no idea how. Kranak hasn't been able to find her. And me? I haven't had time to even look, dammit. And all the while Veda's drifting farther away."

I tossed my keys on the bedside table, let Penny out, and then picked up the portable in answer to the phone's blinking red message light. As I listened to my voice mails, I shucked my clothes, pacing back and forth, only half listening to the litany of "to do" lists from Bertha and Kranak and Donna at work.

"Tal," Gert said in an unnaturally serious voice. "Call me. Fogarty's assistant has been arrested. Boston PD hauled him away. Ieeee. In handcuffs, no less. Fogarty's mum. Lotta shit's coming down."

Gert beeped off. Geesh. I couldn't imagine …

"Message recorded …" Another one was coming in. They seemed endless.

"Hey, Babe. You okay? Missing ya." Hank. "You packed yet or not?" said his recorded voice. "They're having a heat wave out in Taos, so throw in some cooler stuff. Love ya, hotshot. Bye."

Damn. In two days I was supposed to leave for New Mexico with Hank. Our first vacation together. And I had forgotten all about it.

Boy, if ever I needed a vacation ...

I flipped open the back door. Penny trotted in and dived for her water bowl. She beelined it for the bedroom while I brushed my teeth and splashed some water on my face.

I chuckled. Penny and I were like old best friends. If only she could talk.

I scooted beneath the down comforter, almost too exhausted to sleep. I flipped off the light, closed my eyes. I saw a child struggling with a shadowy shape. I blinked my eyes open, preferring my bedroom's reality. I was miserably, disturbingly awake.

I longed for the Maine cottage's stream of moonlight, and the sound and scent of the sea that came from the open window. The chirp of insects and pinkletinks, the pungent smell of low tide, the sense of space and infinity that was the paradox of the Maine woods.

I missed Hank's moist breath on my thighs and his tongue slipping ...

"Damn."

Penny came to attention.

"It's nothing girl." I scratched behind her ears. "Nothing. But I can't go on vacation, Pens. Not now. No way."

Six A.M. the following morning, I tugged open the passenger door to Lauria's black SUV.

"I feel like crap," I said.

"Dare I say ...?"

"Don't." I hoisted myself into the passenger seat beside Lauria. The tang of old cigarettes made my stomach lurch, while my tastebuds ached for that remembered habit I'd given up years earlier.

"Where's Penny?" Lauria handed me a tall cup of Dunkin' Donuts coffee.

"Thanks. Bella doesn't like her. So I left her home."

"Unusual about the child disliking Penny for her missing leg." Lauria drove the SUV down Appleton and melded into the mornings' traffic.

"I agree."

"You sound lousy."

"Oh, but I feel just *peachy*," I said.

"Sarcasm so early, Tal?" she said. "Rough night?"

I thought of Hank and what I had to tell him about our vacation. "I suspect my day will be even rougher."

Chapter Fifteen

We sped up Route 93 headed northwest. At nine o'clock, the traffic going south into Boston was backed up for miles. I never envied the commuters.

"How's your mom?" I asked.

Lauria smirked. "She's got a new boyfriend. Christ, she drives me crazy."

"She needs the company, Kath."

"She's driving me up the wall. She's sixty-five. Swear to God, she's discovered sex toys. She needs to settle down and act like a—"

"Grownup? C'mon. Maybe your mom needs to live a life she never had."

"She should get a life. Don't start with me, please. Next thing, she's going to want to move in. I can't do that."

"How come?" I asked.

Lauria pumped the gas. The speedometer reacted by hitting eighty. She reached for the pack of gum in her cigarette tray and flicked out a stick of Juicyfruit. I knew Lauria well enough to know our discussion was at an end.

She pointed to the notebook on the dash. "Open it."

I flipped it open and scanned the first page. "The Marshes history." I read. "Pretty thin stuff."

"Yup," she said. "Their history ends ten years ago."

"You think it matters?" I asked.

"Everything matters," she said. "Since we haven't got squat to go on."

A car cut us off.

"Damn," she muttered.

"You ever want to give auto bozos the finger?" I asked.

"Sure," she said. "I'm human, Tally. But it's not worth it."

"No. But sometimes …" I returned to my reading. "Nothing else much here. They've lived in Temple for five years. Bella's a good student. All As, in fact."

"Rose was, too," Lauria said. "The girls went to the same school. I would bet that Eva Lange attended there, too. We've got teams of agents scouring the area, as well as local and state police. So far, they've come up empty."

"We've got to get Bella to open up. I'm deeply worried about Eva Lange. I have a bad feeling. It's atypical that he let Bella go. But everything about this guy is atypical, from leaving Rose at the morgue to the lamb."

"I know," she said. "So why … why *did* he let her go."

"The 'why' is key to finding this killer," I said. "His signals are mixed, his agenda murky. I'm not getting him. Not at all. Let's say he drugged Bella with brownies. That whole stasis thing interests me. The fact that he didn't put her out. More like a twilight sleep. There's a reason he kept her awake."

"Yup," Lauria said. "I'd like you to go out with me and interview Eva's foster parents. One of my guys did the prelim, but I'd like your take on these people. You game? Temple's practically there. We could go right after we see Bella. Maybe we'll have more to take with us, y'know?"

I rechecked my watch. Nine-thirty. I needed to get to work—I had piles to do—and I desperately wanted to see

Veda and to learn if Kranak had found out anything about the dead nurse. But a missing child? "Of course I'll go."

The drive seemed to take forever. We hopped onto Route 3, again busy with traffic headed east toward town, then onto 101A, then onto the 101 bypass that had us avoiding the middle of some town. Few cars were on the road, and the sun was obscured by leaden clouds.

"Kathleen, have you ever—*Shit!*" Something hit us, hard. Coffee flew from my hand and splattered the windshield.

"Fuck!" shouted Lauria. Eyes narrowed, jaw clenched, she tugged right, then left trying to get the hulking SUV back under control.

I clutched the door's grab bar with my right hand, my left arm stretched forward, trying to hold myself in position. My seat belt bit into my shoulder.

The world became surreal in its slowness as adrenaline juiced my body. The side mirror showed a beige van with a staved-in front end, as if he didn't care, as if it were purposeful.

"The car behind us!" I screamed. "Kath, he's coming again!"

She tried to change lanes, but at that moment another thundering hit.

My neck snapped back into the headrest, and then our SUV swerved, tilted, and flipped onto its side. I glimpsed Kath still clutching the wheel, trying to steer, and we tilted again, a forty-five degree angle and slid and bumped and the burst of an air bag ...

I swam and swam and swam upward in desperate need of air. I tried to reach the surface, but it was far, so far. I gasped, smothered, gasped again as I clawed at something that wasn't water. But I couldn't breathe.

I punched, pushed, and a sudden shift.

I gasped in a breath. Then another. And another.

I collapsed, quiet, against the powerful white thing that had held me prisoner. My body ached, burned, even, yet there was no flame. I was cold, *cold,* and I couldn't see. I brushed my arm across my face. Wet. I did it again. Opened my eyes to ... red. Blood?

I gasped. "Kathleen!"

I heard nothing, not even another's breath.

"Kathleen!"

And there, in the quiet, a moan.

"Hang on, Kath." My torso was trapped, but my fingers felt the suede of my purse. I walked them inside and found my cell. I eased up my arm—God, it hurt—and flipped open the phone with my thumb. I had no idea if the cell would still work after being submerged in water.

"Gert," I said, hoping the phone would recognize the voice activation. *"Gert."* When I heard the rings, I cheered for the voice dial I'd taken the time to create but a bare month earlier.

"Hey, Tal! Ya not gonna believe what happened with—"

"Gert!" My voice sounded labored, breathy. "Down an embankment. Route one-oh-one. Accident. Make sure they take me to Hawthorne ... *Hawthorne....* Send ..." My fingers spasmed. I dropped the phone. *Shit.* "Gert!" I tried to shout, but what emerged were the sounds of a breathy child. I tasted blood, from somewhere, and fell ...

I am with Rose. Her hair is long and black and lovely, and when she smiles up at me, her silver braces glitter.

"You know," *she says.*

"But I don't ..."

She takes my hand. Her stubby nails are polished pink with purple flowers. She leads me to a bench seat between two large maple trees that burst red with autumn color. Rose smiles up at me, this time lips closed. Eyes almost closed, too, as she tilts her face to the fresh breeze of a new season.

I stroke her hair, and she leans against me. Snuggles, really.

Oh, she's a sweet child, and my heart aches because ... Why?

I try, but I can't remember.

A burst of pain tugs me away. But Rose holds on tight to both my hands, and I stay seated beside her on the bench.

"You can help Eva if you try," she says. "You know. You do."

And I believe, although I can't capture the thought that's brewing in my mind.

We walk down a path lined with oak trees as their leaves sway to the forest floor. We hold hands. Hers is small and warm in mine.

Rose hums a tune, one I know.

"What is that, Rose?" I ask.

She smiles and hums louder. She releases my hand, fans her hands in front of her, kicks out the heel of her left foot.

If she'd only say the words.

He smile widens. She prances between the majestic oak trees, and in the distance I see what looks like a castle. I can hear the humming now, and words form in my head.

The song's there ... almost there.

"I'll understand then, yes, Rose?"

"Yes!"

Oh, my tongue tingles with anticipation of—

Blinding pain, and I screamed for Rose and the trees and the leaves and the song. Gone.

Something swayed, and something else held my mouth prisoner. I pushed at it, but I was prevented from moving it. I focused. Someone in uniform. Beside me. I'm strapped in. *Panic.* I try to move. Can't!

A hand. A voice. "Sshhhh."

I blink again, sway. Me, on a stretcher. An ambulance. I searched for Lauria with my eyes, but couldn't find her.

I tried to say "Kathleen," but the EMT shushed me with her fingers and a smile.

Where were they taking me? "Where?"

She nodded. "St. Joseph's in Nashua."

I shook my head. "*No*. Hawthorne. Hawthorne. *Hawthorne*."

She smiled. What the *hell* did that mean?

She jiggled something on the plastic bag hung beside me, and a dark velvet cloak enfolded me.

I never knew outer space was so thick or filled with clouds or that I could breathe. I sighed. Who knew? I chuckled.

Someone chuckled back.

I blinked. The glare, awful. I squeezed my eyes tight, but a familiar voice said, "C'mon, Emma, open up."

Emma? I wasn't in space, then. Damn, that had been so cool. So ... I cranked up my lids, and now I was certain I was in the grip of a hallucination. My old Winsworth pal, Carmen Cavases, stood over me dressed in a baggy Elvis tunic. *Elvis?* Why dream of Carmen? What kind of Freudian weirdness was going on here? What ...

"*Mi amiga*," the Carmen apparition said. "I'm real."

"Ridiculous," I said, only it came out a mumble. "You live in Maine."

"*Maldito sea!* Tally, open your eyes."

Now *that* was the Carmen I knew and loved. "What the—?"

"The accident, babe?"

An avalanche of memories buried me. Horrible things. Minutes later, I surfaced and looked around. I lay in a hospital room, my bed by a picture window, with Carmen curved over me like some gargoyle. Two bags of glop hung from a stainless coat rack with tubes snaking from the glop to needles that were taped to the inside of my left elbow. Didn't they know I was a lefty, dammit?

I felt grouchy and frightened and fuzzy all at the same time.

"Stop looming," I said.

She smiled. "That's more like it."

"It doesn't feel anything 'like it,' dammit! Where am I?"

"Hawthorne Hospital."

Thank heavens I'd gotten through on that. "How did I get here?"

"Ambulance, duh."

"No, I mean—"

"Your pal, Gert, made sure you got here."

I paused. I'd been … Yes, I'd been on the phone with Gert. And Kathleen … "How's Kathleen?"

She compressed her lips, shook her head.

Fear smothered me. "I need to know."

Carmen checked my IV lines, avoided my eyes. "She's at Mass General. Intensive care. She's bad, Tal."

I pushed up on my elbows, accompanied by grunts of pain. "Will she …?"

"They don't know."

I tried to process Kathleen Lauria injured. She was invincible, so how could she be mortally wounded? I inhaled a sob. *Damn* SUVs that roll over.

Carmen pulled an orange vinyl chair over to the bed and sat. She's a big woman—tall, big-boned, and majestic—with a flame of red hair that she'd bound into a French twist. She's beautiful, too, with hands that show years of work and care running a natural food restaurant and farming her land. Which was why I didn't get the nurse's costume.

She leaned in close. "I'm undercover."

"Oh, *great*. Not! How the hell do you—"

"Here's the story, *compañero*. You're at Hawthorne Hospital, and you're doing just dandy. I got a job as Veda's private nurse." She grinned. "You didn't know I was a nurse, did ya? The profession didn't suit. Not t'all. But it comes in handy from time to time." She winked.

I now knew, definitively, I'd tumbled down the rabbit hole. "Are you nuts?"

"Wicked nuts." She grinned. "Hank put me up to it. Told me all about Dr. Barrow and the murdered nurse. And you. He suggested I come down and keep an eye on Dr. Barrow. I thought it was a pretty cool idea. See, we'd planned this all out before you managed, in your own special style, to end up as Swiss cheese in the very same hospital as your foster mum."

"My God. Hank! Our big vacation." I moved the wrong way and yelped.

"Cancelled," she said. "The man's bullheaded, but not dumb." She squeezed my arm just as another nurse entered with a physician in tow.

"What are you doing here?" he barked at Carmen.

"Just checking." Her bimbo tone was most un-Carmen-like. "I thought I heard a noise. Bye."

The physician watched Carmen leave, and then said in a way-too-jocular tone, "Ms. Whyte, welcome back to the living."

"Fortunately I was never dead," I said. "What's wrong with me?"

He scratched his shaved head and said, "You'll be released in a couple to three days." He flipped the chart he lifted from the foot of my bed. "Concussion. Sprained arm. We had to remove your spleen, I'm afraid. We performed a laparoscopic splenectomy."

I felt around and found the tender spots on my belly. I winced. Whoever had done this to Lauria and myself would not go lightly into the night.

"How long have I been here?" I asked.

"Three days," the doctor said. "We kept you sedated."

I had no memory of it. Three days—vanished. Gave me the creeps. "Why?"

The doctor pursed his lips. "You were so emotionally agitated, we believed it to be for the best. You'll be released in two to three days."

"Are the police here?" I asked.

The nurse glanced toward the door. "They haven't left."

"Kranak?" I asked.

She snorted. "How did you know?"

I smiled, and thanked Buddha, the Lord, and all the gods for friends like Rob Kranak. "Send him in, please."

"We need to talk about your care," Dr. Whomever said. "You need to address some issues."

"Not now, I don't," I said. "Right now I need to see a friend."

Kranak wore a rumpled brown suit, and crumbs dotted his blue shirt. Although his hair was Brylcreemed to attention, sunglasses hid his eyes.

"You look like one of the Blues Brothers, Rob."

He didn't smile, but removed his sunglasses. Red spidered eyes that projected exhaustion.

"You look awful," I said.

He tossed me a grimace. "You would, too, if your pallie got herself nearly killed."

I opened my arms for a hug, and instead got a pat on each shoulder.

"Can't," he said. "Don't wanna hurt the patient."

He honked into his handkerchief—that was wrinkled, too—and said, "Hay fever."

I teared up at his cocktail of pain and worry. "I'm okay, Rob. Really. And I'll take a rain check for the hug I really want." I held out my hand for his, which shook just slightly as he took mine. Now I was the one worried about his diabetes flaring up. He wasn't taking care of himself. That was obvious.

"Don't," he said.

"You know me too well."

"Yeah."

"Are you really okay?" I said.

He sat in the chair Carmen had vacated and pulled out his slim notebook. "Let's talk about you, kiddo. We haven't learned much, I'll tell ya. No witnesses. Christ, New Hampshire's the sticks."

"I like the place. Go on."

He flipped open his notebook. "You were hit by a Chevrolet Astro cargo van, circa 1996 to 1998."

"Hit?" I bunched the sheet between my fists. "Of course. Now I remember. When I woke up, I thought we'd just rolled over. I saw the van in the side mirror just as he hit us the second time."

Kranak nodded in agreement. "They got it figured the guy was after Special Agent Lauria."

"Who's 'they'?"

"FBI, state boys."

"Is that what you think?"

His compassionate eyes wouldn't meet mine.

And I knew. "You believe it was me the guy was after, not Lauria."

He shrugged, quintessential Kranak.

Me. And I was seared by the idea that if I was the target, I was the one who'd put Lauria in harm's way. I turned away from Kranak to process the pain.

Chapter Sixteen

Kranak remained silent, as did I, for a long while. And then I caught his eyes and held on hard. "So how come you think the van was after me?"

"Christ, Tal, gimme a break. You're banged up. Screwed up. We can talk about this later."

"Later doesn't exist."

He flapped his tie. "The dead nurse. What's going on with Veda. I don't trust nobody. Like you say, it's a gut thing."

"Bertha! Penny! The vet!"

He squeezed my shoulder. "Take it easy. They're fine. Fine. Your Aunt Bertha's moved in with some niece or other and Sculptor-boy is watching Penny. He talked to the vet, too. No news."

I exhaled a breath I hadn't realized I'd been holding. "Thank heavens. And don't call Jake 'Sculptor-boy.' Now all we have to figure out is the *who*."

"Not 'we,' babe. No way." He kissed my cheek, and then headed for the door.

"Rob, wait!"

He didn't turn, but gave a wave over his shoulder.

"Dammit! I just have one request!"

He stopped, slumped, and bellowed a sigh.

"*One* thing," he said as he turned. "That's *it*."

"Promise," I said. "One thing. Go up to Temple, New Hampshire. Take someone with you. I'd take a woman. That'll work better. Talk to Bella Marsh. I think she knows where Eva Lange is. She doesn't realize she knows, but she does. That's where Lauria and I were headed before …"

Kranak frowned, brushed fingers through his bristly mustache. He was stalling. He didn't want to do this. After all, it was the FBI's case, and he generally despised them. All except for one murdered agent whom he'd loved.

"For me, Rob. Do it. Please. Eva's life … it's teetering. I know it is."

"You and me, we're not having a good day here."

"Not having a … Ahhhhh. I get it. So what's the story?"

"We tried. We knew that's what you and Lauria were up to, so an FBI agent and me, we went up to the sticks to do just that. They're gone, Tal. The Marshes. Whole kit and caboodle. We got nothing on the Eva kid. Nothing. We're on it, but we're fucked."

That we were.

I was exhausted and in pain, but I needed to accomplish certain things. I buzzed the nurse, and I waited … and waited … and after a half hour, a middle-aged nurse with deeply etched frown lines finally materialized.

"Glad I wasn't teetering on the brink," I said.

She hugged a clipboard and donned a smile that could melt polar ice caps. "What can I do for you, honey?"

"Call me Tally. I'd like my cell phone."

She shook her head. "Not a chance."

"I just need to look up some numbers that's on the phone."

"I'll have to check."

"Please do. And I want a report on Dr. Barrow. In fact, I'd like to go see her."

She tilted her head, apparently listening to some distant symphony. "I'll have to check."

"Really." I hoped my sarcasm would relay how annoyed I was. "Okay. Last thing. I want this catheter out. Now. Please. I'd like to get up and go pee."

The smile faded. "I'll have to check on that, too."

I reached for my urine bag, about to throw the thing at her.

Fear skated across her face.

"Look," I said. "I know you're overworked. I understand how hard nursing has become as a profession. I know things aren't easy for you. But I am so frigging frustrated. I really wish you'd bag the doctor who's pulling your strings and help me out here."

She leaned toward me, a hand on the bedrail beside me, faces so close our noses almost touched. She dropped her nurses mask. "Don't you see, I'd love to do all the things you requested. All of 'em. But if I acted on my own, I'd be dog doo. I'd end up paying in lousy ways. And it sucks. And it's only getting worse. When I started twenty years ago, things were better by a lot."

She straightened, brushed a hand down her rumpled tunic, hugged the clipboard tight, and readjusted her professional persona. "I'll try to help you, but, honestly? I doubt I can."

I held out small hope that any of my requests would be granted. Beat from one too many battles, I let my lids slide closed.

Somebody was pinching the soft flesh of my inner elbow. "Ouch, dammit!"

"Ssshhh!" came the hissed reply.

I blinked twice, but all I saw was an apparition hovering over me, blocking out the light.

I opened my mouth to yell. A hand slammed over it. I reached for the wrist so I could push it away. I dug in my nails. Couldn't get breath. Couldn't—

"Dammit, Tally, it's Carmen. Stop it!"

"Can't breathe," I said, which came out like a mouth full of marbles.

The hand flew away, and I rubbed fingers across my sore lips. "Some nurse. You practically suffocated me! What the hell time is it, anyway?"

"It's three A.M., and you're way too loud. *Quiet!* And listen." She pulled the chair over. "I went out to grab a juice about an hour ago. You know, she's got that cop guard, twenty-four/seven. So I go back in, and I'm really quiet so as not to wake her. I didn't pay any attention to the cop, y'know?"

"Is she okay?" I said. "Your tone is scary. I don't like it."

"You shouldn't like it. Veda was almost on that big boat to Valhalla. Just listen. So I'm back in the room, and I'm wicked quiet, and I'm sitting in a different chair, the one in the corner, so I can drink my juice and eat my granola bar and not wake her. Y'know she's safe, right? There's a boy in blue outside the door. What can happen."

"*And?* C'mon, Carm, hurry up with this."

"Can you picture I'm in the shadow? So the door opens, and this girl, this nurse, comes in. She stands right in the doorway, and with the light shining behind, I can't really see her. But she's pretty, y'know? Somehow I know that. She's carrying something, and when she steps into the room, I see it's a hypodermic. But she's not just carrying it. It's against her belly, like it's hidden."

I reached for Carmen's hand and held it tight. "Geesh, Carm, you're making it sound like a soap opera. Get on with it!"

"Ayuh. So Miss Nursie closes the door really gently, and

I'm wondering where the hell is Mr. Cop. It's really dark, but my eyes adjust to the glow of all the machines and the night-light. So I can see a little. And here I am, hidden, sort of, but mostly because all she sees is your mom. And I'm a little pissed, y'know, because her hair's in a long braid, just like I usually wear it, and I don't know why that bothers me, but—"

"Carmen!"

"Sorry. So she tiptoes to the bed, soft and secret-like. She looks down at Veda. Swear to God I saw a tear on the babe's cheek. Which is really bent, considering she raises the hypodermic and is planning to inject something into Veda's IV tube."

My belly cramped. "She's okay, right? She's fine? Veda's fine?"

Carmen smiled, squeezed my hand. "Fine. Relax."

"Oh, yeah, right. Sure. I can relax during this tale of horror. Can't you for once speed it up?"

Carmen smiled wider. "C'mon, Tally Whyte, half the fun's in the telling. So anyway, I jump up, and as we both know, I'm no petite Louise, and I say 'What the fuck are you doing?' which might not have been the brightest thing in the world."

"Just go on," I said.

"So her hands fly up and she says 'Oh!' in surprise. And I say 'Yeah!' and she scoots out of the room. I go after her, trip on something, go flying. Man, it hurts landing on that damned linoleum floor. I push myself up and run after her. But she's gone. I mean, I can't find her anywhere."

I sighed. I took her hand and brushed it against my cheek. "Thanks, Carmen, for being there. Thanks."

"There's more." Her green eyes glittered.

"Go."

She reached inside the pocket of her tunic, slid out a baggie and held it up. Inside was a bent hypodermic needle and plastic syringe.

"That's what I slipped on," she said. "I'm thinking that when I surprised her and her hands flew up, off went the hypodermic."

I echoed her grin. "Nice. Very nice."

We giggled, much like we'd done as kids, when suddenly the horror of what had almost happened to Veda overtook me. "I can't believe I'm laughing. My God, Veda was almost killed."

"I know," she said.

I pushed myself up in bed, winced. "Damn. What was the cop doing all this time?"

"Having a little drug-assisted nap, I suspect," Carmen said.

Fear tightened my throat. "So if you're here, who's watching Veda!"

"Ssshhh. We're cool. I called your friend, Kranak, told him the high points. He sent somebody over to watch your mom. As soon as Kranak gets here, I'm to give him the needle, so to speak."

"You can't resist those, can you?"

"Naw." She grinned.

I heaved out a sigh. "Wow. At least we can relax."

"Right." She nodded.

I recognized the nod for a lie. My dear Carmen was keeping something from me. Something big. Hmmm. If I confronted her, I'd get nothing. She was more stubborn than I could ever hope to be, and immovable as the Tetons. Whatever it was, was bad. And I'd have to trick it out of her. First things first.

"Do me a favor? Please remove this awful catheter."

Without even one quip, she did the deed.

"Kranak should be here by now," I said. "Let's go see him."

She nodded as she stood. "Sure."

"He'd be with Veda, right?"

"Ayuh." She headed for the door.

"Well, I want to see her, too."

She turned and winked. "All in good time. You've had a big few days. You need to rest. I need some, too, after all my adventuring. How about this—I'll come get you in the morning and you can see them both. Night."

I waved. "You're right. I'm not up to snuff. Thanks, Carm. Night." I closed my eyes.

When the door whooshed shut, I opened them. I'd be damned if I wasn't seeing Kranak and Veda that night. I couldn't imagine what else was going on, but I wanted to know.

I again closed my eyes and began to count to one hundred. The sound of a door opening, and through my lashes I saw Carmen peek in. Good thing I'd waited. She'd have wrestled me back into the bed.

On one hundred, I sat up. A needle was poking into the soft tissue of my inner elbow. I undid the tape and tugged it out. Ouch. Drops of blood oozed from the puncture hole.

I shivered when my feet hit the chilly linoleum. My butt was chilly, too, and I tottered over to the closet where I figured some human clothing might be hung. No such luck. Geesh. I was dizzy, to boot. I took a couple steadying breaths.

I somehow managed to get back to the bed. I pulled off the top sheet. My side felt like a knitting needle was scraping around in there. I wrapped the sheet toga-style and headed for the hall. Actually, staggered would be a better term.

I opened the door a hair. The hall was clear and quiet, reminding me of OCME at night. I was in 234, Veda in 347. She seemed like miles away. But, dammit, I was going to see her.

By the time I stood down the hall from her room, I was shaking from exhaustion. This was a larger adventure than my body was in the mood to take. I leaned against the wall, panting and sweating.

A woman in khakis, blue button-down shirt, and sneakers sat on a chair in front of Veda's hospital door. She was either FBI or a Massachusetts state cop.

Here I was, looking like a Roman hooker, no ID, and trying to gain entry to the state's Chief Medical Examiner.

"Hello," I said, attempting a saunter while the wall held me vertical.

Veda's watcher sprang to her feet, gun drawn. Her eyes widened, and she lowered her nine millimeter. "Ms. Whyte?"

A feeble smile popped out. "You know me! Thank heavens. I need to see Dr. Barrow."

"Let me help you."

"Oh, hooray. Please do." This was way too easy. Something was up.

She took my right arm and supported me while she opened the door. We slowly walked inside.

"Maybe you'd better sit first," she said.

"I've got to see her."

She shrugged and led me forward. I leaned on the bottom of Veda's bed and stared up at her. The light was but a dim glow, but showed me enough. Her cheeks were flushed, her hair unbound and askew. She'd pulled the sheets and extra blankets up to her chin, but her shivering was unmistakable. A nurse was fiddling with her IV.

"Good gracious!" the nurse said.

"Dr. Barrow. She has a high fever, yes?"

"I really can't say," replied the nurse.

"To me you can, dammit," I said. "All the papers are in order. I've got power of attorney and all the other crap one needs nowadays. I need to know what's up."

The nurse stiffened. "You don't have to get nasty. Dr. Barrow has a fever of one-oh-three, and it's still going up. We've been unable to bring it down. I'd say you should look out for yourself, ma'am."

"Huh? I'm okay."

The cop cleared her throat. "Not exactly." She pointed to my side.

I looked down, and grew dizzy from the blood staining my toga.

* * *

"Can you *never* behave?" Carmen's familiar gruff voice pulled me to consciousness. I opened my eyes just a slit to scope things out. I wasn't in my regular hospital room, but in a chair, and some evildoer had replaced the IV in my arm.

"I found something out," Carmen said. "I wasn't going to tell you, but since you've decided on adventuring, what the hell."

"And ...?"

Her brow furrowed. "Earlier. Days ago. The day Veda lost it. Um, they found a massive amount of heparin in her blood."

"Heparin? Veda's not on heparin. It thins the blood, right?"

"Yes. It can kill. It can also cause a bleed, which—"

"Which can cause brain damage."

She compressed her lips and nodded.

It took me a minute to process what Carmen had said. I didn't want to believe it, hoped she was wrong. "Carm, I ..."

A voice behind the drawn curtain grabbed my attention. Veda's voice. Whispering in her native German, a language she never, ever spoke.

I frowned, but found no words.

Carmen crossed her arms over her large breasts. "You know how sick she is."

I nodded. "And I'm terrified."

Chapter Seventeen

"Which is why I didn't tell you about the heparin last night." She slid her bum onto the bed. "It's bad, Tal."

"I'm glad I'm here now," I said. "It seems like eternity since I last spoke with her. Since we shared a joke. Two weeks ago, she was fine, normal, sharp as a scalpel. I miss her, and at the same time, I feel guilty because she's here, not gone."

Carmen's frown lines deepened.

"I'm glad you're here, pardner," I said.

She winked. "Hank's damned smart. I'm glad I'm here, too. Whew—haven't had this much excitement in years."

I chuckled, and my side stitched. "Crap. Get me over to Veda. Please. I want to sit beside her."

I made it with Carmen's help.

"I'll keep watch for Nurse Ratchet," Carmen said.

"Deal." I took Veda's hand. It burned. "Oh, Vede."

Her eyes grew wild, pinballing around the room. *"Ich will nicht geh'n, Papa!"*

"What are you saying, Vede?" I frantically opened drawers, found a pad, but not a pen. "It's Tally. Speak in English."

"*Nein. Ich werde nicht geh'n!*" she hollered.

I wished I could write it down. I only recognized a few words. "Go where, Vede? What can I do? Please!"

"*Die sind böse und werden uns umbringen,*" she said. "*Die haben Purtzel auch umgebracht! Ermordet! Die haben alles mitgenommen. Papas Bücher. Muttis Silber. Unser Spielzeug.*"

"Vede! You're safe. You're in America." I wrapped my arms around her shoulders and hugged her tight.

She pushed me away. "*Ja. Das werden sie. Ganz bestimmt. Wo sind die beiden Mädchen am Meer geblieben?*"

"I don't understand. Can you speak in English, please? Please?"

"*Die schönen Mädchen am Ufer! Ich hab' es geseh'n. Sie haben es. Du musst ...*" She stuttered an inhale and her eyes rolled up so only the whites showed.

"Carmen!"

Veda stopped breathing.

Carmen pressed some buttons and began pounding Veda's chest.

Someone dragged me out of the room. I was clammy with terror until a nurse appeared and said Veda was back with the living and resting comfortably. That's when I threw up in the hospital corridor and they wheeled me back to my room.

The following morning, I physically felt much more human. My side throbbed, but didn't feel like a serrated knife was sawing me in two.

I phoned Veda's room. "How's she doing?"

"Better," the nurse said. "Her fever's down to one-hundred-one. Her color's much improved."

Tears of relief stung my eyes. "Great. Good. Um, I'll be up in a bit."

I called Gert at work and then went up to visit with Veda. She *was* better, and she was speaking in English. But the vagueness that I hoped had dissipated remained.

By the time I got back to my room, Gert was stretched out on my hospital bed watching some soap opera.

"Yummy stuff?" I said.

"Yeah," she said as she unwrapped a piece of Bazooka. She slid the bubblegum into her mouth, scanned the Bazooka Joe comic, and smiled. "Good one." A huge pink bubble erupted from her mouth, and she popped it with a pink-polished nail. "Here are your clothes." She grinned and handed me the bag.

"Thanks, kiddo. I'll be out in a sec."

While I showered, I thought about different points of attack for Veda's situation. "You ready?" I said to her as I emerged. Boy, it felt good to be wearing human clothes again.

"At your disposal, Tal."

And off we went to hunt a killer.

Gert and I sat in my office at OCME. I was shocked by the feel of a house unwatched. Hard to imagine what Fogarty was doing or why the desk sergeant wore a wrinkled uniform or why duct tape covered the coded lock to the inner sanctum. I was afraid of what I'd see if I went back to the cooler and autopsy suite. Penny sat on my feet, and I couldn't hug her enough. Her lump remained, but it must be nothing. It had to be.

Midway through my telling of the murdered nurse and the mystery nurse's warnings and the further attempt on Veda's life, Carmen strolled in.

"What are you doing here?" I said.

"Pretty obvious to me." She pulled up a chair alongside

the couch. "A nurse-FBI agent is spelling me in Dr. Barrow's room, so I assumed you needed me down here."

"What kind of accent is that?" Gert asked in thick Brooklynese.

"Whatcha gonna make of it, little lady?" Carmen replied in her best Maine-speak.

"Maine meet Brooklyn," I said. "Now lets get on with it."

We plowed through the files for Veda's possible attacker. Stacks from a thirty-year career dwindled slowly. We poured over each folder, setting aside files we considered "possibles." That pile grew and grew.

Around one-thirty, I had trouble keeping my eyes open.

"Surgery knocks you out," Carmen said.

"I know, but—"

"Take a nap," Gert said. "We'll keep going."

When I awakened, Gert and Carmen wore glum faces. "What's up?"

Carmen lifted her chin. "Look."

I saw three stacks of two-foot-tall files and one tiny one. "I'm afraid to ask."

"The problem," Gert said, "is that Dr. Barrow has been around a long time. That little pile contains the ones we ruled out. The three big ones are—"

"The contenders."

"Contenders?" said the voice from the doorway.

I looked up to see a grinning Tom Fogarty looming at the entrance to my office, his lackey Judy Ethridge standing beside him.

"Well, well," he said. "Lookie what we've got here."

"What we have here is none of your business," I said.

"Tsk, tsk," said a smiling Fogarty. "Sad when the mind goes. Of course it's my business as acting chief ME."

"Fuck you," I said.

His oatmeal face lost its smile. "No, sweet cheeks, fuck *you*. Those files are the property of OCME. Hand them over."

"If I don't, what'll you do, take them?" I pushed up from the couch, wobbled a bit. But that was okay. Fogarty still shrank from my stare.

"Charley!" Ethridge yelled.

The technician appeared and slinked through the doorway, hands in pockets, face flushed.

"Those." Ethridge pointed to the stacks on the floor.

My hands itched to strangle her. I lurched forward.

"Hey, Tal!" Gert said.

I turned. Gert was sitting on my desk, leg swinging, filing her nails. "Not worth it." She blew a purple Bazooka bubble, and then sucked it into her mouth.

I whooshed out a breath. "Right. Go ahead, Charley. Take 'em."

He scooped up stacks in each arm and beat a quick retreat.

"Happy?" I said to Fogarty.

"Not yet," Fogarty said. "I checked MGAP's contract. While you're an independent agency, you also can be evicted if we need the space. We do. You have a month to clear out your crap." His pale eyes glittered and the smile returned.

I walked toward him, forcing myself not to sway with the pain in my side. "First off, you'd better get *your* house in order. Things are a mess. Veda will have a fit when she gets back."

"Veda won't be coming back," Ethridge said.

Fogarty's grin faded. "I visited her this morning. She looked well. Very well. But she won't be returning to OCME, Tally Whyte. She's gone somewhere that neither of us can travel."

"You're wrong," I said. "Veda's incredibly strong. She *will* be back."

His lips thinned. "She's my friend. I miss her. But you? You're out of here."

*   *   *

"I wish I had some Lysol to clear away Fogarty's stench," I said to Gert and Carmen after Fogarty and Ethridge had left. "Of course Veda will be back."

"Yeah," Gert said. "She will. MGAP is not going anywhere, either." She nodded to Carmen, who went and shut my office door.

"What's up?" I said.

Gert grinned as she slid off the desk. She lifted a manila folder that had been resting beneath her butt. "This," she said as she handed it to me.

The name on the folder read: *Noguchi, Teresa*.

"You're kidding?" I said.

Carmen laughed. "We thought it was mighty cool, finding it. We were going to surprise you. That shit Fogarty won't even know it's missing."

"Veda worked the case?" I said.

"Did she ever," Gert said.

I read over Veda's case notes while Gert played lookout. Teresa Noguchi and her brother had a car accident several years ago here, in Massachusetts. Teresa was paralyzed and the brother died.

He'd been driving. Veda ruled his an alcohol-related death. Teresa insisted they'd been pursued by thugs. Veda's chicken-scratch shorthand told me she'd hooked Teresa up with a counselor in New Hampshire and a physical therapist friend.

Yet the file held an angry letter from Teresa and John Noguchi, saying that they protested Veda's ruling and the brother's death should have been ruled a homicide.

It might or might not be true about the case being a homicide, but deciding that aspect of things wasn't in Veda's purview.

I wondered if they still blamed her.

I wasn't sure if the file added up to anything. Then again, I seldom bought into the idea of coincidences.

* * *

Penny whined.

"I'll take her out," Carmen said.

"Thanks," I said, "but I'd rather."

We crossed the parking lot and went through the back gate so she could trot around on the grass, smelling intriguing smells and doing her business.

While Penny chased several pigeons into flight, I reveled in the warm breeze. My ankle turned on a rock. I lost my balance, grabbed the chain-link fence. Again I was tumbling over and over in Lauria's SUV, the sensation so real …

"*Ke mne,* Pens! Come!"

She hugged my side as I half-ran, half-stumbled back to my office.

I called Mass General.

"Please connect me to Ms. Kathleen Lauria's room," I said.

A pause, then some clicks. What was …

"May I help you," said the harsh male voice.

"I'd like to talk to Kathleen Lauria."

"Who is this," he said.

"Tally Whyte. A friend."

"Sorry, ma'am, Agent Lauria's condition is unchanged."

Unchanged. *Everything* had changed. Veda, Penny, Lauria, little Eva Lange, Rose. *Damn, damn, damn.*

Outside my window, the maple wore buds, green and rich, like a web of emeralds. A robin searched the ground at the base of the tree.

Yet I longed for what was. For winter, just passed, and snow and sleet and bare trees and no robins. I wished for dogs and friends and mothers, all healthy and full of life. And children playing, not laid out on steel tables.

I saw the world spinning more slowly, then pausing, and then reversing itself to find that time when everything wasn't broken.

Of course, that would mean going back twenty-some

years, to before Dad was murdered, which would also mean never having met Veda or owned Penny or become a homicide counselor or lived a life shaped by his death.

I always feared the monkey's paw—the trap of wishes granted and the past returned.

I stared out the window and a boy in red shorts skipped by. I could almost see his goose bumps. He was eager for spring.

I wished I was.

Chapter Eighteen

I swear Nurse Carmen slipped me some drug, because after the Noguchi revelation, we went back to my apartment, and I slept almost twenty-four hours. I hated losing a day, but boy, did I ever need that rest.

That night, on our way to dinner, Carmen drove me to see Kathleen Lauria in intensive care. An FBI agent guarded her, and I was allowed only five minutes. IVs snaked into her arms, and the respirator helping her breathe went *ka-thunk* over and over, like some demented metronome. I spoke to her, telling her I was fine, and that I missed her, and that she'd be in big trouble if she didn't get well soon.

I got no reaction.

"She could still wake up, Tal," Carmen said as we parked near Bella Davide Cantina in the North End.

"I know. I hope ... yes."

Carmen and I feasted on cavatelli and capalettis and bra-ciola and baby green salad and garlic bread.

"God, that was good," Carmen said. "This stuff screams organic, y'know."

"Even so, I like it." I laughed. "Oh, don't look so pruney. It's great stuff, just like yours is yummy at Town Farm."

She snorted. "I checked your fridge. Your diet sucks."

"Spoken like the organic chef you are."

"Heavenly." We smiled as the waiter delivered our Neapolitans and thick, dark coffee.

We ordered grappa in coffee, and after the waiter delivered it, we felt ready to dive into some heavy-duty brainstorming.

"One." I held up a spread-fingered hand. "Someone somehow damaged Veda while she was in Hawthorne hospital."

Carmen nodded. "My guess, as a nurse? I'd say it was a failed attempt to kill her."

I nodded. "Two. A nurse who said her name was Brooke *told me* someone was trying to kill Veda."

"Right."

In that instant I felt eyes on me, harsh and intense. I shook my head, trying to rid myself of the discomforting sensation. It remained.

Carmen appeared oblivious to the malevolence I was sensing. "Three," I continued. "A nurse named Brooke was murdered and thrown in a Dumpster. It was a different nurse than the one I met."

"That's creepy, Tal," she said.

I peered around the restaurant, but the darkened booths and candlelit tables prevented me from seeing much of anything.

"Tal?" she said.

"Sorry. There's just something … Whatever. Yes, it's creepy. The nurse we found in the Dumpster was the real Brooke. Ergo, the woman who talked to me about someone murdering Veda wasn't a nurse at Hawthorne."

"Anybody can sneak into a hospital." She nibbled on a bread stick.

"People want to stay *out* of hospitals, not get into them.

Four. We've got someone who two nights ago tried to stick a hypodermic into Veda's IV line, most likely to kill her. Which is what you think, yes?"

Carmen nodded, and took a sip of wine. "From the look of her, I'd say it was your girl, the faux Brooke."

"Did you just say 'faux'?"

"Of course I did. We Mainers have class." She winked. "The woman matched your description."

"What's confusing is why would the killer try to warn me? Look, we've got a terribly ill woman here. An older woman."

"Go on," Carmen said.

"I've been looking at this relating to something that's happened. A revenge thing."

"I agree," Carmen said. "Maybe the secrets are in the Noguchi file."

I tossed my napkin onto the table. "I believe that's a key. One of them. The day Veda was hospitalized was the day Rose was found in our cooler. But why keep attacking Veda? I mean, she's pretty much debilitated right now. Maybe … maybe it's not about something that she's done, but something that's going to happen in the future. Which is why he—she—keeps going after her."

Just then, someone entered the restaurant accompanied by a sharp gust of wind. Candles flickered, and in the dancing light I saw a familiar face: Harry Pisarro. Mob boss, sexual predator, and all-around nasty guy, but also a man who'd lost a beloved daughter.

I'd thought him a friend once. Now I knew better.

Two bulked-up hoods in black pants, black T-shirts, and black leather bomber jackets flanked him. Joseph Arpino, the restaurant's owner, hustled over, head bowed, obsequious as hell. I wanted to barf.

I gave them my back with the hope that Pisarro would ignore us. "Go on, Carm. You were about to say something."

Her eyes narrowed. "Can't. We've got a wicked bad guy coming our way."

Prickles washed across my shoulders. I would not give him the satisfaction of turning.

Pisarro paused at our table.

"Ms. Tally. So good to see you." His brilliant white-capped teeth gleamed in the candlelight. His uniform matched his flunkies, right down to the sockless feet with tasseled loafers, but the fit and sheen of his loafers said bucks, where theirs didn't.

"Hello, Harry."

"Problems over at The Grief Shop, eh?" His smile widened. His white mane of hair glistened.

"None that I'm aware of." I took a sip of grappa.

"Word in the community has it that Dr. Fogarty is about to be arrested. For what, I couldn't say."

Hell. Harry Pisarro was seldom wrong.

He leaned forward, moved a hand so his index finger went back and forth over mine. "Aren't you going to introduce me to your friend?"

"Actually, no, Harry." I turned toward him. "Maybe you'd like to take your friends and have dinner now. Good seeing you."

He chuckled in the soft way that recalled his hands on my breasts. I shivered. "And good seeing you, Ms. Tally. Tell Dr. Fogarty I send my best."

I tossed down some dollars that included the tip, signaled Carmen, and vamoosed.

Outside, the fresh air felt bracing after Pisarro's stench.

"That was one creepy guy," Carmen said.

"Yup. If Pisarro's right, Fogarty's dead meat. I can't stand the man, but I don't want to see Veda's second-in-command taken away in handcuffs. Good God, what the hell could that idiot have done?"

* * *

Back at OCME, I checked with Charley, who was manning the desk. Fo-garty had left The Grief Shop much earlier in the day.

"Did he leave you a number?" I asked.

"Naw," Charley said. "Never does."

In my office, I found Fogarty's home number and called. I got his machine and left a message for him to call me pronto. Carmen raised a finger.

"What?" I said.

"How about your friend Kranak?" Carmen said. "He's a wise one."

"You think?" I said.

"That he is." She winked. "Hank had better watch out."

I laughed. "No way. Kranak and me? Naw. But you're absolutely right about him knowing something." I called his cell. Unless he was on a case, he'd be on his boat. He picked up after three rings.

"Leave me alone," he said. "I need my beauty sleep."

"That's an understatement."

"Cruel, Tal. So waddya want?"

I was startled by the urge to say "You!" What had Carmen done to me?

"Hey, Tally? You napping?" Kranak said.

"No, um, do you know anything about Fogarty being in trouble? I just heard—"

"Where've you been? He's in jail."

I sat on the couch. "*Jail?*"

"Some Boston cop with an NYPD-ego thinks the doc's in bed with Harry Pisarro."

"So who's running OCME?" I said.

"Damned if I know."

I felt like going home. I doubted that anyone but Charley was at The Grief Shop, but hoped someone was around who knew who was in charge. My sprained arm ached and my painful incision reminded me I was in the hospital a couple days ago. Why had Kathleen Lauria's injuries been so much worse?

I found Didi Cravitz, our forensic anthropologist, hard at work on a reconstruction of a Jane Doe whose bones had been locked in an abandoned suitcase at the chichi Copley Plaza Hotel.

I pulled up a chair next to where Didi was performing her magic.

"How is Dr. Barrow doing?" Didi's eyes never left her work.

"Each day she gets stronger," I said.

"Very fine." Her attention returned to the woman coming alive in clay beneath her fingers.

"Beautiful," I said.

"But sad. See?" She pointed to the woman's cheek. "Broken. By a fist, I suspect. We think she was beaten to death during a robbery."

"Robbery?"

"Yes." She scraped the back of her hand across her high forehead, leaving a smear of clay. "Her left hand still clutched the strap of a Chanel handbag."

"Have you heard about Dr. Fogarty?"

Her plushly wrinkled face tightened into a sneer. "I certainly have."

"I thought you liked Tom?"

"I do. I believe his arrest is a mistake. No, it's that Judy Ethridge. We received a memo from Tom. She's in charge now. I can't stand that woman."

Didi was the gentlest of souls. "Because ...?"

Her bespeckled eyes fastened on mine. "First, I despise a woman of science who would waste money on fake boobs."

"It's not a crime, Didi."

She tightened her lips. "No, but this is: she was cruel to Bob."

"You mean the cleaning fella who had polio?"

She nodded. "Ethridge threatened to fire him if he didn't move faster."

"But—"

"Exactly.

Fogarty-the-Idiot might be in jail, but a devil—in the worst sense—was in charge of OCME.

The following morning I woke up with a pain in my side and an ache in my arm. Worse, Penny seemed lethargic.

I shucked off the covers. "Pens?"

Her golden-brown eyes lifted to mine. But instead of moving, she sighed and rested her muzzle on her paws.

I flew out of bed. "Carmen!"

"In here."

I found her in the kitchen making some nutritious something-or-other that looked fabulously delicious. Except I couldn't eat a thing.

"I'm taking Penny to the vet."

She dropped the spoon, turned off the stove, and brushed her hands against her jeans. "Let's go."

"No, you stay."

She raised an expressive auburn eyebrow. "Yeah, right. I'm driving. Period."

I sat shotgun, Penny in the middle, head resting on my lap. I stroked her forehead. When we arrived, Carmen and I helped my sluggish pup out of the 4Runner.

Dr. Joby's assistant took one look at Penny and motioned me to lead her out back. Once in the small, pine-paneled room, I scrunched down and said "*Zustan*, Penny. Stay."

She did, of course, giving me the most dreadful look—as if her dignity had been breached—while the assistant took her temperature.

The tech frowned.

"What?"

She shook her head.

"C'mon, what?"

"It's high," she said.

As I hugged Penny, I wondered if this was connected with her lump or some new and nasty kink.

Beth Joby arrived and consulted in whispers with her assistant.

The vet scrunched down in front of Penny, examined her gums, ran a hand over the lump, and pressed her fingers to Penny's belly.

"We're going to keep her for a bit," Dr. Joby said.

"How long?" I couldn't even ask why.

"A day," Dr. Joby said. "Two at the most, I'm sure."

"What is it?" I asked.

The vet shook her heard. "We don't know. Most likely some treatable infection, perhaps caused by her lump."

I hugged Penny. "*Hodny*. Good girl."

"You look pretty banged up," Beth Joby said after I'd left Penny with her assistant.

The accident. Rolling over and over and ... "This is worse."

"I know."

Chapter Nineteen

I walked to the 4Runner. Carmen spotted me and opened the driver's door.

"Scoot over," I said. "I need to be behind the wheel."

She scooted, and I crawled up into the driver's seat and clutched the wheel. "I've about had it. Rose and Bella and Eva. Veda and a dead nurse and Pisarro and Lauria in the hospital and Fogarty in jail. Now Penny. Again." I leaned back and scraped fingers across my scalp. "Gert's holding down the fort at work. If I don't do something proactive, I'll pop. You coming or not?"

Her eyes widened. "Sure. Let me pick up my car so I can get to the hospital later."

I varoomed out of the parking lot, and the feel of power gave me great satisfaction. Once Carmen had gotten her car, we hopped onto 93. I punched on the radio, found some hard rock, and let it wail. I slapped the steering wheel and forced myself to get jazzed.

My cell phone bleeped. "Tally Whyte."

"Where are we going?" Carmen said.

"The Noguchis."

In the week since I'd been to Temple, New Hampshire, less snow dotted the shaded banks alongside the roads. But spring remained elusive.

I parked in the driveway. No sign of Mrs. Noguchi's handicap-fitted van. The sun shined brightly on the drab lawn that seemed fitting for a house in mourning. Closed drapes curtained the windows, and no light gleamed from inside the house.

I expected to hear the bark of their yellow lab, but heard nothing.

Silas would have left for school, John Noguchi for work. But I was here to see Teresa Noguchi. Was she really out on an errand or inside the darkened house, hiding from the pain and grief of losing her daughter?

I filled Carmen in as we walked up the path. She'd be a fine companion, but she wasn't Kathleen Lauria, who would always have my back.

Let Kathleen be okay. Please.

The front door was painted a bright and bloody red. I banged the brass fish knocker, but the house remained silent. I banged again. Nothing.

"They could be gone," Carmen said. "After something like this."

"I know. But Mrs. Noguchi is in a wheelchair. Her van's not here, but she could still be. The Marshes took off, but somehow I don't see the Noguchis doing the same. Let's walk around the house. You go that way, and we'll meet in the middle."

I walked counterclockwise around the antique colonial. Every shade was drawn, ever curtain pulled. I didn't like the feeling I got from the house.

I halted beside a pink-curtained window, pressed my hand to the clapboards. I felt a heaviness, so breath came hard. It was as if I were being pressed against the house. Peeling paint—a window needing to be scraped.

Break it!

I shook my head. What was I thinking?

Break it!

The voice became more insistent, almost a shout.

Break it!

I scooched down, and my hand felt the cool hard ground, and then a large smooth stone. My fingers wrapped themselves around the stone, raised it up, and smashed it against the window. Once. Twice. Three time's the charm.

Wood and glass shattered, and I wove my hand inside and found the latch. I unlatched it, and then shoved the window hard. I hated the way old windows stuck. With a startling suddenness, the window flew up.

Good!

The voice was plain and pleased and definitely not mine. Except ...

I bagged the analysis. Now all I had to do was get inside.

My sprained arm wouldn't support my weight, so I couldn't just hop up. A quick check around the side yard showed me an old apple crate, wood stained and weathered.

I dragged it over with my good hand and stepped on it. The crate was just high enough so I could brace myself with my good hand and fanny-hop onto the sill.

Up I went, and I was about to swing my legs through the opening, when ...

"What the fuck are you doing?" Carmen said.

I shook my head. "I'm ... I guess I'm breaking and entering. Or something like that."

I again began to swing my legs. Carmen grabbed them.

"Hold on," she said. "*What* are you doing?"

I rubbed my forehead. "I don't really know, Carm. All I know is that I have to do it."

"*Twilight Zone* time?" she said.

I bit my lip. "A little. Yeah."

She shrugged. "I always liked that show."

In I went. My side killed as I tumbled to the floor. I caught my breath, got to my knees. I was blind, the room was so dark. But I remembered it from my first visit.

The faint scent of roses infused the room.

I groped on the floor to find my bearings so I could stand. Instead, I found something soft and sticky-warm. Oh, hell. "Carmen! Flashlight! Hurry!"

Seconds later a beam of light sprayed across the room. And there was Mrs. Noguchi, sprawled on the floor, blood pooling beneath her. I checked for a pulse, found one.

"Call nine-one-one. Tell them we need an ambulance and to frigging hurry!"

Carmen and I sat in the emergency waiting room of the Monadnock Community Hospital. Just like with little Bella Marsh. The strange circularity about all that was beginning to gnaw at me.

So why hadn't I connected the dots? What wasn't I seeing?

"I'm going to call Kranak," I said. I told him about Teresa Noguchi, and even though it was out of his jurisdiction, he'd call for the reports on the scene.

"Be sure to check on Teresa, will you? They'll tell you more than they will me."

We signed off, and a few minutes later, Carmen got up.

"I'm going to go get us some food downtown," she said. "At some natural food place called Maggie's. You okay alone?"

"I'm fine. Go."

"Has it occurred to you that you have a tendency to break into houses and find dead people?"

She was recalling an old case I'd been on. I growled. "Mrs. Noguchi isn't dead."

"Just about," she said. "You gonna ever tell me why you did a B-and-E?"

I paused. I'd probably sound like a nutcase. Hell, that

wouldn't bother Carmen in the least. "Rose. Rose Noguchi told me to."

Carmen was long gone to downtown Peterborough when I jumped at the sound of pain behind me. A couple entered, the woman cradling her arm in an awkward fashion.

No John Noguchi or his son. I was growing noodgy waiting for them.

A doctor poked his head into the waiting room. The gal in charge nodded to me, signaling that he was the one treating Mrs. Noguchi.

I crossed the room. "How is she?"

The doctor looked me up and down.

Blood smeared my jeans and blouse. "I'm the one who found Mrs. Noguchi. I called it in."

He tugged at the colorful bandanna covering his hair. "Are you a relative? Friend?"

"Sister," I said. We locked eyes. He read the lie in mine, and I saw that he would accept it in his.

He nodded. "We don't know if she'll make it yet, I'm afraid. Due to her disability, her ability to fight something like a wound and blood loss isn't as great as a person in full health."

"She just lost a daughter," I said. "Her family needs her. And she needs them. Anything you can do … Thank you." I turned away. I ached for the woman who'd lost a child and for the father and son who now might lose a wife and mother.

I hesitated, and then I turned back to the doctor. "She, um … the wound wasn't self-inflicted, do you think?"

"I read about the Noguchis's loss in the *Ledger*. For what it's worth, given the trajectory of the bullet, I doubt she shot herself. An expert could tell, of course, but for her to have held the gun, with her arm twisted around back, and for her to pull the trigger would be pretty awkward."

"Thank you, doctor."

A weight lifted that Teresa Noguchi hadn't tried to commit suicide. That raised the question of who had tried to kill her and why.

If possible, Rose's sweet voice in my head grew louder. *Please help.*

Carmen returned with a brown bag filled with granola bars and juice. We made a little picnic in the waiting room.

"Weirdest thing," she said through a mouth of granola bar.

"What?"

She pulled out a pomegranate juice and handed it to me. "I'd swear I saw that Mrs. Marsh in downtown Peterborough."

I straightened. "Mrs. Marsh? The family disappeared. Vanished."

She flicked her braid. "I remember. You showed me their photo. That's why I thought I recognized her."

"Was she at the health food store?"

"No. I got lost downtown and ended up in somewhere called Depot Square. I sure didn't see any depot, but whatever. This gorgeous gal was coming out of a clothing store, a place called The Renaissance Room. Just my style if I was richer and hipper." She slapped her thighs. "She was wearing jeans and a scarf, easy to follow, y'know. Distinctive."

"So where did she go?" I said.

Carmen shrugged. "I lost her. I know, bummer. I think she spotted me. I'm not some tiny wallflower."

"No, dear Carm, you're an epic goddess. You did good, though. Good.

After we ate, Carmen left for Hawthorne Hospital to guard Veda. I remained in hopes that John Noguchi and his son would show. I dozed.

Someone shook me in a rough, almost violent way.

"Hey," I said. "Cut it out!"

"Where is she?" A rumpled and dirty John Noguchi stared down at me, his eyes panicked.

"I don't know, John," I said. "Maybe in recovery. They operated."

He continued to shake me and began to shout. "Why! Why!"

I reached for his hands. "Let go of me, John!"

"Father, stop. Stop!"

I was suddenly free and staring into the face of a tearful Silas Noguchi.

"How's Ma?" Silas said to his father.

"I don't know!" Noguchi said.

"Calm down, Pop. Don't beat up on Ms. Whyte."

Noguchi bit his lower lip. "I'm sorry. Forgive me, Ms. Whyte."

"It's okay," I said. "Sit, please."

Noguchi slumped back on the couch. His son slung an arm over his father's shoulder. "Mom's been so sad since Rose. We shouldn't be surprised."

His father bristled. "Yes, we *should*. Where did she get a gun? And the strength and energy to fire it? Where?"

"Pop, I—"

I cleared my throat. "I don't believe Mrs. Noguchi tried to kill herself."

"Huh?" Silas said.

"It's unlikely your mom did this to herself," I said. "Ask the doctor. He knows more."

John Noguchi's face tightened with anger. "Then who?"

"Exactly," I said. "Keep your family safe. Before I go, I'd like you to tell me about your family and Dr. Barrow."

Noguchi shook his head. "It's not for us to say. Ask her."

"But, Pop," Silas said.

Noguchi wrapped his hands around his own wrists and shook them forward toward Silas. *"No!"*

"All right," Silas said.

"All right nothing, dammit." I sat down beside Noguchi.

"Look, John, I need to know. Veda is my foster mother. She's very ill. I must know if what's happening to her has anything to do with you and Rose and the Marshes."

Noguchi put his hands in a position of prayer and tapped them against his lips. "I can't," he finally said. "Don't you see what's happened to Teresa? You must ask your foster mother or wait until Teresa is well. She may choose to tell you. I cannot."

Accompanied by an overwhelming sense of frustration, I changed into a clean pair of jeans and a button-down shirt that I always kept in the 4Runner and drove from the hospital. I obviously only understood a part of the connection between Veda and the Noguchis. I lacked an element that I suspected would explain both Teresa's shooting and the attempt on Veda's life.

If I were at the office, I could do a background check on John and Teresa Noguchi. I called Gert, who volunteered with glee. She loved what she called "cloak and dagger" stuff. I was sick of it.

Instead of turning right out of the hospital parking lot, I turned left and drove to the village of Peterborough in search of answers.

Chapter Twenty

I drove around Peterborough until I found what Carmen had described as Depot Square. The town was small and fun and funky, with neat shops that I wanted to explore and great-looking restaurants and a one-screen movie theater, and what looked like a bookstore to die for, The Toadstool.

I hooked a left into the square's U. On my right, just like she'd said, was a shop called The Renaissance Room. I parked in front and took my time before I entered the shop. I didn't want to mess this up.

Gorgeous clothes—unique and funky and expensive—hung from small racks or posts. Velvets and satins and chiffon and organic cottons made my mouth drool, as did the wild hats scattered around the shop.

"May I help you?"

The woman's soft-sweet eyes beguiled me. She wore one of the shop's fantastical creations, and her black hair, scrolled up in an intricate do atop her head, glistened in the warm light.

"I'm not sure," I said. "How about I look around for a bit?"

"Be my guest. Just call if you need me."

I wove through the shop with the growing sense that there was no way the tightly wound Marlene Marsh would buy a single item from this shop.

My pink bubble of hope deflated. It would be stupid not to ask, so I approached the gal with the midnight-black hair and described the tall, blonde Marlene, with her striking patrician looks.

The shopkeeper shook her head. "No, I'm sorry, but I can't recall anyone like that. There *was* a woman in earlier today who was stunning, and quite tall, but her hair was black, like mine."

"Really? Did she buy something?" Maybe she'd charged it.

The shopkeeper's bee-stung lips tipped into a smile. "Not from me. But she did do a reading with Pricilla."

"Reading?" I said.

"The tarot."

I sure didn't picture Marlene Marsh getting her tarot read. "Is Pricilla here?"

She shook her head. "I'm not sure when she'll be back, but she takes appointments." She handed me Pricilla Magee's card.

I called Pricilla Magee and made an appointment to see her in an hour.

I gobbled a sandwich at the intimate Aesop's Tables, which was inside the bookstore. I drooled at the stacks of books I was dying to browse.

Instead, I called the Langes, the missing Eva's foster parents. Lauria had said they lived in Peterborough. No answer. I still had 45 minutes before I met the tarot reader, so I wandered the stacks' feast of fiction and nonfiction.

I hadn't relaxed for days, and it felt great just to chill for a while. The carousel I'd been riding seemed to be spinning faster. It felt good to get off, if only for a few minutes.

I was examining the section on Zen when I spotted a sky-scraper of a woman. My recognition bells clanged.

Was it possible that Marlene Marsh had wandered into The Toadstool?

I inched closer. The woman wore spiked heels and tight jeans and a Pucci scarf around her head in the style of Grace Kelly. Her plum silk blouse was subtly expensive. I moved closer still.

She looked nothing like Bella's mom. Yet, I'd swear … She also gave off a furtive vibe.

I turned my back on her, just for a sec, and clipped up my wild hair. I dragged my beaten-up pink Red Sox hat from my bag and tugged it on. I hoped my Merrells and jeans would further disguise the professional Tally she'd met days earlier. When I turned back, the woman was running her finger across a page that seemed to absorb her completely.

I continued to study the Zen books, but took my keys from my bag, ready to leave the instant the mystery woman walked from the store.

The woman continued to read, her red-painted finger tracing the words. My watch told me I had less than thirty minutes before my appointment. I could always call it off.

The woman slapped the book closed and tucked it in the crook of her arm. She made her way to the cashier and stood in the short line, shifting her weight from one leg to the other. I moved closer, picked up a cocktail-table book and opened it, the better to obscure myself. But she never looked my way.

She paid in cash. Her fingers strummed the counter while the clerk rang up the sale. She then stretched her long legs in a trot and left the store.

"What book did that woman just buy, may I ask?" I said to the cashier. "It might have been the one I was looking at, too."

"*For the Sins of My Father: The Legacy of a Mafia Life*. We don't have another, but I can easily order you one."

"Huh. No, that's not the book I was thinking of. Thanks so much. Great store!"

Sins of My Father! No coincidence. I caught the woman sliding behind the wheel of some Volkswagen. Not a Bug, but an SUV-type.

I forced myself to slow, when all I wanted to do was run toward the 4Runner. I finally slipped into the driver's seat. The VW pulled out; I waited three beats, then followed.

As I drove, I called Pricilla Magee to cancel my appointment. Then I concentrated on the VW's progress.

We drove out of Depot Square, turned right, and then left onto Route 202 heading north.

Traffic was light as the sky blackened with storm clouds. We passed the street to the hospital, climbed a small hill, and by the time we went through a light by the high school, the rain had begun to pour. Further on, signs for a town called Hancock appeared, then Bennington, then we entered a village named Antrim. She bore left at a fork, then another left soon after. The road was suddenly empty except for my SUV and hers.

I pushed my windshield wipers to a higher speed.

This was probably foolish as hell. The woman most likely wasn't Bella's mother. I didn't remember Marlene Marsh being so tall. But what if she was? And what if she could lead me to Bella, and maybe even Eva Lange?

I donned my earpiece and punched out numbers on my cell. Kranak might have heard some news about Teresa Noguchi. And I could give him VW woman's license plate.

"Who's the plate for?" he said.

"I don't know. But I might be following Marlene Marsh."

"What the fuck for?" he said, his irritation coming through loud and clear.

"I think the Marshes are our best bet to find Eva."

Silence on the other end and the pounding of rain on the roof filled my ears. I grew chilly with fear. "Rob, what?"

"Nothin', nothin'. Just … well, let it go, kiddo. Forget the Marshes. You got stuff brewing here."

"Like *what?*"

"Nothin'. Just get back, huh."

The SUV ahead slowed, and so did I.

"C'mon, Rob. You can't just say that. Is it Penny? The office? *Veda?*"

"Nothing's changed with them, far as I know. Just come on back."

"What about Teresa?" I was afraid to hear. "You said you'd call, Rob. Is she—"

"She's gonna be fine. A-OK, y'know. At least the docs think so. You're the one who saved her life, Tal. She'd bled out."

I blinked fast, relief burning my eyes.

"You there?" he said.

"I'm here, all right. Did she or didn't she try to kill herself?"

"No way. No gun anywhere in the room. The trajectory of the wound doesn't work either. I talked to New Hampshire forensics. They're havin' a field day. You got any ideas who?"

I looked in front of me. The VW remained a couple car lengths ahead. "I've been thinking about it. It's got to be connected with Rose's death and Eva's disappearance. Um, did you know that the Noguchis know Veda? That they've been in touch with her more recently than their old court case would warrant?"

He whistled. "That's a leveler."

"The father, John, refused to tell me the connection. Said I had to ask Veda. He looked pretty intense. Listen, I've got to run or I'm going to hit a tree."

"Where are you?"

I told him. "I can still see the VW."

"That is the dumbest—"

"Gotta run. The rain's crazy. I can't see squat!"

"Hold on! Your Aunt Bertha's been trying to reach you. She's wiggy over it."

I pulled off my earphone. How many more things could I worry about?

Ahead of me, the SUV came to a halt, and then made a right. A minute later, I did the same and found myself on Route 9, headed east. It was no back country road, but an almost-highway. The Volkswagen sped up, and I did the same.

Minutes later, a sign signaling Hillsborough appeared, and then the skies began to pelt my truck with a combination of rain and hailstones. I cursed.

The world became a smear of color and light. Impossible to tell, but I thought I still had the VW in my scope. Up ahead, I spotted the gleam of traffic lights. Then another sheet of rain and hail made the lights disappear.

I pushed on my turn signal, so I could pull over until the storm passed. But then where would I be? I slowed to a crawl. She'd have to slow, too. The rain sheeted across my windshield. The car felt hot and musky from my sweat and Penny's fur and overuse. The copper scent of Teresa Noguchi's congealed blood on the clothes I'd tossed in back grew stronger.

As I inched along, I thought about the book bought by the long-legged woman. *Sins of the Father*, yes. Mafia? I hadn't seen that coming. The Marshes weren't Italian. So what would the Mafia have …

A red light swaying in the wind halted me. I pounded the brakes, and the 4Runner screeched to a halt. I was the first in line. No Volkswagen SUV. I peered around—down the road, right, left. Nothing. *Damn.*

The light winked green, and I hesitated. Should I go forward? Turn left toward what looked like another highway? Maybe she'd gone right? Or into the McDonald's parking lot.

An explosion! Glass shattered, and I pulled to the right,

anything to get away from flying bullets. I punched the gas, just as another explosion hit. A spray of glass coated me from behind.

I pulled hard to the right, then forward, and—*smack!*—right into a metal guardrail. My whole body shook as the truck's frame shuddered.

I ducked down, peered all around. The rain was coming too fast for me to see much of anything.

The 4Runner swayed, and I reached up and flicked the wipers faster. *Hell!* I'd bent the guardrail, nearly broken it, just above the bank of a madly swirling river.

A hit from behind!

The truck slammed into the guardrail that was inches from coming apart. I stood on the brake and pushed the 4Runner into park. My arm was killing me. My side, too.

Another hit and the shriek of metal ripping.

Dammit, they weren't going to get me this time.

I slapped the truck into reverse and floored it.

The 4Runner lurched, jumped, revved backwards all in one bizarre moment. I flew across two lanes of highway and into an embankment.

I looked around and just ahead was the VW SUV leaving rubber as it raced from the scene.

I sat for a moment, shaking so bad I couldn't see. Finally, I white-knuckled the steering wheel and inched my way across the road and into the parking lot of a car dealer. I rested my cheek on the steering wheel and closed my eyes.

I was safe, unharmed. Oh, boy.

A few more minutes, and I opened my eyes. Rain continued to pelt the car. A sign for Peterborough pointed the way, and I headed south. Although I'd called to cancel, maybe I could still catch up with Pricilla Magee.

I sat at the back of The Renaissance Room amid velvets and silks and faux tiger-striped fur and relaxed with the taste of fresh-brewed green tea. Opposite me at the small table sat a fortyish woman with red hair, soft green eyes, and a serious smile.

"Your arm, your walk," she said. "You've been banged up a bit, I see."

"A car accident, I'm afraid."

"You want information," she said.

"I do, Pricilla. I hope you can help me regarding a woman that you did a reading for earlier today."

She nodded. "I appreciate that you're on an important mission, but I don't give out my client's private information."

I explained about the Noguchis and Rose, the Marshes and Bella, and now how Eva Lange was taken.

She took my hand. "May I?"

"Sure." I relaxed while she held my hand, first palm down, then palm up. She ran two fingers down my palm, and I giggled.

"Tickles." She smiled.

"Yes."

She gently placed my hand on the wood parquet table. "I don't presume to know you, Tally Whyte. But I do believe that you are sincere and honest and tell truths that others might avoid telling. That's admirable."

I shook my head. "I'm not always admirable. I prevaricate and I mess up fairly frequently. But I try to live a kind and honest life. That's about all I can say."

There, that serious smile again. "The woman I read for told me her name was Mary Dean. It was not. She was worried about some deaths. She didn't tell me which ones, and I couldn't tell her that they would or would not end. Much of what went on between us was playacting, something that I don't care for very much. I can say no more."

"I don't have a picture with me, but if I can find a computer hookup, I could show you Marlene Marsh's photo."

She reached beside her and pulled a laptop from its case.

She opened it, and pressed a few buttons, then tuned it my way.

"Wi-Fi?"

"Yes. Don't you love it?"

I tapped some keys, and there was the photo of Marlene and Andrew Marsh the day they'd pleaded for their missing daughter's life. I swiveled the computer back to Pricilla. "Was that the woman who had the reading?"

She stared at the image a long while, and then looked at me dead on. "Yes, that's her."

I sighed. "Thanks. I was hoping we had a lead on the Marshes."

"You do." She pointed to the screen, to Andrew Marsh. "*He* was the woman who I gave a reading to. Something was off, but I confess I never guessed that she was a he."

I'd seen him for myself and never guessed. I thanked her for her graciousness. Andrew Marsh had paid in cash and had declined to join Pricilla's e-mail or snail mail list.

"Outside of the reading, which I hesitate to repeat, he—she—mentioned the family going 'up north' in New Hampshire."

"Did he mention specifics? Anything that might give me an idea where they are?"

"A town near Mount Washington. She—he called it 'funky.' "

"Any thoughts?" I said. "I'm not very familiar with New Hampshire."

She chuckled. "I'm funky, but I don't know northern New Hampshire any better than you do, I'm afraid."

She rested a hand on my forearm. "Would you like a reading?"

"Maybe someday. I have a feeling, whether the tarot is real or not, you have a gift."

She nodded with grace. "Thank you. So do you. One moment." She took my hand again, this time closing her eyes. When she opened them, they narrowed with concern. "Someone's watching you. A little girl. I don't know why."

Rose.

She stroked the palm of my hand. "Something else. Be sure to go to the opening of the exhibit. Any idea what I'm talking about?"

"Not really."

She smiled, this time broad and clear. "You will."

Chapter Twenty-one

I arrived home physically and mentally exhausted. I checked my messages: Aunt Bertha, Hank, Gert and Dr. Joby had called. I listened to Dr. Joby say they were keeping Penny for a day more. Tests. And—they wanted to warn me—they might have to operate on her leg.

Fear tickled my heart, but I trusted the vet.

The apartment felt empty without Penny. Negative space. The absence of joy. No sound of clack-clacking nails on hardwood floors. No whining to go out. No cold nose pushing me for an ear scratch.

I'd pick her up tomorrow.

I dialed Aunt Bertha. "Sorry it took so long to get back to you."

"Not a problem, dear Tal."

On the phone she sounded so like Veda I got chills. "What's up? What can I do for you, Auntie?"

"Not a thing. I'm going to visit cousin Jean in Philadelphia. I just wanted you to know."

"What? How are you getting there?"

"Jean is driving me."

"What about Veda, Aunt Bertha?"

She sighed, and I'd swear I heard a match strike, then a long inhale on the other end of the phone. Bertha hadn't smoked for decades.

"Aunt Bertha?"

"Haven't you noticed my sister isn't well?"

"That's somewhat of an understatement, Auntie." I scrunched the phone between my shoulder and ear and poured a couple fingers of Rebel Yell. I added two ice cubes and swirled the glass round and round. I stretched out on the couch. "That's why I don't understand why you're leaving her."

"Because, *Liebchen*, my beloved sister will not get well."

"Sure she will."

Another inhale, then a sigh. "No, she will not. And I will go with Jean for a week or so—I must build up my strength—and then I will come home to care for my dear Veda for the final push."

I sipped my drink. Final push? Bertha was being her usual histrionic self. I wished Veda were here to calm her down, to show her how she was exaggerating. "I'll come visit you tomorrow."

"Not to worry. Jean's already here and her usual sparkling self. We're going to see Veda, and then off we go. You have enough, what with my sister not running *that place*. And the poor little girl dead and all."

"Rose? She's been dead for—"

"Ach, no. Not the little Rose. The new one. The little child with the German name. Eva something."

Oh, no. That's what Kranak hadn't wanted to tell me on the phone. I *knew* he wasn't giving me the whole story. "I love you, Aunt Bertha."

"I love you, too, dear one."

My aching side and arm told me to rest, but I had to see
Eva Lange.

I parked close to one of the huge TV lights that beamed
across the lot at OCME. TV trucks with reporters yammer-
ing and Boston cops and CSS trucks and cars with state
seals swarmed the lot. The place looked like a circus run
amok. I sauntered across the lot, hoping to avoid attention.

"Hey, Tally!" shouted the Channel Five reporter.

"Hey," I waggled my fingers at her and picked up the pace.

"Wait up!" She zoomed over, mic in hand, cameraman
and lights trailing. "They've allegedly found another dead
child. What's your take? Is this some serial killer?"

"I have no 'take.' I've been gone all day and have some
paperwork I've got to retrieve. Sorry." I scooted through
the doors and got stopped by a state cop I didn't know. I
flashed my OCME ID card and squeezed inside.

The lobby swarmed with law enforcement and officials.
No crime scene tape, so I presumed that Eva hadn't been
left in the cooler. So where had they found her, poor child?

I bent over Eva Lange. A cool breeze from the blowers, with
just a hint of fetid air, washed against my body. I flexed my
latex-covered hands. Nerves. Sorrow. I had so wanted to
save her.

Blonde hair bound in a single braid, fair skin, a small
mole high on her left cheek, eyelashes so pale I almost
couldn't see them. Grey lips that naturally tilted up. A child
who'd smiled a lot. Her hands remained in their brown
bags, ready for forensics to gather material beneath her
nails and on her palms and the tips of her fingers.

I touched Eva's shoulder and became terribly aware of
the absence of life, the flesh dead and unresponsive. Kranak
stood beside me.

"Did she have a lamb with her?" I said to Kranak.

"Yeah," he said. "Sucks that we couldn't save this one."

"I know." I pointed to her bagged hands. "Did he write on the palm again?"

" 'Sins of the father.' Just like the first one."

I brushed a stray hair from her cheek. "Such a short life. When's the autopsy?"

He checked his watch. "Fogarty says he's doing it, the dickhead."

"He's back?"

"Posted bail, I guess." Kranak's eyes roamed the room lined with bodies on gurneys. "He's still in charge of all this. I wish Veda ... We should get outta here."

"Okay. She wasn't left here like Rose?"

"Nope. A bunch of tourists found her in the Old Granary Burial Ground."

"Isn't that where Paul Revere and Samuel Adams and a bunch of other famous revolutionaries are buried?"

He nodded. "He'd wrapped her in gauze. Couldn't be missed. C'mon, we gotta scoot."

I bent over Eva and said my silent prayer of sorrow. I hoped Rose would take care of her.

I will.

Geesh, Rose was in my head way too often lately. Imagination could only take me so far. "Rob, did you say something?"

"Nope." He pushed the heavy door open and nodded for me to go first.

I left the cooler and walked straight into the chest of Tom Fogarty.

The man looked shrunken, pathetic, yet at the same time all puffed up, like some bird putting on a display of power.

"Oh, Tom." I felt pity for the man. And annoyance. "Why did you put Judy Ethridge in charge of OCME?"

His face tightened. "Because Dr. Barrow put *me* in charge."

I hooked my arm through his. "You're putting the whole program in jeopardy. Don't you see that?"

"What I see is you trying to interfere again. If something

happens to me, Dr. Ethridge will officially become acting chief."

I inwardly groaned. "Judy Ethridge is an inappropriate choice. You know that's what Veda would say."

Ethridge materialized out of nowhere. "But Dr. Barrow isn't here."

I towered over Ethridge, whose pale thin looks and fake breasts gave her an angel-on-steroids appearance. I despised her vast ego and negative moral compass.

"Didn't Tom ask MGAP to clear out its offices?" she said.

"Tom might have some power," I said. "But you sure don't."

She smiled, and her eyes glowed with self-satisfaction. "How wrong you are. Now, get out."

I blazed with anger. "Why you arrogant little bi—"

A tug on my arm and Kranak hauled me down the corridor.

I huddled in Kranak's' office, sipping some bourbon-laced coffee and fuming.

"What the hell got into you, Tal?" Kranak said.

I wanted to strangle Ethridge and Fogarty, and Kranak, too, for pulling me out of there. "More than Fogarty, she's a threat to OCME. I'm beat, too. What a day. Screw Ethridge and Fogarty. Let's talk about Eva. Obviously she was killed by the same people or person as Rose."

"Seems so," he said.

"When's Fogarty doing the post?" I asked.

"In a few minutes. Go home. I'm gonna go watch."

"I'd like to be with Eva for autopsy."

"Not today, kid. I'll take care of her. Get some rest. You need it."

"I need more than that." I wanted to stay, but Kranak was right. I slung my bag over my arm and tugged on my jacket.

"Watch out for those asshole reporters." He hugged me good-bye, and I relaxed in his embrace.

He smelled of chocolate and cloves, and his six o'clock

bristle and bushy mustache tickled my forehead. His awful blue suit jacket, soft from years of wear, caressed my cheek.

I held him tight. Maybe too tight, in a hug that was more familiar than breath, yet not the same. Not the same at all. My nerves, all tingly and raw, felt Kranak's blanket of comfort. And something more.

I tilted back my head. And where I'd always looked up into friendly brown eyes, I now saw heat bubbling from their center.

I felt the heat, too. My belly clenched.

I slung my arms around his shoulders and stood on tiptoe and tilted my head, just so, and framed his lips with mine. He pressed against me, and his shudder was answered by one of my own. He bent me backwards onto the carpeted floor, and I let him, and all the while I never released his lips, which were moving fast and hard over mine.

His tongue was suddenly inside my mouth. I welcomed it and touched it with my own, first tentatively, then with a fury answered by a desire that made me whimper. He cradled me, and all I wanted was his fingers on me, and there they were, exploring, and I shivered again with the rapture of his caress.

"Isn't this just the cutest thing I ever saw."

Ethridge. We sprang apart, both panting. I ached to strangle her.

"You should knock," Kranak said. "CSS isn't yours."

Ethridge smirked. "I just came by to tell you Tom was starting the post on the Eva kid. At your service, Sergeant."

"Get lost," he said.

"Sure looks like you don't need any more servicing."

"Get the fuck out!" he bellowed.

My hands shook as I rebuttoned my shirt. Kranak brushed them away, and gently took over.

"What did we do, Rob?" I said.

His hand brushed my hair. "I've always loved it wild. Your hair."

I cupped his hand to my cheek. "I don't know about this."

He smiled, and I recognized that wistful Kranak smile that said his expectations were low.

He got to his feet and pulled me up. His hands told me it was hard to let go. For me, too.

I straightened his tie. "Rob, I ..."

"I'm gonna go watch Eva now. Go home."

Carmen greeted me at the door of my apartment. "Where the *hell* have you been?"

"Sorry." I left clothes in a trail, turned on the bath, and closed the bathroom door. I sat on the toilet lid while the bath filled, scrunched over, trying not to think about anything at all.

The door flew open. Carmen in Valkyrie mode.

"Carmen! What the hell?"

She walked over, hands out, holding glasses and a bottle of red wine.

I took one. "Thanks. Now go away."

"Go away? I've known you for twenty-five years. You think some door's going to keep me out?"

"But—"

"You take the tub. I'll use the toilet chair."

Steam rose in the bath and the hot water relaxed muscles I'd forgotten I had. The wine relaxed me more. I finally was ready to tell Carmen about Eva, but not about Kranak. Definitely not Kranak.

She took a sip of wine. "I shoulda brought the hard stuff. I hear these terrible things, I think about my kids. I can see them right in front of me. I picture them playing together, and then some creep coming and taking them and ..." She emptied her glass and refilled it. "I miss them, Tally."

"How could you not?" I said. "Maybe it's time to go home, back to Winsworth, to your kids and husband."

She rubbed her palm up and down one knee. The room grew quiet, but for the cascade of water pouring from the tub spout. I shut it off.

I'd meant what I said about Carmen returning to Winsworth. I'd miss her, but I could hire someone to watch over Veda.

"I wonder, Carm, who's after Veda. My gut says it's somehow connected with the Noguchis, and they're connected to the Marshes. Unless ..."

I sucked in a breath. *Tom Fogarty.* He'd never crossed my mind as wanting to harm Veda, yet could he? *Would* he? No, of course not. But he loved the power and glitz that came with the chief's job.

"What's that demented brain thinking, Tal?" Carmen said.

I chuckled. "Demented, is it? Ya got that right. I'm contemplating Tom Fogarty and Veda. I could almost see him for the attempt on Veda's life."

She snorted. "Works for me. He's a doctor. He could get a hold of heparin. Maybe that Ethridge was the woman I saw that night at the hospital."

I pictured it. "Except although Fogarty's a foolish man, he seems to adore Veda. I always believed it was genuine. But I like your idea about Judy Ethridge. Lots."

"I want to stay, Tally," Carmen said.

"To stay here, with Veda? Are you sure, Carm?"

"Ayuh. Don't see how I could leave a friend struggling in such a muck."

"A muck, is it?" I smiled.

"Big one. Sorta like mud season in Maine"

I laughed, and it felt good. "Yes, it is, isn't it? I realize how much you must miss Sadie and Tommy." The thought of kids flashed through my mind, and I was glad for the steam that billowed around me.

"Someday for you," she said.

"You're uncanny. I hope so." I paused. "Um, how was Veda today?"

She topped off my wineglass. "I've seen her better."

I twirled my wine, stared into the rich red liquid for answers I knew wouldn't come. I finally looked back at Carmen. "Bertha thinks Veda's going to die soon."

Carmen looked me straight in the eye. "She might, Tal. Or she could live another twenty years. Know what I mean, *compañero*?"

"Another twenty? I wouldn't want that. Not unless she gets better. All better. Mentally better." I sucked in a sob. "But I *do* want it. I don't want her to go. She can't go."

She sighed. "Everyone must go, Tal."

I pictured Eva and Rose and the dead nurse and ... "Yeah, I know."

"Have you made any—"

The beep from my cell phone interrupted her.

"Get it for me, huh?" I said.

She picked up the phone, pulled her granny glasses from her overalled pocket, and slid them on. "It's you're buddy, Kranak."

I was tempted to ignore the call. What would I say to him after ... "Sure, give it to me." I handed her my glass, dried my hands, and flipped open the phone. "Hey, Rob."

"Hey, Tal. That little Eva? The kid got killed same way as Rosie. Suffocated. No labs yet, but I'd bet she'd probably been drugged like Rosie, too. She had a soft death."

Not a happy note, but at least Eva hadn't suffered in death. "Thanks, Rob. Makes me sad."

"Something else," he said. "She was abused."

Crap. "That sure as hell isn't a soft death."

"Not the killer. It's not recent. Not like last week recent. But before that? She's pretty scarred down there. Ripped up. She was with her foster parents for about three years. I'd guess they were the ones."

"*Damn*! Nothing is more hateful than that."

"Yeah. We're heading out that way in the morning to interview the foster parents. Thought you might like to tag along."

"You betcha," I said. "Um, about earlier, Rob. I—"

"Yeah. I know. See ya around eight."

Chapter Twenty-two

I handed the phone back to Carmen. "Life can sure suck."

She snorted. "Ya got that right. Ayuh."

I filled her in on Eva's apparent abuse. "Kranak suspects the foster parents or one or both or a foster sib or ... The child wasn't safe there at all."

Her face blanched, turning her freckles to constellations. "*Madre de dios!* I could kill people like that."

"I know. Ironic, but it sounds like Eva's death was far easier than her life, and ..." I thought about that, about her life, then her kidnapping and her death. A puzzle, a strange one at that ...

"Tal?"

"Like Rose," I said, "Eva was a sacrificial lamb. The sins of the father. Making up for those sins. I wonder if they took her *because* she was being abused. Her life was a constant misery, and so this ... sacrifice ... could actually be perceived as an act of kindness."

"Boy," she said. "That's messed up."

"Yes. But in a way, it's not, you know. Not the way these people would think."

"You realize you're not saying 'he' anymore, but 'them' and 'these'?"

"Much as I hate it, my mind keeps going back to the Marshes. The way they've disappeared, wouldn't let us talk with Bella. His disguise. I don't know." I pushed to my feet. "Time to do some research and give a friend a call. This is key. It could lead us to Rose and Eva's killers."

I swaddled myself in a towel and climbed out. Carmen slapped a heavy hand on my shoulder.

"What?" I said.

Her eyes glittered. "This is all well and good, little Emma. But something else happened today."

I shook off her hand, dried myself, and pulled on the pj's that hung from the bathroom door. No one had called me Emma in a long time. "C'mon, Carm."

I gave her my back and marched into the kitchen. I took a Diet Coke from the refrigerator.

"That stuff's crap."

I rounded on her. "And you're relentless. Just leave it."

"I'll leave your crappy addiction alone. So what else happened today, Tally Whyte, that makes you blush and stammer? What?"

"Nothing."

"Yeah, right. I'm not gonna let this bone go."

"Let it alone." I turned away, walked to the bedroom, and shut the door.

Carmen swung it open. "With all this frickin' stuff going on, you're going to tell me, dammit all."

I rounded on her. "Fine. Fine! I almost made love with Kranak. That's right. Look shocked as shit. You aren't the only one. If Ethridge hadn't walked in, we would have done it on the floor of his office. And I don't understand. Not at all. This is a guy I've worked with for years. A friend. A dear friend. So what happened? And what about Hank, the man I love. I think I love." I shook my head. "Thought I loved."

I slumped down on the bed.

Carmen sat beside me. "I don't know, either. But if you and Kranak get together, I know it'll just about kill Hank."

The following morning, Carmen was long gone when I left for The Grief Shop. In just a week the leaves had begun to unfold the promise of spring. The sun pulsed higher in the sky, and when I left the truck in the parking lot, the scents of the young season quickened my step.

Maybe today would be the day when Veda began to heal. Maybe she was just waiting for the new season to bloom. Spring was her favorite, she often said in that rich way she had of expressing herself.

Yes, maybe today would be the day.

Fogarty ran that morning's meeting, with Ethridge glued to his side. They turned Veda's taut daily meeting—where cases were assessed and divvied up—into a painful, ponderous project.

Kranak caught me in the hall on the way out, and my cheeks bloomed with heat.

I found myself anxious and excited to be that close to him. I leaned toward him. I wanted him to touch me. "Are you going now?" I said.

"To Peterborough and the kid's parents, you mean?" He shook his head, dug his hands into his brown suit jacket. "Gotta wait for the New Hampshire state boys. They want a piece of the pie."

"Doesn't everyone always? I hope they don't take too long."

We headed down the stairs and stopped in the lobby. We walked the way we'd always done, talked just like the old friends we were, except everything had changed.

Kranak's lips had taken on a new and alluring shape, and his eyes called to me in a way that made me want to drown in them. I started to rest my fingers on his arm, but pulled back. I was terrified I'd touch him in some inappropriate way. Give him some stupid signal I didn't mean.

But maybe I did, and maybe he'd reject me and ...

I opened the purse I'd slung over my shoulder and pretended to look for something important. "You'll holler when you're ready to go out?"

"Yeah. I'm gonna need you to take a read. I'll get these pricks. You shoulda seen the little kid's scars. On her privates. On her arms and belly." His large hands curled into fists. "I'm gonna get 'em all right."

"I know you will, Rob." I leaned in, felt his warmth. I smiled. "Yes."

His hands reached for me. But instead of finding me, his palms rubbed together, like two birds, fearful of crashing, stopped mid-flight. Then he cocked a finger at me, like shooting a gun, only worse. It felt a lot worse.

"See ya." He strode off toward his office.

The soft laughter from behind made me turn.

Ethridge, her arms crossed, her face cold and smiling.

"Screw you," I mouthed.

She laughed harder.

A normal morning. Well, almost. It felt peaceful, even though a drive-by and a suicide filled MGAP's day. I took the drive-by and Gert handled the suicide.

Sad thing was, nobody showed for the emaciated Vietnamese boy who'd littered his arms with tattoos of sexy Asian girls and bloody knives.

Hours elapsed. I ate a bagel with lox and cream cheese at my desk as I fired through a Mount Vesuvius of paperwork— pink, blue, and yellow. I worked on the assignment board, and I signed up several of our counselors for an evening "brush-up" class I was giving for law enforcement and others who'd taken my course on homicide counseling at Northeastern.

Around two, reception buzzed with the drive-by's detective on the line, and I learned that no one would be showing for the Vietnamese boy's ID. He was a street orphan.

I went to visit him and to see Eva again. Society had betrayed both children in different, yet equally dreadful ways.

My voice mail light blinked red when I returned to my office. Not Kranak, but the vet. I could pick up Penny anytime.

I shelved the paperwork and flew.

I couldn't stop hugging Penny.

"Look at that tail go!" Dr. Beth Joby crossed her arms and beamed.

"I am so happy to see this doggie."

"That we know."

I buried my face in the soft fur of her neck and inhaled the essence of Penny. She vibrated with joy. I did, too.

"She looks good." I smiled at Joby.

"Doesn't she?" She scratched Penny's left ear. "You haven't even asked about the surgery."

"Surgery?"

"Her leg?"

My eyes snapped to Penny's leg with the lump. Except it was bandaged and flat. Flat. "My God, it's gone. The lump, it's gone."

"Yup."

I gently ran my hand up Penny's leg. "I can't believe I didn't notice."

Beth Joby's soft smile traveled to gray eyes wise with knowledge of pets and their people. "I can."

I slumped into the narrow bench attached to the examining room wall. Penny lay at my feet. She was happy just to be with me. I felt the same.

"I was sure … I believed she had cancer. I thought I'd lose her."

Joby took the bow-back chair. "I thought you might, too."

"I've been holding my breath about this."

"Hard not to."

I grazed the rough bandage with my fingertips. "All gone. So what was the lump all about?"

"It was a benign nerve sheath tumor. Animals get them. So do humans."

"I've never heard of it."

"It's not uncommon. She's fine. We took it out yesterday. There's no reason to think it will return."

My phone beeped.

Joby slapped her thighs. "Go ahead. I've got a lineup of patients to attend to."

I flipped open my phone. "Tally Whyte. One second, please." I hugged Beth Joby as hard as I could. "Thank you for saving Penny's life. You've saved mine, too."

She waved good-bye as I lifted the phone to my ear. "Sorry to keep you waiting. How can I help?"

"Ya gotta come back to the office," Kranak said.

"Where are you, Rob? You're not on your cell phone. What's up?"

"Nothing. Just come."

Penny poked her cold nose beneath my left hand. "I'm not coming, Rob. Not until you tell me what the story is. Something's bad."

"Yeah."

"Veda!"

"No, no. Not the doc. It's ... Christ, Tal, can you once just do as I say? Just this once."

"You promise it's not Veda."

"Promise."

For the second time that day, I flew.

I trotted across the OCME parking lot, Penny by my side. She limped, but it was okay. As we walked through the doors, I gave her a reassuring scratch behind the ears.

The lobby was quiet, hushed, and my neck hairs bristled

with the odd tension in the air. I didn't see Kranak, but instead my eyes found Gert. Her face was parchment stiff and white. Her hands were in front of her, one wrapped tight over the other.

"Gert?" I crossed the lobby.

Her eyes fell to Penny, and she melted like a spring rain on old snow. She dropped to her knees and hugged Penny. "She's okay?" she said.

"Penny's fine." I explained what Dr. Joby had told me.

Gert burst with watery laughter when Penny nosed her pocket for a treat, an oft-repeated dance the two performed.

"Gert?" I said, and she snapped me a look both sad and fearful.

"Please wait," she said. "Sergeant Kranak's on his way."

"It's so bad you can't tell me?"

She pushed to her feet and brushed at her short black skirt, now covered in dog hair. She wouldn't look at me, but kept tracking her eyes from her skirt to the door and back again.

"Gert, this is—"

She tucked her chin. "Why don't you give me Penny for a sec."

I turned to see Kranak plow through the side door of OCME. I handed Gert Penny's leash and walked toward my friend.

"Rob?" I couldn't get more out.

"Tally!" boomed another voice, one annoyingly familiar.

I turned and Fogarty stood before me. "What, Tom? Can't it wait?"

He brushed his nonexistent beard. "I just wanted to say how sorry I was to hear about Special Agent Lauria."

"Shut the fuck up!" hollered Kranak.

I whipped around just as Kranak barreled into me. "What the—"

He hugged me tight, and I knew that Kathleen Lauria

was dead. I held onto him. Tight. Buried my face in his shoulder. "No," I whispered. "Nonononono."

An hour later, I sat beside Penny, arm slung around her shoulders, while Kranak's Crime Scene Services truck zoomed up Route 3 headed for Peterborough, New Hampshire.

We were on our way to interview Eva Lange's foster parents. New Hampshire state cops had agreed to play backup, and when we were done, they planned to arrest both parents on child abuse charges.

That's what Kranak had told me.

All I could think about, all I could *see* was Kathleen Lauria in the movie of our friendship that kept playing on a self-repeating loop.

I couldn't lose the cotton candy feeling in my head. Kranak would speak, and, oddly, I'd answer. But what either of us said I couldn't recall.

At a stoplight in a town named Wilton, I panicked. I flipped open my cell phone and dialed Carmen.

"Is she okay?" I blurted into the phone.

"Veda's holding her own, Tal," Carmen said.

"Keep an eye out, especially today."

"I do and I will. Nothing has changed here. I will take care of her. Know that."

"Good. Fine. Yes. Thanks so much, Carm."

"Are you all right?"

"No, I'm not." I told her about Kathleen. "I'm so glad you're with Veda. So glad."

We signed off, and I rested my cheek against the passenger window. The glass was chill. It felt good. When I sighed, mist formed on the car window. Penny whined, and I pet her.

But none of that mattered. Kathleen Lauria was a rock. Way too young to die.

"We're almost there," Kranak said.

I blinked a couple times and saw we were headed down the steep hill toward the village of Peterborough.

"So ya know what you're going to say to these creeps?"
I hadn't a clue.

Kranak made a sharp left before we hit town. The street
switched back, so we again were climbing the mountain.
The road was hard-packed dirt, and dust billowed around
us. We passed a farm with fat wooly sheep grazing in a large
pasture and a white farmhouse and low-roofed red barn.

Just beyond the barn, we turned right and drove down
another long dirt road lined with overgrown forsythia and a
huge beech tree and an old stone wall where aged snow
clung between the stones. Two tall oaks appeared, and at
the end of the road crouched an old red Colonial that
sagged with age and neglect. A beige minivan was parked to
the left of the house, in front of a shed door.

"I got the lead," Kranak said. "But you do your homicide
counseling thing. Okay, Tal?"

"I guess. I ... today is a bad day for this."

He rested a hand on my shoulder. "It's the only day. The
New Hampshire boys can't wait to get their hands on these
creeps."

I stuttered a sigh. "Sure. Do you know what happened?
Kathleen, I mean."

He bowed his head, and then his eyes found mine. "They
said it was a rampant staph infection. The accident ... it
made her weak. No way could she fight the infection."

A movement to my right. Atop the stone-stepped path
that rose to the front door, a women stood on the stoop, no
jacket, rubbing her arms and peering at us with eyes that
felt intent and panicked.

"Let's go in," I said. "I'll be fine."

His callused hand brushed my cheek. "You always are,
Tal."

Chapter Twenty-three

I sat sipping lukewarm tea from a porcelain cup. A pale sun streaked onto a living room that was at heart antique Colonial, but seemed frozen in 1970s mode. The room sparkled, which made me wonder how three foster children lived in such pristine ugliness.

Mr. Lange sat across from us on an immense leather recliner. Mrs. Lange sat at the opposite end of the L-shaped sofa, her milky pale hands restless. She couldn't sit still, and the skin across her bladed cheeks often tightened in what looked like fear.

She was a blur of motion, jumping up for any sound from the far reaches of the house. She gave all the signs of a person in flight mode.

I wondered if Mr. Lange harmed her, too.

"Sit the frig down, Beth!" Jonas Lange barked, then pushed the recliner back as far as it would go. Then he popped it back up again.

Beth Lange glared at her husband, but she sat, and Jonas Lange snapped a nod, as if acknowledging her defeat.

"The children are upstairs," Beth Lange said.

"I'd love to meet them," I said.

Her face fell. "Oh, they're napping. I'd hate to wake them up. They're so sad about Eva."

"I understand. But we'd still very much like to see them."

"Maybe later?" She smiled. "Would that be good?"

"Later would be great," I said.

On the one hand, her emotions felt real. They weren't. Instead, we were watching a well-orchestrated drama.

I leaned toward Kranak and whispered behind my tea cup. "Something's off. Use care."

Kranak raised an eyebrow, nodded.

"We're so sorry about Eva," I said.

"Me, too." Lange wiped his eyes with a brilliant white handkerchief. "She was a sweet little thing."

The air clouded with Kranak's fury. I rested a hand on his knee. "Do remember, Sergeant, what I mentioned earlier. You know?" I turned to Jonas Lange. "So Eva took your name?"

"Yeah," he said. "She was a little Jew girl. Her name embarrassed her, so we changed it to Lange. You understand."

Kranak nodded. "Sure we do."

"Lange is Danish?" I said.

Beth laughed, deeper and more assured than her current persona implied. "German," she said.

German. Of course.

"Somethin' wrong?" asked Jonas Lange.

"Wrong? Um, no. When did you change Eva's name?"

Beth Lange leaned toward the window and pushed back a drape. "The day we got her," she said.

I looked at Kranak, willing him to be ready with the right question. Something was going on with these people deeper than Jonas Lange's abuse of Eva. I wished I'd brought Penny inside, instead of leaving her in Kranak's truck.

"Do you know a family named Noguchi?" I asked.

"Japanese, right?" Jonas Lange said.

I nodded.

"Lemme think," Lange said.

Beth Lange popped up from the sofa and disappeared into the kitchen. I smelled cookies baking, but even that felt wrong.

Jonas Lange frowned. "Do we, Beth?" he hollered into the kitchen. She returned brimming with smiles and wearing a Mrs. Cleaver apron. All she needed were the pearls.

"Let me see," she said. "I'm not aware of any Japanese children in the area."

"How about the name Marsh?" Kranak said.

Jonas Lange grinned. "Yeah, the Marshes we know. Met 'em at Eva's school. Fine folks. Really fine."

"Did you ever hurt Eva?" Kranak asked.

Electricity jumped between the two men. A bell dinged in the kitchen, and Beth Lange disappeared.

Lange slapped his recliner forward. "What are you talking about?"

"You know what I'm talkin' about," Kranak said.

"That's disgusting," Lange said.

"Yeah." Kranak sat at the edge of the couch leaning forward. "It sure is. And we got us a dead kid here, one who's been sexually abused a few hundred times."

I leaned toward Kranak. "I'm going to check on Mrs. Lange."

"Stay here," he hissed.

I slapped his knee. "Be right back."

As I walked past Jonas Lange he grabbed my wrist. Kranak's gun flew into his hand.

"Let her go," Kranak said.

Lange did. "I just wanted to talk to Ms. Whyte," he said. "I don't know where you're getting your ideas, but I never touched the kid. She was my daughter, ya know?

"I'll be right back," I said, and hustled out of the room.

* * *

Burnt-cookie smell teased my nose as I entered the kitchen.
My quick scan showed the kitchen was empty. Damn. I ran
through the first floor. Laundry room, den, bath, family
room. Nada. I flew up the stairs. On my right, picture-
perfect kids rooms in such pristine condition I doubted a
child had ever stepped foot in them. A swift check told me
they were empty. The same for the hall bath. She had to be
in the master bedroom. She couldn't have left the house
without us hearing her.

I entered the large master and stopped, listened. Silence,
so loud it ate up the air in the room. While trying to remain
quiet and still, I tracked the room with my eyes. Bathroom,
two-door closet, bed, windows, chairs, dresser.

"Hello?" If anything, the silence deepened.

A sudden scent of roses. I turned, expecting … *Rose?*
Of course, nothing was there. But the scent lingered, the
same one I'd smelled in Rose's room. What the hell was going on? I got no sense of Beth Lange, yet Rose Noguchi
seemed … here.

Oh, boy. I took a deep breath and wondered if I should
sign up for some parapsychology show. More likely a
Looney Tunes cartoon.

But Rose, she had a profound kindness that I'd swear I
could feel.

I shook my head, trying to return to the here and now.

I got down on my knees and peered under the bed. Nothing. I rummaged through the closets and the bathroom. Not
a soul. Where was Beth Lange?

The New Hampshire cops would arrive any minute.

But I was afraid to leave. To leave the two remaining foster children with Beth Lange. Where were the children?

I tilted my head back. The ceiling was papered. Strange.
Even stranger, the pattern was a flurry of lilacs and hya-
cinths and busy as anything. Made me wonder.

I stepped onto the bed and ran my hands across the ceiling. My fingers felt a crack, almost invisible, but not completely once I knew where to look. I scraped them further along and brushed against what seemed to be a recessed handle.

I took a breath and pulled.

The door creaked open, and folded stairs thundered down so I had to jump out of the way. Good God, impaled by a staircase.

"Tally!" Kranak shouted.

I leapt off the bed and ran to the hall. "Sshhhh." I peered over the second-floor railing. Kranak was looking up at me, his one eyebrow raised.

"Well?" he hissed.

"Beth Lange's disappeared. Someone's in the attic."

"Stay there," he said. "I'll come up and—"

"Just let me." I retuned to the bedroom, slipped off my shoes, and climbed the rickety stairs.

I peered into a cavernous space. The attic, dark and chill, felt more like a dungeon than an aboveground space. My skin goose bumped.

The smell, not roses, for sure, but oil mixed with an unhealthy mustiness. I'd swear I smelled fear, too.

I waved my left hand for a string light, found nothing, but when I pushed against the floor, I felt a switch. I flicked it on.

A king-sized bed filled part of the floor. Bolted down, it rested on a Persian rug and was surrounded by three white fake walls. Two large studio lights were aimed at the bed, as was a small video camera screwed to a tripod.

A stage set. My stomach heaved. I imagined Eva in that bed, crying, fearful. I squeezed my eyes, and yet the image burned into my brain. This was a black and bitter place.

A sound, maybe a thump, drew me higher up the stairs, to the top. Way off in a corner blackness, I saw the outlines of what might be a room. I could imagine what horrors *it* held.

No wonder the killer saw Eva's death as merciful.

Another sound—a sob?—and I walked across floor-boards toward the hideous bed. I saw no one, but my anxiety only increased.

"Kranak!" I hollered. "You'd better—"

A creek, a slam. Total blackness blanketed the space. "Shit." Someone—I'd bet Beth Lange—had flung up the stairs, closing the attic door.

I took a couple of deep breaths. I couldn't see a thing. But I could hear, and that sob came again.

I waited. Small beads of light filtered through the attic boards to my right and my left. Not enough to help me see, but reassuring me that I hadn't slipped into hell.

I rested my hands at my sides. The bed was to my right, and the sob had come from straight ahead, right where I'd seen that room.

I walked forward. A board creaked, and I jumped like an idiot. I was sweating. Where the hell was Kranak?

I moved forward again, another step then another. More creaking boards, but nothing else.

The air moved, and I let out an "Eek!" It moved again, close, but not touching my face. Not a person. Bats. Just peachy. I liked bats—outside. Not trapped with me in some creepy attic.

"Crap." I sighed. Maybe I should just wait for Kranak's rescue. But something or someone was over there, near the end of the attic. And they were afraid.

I moved forward and sensed a wall just as I banged into it. Ouch. Then silence.

My hands found the door, a knob. But the door wouldn't open. Right. That would have been way too easy.

I slid my fingers up, then down the door. When they found a padlock, I wasn't surprised.

"Hello?" I said. "My name is Tally Whyte. I'm here to help you."

"No you're not!"

A child's voice, scared, high pitched, yet belligerent. Feigning a bravado he didn't feel.

"Please. I really am here to help. I'm from the Massachusetts Grief Assistance Program, and I'm here with a police sergeant. I'll get you out of there."

"No!" the boy yelled. "*She* said the Dementors were coming to get us. She said so! She's always right. Go away, or I'll hurt you."

He said "us." The two children were in there. I pressed my cheek to the door and willed the feeling of kindness through the boards. "I hope you won't hurt me. I want to let you out and help you find a new home. A safe home."

"That's what they said to Eva! And look what happened to her."

They. What a break if the child had seen Eva's abductors. But I had to get him or them out of there. That was the priority.

I had nothing on me, couldn't see. "Listen. I'm going to holler for a man named Sergeant Kranak. He's a police sergeant and very good at helping people. I'll be right back."

A sob.

I found my way back to the stairs, got down on my knees and pushed. They didn't budge. I sat, pounded with my feet. No luck there, either.

That was when I smelled the gas. The aroma was faint, but sharp. Oh, boy.

I crawled back to the door where the kids were held.

"Kids, do you know where there's a key out here?"

"No key. She never keeps a key up here. You're not gonna help, are you? You're going to leave us. So just say it."

"I'm going to help. I won't leave. Listen, I'm going to kick in the door. So get back. Get away from it."

I sat on my fanny and raised my legs like a battering ram.

Once, and the kids inside shrieked. "I'm just kicking in the door."

I kicked again and again, and suddenly the door flew away from my feet, and a furry growling something knocked me flat on my back.

"That's Zork," the boy said. "He can rip your throat out."

The dog's breath was hot and moist on my face as he pressed me to the floor. Light from inside the boy's small prison reflected on sharp teeth exposed by Zork's grimace of fury. Low growls rumbled from his throat.

I swallowed hard as I tried to project love and kindness. Tough, when fear was the predominant emotion. My heart fluttered motorboat fast.

"How about you get Zork off me," I said.

The dog growled, moved his muzzle closer to my face. His yellow eyes glinted in the soft light, and I saw determination.

"No!" the boy said. "I won't! *Pass auf!*"

What was that? Not Penny's Czech, but ... a *German* command. Yes. I heard myself pant, felt the child's simultaneous fear and power. *Pass auf.* I knew that. It meant ... *guard.* Yes. I'd learned all the commands—German, French, Czech, Dutch. If only ... think, think.

"I smell something funny," the boy said to someone inside the cell. "We have to leave. Come on."

"No. I'm scared," came the tiny voice.

The voice was soft and frightened. A child's voice. A little girl's. Think. Think. *Such rauschgift?* Maybe that was ... no. That meant find narcotics.

How to say *hodnay*—good—in German?

"*So ist brav!*" I blurted out. I softened my voice. "*So ist brav*, Zork. *So ist brav.*"

"Shut up!" the boy said.

"I have a Canine Corps dog. Her name is Penny. She's in the truck in your driveway. She's a good girl. Zork seems like a fine fellow. I really won't hurt you or your sister—

"She's not my sister!"

"I won't hurt any of you. I am here to help you. Promise." The scent of gas, stronger now, tweaked my nose.

Silence, then, "No! *Pass auf!*"

Oh, geesh. The place was filling with gas, the dog about to eat my face, and the kids in grave danger. I had to make a move. "*So ist brav*, Zork!" I pushed to a sitting position. At least the dog didn't instantly rip my face off. Zork continued to growl and stand beside me. Where the hell was Kranak?

"We have to leave," I said. I got a good look at the boy. He'd been made-up to look like a girl, down to the patent leather shoes.

A little girl, maybe five, appeared at the door to the room. "I'm scared, Curt. Can we go?"

He hugged the girl and began to sob. I reached for them, and Zork sprang.

"*Lass es!*" said Curt. "Leave it!"

"Come on, now," I said, reaching for calm. "Let's find a way out of here."

Curt nodded.

"I'm sorry for all that's happened to you," I said. "Don't give up. Things will be better."

"She's nice," came the little girl's voice.

"So was Mrs. Lange," he said, his voice full of bitterness. "At first."

I didn't know if it was my imagination, but I'd swear I smelled the gas seeping through the floor boards. Of course, if it were lit …

We had to find a window. But no, the only way down was death from the third story of the colonial home. I began pacing out steps back to the stairs, accompanied by the click-clack of Zork's nails and the padding of small feet.

I found the stairs, tried them again. They wouldn't budge.

The monster woman planned to blow us up. Or gas us. Or burn us alive.

Curt tried the stairs, too. He pulled and pulled, and I pulled with him. Together, maybe … I finally put my hands on his shoulders. "We can't open it, Curt. Let's save our energy."

Chapter Twenty-four

The gas smell was so strong my stomach flip-flopped. I felt slightly dizzy, and the two children began to whimper. So did the dog.

I had to think.

"I saw something once," the little girl said.

I crouched down. "Tell me, hon."

"*She* said it was a ghost," Curt said. "But … I'm not sure it was."

"Where did you see this thing?"

The child pointed toward the rear of the house. "Way back there."

She meant the far end of the attic. "Come on. Let's all hold hands and go check. Curt, why don't you lead the way."

"I can't," he said.

"No?"

"There's … something bad over there."

"That's okay to be afraid. But we have to do something.

Take my hand, and I'll lead." We made a chain and walked across the attic, following the light that slipped in from loose clapboards.

Old colonials often had servant's stairs, I explained to the kids. I got down on my hands and knees and felt the floor for any cracks that might be a doorway.

The attic smelled foul, and back in the center of the room, I swore I saw a glow from below.

"I want to go!" howled the little girl.

"We will," Curt said. "Hang on, Lena."

My fingers brushed something different. Not wood, but ... I groped for the place I'd found. Rope! A rope pull.

"Get back, kids." I crouched and put both hands around the rope and pulled up. It didn't move. "I think it's stuck. C'mon, Curt. You, too, Lena. Help me pull."

Curt grabbed a piece of the rope and Lena put her arms around one of my legs.

"On three. One, two ...."

The door flew open, as if ... *oh, forget it, Tal. Don't get spooked now.* "We did it!" I said.

"I didn't do anything," Curt said.

"Sure you did. So did Lena."

I peered down into blackness. But the blackness was different. A *something* was there.

I lifted the flap back further and as gently as possible. Even so, it creaked.

"Hang on, kids. I'm going to go check it out."

Again I ran my hands across the floor. I found emptiness, and then a wood stair. And another.

I sat my bum on the first stair, feet on the second, and hiney-walked down.

The stairs were old and incredibly narrow. The heads of nails scraped my butt. As I moved down, the gas smell increased.

I had to stand at the bottom, as the door and the staircase

pressed close together. The smell of gas clung like a plastic bag over my head. I didn't get why we hadn't already exploded.

I wrapped my hand around the doorknob. Not hot. A good sign.

But I couldn't get myself to twist and open the door. All I could think was *had Mrs. Lange booby-trapped it?*

"Are you okay?" Curt hollered down.

"Fine!"

I had to turn it. Had to.

"Something's coming!" screamed Curt.

"What?" I yelled.

"Up here," Curt said. "Coming up here!"

I ran up the stairs. The thumping grew louder and louder. *A helicopter?*

"You in there Tally?" boomed Kranak's voice.

"Yes!" Not loud enough. Where to yell from?

Curt took my wrist and walked me to the wall. "Here. There's a window."

I felt around, found some boards. "Pull, Curt."

"Me, too," said Lena.

We all pulled, and I leaned back, my right foot pushing against the wall. The board flew off, we fell to the ground, and watery, gray light streamed in from a small attic window.

I punched out a pane of glass and screamed as loud as I could while waving my red scarf. "Here, Rob! We're in here!"

"Don't leave the attic." His voice boomed from a loudspeaker.

"Then how do we get down? I've got two kids and a dog up here with me."

"You guys get back," he said above the thump of the helicopter. "We'll break in and get you."

We moved back and glass and wood splintered as a large

man wearing body armor that read SWAT flew through the window and stumbled onto the floor.

He straightened and wrapped an arm around Lena. "I'll take this littlest one first."

Lena shrieked, but then she laughed as the man swung back out. Curt, Zork, and I watched her rise into the air, and then disappear into the helicopter.

Curt ripped off his dress. "I won't go like this."

The man catapulted back in through the window and wrapped an arm around Curt.

"Not without Zork!" Curt screamed.

"I'll take him with me!" I said. "I won't leave him. Now go."

Holding Curt tight, the rescuer swung out the window, rose on the cable, and the pair disappeared into the helicopter.

The overpowering gas scent nauseated me, and I rested a hand on the window casing. Stars danced before my eyes.

"You ready?" hollered the man dangling from the cable. He steadied a red metal basket. "For you and the dog."

I blinked a couple of times, aware of how woozy I felt. Then, the world was blanketed with silence. No thumping helicopter, no shouting man, no sound whatsoever ... except for the creak of a doorknob turning.

"Ready!" I shouted, frantic to get out of the house.

The basket was almost to us. We had to go. Then or never. "Zork, *hopp! Hopp.* Jump!"

He leapt, and the basket wavered as he landed. Thank God.

I climbed onto the windowsill, hands on the window's frame, and jumped, too.

I was flying, the basket careening wildly as an explosion behind me voomped a gust of air. Then the basket was flying toward me, but in slow-motion, and I reached and reached and ...

Strong arms hooked around my forearms, like we were

trapeze artists, and I was pulled into the basket, which suddenly leapt higher and through the air.

I screamed and wrapped my arms around the dog, burying my face in his fur. We'd die, but at least—

"Tally, look," boomed Kranak.

The wind whipped and the noise was incredible. I peeked. Splintered pieces of the house burst upward, while what looked like the house sawed in half collapsed into itself.

A flying clapboard came at me and something smothered me and …

I couldn't breathe. I pushed and pushed, but …

"Move Mr. Zork, please, kids," said a familiar voice.

A weight released me, and I sucked in a huge inhale.

"Wake up, Ms. Sleeping Beauty."

The voice was rough and rich and filled with affection and worry. Kranak. I wanted to scrape a hand across my eyes, but both my left and right were held tight in warm, cradling ones.

I blinked my eyes open and found myself staring at a moist pink tongue.

"He was sittin' on ya," Kranak said. "He protected you when that clapboard came at you. Amazing."

"Zork," I said. *"So ist brav."*

The dog whimpered.

"Penny?" I said.

"She's fine," Kranak said. "Relax."

"Sure, that's me," I said. "Ms. Relaxed."

The helicopter fluttered onto the ground. A blanket-wrapped Curt held my left hand, while Lena gripped my right so tight it almost hurt.

I squeezed their hands in thanks. "Kids, you were great. So brave. I think I'll sit up, okay?"

Kranak grunted. "The loony Mrs. Lange blew—"

"She wasn't loony," Curt said, avoiding everyone's eyes. "She was a monster."

"Well, kid," Kranak said in a much-softened tone. "She won't be monstering anymore."

Hours later, after we'd gotten Curt, Lena, and Zork checked out at the hospital and settled with New Hampshire family services, we drove back to OCME. Darkness seeped into Kranak's truck, and I rested my head on Penny and tried not to doze.

I woke up as Kranak pulled into the parking lot.

"Let's talk in the A.M.," he said.

"Yes, let's. What I don't get is how I smelled the gas for a long time, but she obviously waited to light the match."

Kranak leaned against my 4Runner, his body shielding mine from the sharp breeze. "She wanted to find her cat. I got the old man out, but I never saw the bitch again. All I heard was her calling the dumb cat. Funny thing, the tabby made it out."

"The cat saved our lives." I turned to open the door to the truck. Kranak brushed his hand over my hair in the most terribly gentle way. Tears dampened my eyes, and I turned back. "*You* saved our lives, Rob."

He brushed my hair again. "I was scared."

I couldn't see, not even with the parking light glare, but I knew what his eyes were saying. I'd known this man too long not to understand.

I leaned forward. "Oh, Rob." Our lips met, his hard and tight, mine soft and compliant. His tongue invaded my mouth, and I pulled him closer.

God, it felt good, the way he pressed me to him, pulling my body tighter and tighter to his.

He pushed me away. "What are we thinkin', Tal? What are we doin' here?"

"I don't know. I ... " At that moment, no one existed for

me but Rob Kranak. I cupped his face and kissed him hard. The world dissolved into hunger and need.

"Tal?" A new voice. "Tally?"

I gasped, released Kranak, and turned. He was just a silhouette, but I'd recognize Hank Cunningham anywhere.

Kranak vanished, and minutes later Hank stood beside me.

"Carmen called me," he said. "She thought I should come down."

"I'm glad you're here." I slipped into the 4Runner, unable to kiss him. He'd seen. What had I done? "I'll meet you at the apartment."

Hank followed my truck. Normally I would have ridden home with him and left my truck at OCME. Not that night. How could I explain to my sweetheart why I'd just kissed another man?

I'd almost died that day, and instead of death, Kranak filled my mind.

Carmen was at the apartment, giving me precious minutes to gather my forces. They weren't gathering. What could I possibly say to Hank? I hadn't a clue, other than a bucketful of meaningless excuses.

I made a dash for the bathroom to "freshen up." I'd freak out if I'd caught him kissing someone else. I counted on him, expected him to behave in a certain way. I trusted him.

He'd done the same for me, and I'd messed up. Big time.

A bruised-looking stranger with wild, filthy hair and a dirty face looked back at me from the mirror. Kranak kissed *this*?

There I went again, thinking about Kranak and not Hank. But I adored my Maine sheriff.

"Tal?" came Hank's voice through the door.

"Coming!" I scrubbed my face, ignoring the pain from various bruises and a cut on my chin that burned. I didn't even try for makeup. I shucked my ripped clothes and pulled on some sweats. What? Was I trying out for Gold's Gym? I pulled them off, and slipped my nightgown and robe on. More comfortable. Easier on my bruises. Who was I kidding? I hoped the filmy outfit would soften Hank's fury.

"Tal?" Hank hollered. "You okay?"

I opened the door with a dramatic flourish and a plastered-on smile. "I'm fine!" I turned to Carmen. "Carm, I ..."

She wasn't there.

Hank hooked his thumbs over his belt. "She cut out so we could be alone. You *do* want to be alone, right?"

I blinked and kept on blinking.

"Something in your eye?" he said.

That's when I got the anger ... and the sadness. I hooked my arm through his. "Let's sit, huh?" I drew him to the couch. He disengaged my arm and sat at the far end. Taking my cue from him, I took the other end. Penny laid her head on my lap.

"Penny?" he nodded toward her.

"Oh, my gosh. I didn't tell you." I filled him in, and the relief made me tear up again.

"Good stuff," he said.

"Yes."

Arms folded, he chewed the end of his mustache. "You love me?"

"Yes, I do. But ... oh, Hank, I don't know what's going on inside me. I feel like one of those veggie cocktails, all that stuff mixed together in a mess."

He chuckled. "You make the worst analogies ever." His smile faded. "Kranak's tough competition, Tal. And I'm not one to compete in that kind of race."

I moved to pat his Buddha belly.

"Don't," he said. "Don't be cute or sweet or whatever it is you're doing."

I scraped fingers through my matted hair. "See, I don't

know what it is I *am* doing. You know all that's been going on. My feelings are jumbled. My head's whirling."

He stood and pulled his keys from his pocket. "Have you slept with him?"

"No!"

"You will."

I held out my arms. "Hank, don't go. Please. Help me understand what I'm feeling here. You mean the world to me."

He unhooked his keys from his belt. "Those are friend words, not lover words."

"Crap. Hank, please. I messed up. I'm sorry. I'm confused, and I …"

He sighed, and then hugged me hard. His smell, his body, the softness of his mustache—everything about him spoke of beauty and love and passion.

He released me. "Call me when you know."

I slumped on the sofa, aware I was messing up my life, but not knowing how to unmess it.

Carmen reappeared. She loomed over me, foot tapping. "Your car isn't that comfy."

"You've been sitting in the car?"

"Where the hell else? You screwed up, huh."

"I am one giant mess." I filled her in about Kranak and the kiss and Hank seeing the whole thing.

"You know, all your guys have 'k's in their names. Is that, like, a theme?"

"Not funny."

"So what's going on?" She flopped beside me and slung an arm around my shoulder.

"Ouch. I've had a helluva day." That's when I told her about Mrs. Lange and Curt and Lena and Adventures with Helicopters.

She waggled her hand. "Whoo-hoo. That's big. I'm sure

glad you lived to tell the tale. So which is it, Kranak or Cunningham?"

Penny whined. I walked to the French doors and let her out back. I switched on the spotlight, wanting to keep an eye on her. My pocket garden looked ghoulish in the evening light. The bed of lilies and coneflowers needed cleaning out. I should have blanketed it with hay over the winter. Somehow the garden always came back each year, despite my neglect.

Penny did her thing, and thundered back up the stairs, eager for a dog cookie. "Here you go, girl."

Satisfied, she curled up beside the fire that Carmen had lit.

"Stop stalling," Carmen said.

"Hank or Kranak?" I said. "Laugh, but it sounds like apples and oranges. I love them both. I *thought* in different ways."

"You're going through a lot, Tally. Kranak's here."

"He's always been 'here' for me."

"Hasn't Hank?" She poured us each a bourbon on the rocks. We clinked glasses. "To life."

"Yes," I said. "Hank's been here for me, too. But it's different."

"You'll figure it out."

"They deserve better."

"You can't always get what you want," she said. "Speaking of … let me fill you in on what happened at the hospital today."

I placed another log on the fire. "Go."

"I was in with Veda when—"

The phone beeped. "Hang on." I didn't recognize the caller ID. "Tally Whyte here."

"You must go!"

"Veda?"

"Go. There is still time. *Morgen. Ja.*"

"English, Veda."

"There is time. You must. Tomorrow. *Ja!*"

"Veda, what—"

"Nein! Nein!"

"Veda!"

The line went dead.

We raced to the hospital.

Chapter Twenty-five

Carmen and I ran down the hospital corridor. When I spotted Veda's state police watcher, I slowed.

"She'd better be okay, dammit," I said to Carmen.

"I don't trust these people," Carmen said. "Not the cops, not the hospital staff."

"You're paranoid, Carm."

She shot me a dark look as she held her side. "This racing around is killing me."

"It's good for you," I whispered. "But something happened in Veda's room. I'm going to ask the cop before we go in."

"Officer?" I said. He didn't react as we approached. "Officer!" I pressed a hand to his shoulder. He tilted sideways on the chair and crashed to the floor.

"See to him!" I said to Carmen as I slammed through Veda's door. "Veda!" All I heard were her damned hospital machines.

"Veda!" I ripped back the curtain around the bed.

The bed and Veda were gone.

* * *

"At least he's alive," I said to Carmen as we pounded the hospital corridors.

"He's out cold," she said.

"The troops are on their way," I said. "I can't believe someone had the balls to kidnap the state's chief medical examiner."

"Not to mention Tally Whyte's foster mother."

"You're right. That was their real mistake."

As soon as I'd gone hollering into the nurses' station, Hawthorne Medical Center had sealed off all exits and entrances. Or so we'd been told. One could only wonder, when right under their noses a cop was drugged and a woman kidnapped from her room.

The corridor was bright. They'd raised lights they normally dimmed at night. We passed staff equally frenetic, most looking for Veda.

Lord, I could hear her voice in my head. Would I never hear that voice again? I stifled a sob.

"What?" Carmen asked.

"Nothing. I'm cool."

Down another wing, and I began seeing officers in uniform and plainclothes detectives and even staff from OCME.

I pushed open the door to the stairs and almost slammed into Kranak.

"Rob!" I made fists of my hands, so as not to hug him.

He rested his hands on my shoulders. He wore his rumpled blue suit and an awful tie. "We'll find her, babe," he said.

I smiled at the old, familiar joke. "Don't call me babe."

He chuckled.

"She's alive, Rob," I said.

He nodded.

"She *is*. Whoever snatched her could just as easily have killed her. But they took her. I bet they masqueraded as a tech who was moving her for tests."

"Why don't you rest?" he said.

"Rest? Right. We'll catch you later. And thanks."

He hugged me, and I caught the sour smell of booze. I wanted to curse or cry. Damn him.

We'd made it to the basement level. Someone, a municipal cop, maybe, said he'd gone through the basement and found nothing. But no way would I let an inch of that hospital go unchecked by me.

Carmen flopped into a pink plastic chair that lined the hall of the first corridor. "Just for a minute, Tal."

I looked at my friend and saw exhaustion droop her eyes and curve her back. I slumped beside her and slung an arm across her shoulder.

"She's gone," I said. "And I bet she's afraid. She's so changed. She never feared anything, and now ... she's a different person, but still my Veda. She saved me, Carm, from a life in hell. She was the one after my dad was murdered who rescued me and brought me back to health. She gave me a purpose and a will to live. And now, I can't even—"

"Don't say it! You're doing everything you can. So I'll get off my butt and we'll keep looking."

"You're exhausted."

"Like hell I am. Don't you think for a minute I'm some pantywaist."

She was about to punch my arm, when I heard a shuffle down the corridor. I held up a finger and mouthed "Wait."

As I pointed down the hall, another sound, maybe a groan. I wished for my pepper spray, which I'd left at home. I held a finger to my lips. "Sshhhh."

We stood as one and moved silently down the basement hall.

Another groan, and Carmen pinched my arm. She pointed to a door two down on the left.

As we neared the archway, behind us, someone slammed open the basement stair door.

"Shit!" Carmen said.

The hall lights flickered once, twice, and went out.

Seconds later, a breeze, chill and damp, brushed my face.

"He's taking her outside!" I ran toward my memory of the doorway.

I hung a left in the dark and slammed into something that knocked me on my back. I groaned, but pushed myself up.

A hand slammed me down, and I felt linoleum against my head and hot breath on my neck. A knife? A needle? I steeled myself for pain.

Instead the lights again flickered once, twice, and I glimpsed someone carrying a white-sheeted body out the basement door.

I rolled to my feet and staggered across the large supply room toward the exit door. I pushed the handle downward. The door wouldn't budge.

"I can't get it open," I said.

Behind me, Carmen said, "Coming," then wrapped her hands around the handle and pushed with me.

"Wait," said the male voice. "Move out of the way."

A man wearing jeans and a flannel shirt inserted a key into the lock. He turned it, I pushed, and the door flew open.

A dark van peeled out of the parking lot, and I ran after it, hoping to see something, anything that would give us a clue.

The night was dark, the windows blacked out, and the bulbs that lit the van's license plate was smashed.

The van disappeared, and I just stood there, paralyzed by a sense of utter helplessness. I called Kranak on my cell, but I was too late. Too late.

Not the state cops, nor municipal ones, nor the FBI—no one could believe that the Chief Medical Examiner for

Massachusetts had been kidnapped. Veda was a legend, an icon to many for as many reasons.

Yet as officers and agents fanned across the state that night, I knew it would take more than a little help from fate to find my foster mother, who now was reduced to an ill old woman whose mind was fading and whose physical resources were few.

The following morning, I groaned awake filled with aches and pains from helicopter flying and van chasing, not to mention my sprained arm and my operation. Penny lay asleep at the foot of the bed, sprawled on her back, lacking any semblance of dignity.

How wonderful to see her there for the first time in weeks without that fist of fear in my belly.

I tried to free my body from my nightgown, which was wrapped around me like an Ace bandage. I finally pulled it over my head, tossed it on the floor and flopped back against my pillow.

I'd had such a strange dream....

I walk in a field of lavender that comes to my waist. I am surrounded by it, and the feeling is one of peace and contentment.

I am surprised that it's my father's field. He and Mother are professors at the university, the lavender field is his hobby, his passion, next to my sister and me, of course.

I stand inside our cottage in France where we go to vacation. Father speaks wonderful French, but I'm not so fine at it, and the words stick on my tongue.

The walls are thick and uneven and painted bright, sunny colors. The doors are turquoise and red, and I like the one best that leads to the kitchen because it's a double door, and I can sneak beneath the lower half and sometimes steal cookies from Anna, our maid.

I peer out a small-pained window filled with bubbles in the glass.

Clouds shaped like warriors march across the deep blue sky, and I'm suddenly standing in the lavender field. I worry about getting my new frock wet.

I dash into the house just as the rain begins to pelt the crop that now waves wildly in the wind.

Father hugs me and lifts me and twirls me around, and we walk hand-in-hand to the small parlor where my favorite …

I gasped. The telephone. I groped for the phone. I wished I hadn't been interrupted. The man in the dream wasn't my father, and I wasn't that child. France? I'd never been there.

But I'd smelled the lavender and seen those clouds and entered that small cottage, which held such promise of things that were good in life.

I tried to cling to the comfort of those feelings as I lifted the portable from its cradle and slid out of bed.

Kranak. No news.

I sighed, and punched out the numbers for Bertha. I hadn't been able to reach her the previous night, and I sure as heck hadn't wanted to leave a message that her sister had been stolen.

"It's Tally, dear Bertha."

"I know, *liebchen*," she said. "All about it."

I couldn't tell her I was terrified. "She wasn't well when she was taken, Auntie."

"No. But my sister's a survivor, that one." She chuckled. "She will not die in someone else's arms."

"She's not going to die."

"She is going to, dear Tal," she said. "*Ja*. You must pre-pare yourself."

"A month ago she was running the medical examiner's office."

"I know the signs, Tally. The camps … We learned the signs well."

Bertha might be convinced, but I wasn't.

"Call me when you know more, my darling," she said.

"I will."

I couldn't help Veda, not now, anyway, but perhaps it was time for me to learn more about a lot of things.

I knocked on the back door and was greeted by a hug. My old professor and friend, who wasn't old in the least, pulled me into her arms and hugged me for long minutes.

Finally, the concerned face of Dr. Barbara Beliskowitz stared up at me. One of the top forensic psychiatrists in the country, Barbara awed me with her acumen at sussing out motives and methods.

"Come in. Come in." Barbara's deep, honeyed voice was a balm to my soul. I hadn't realized how much I needed to see her until that moment.

We grabbed mugs of steaming chai, and I handed her the cookies I'd picked up at the neighborhood bakery. Her favorites. That brought out one of her big, toothy smiles that rose all the way to her intelligent gray eyes.

I put the chai on an end table and sank into one of the huge couches in her art-filled living room. The smell of jasmine brushed my nose. "That smells great."

"I love it, too." She sipped her drink and waited, something she did with infinite patience.

I filled her in on Veda and my love life and work. "But those things I somewhat understand."

Her eyes smiled. "Even your feelings about Rob Kranak?"

I shook my head. "I'm here because I need your help unraveling an impossibly tangled skein that has to do with the murders of two children. Homicides that I fail to understand, as much as I've tried."

"I'll do my best."

I finished the chai and leaned forward. "Here's where we're at." I told her about Rose, and how she'd been left in OCME's refrigerated room, and about *Sins of the Father* inscribed on her hand and the lambs they carried. I explained about Bella's kidnapping and release/escape, and about Eva, the killer's latest victim.

She sat back on the sofa, her face frozen in sorrow. Telling it all again broke my heart, yet it made me see that I was missing a key element, a concrete motivator.

"A concrete motivator," she said. "Yes."

I hadn't realized I'd spoken out loud. "That specificity is what's missing. Sins of the father is one thing, but what sin? What father? And why would these particular children expiate the killer's guilt?"

"Absolutely," she said. Her scruffy alley cat leapt into her lap and began to motorboat. She stroked the cat's fur. "Remember, he released Bella Marsh...."

Barbara got up and paced. "That disturbs me. Something's way off."

"It is. I think it could be the Marshes. They took Bella, but they couldn't bring themselves to harm her. Thoughts?"

Barbara was silent for long minutes. "Given Bella's return, and the family's disappearance and what happened to you in Peterborough, I'd say, yes, it's highly possible they're involved."

"Could *they* be the killers?" I said. "That's the real question."

"I can't answer that. Find the 'why,' then you'll know."

"You're right, of course."

"The killing has less to do with the individual child and everything to do with what they represent."

"What they represent. What they symbolize. Or, what their parents—"

"or grandparents—symbolize."

She laid the cat on the floor, walked to the couch and sat beside me. "Here's what you have to do, Tally. Forget thinking about these innocent children as people, something you do so well. And start thinking of them as symbols. I believe that only when you *dehumanize* them and turn them into icons, will you be able to see the truth of the case."

"You're telling me I need to depersonalize them? They've been children to me ... people. But to him or her, they're simply—"

"—Goals, steps—"

"To some specific atonement!"

"Yes!"

I leaned back, and Barbara's basset hound inched onto the sofa, her huge body making every effort to appear small and insignificant. I hugged her. "Susie thinks she's a chihuahua, right?"

Barbara rolled her eyes. "Sometimes. And sometimes she just pretends she's invisible."

"He'll kill again," I said.

"It's highly possible. If you can figure out what the killer's atoning for, maybe you can stop him."

Chapter Twenty-six

When I arrived home, Carmen handed me a note from Kranak, a glittering cocktail dress and a large linen envelope. "Hand delivered. The envelope, I mean."

"You're kidding me?" I read the invitation to the opening of the Holocaust and Gaman Art Exhibit at the Wirth Gallery. It was for that night. Veda was listed as one of the main sponsors. Veda.

I ripped open Kranak's note. Although the boy, Curt, was filled with information about the Langes, he had not seen who'd taken Eva. The "they" he'd referred to were the Langes.

I'd hoped ... I walked to the cabinet, dotted with half-used liquor bottles. "Bourbon?"

"Two fingers," she said.

I poured one for each of us, added some ice, and handed her a glass. I raised my hand. "To you."

She clinked my glass and downed a mouthful.

"You look guilty as hell," I said. "What's up?"

"I've got to go, Tally." She finished the bourbon and poured herself another finger. "Home. In the morning."

My stomach clenched. "Must you?"

"The kids, Bob. I need to get home. Veda's … gone. I didn't do enough."

"Are you kidding? You went over and above."

She flopped onto the couch and crossed her ankles on the coffee table. She peeked up at me, an ironic smile on her face. "She was kidnapped, for Christ sake."

"No one, not a soul could have seen that coming," I said. "You kept her alive."

"Yeah, I probably did. I helped. It was a good thing, me coming. Now, it's *adiós, mi amigo*."

I wanted to scream "Stay!" Instead, I smiled. She'd been great, marvelous. "I understand. I do. You've been more than a friend. You've been valiant."

She winked. "You always had class. Look, I'll come back if I can."

I hugged her. "Good."

"Don't get all mushy on me, Tal. Shit, remember when we got drunk that night in Winsworth?"

"*Not* a pretty memory. And not tonight. Let's light a fire."

We got kindling and a couple logs, and soon a fire crackled in my historic fireplace.

Carmen swooped up the dress she'd laid on the back of the couch. "You'd better get this on."

"Ah, the gallery opening. That's the last thing I want to do today. There's no way."

"Fine," she said. "So bag it. I don't blame you. It's just Veda …"

I took a sip of bourbon. "I know. But she'd understand. I'm exhausted." Penny curled up on the couch beside me.

"Veda's been all over the news," Carmen said. "Pictures, everything."

I flicked on the clicker, channel surfed for the news at seven, sighed. There was Veda, looking full of energy, her intense black eyes fire bright. A quick cut, and a reporter was interviewing Ethridge, who stood with a silent Fogarty at her side. She mouthed platitudes into the microphone that to my ears sounded gratingly insincere. Fogarty looked devastated.

"Every time I see that woman," I said, "I want to barf."

"That's what you get for refusing to talk to those reporters."

I grumped, took a large sip of bourbon. "I suppose so. At least Fogarty's occasionally sincere. But Ethridge? She's a piranha."

"She looks creepy. Like an icicle with big boobs."

"She's good at posing," I said. "I'd swear she has it in her to kidnap Veda to get what she wants."

Then a different reporter showed a recent photo and repeating how Veda'd been kidnapped, how the FBI was involved.

Numbers flashed onscreen, and a Web site, too.

The old Veda would laugh that she'd made national news. The new Veda? I groped for the pack of cigarettes I kept stashed in the box on the end table. They'd be ancient—I hadn't smoked in years—but I didn't care.

The box was empty. "Carmen!"

Her beatific smile told me she'd tossed them. "Dammit, I need a smoke."

"No, you don't."

As I gave her the finger, the phone rang. I checked the caller ID screen.

"Reporters, I bet," Carmen said. "All day."

"It's a New Hampshire number. Pricilla Magee. The tarot reader." I snatched up the phone. "Pricilla, hi."

"Hi, Tally. I'm so sorry to hear about your foster mother."

"Thanks. If you have any insight ..."

"None, I'm afraid. But I'll do a reading for her, just in case."

"Thank you."

"Remember what I told you?"

"You told me lots of stuff."

"Please go to that opening."

"The gallery. I—"

"Just go."

Carmen and I peeled out of the taxi with little grace. I wore the handsome black sheath Carmen had chosen, and I paled beside my spectacular friend. Her auburn hair glowed above a ruffled green gown made of satin and lace. All I could think of was a Valkyrie about to do battle.

"You look amazing," I said.

"I do, don't I?" Her grin was Cheshire wide.

If anything, the crush at the Wirth Gallery was even larger and more glittery than the last time I'd visited. Men in tuxes and women coated in gems gave way to even more fabulous costumes.

The gallery throbbed with money and prestige. I could smell the egos colliding. At the moment I was ready to run, Carmen gave my elbow a discreet shove.

"Stop it," I hissed.

People waved. I waved back and wove deeper into the crowd. I saw my landlord, Jake, flanked by two glamorous models, one on each arm.

I mouthed "C'mon" to Carmen, and off we went for a chat with Jake.

"How come you're here?" I asked him. "This historical stuff isn't usually your cuppa."

He hugged me, and whispered how sorry he was about Veda into my ear.

"Thanks." I introduced him to Carmen. "So, why did you come, Jake?"

He shrugged. "The Holocaust. It's a fundraiser for Spielberg's Shoah Foundation. The Japanese connection with the Internment Art. I've always been fascinated by that."

I laid a hand on his cashmere turtleneck. "Really."

He grinned. "It's art politics, Tal. Everybody's gotta show up to this thing, or else. You?" he said.

I couldn't explain Pricilla Magee's insistence, so I told him about Veda's involvement. Minutes later, Carmen took point, and we navigated our way through a room of art painted by Holocaust victims or about the Holocaust. Some were charming and gay, others so bleak I could barely look at them, their visceral power pulling me back to that dark moment in history. The variety was huge. Many of the works had red "sold" dots on them.

I still hadn't seen why Pricilla Magee insisted I attend.

The chatter in the room was fever-pitched, but as I squeezed in front of the paintings and sketches, I pictured Bertha and Veda, children in the camps. I moved on, cloaked in a terrible misery.

Nick and Stan Wirth had dedicated the exhibit's second room to the Japanese-American victims of internment by the U.S. government during WWII and the amazing art they produced. The subject was the art of Gaman, or "enduring the seemingly unbearable with patience and dignity."

If possible, this room was even more jammed with humans—all talking at once—than the last Wirth event. Artfully placed around the room were carvings of birds, and elephants, and geishas; of herons and teapots and hearts made from shells; of Butsudan chests and Sennibari vests. I recognized the petite woman in the corner as the author Delphine Hirasuna, whose book, *The Art of Gaman*, was the basis for the exhibit. Another day, I would've enjoyed meeting her.

I scanned the room as I walked past the exhibit pieces. I recognized Alex Wirth, Nick's son, and waved. I spotted several Boston luminaries. One gave me a wave, and I returned it.

The art compelled me. Each piece was beautiful in its own right, and I had difficulty imagining such beauty coming from people experiencing such heartache.

One carving, in particular, snagged me. The heron was beautiful, but it was the name—Ken Noguchi—that stopped me. The blurb beside it said that Ken Noguchi was interned for two years before being drafted to fight in the European war theater. He fought for his country—after all, he was an American citizen—in the 442nd Regimental Combat Team, a racially segregated battalion of Japanese-Americans that the army created for the Nisei, American citizens of Japanese ancestry.

The text and the art were spellbinding, but it was the donor's name—John Noguchi, son of Ken Noguchi—that riveted me.

"Only connect," E. M. Forster wrote. I was surrounded by connections, yet I was missing some of them. I could feel it.

Carmen pinched my arm. "Look, isn't that the White Witch?"

I followed Carmen's finger. Ethridge, wearing a white knit dress that emphasized her enlarged breasts, held forth to a group of media leeches, while Fogarty gazed worshipfully at her.

Pawn or player? I wondered who was which. I couldn't help but contrast their peacock behavior with Veda's down-to-earth persona. It was as if Ethridge were reveling in Veda's illness. She was sharp. After all, she'd played the mouse for years. She just might be capable of harming Veda to attain her goals.

"Let's go find the Wirth brothers," I said. "Then we can get out of here." I led Carmen toward the third room where the legacy Holocaust paintings were on display. A tall flicker to my right stole my attention.

A woman lasered me through her retro cat's-eye sunglasses. She was tall and willowy and glamorous. Her flowing brown hair draped over one eye, à la Veronica Lake, and her plump lips glistened with vixen-red color that pulsed against skin artificially porcelain white.

She looked like every man's fantasy come to life, but I'd swear "she" was the person I knew as Andrew Marsh.

I learned toward Carmen. "It's *her!* The gal I saw in The Toadstool, the one Pricilla Magee identified when she saw my photo of Andrew Marsh!"

Carmen peered over the crowd. "No way," she said.

"I'm telling you, she's a he," I said.

She snorted. "I should look so good."

"If it *is* Andrew March in drag, then why is he here?"

"What does it matter?" Carmen tugged at her strapless top. "Stupid dress."

"Matter? Because he's hidden his child so she won't talk to the police. And because he's involved in the deaths of Rosa and Eva. I believe that."

"If you're right, it makes no sense that he'd expose himself."

"Exactly. I'm going after him."

"Call your friend, Kranak."

"Hell, no." I began to thread my way through the crowd.

"Wait!" Carmen said.

I kept trying for speed, but was blocked by a roomful of schmoozers, half of who knew me and wanted to chat. The human riptide was preventing me from reaching Marsh, no matter how many sweaty bodies I pushed out of my way.

I cursed and plowed forward. We were less than ten feet apart.

My quarry looked frantic. Her lips mouthed something I couldn't get. "You *must*—"

"Tally!" shouted a familiar voice.

To my left, a madly waving Stan Wirth stood beneath the doorway arch.

"In a sec," I hollered to him, and pressed on toward Marsh.

The bang of a gun! I jerked. Screams and shouts and hands covering heads and … laughter?

"Nothing, folks. It's nothing!" A grinning Andrew Wirth

help up a magnum of champagne that frothed over the bottle's rim.

Geesh. Scared the hell out of me.

When I looked back at the striking brunette, a woman I'd swear was Marlene Marsh was hauling her out the door. They were running from something. I squeezed after them, pushing and shoving.

I reached the door and caught the brunette in flashing red heels screeching at someone out of sight.

"Andrew!" I hollered. I raced up the gallery steps to street level. Again a woman I was sure was Marlene was tugging Andrew toward a yellow cab.

"Wait!" I ran.

Andrew shrieked when she pushed him into the backseat. People stared, but no one stopped.

Marlene Marsh gave me one look before she dived in after her in-drag husband. The cab sped off.

I stood for a moment on the sidewalk, chest heaving for breath.

How strange. I'd seen Marlene quite clearly in the glow of the streetlamp. Her look wasn't what I'd expected. No hatred or anger, but rather sorrow.

Rather than illuminate, it confused me even more.

Chapter Twenty-seven

Having failed to catch the Marshes, I went in search of Nick Wirth. Carmen and I entered the room where he'd shown me the art stolen from Holocaust victims. I peered over heads for Nick and Stan. Had Nick visited Veda before her kidnapping and found her changed?

"Holy shit," Carmen said. "Look at these things."

"I know. Monets and Picassos and Rubens. Many of the German and Austrian and Polish Jews of their time loved to collect fine art. Some of the artists, like Picasso, were considered experimental back in the day. It's amazing stuff. The Nazis stole and then sold the works, many of which ended up in European museums. These pieces here have been returned to the rightful owners' families. The Wirth brothers are selling the art for those families. Some feel the work is tainted. Some just need the money."

We passed a guard, and again I saw Nick's son, Alex, now deep in conversation with Nila Wendall. I walked over and introduced Carmen to Alex and the artist, then excused myself when I spotted Nick.

He'd donned an elegant tux and quietly held court. So different from Stan, who stood beside him gesturing enthusiastically to a clutch of art devotees. I hadn't realized earlier what he was wearing. Good God—a black turtleneck, black linen jacket, black pants *and* black leather-harness motorcycle boots. The man had to be over eighty. Dear Stan, *what* was he thinking?

"Tally Ho!" Nick's embrace choked off all thought. His wonderful lime scent drew me in, and I hugged him back.

Stan pecked me on the cheek. "Must run. Talk to Nick."

Nick hooked an arm in mine and one in Carmen's. "You're a gorgeous pair!"

"Ah, Nick," I said. "So good to see you. Yet another crush."

He pushed up his wire rims by the nosepieces. "Of course. A must-do. You look rather flushed, m'dear."

"Yes, well, it's been a startling evening so far."

"I know just what you mean. The governor and the mayor. Even Barbra Streisand was here earlier. We had to turn away reviewers from the *Times,* not to mention the *Globe* and the *Herald.* The owners don't want publicity. Isn't that marvelous? Talk about cachet. We couldn't be more pleased." His face sobered. "Have you heard anything about Veda."

I shook my head.

"Can I do anything to help? Anything at all?"

"I wish. That's a kind offer."

"I'm crazy about her, you know."

I rested a hand on his arm. "I do. I'd like you to meet my friend."

I introduced Carmen, and the three of us did a tour of the room. Since my last visit, Nick had hung eight-by-ten photographs beside the paintings.

Black-and-white images of corpses and human skeletons and emaciated children; photos of Auschwitz-Birkenau and Mauthausen and Belzec, Treblinka and Dachau, Sobibor and Bergen-Belsen; of GIs' shocked faces, the gas chambers and crematoriums; and more, much more.

"Oh, Nick, this is incredible. Horrible."

"Yes." He brushed a hand across his eyes. "No one should forget."

"No. Never." Here, again, red circles dotted the art. "Fabulous money changing hands."

"Yes. It will help them, the lost ones, in particular."

"I understand. Has anything—"

"Wait. I'd like you to meet Marie Pinkus. Her father …"

We met a wizened woman with dark eyes and a haunted smile and then a young man whose grandfather had survived the camps. On and on, Nick introduced us to groups of people, always mentioning Veda and her collaboration on the room and the show.

Feeling out of sorts and time, I finally put a hand on his arm. "Nick, wait. This is amazing, wonderful. But Carmen is leaving in the morning, and I've got some heavy cases going. I must ask you some things."

He snagged glasses of champagne for the three of us. "How can I help?"

"Has anything strange … out of the ordinary happened tonight?"

"Not a thing. I'd remember. Believe me. But I'll check with Stan and Alex. We try to cover different areas of an affair. My great sadness is that Veda couldn't be here, as she was such a huge part of assembling the Holocaust collection."

"I know." I'd hoped he'd know more. "You've had lots of sales."

He smiled, its warmth a reminder of why Veda found him so charming. "Oh, yes. It's amazing to me how many are able to pay such insane prices. These works are prizes in the art world. Even this one, clearly marked 'Not for Sale' was offered for." His long fingers brushed the Gauguin of two girls by the seashore.

"It's stunning," I said.

"Yes. It's from my personal collection. I planned to gift it to Veda at the close of the exhibition when I proposed. Yes, Tally, I was going to ask her to marry me. Now ..." He removed his glasses and rubbed his eyes.

I rested my hand on his arm. "They'll find her."

"Tally Ho, it's not that she's missing. It's that she's *gone*."

I shook my head. "She'll get better."

"Come, child, I've talked to her," he said. "In the hospital. She's ... not the same, Tally. Not our Veda."

I paused, then "No. No, she's not." Before I got too morose, I shifted the subject. I described Marlene and Andrew-as-a-woman Marsh. "Have you seen them?"

"Not that I recall," Nick said.

"See if Stan or Alex saw that couple, would you? It matters."

"Of course. Do you care to explain?"

"I can't. Not yet."

When we left, we carried with us the Wirth Gallery's guest list. Outside, the night pulsed with city lights. I pictured Kranak on his boat and wondered what he was doing or if he was alone or if he was with ...

A taxi responded to my waving arm, and Carmen and I piled inside.

"I'm glad to be out of there." I powered down the window and let the night air cool my face.

"Uh-huh," Carmen said.

After giving my address, I leaned back in the cab.

"I don't trust any of those artsy-fartsy types," Carmen said.

"Geesh, Carm. They're good people."

"Ayuh. I'll shut up."

"You'll never shut up."

She snorted.

I sighed. *Something* had gotten her going. "So what is it?"

"You don't want ta know."

"I do so."

The cab pulled in front of the apartment and we headed for the front door. I reached for Carmen, slowing her down.

"The light's out," I said. "Dammit."

"The porch light? All it needs is a——"

I pulled her away from the streetlamp into a crevice of dark. We'd make perfect targets. I slipped my cell phone from my purse and flipped it open.

"Crap," I hissed. "I forgot to charge it again. We can use yours."

"I didn't bring the stupid thing."

"Swell."

"C'mon," she said, tugging my arm. "Let's go in. Whatever it is, we can handle it."

I smiled. She was right. We could. "At least let's not sound like a herd of buffalo."

"You're the one who——"

"Oh, come on."

We took off our heels and held them like weapons. I got out my keys and we padded up the concrete steps. I glanced up to the second floor. Jake wasn't home.

Penny! If anyone hurt my dog, I'd . . .

"Quiet," Carmen said.

"Shush!"

I shined my keychain light on the door's lock. No scratches or marks or breaks in the mahogany. So no one appeared to have broken into the apartment. I still didn't trust the light being out.

I looked at Carmen as I turned the key. I raised one of my stiletto shoes, heel outward, and she did the same. I opened the door.

The hall light was out, too, and I felt the switch. It was in the "off" position. I was certain I'd left it on for Penny.

We crept down the hall toward the living room door. A soft glow seeped into the hall from beneath the door. Had I left on a light in the room? I couldn't recall.

I turned the handle. A squeak. I eased the door open. A soft glow from the back of the room. The back deck lamp was lit. It gave off little light, but enough so ...

I gasped. Someone sat on the sofa facing the fireplace. Another person sat in the club chair. A whine. Penny. But not in pain.

They appeared still—statues—but the sounds of labored breathing filled the room.

I held my breath as I flicked on the overhead light.

"Veda!" I rushed to the sofa. She was asleep, Penny beside her. She was snoring of all things. She looked fine. I choked back a sob.

"Tally!" Carmen said. *"Madre de dios!"*

I turned. John Noguchi leaned sideways in the club chair, his breathing labored, his pale shirt coated in what looked like blood.

I felt Veda's pulse. The beat was steady and strong. I drew the afghan over her, scooped up the phone, and ran over to Noguchi.

Carmen had ripped open his shirt. A nasty bullet hole oozed blood.

"I've got to stop the bleeding," she said.

I called 911 as I pulled a clean sheet from the linen closet. "Here."

Noguchi looked ashen in the light. His lips were gray, with lines fanning outward in exhaustion. His closed eyes twitched.

"What else can I do?" I asked. "Maybe some water?"

"No," she said. "This kind of wound. No."

"At least I can get a wet cloth for his lips." I was back in seconds, and as I daubed the cloth across his lips, he moaned.

"John," I said. "Can you hear me."

He nodded, the smallest of movements.

"Who did this to you?" I said.

He head moved back and forth.

"What can we do?"

The index finger of his left hand crooked toward me. I crouched down and leaned in, so he wouldn't strain too much.

"Dr. Barrow," he said, his voice reedy and faint. "Hide."

"You want me to hide her?"

"Yesssss," he whispered. "We were in Littleton."

"Massachusetts, John?"

"No," he gasped. "Hampshire. They found us and ... Marsh."

"The Marshes?" I said. "Are they the 'they'?"

He sighed and lost consciousness.

"Carmen, can you—"

Her lips tightened. "I can't do much. Just keep him comfortable. Let's get Veda out of here."

"Yes. Go wash up and change while I get him a blanket." She looked down, and her eyes widened at smears of blood covering her gorgeous dress. "It was a pain in the ass to wear, anyway."

I covered John Noguchi with a blanket, told Penny to guard him, and then Carmen and I carried Veda up the stairs to Jake's apartment. I unlocked the door, and we laid her on Jake's bed, beneath the covers.

"She's so tiny," Carmen said.

"I know. You don't notice it when she's ... herself. She's bigger than life."

"I wish we'd met before," Carmen said. "But, you know, she's a very lovable and loving woman."

"Yes, she is," I said. "I'm worried about her. She'll be frightened when she awakens in a strange place. Stay with her? I'll go down with John until the EMTs get here. He's in jeopardy, too. If whoever is doing this shot him once, I suspect they'll try again. I'll call Kranak. Maybe he can get a watcher for Noguchi."

She pushed her hands into the back pockets of her jeans. "And Veda?"

I pulled the covers up to Veda's chin. "I think we leave her kidnapped."

She pursed her lips. "I like it, but won't you then become the kidnapper?"

"Better that than Veda dead. The cops didn't do such a hot job guarding her, now did they."

"Ayuh."

A tremble from the bed. Carmen's hand went to Veda's forehead. "Damn," she said. "She's got a fever."

The wail of sirens had me zooming downstairs. Noguchi hadn't moved, and if anything, his pallor was worse. I ran to the door and opened it for the EMTs, who raced inside.

When they left, John Noguchi was breathing oxygen and getting fresh blood. They were taking him to Mass General.

They didn't know if he'd live.

I peered out the front window and watched the ambulance pull away. Boston PD had yet to arrive. On my way back upstairs, I called Kranak and filled him in on everything except Veda. He'd be furious that I kept her from him, but if I told him, he'd take over.

Now Kranak was on his way here, too, and I felt a spurt of guilty comfort. Back in Jake's bedroom, Veda was sleeping peacefully beneath a pile of blankets. Perhaps too peacefully. "Carmen?"

Her lips thinned and she shrugged. Bertha's words echoed in my heart that Veda would soon leave us.

I pulled a chair beside the bed. "Boston PD's coming, so's Kranak. We'll have a full house downstairs."

"What'll you tell them?" Carmen said.

"Not much. I hope Jake will let us keep her up here."

"You hope I'll stay." She ran a finger across Veda's gnarled hand that had crept out from the covers.

"You should go. I can hire someone who—"

"Won't take as good care of her as I will," she said. "Four days. The restaurant, my family. They can wait four days longer. So can I."

"Thank you, Carm." I hugged her.

She sniffled and pushed me away. "You are *so* full of sentimental crap."

"Who, me? I owe you big-time."

"Bet your ass."

I listened, thought I heard the cops. I peered out the window. The street was quiet. I realized I was wiped.

"Remember what I started to tell you in the taxi?" she said.

I straightened. "Taxi? No."

"That gangly kid, Alex? Nick Wirth's son?"

"Yeah. So?"

"You've known him forever, right?"

"In a way. He was at boarding school, and now he's in college. I haven't seen that much of him."

She wrapped a scrunchy around her Titian hair. "He's funky. When we came out of the ladies room, I'd swear I saw him talking to the woman you said was Andrew Marsh."

I walked back to the bed. "Really? Why didn't you say anything?"

"I wasn't sure who the kid was," she said.

I sat on the end of the bed. "I can't believe Alex Wirth knows the Marshes. It's too weird."

She frowned. "Weird? Oh, *really?* Any more than the other weird stuff that's going on around here?"

"Here? As opposed to good old normal Winsworth? Not! Do you remember what went on during my last visit? Huh?"

The door flew open and Jake barged into the apartment. "What the *hell* is happening?"

Simultaneously, sirens wailed outside. Boston's finest had arrived.

"Carmen'll fill you in," I said as I ran down the stairs.

My heel snagged on Jake's Persian rug, and I tumbled down the remaining two steps, hollering "Shit!" The door flew open as I landed on my bum before a plainclothes woman, gun drawn, and a brown-suited Kranak.

"I'm fine, people," I said, assessing that I'd broken no bones. Kranak held out a hand, which I took. Not only did my bum hurt, but I was mortified.

I hobbled into the living room and sank into the sofa. "There." I pointed to the empty chair, which was now stained in John Noguchi's blood. "He was here when we got home."

Kranak and the Boston detective pulled out their notepads, and I held forth. Veda would have been proud. I told all the facts, omitting only that Noguchi had arrived with Veda.

If he lived, he could tell them about Veda.

I prayed he'd live.

Chapter Twenty-eight

Kranak lingered after the Boston detective left with a note-book full of information on John Noguchi, his murdered daughter, Rose, and his wife and son.

Between my exhaustion and my deception, I had trouble talking to Kranak. He bristled with suspicion on his way out, and my guilt lasted until Carmen and Jake came downstairs to tell me they would tag team caring for and guarding Veda. We talked about bringing Bertha home, but decided to wait a day or two.

I crashed around three. It took me forever to fall asleep.

I awakened in a dark room, not my bedroom, but a strange place filled with black wisps that moved like wraiths through the air. I pushed up on my elbows—funny how they didn't hurt from the fall—and peered into the darkness.

Beneath me, the bed was soft and cozy and pliable. All I wanted to do was lie back down. But I couldn't.

I was trapped.

No doors, no windows, no way in or out.

I pushed myself to a sitting position and looked up.

The ceiling was open to the sky. A fresh breeze from the sea blew into the room. If I could scale the walls, I could get out.

I stood on the bed and found I was nowhere near the top of the wall. I bounced, trampoline-like, but couldn't reach the lip of the wall.

I closed my eyes. I was dreaming. Had to be. So I relaxed.

When I opened my eyes again, a ladder rested against the wall beside the bed. I got down and walked over to the ladder. It was smooth wood, soft to the touch, as if it had been repeatedly sanded and oiled. It felt wonderful.

I rubbed my hands up and down. Finally, I began to climb.

The ladder rungs hurt my bare feet, but I didn't mind. I reached the top of the wall just as the ladder ended. I peered down.

Outside was sunny, with puffy clouds frolicking like sheep across the blue sky. Veda stood below me, waving at me, beckoning, wearing a crooked smile, as if she were apologizing for her foolishness of late.

I'm coming!

I was about to dive off the top of the wall, when little Rose Noguchi appeared beside her.

And then I understood. Veda would die, and I would be the one to find her killer ... unless I died, too.

The following morning, I checked on Veda, Carmen, and Jake, and was thrilled to find Veda sitting up in bed while Carmen fed her some oatmeal. Jake was carrying on about something, to the amusement of Veda and Carmen. Penny crawled up on Veda's bed, performed a couple of circles, and nestled against her legs.

Quite the convivial picture, if you didn't think about Veda's attempted murder, the loss of her mind, or the fact that someone was still trying to do her in.

I left them that way, calmed by a feeling of safety I hadn't felt in days.

That sensation abandoned me the minute I walked through the doors of OCME, around eleven.

The lobby appeared unusually quiet, and a security officer I didn't know asked me for my credentials when I attempted to key myself in to the autopsy suites and the coolers.

"Sorry, ma'am," he said, in a far too jovial way.

"Sorry about what, officer?"

"We've got a new lock and a new combination, so unless you're on my list, I'm afraid I can't let you out back."

Ah, that feel of a slow simmer I knew too well of late in this place. "Tally Whyte."

He tapped some computer keys, tapped some more, and then looked up. "I'm afraid the autopsy suites and the coolers are off limits to you."

"Really?" was all I could say.

He saluted me. I almost gave him the finger, but smiled instead and headed for MGAP.

I turned the knob to my office, found it locked, and fished for my keys. "Hey, Gert," I called across the small hall.

I pushed my key into the lock. It failed to turn. I tried again. Ditto.

"Don't bother," Gert said as she dragged me into MGAP's central office.

"What the hell is going on?" I said.

She handed me a mug of hazelnut coffee and wagged her finger at one of the empty chairs.

"Ethridge has reappropriated your office for OCME," she said.

I didn't need this crap. "We rent the space from the state, Gert. It's ours."

"You tell Miss Bitch that."

"At least are all my files out of there?"

"Nope. They're all inside." She smiled. "But I got a locksmith coming. A friend."

"You're brilliant, as usual." I couldn't have a fit about

Ethridge right then. I had too much to do. "Just pretend I wasn't here. Ethridge and Fogarty will hear about it, but I can't get into it with them right now." I looked at the board where we posted the current cases and assignments.

"Things seem pretty quiet at the moment."

"Not too bad." She popped her ubiquitous Bazooka— that day's color was pink—and showed me the book where we kept additional assignments. "Donna's doing great and so is Shawn. We're okay for now, unless there's a big pileup on ninety-five."

"Not funny," I said.

"So, whatja got?"

I told her my plan, and the following morning I was on the road to Littleton, New Hampshire.

The plan—a definite long shot—was to see if Marlene and Andrew Marsh were recognized in the town of Littleton. I drove a rental car north on Route 93, headed for upstate New Hampshire.

Noguchi had whispered Littleton, and I'd been there once, on a trip years earlier. He also said "they" and "Marsh," which I took to mean the Marshes.

They didn't even *know* Veda. But maybe Noguchi hadn't been saying "Marsh" at all, but something else entirely.

The more I thought about it, the more I came to believe that John Noguchi was the real target. I hoped Littleton could give me some answers.

The drive was smooth, with little traffic. I tuned in NHPR, and grooved on the Diane Rehm show. Her interview with an author of a new Betty Friedan biography kept my mind off Veda and dead children and the two men in my life.

Fluffy clouds drifted across the bright blue sky, reminding me that spring was in the air, at least in Boston. I cracked the window and the air surprised me with a hint of winter.

As the miles clipped by, the terrain grew more stark and

more beautiful. Although the landscape was far different from the Maine coast, I pictured Winsworth and Hank and home.

Would I ever be home?

Less than three hours later, Littleton appeared, nestled in the White Mountains close to Vermont. Main Street was quaint and cute, and more Victorian than Peterborough or Temple. I'd call it "funky," the same word used by Pricilla Magee to describe a place in upstate New Hampshire that was the destination for Andrew Marsh. I hoped I was right that the Marshes were hiding out up here and that John Noguchi had spotted them.

I suspected not much went on in Littleton in early April, normally one of northern New England's least appealing months.

So the people in town might recognize Andrew or Marlene or Bella. Or all three. Word got around in small towns. And if I'd done my research, I should get around, too.

This far north, winter dug in deep. Snow always capped Mount Washington, but it also dotted the woods and remained on hillsides and in crooks and crevices where the sun seldom visited.

Main Street's sidewalks bustled with people, and I passed a nice-sized bookshop and drooled at what looked like a fascinating craft store. A Near East dress shop and a bead shop and another craft store. Some video stores, what looked like neat restaurants, a movie theater, and even a Wal-Mart was in town.

A nice place ... a good place to hunker in. Definitely still a funky place.

Why had John Noguchi brought Veda here and who had shot him?

Thayers Inn on Main Street was a huge, white, quadruple-pillared building in a majestic style. An immense cupola, many windows, three floors—wow, it was grand.

Inside, the maroon carpet hushed my footfalls as I wheeled my overnight bag down the dark hall. The old inn oozed age and majesty and just a soupçon seediness. I could almost picture a gunfight taking place in her halls.

I checked in and found myself peering out the window of a first-floor room once occupied by Robert Dole, of all people. Good God! The window gave me a good vantage point of the street, for which I was thankful.

I spread-eagled on the bed, pooped. I'd been racing for days, and the race was yet to be won or lost. No time for resting, for sure.

I got up to straighten my clothes in the mirror and jumped.

I'd forgotten I was incognito as Emma Nash, the antithesis of Tally.

Emma Nash was a confection of Kathleen Lauria when, a couple of years earlier, my life was in jeopardy. Dark straight hair, bangs, flats, red lipstick, glasses, and a Talbot's outfit right down to the bowed shoes straight out of their catalog. I wore eyeliner and mascara and shadow, something I rarely did, and I'd flattened my B-cup breasts to an A.

I heard Lauria's voice. "Hunch over more, Tally!" I flopped back on the bed, so sad I was near tears. My chest tightened and I stuttered out a breath. Kathleen should never have died.

I didn't see her often, but Kathleen Lauria had been a constant in my life after our first brush with death and danger. I hadn't even had time to properly mourn her passing.

I slipped off my shoes and massaged my feet with the peppermint cream I always carried. The tingling revived me some.

Time to start the hunt.

I walked down Main Street carrying my purse and a photo of Andrew Marsh that I'd doctored in Photoshop. In the photo he wore a similar outfit to the one I'd seen him in at The Toadstool. He looked pretty darned good as a woman.

I also carried a picture of Andrew, the man, as well as Marlene, his wife. I'd even Photoshopped myself as Emma Nash into a photo with the couple.

I tried the craft store and the Indian shop and the natural foods store. No luck. Fueled by a PowerBar, I continued on to a women's clothing shop, a bike store, and the bookstore. All were strikeouts.

I took a break around four and called Carmen. Veda was doing well, her fever, broken. When I accessed my messages, Kranak had left several. I was tempted to call, but I didn't know what to say to him.

Back at it, I tried the furniture store and a kitchenware store that was to die for. More blank stares and shrugs at the photos.

Around six I hit a bunch of pizza parlors and the grocery store. That night I ate at The Beal House, an antique inn with great food and atmosphere. No one recognized the Marshes.

Talk about a bunch of strikeouts.

I climbed into bed with Hillerman's latest novel, but instead of reading, I spent a few minutes on the self-pity train. I missed Penny and Hank and Kranak and Veda and Bertha and Carmen and Gert. I missed MGAP. I told myself to think, but knew that wouldn't work.

I yelled at myself to stop it, read a chapter of the novel, and doused the lights. I turned on my belly and slept.

The following morning, I awakened believing I was off base. Maybe the Marshes had never been to Littleton. But then why would John Noguchi come here? Why say "Marsh?"

I toured more shops, the library, and several banks, again with no luck. Wind snapped at my skirt as I left the library. I pulled on my baseball cap to prevent my wig from experiencing liftoff. I returned to the bookstore and gathered all the free fliers and bought a variety of newspapers hoping to learn something. I left my name and cell phone with the girl on the desk.

I felt a strange, ill-defined urgency. I was off in my theory about the deaths of Rose and Eva. Maybe the Marshes weren't involved. But I was sure they were. If I only understood *why* the children were dying.

The killings felt so orchestrated, the timing so perfect.

Time ... It was nibbling at my heels. Carmen would leave in a few days. I was MIA at work, which would set off alarm bells with Fogarty and Kranak.

Frustrated at unearthing no leads, I packed up, checked out of Thayers Inn, and headed for Temple, NH.

One wrong turn and three hours later, I pulled into the Marshes' driveway. I tugged my wig off and released my breasts, and felt half-human again.

Next door, the Noguchi home was dark and silent. A large maple branch had fallen on the front lawn. No one there to remove it. I hoped John Noguchi was improving. Teresa, too. And how was Silas coping?

The Marsh's yellow house looked even more deserted than the Noguchis's. Someone had shuttered all the windows on the Marsh house. I drove around back, so the car was hidden from the street. It had rained, and tree trunks glistened, and puddles pocked the driveway and walk. I slipped my flashlight and latex gloves into my pocket and stepped from the car. My left foot sank into the mud.

The glories of spring in New England.

I locked the car, pulled on my gloves, and walked to the back door. I heard Kranak's voice chiding me, and I mentally told him to quiet down.

I first tried the back door with no luck. But old houses often had ill-fitting windows that failed to lock, and sometimes people wouldn't even bother to lock them. I hoped I was in luck with the Marshes. I began with the window next to the door, but couldn't budge the shutters. I moved counter-clockwise around the house. On the third window, I pulled open the ill-fitting shutters and pushed up an unlocked, double-hung window.

I climbed into a darkened, shade-drawn room. A musty smell infused the air. I sneezed. "Damn."

Dark permeated the house from the shutters being closed. I was tempted to turn on some lights, but instead flicked on my flashlight. I aimed the narrow beam at the floor and then the walls. I remembered this house well.

I stood at the rear of the mudroom. A basket held mail and papers, and I rifled through them. An air traffic controller's newsletter, some fliers on literary and historical meetings, stuff from South Meadow School addressed to Bella Marsh's parents, a *Newsweek* dated the week the Marshes had gone missing.

I left the mudroom and entered the kitchen. The old house felt damp and chilly. I imagined Rose and Bella at the old black oak table eating milk and cookies.

I saw Rose's face clearly, more clearly than Bella's.

A sense of urgency had me opening drawers and doors, finding nothing, and moving on down the center hall to the parlor on the left, where I'd been before. The damask couches and oil portraits looked the same, and I was surprised that the Marshes had left the silver tea service on the sideboard. They'd certainly departed in a rush.

I peered in drawers and opened doors and looked behind expensive-looking paintings. I found nothing. My quest felt futile. In an old house like the Marshes, it would be easy to hide anything that wasn't meant for a stranger's eyes.

I crossed the hall to the second parlor that they'd obviously used as a family room. My flashlight scanned comfy couches and a large TV flanked by well-stocked bookshelves. I examined the history-heavy titles, but found nothing noteworthy. A smaller floor bookshelf was stuffed with books for kids, and my heart squeezed for Bella. A long dining table filled the back of the room and a door led directly to the kitchen.

More searching, more futility. In the two days I'd been gone from Boston, I'd found zip.

Boards creaked as I made my way upstairs. I worked my way through the huge master bedroom, Bella's room, and the guest room. I was about to enter the hall bathroom, when a draft of icy air suddenly brushed my face.

O-kay.

I stepped quickly back into Bella's bedroom and doused my flash. I took shallow breaths and waited. Maybe I was crazy, but I was convinced that the cool air was a warning from Rose.

The creak of a stair tread got my attention.

Oh crap.

I got out my pepper spray. I could hear Bertha and Veda saying how I should carry a gun.

I eased back into the room. Whoever was there, for whatever reason, I knew it wasn't healthy for me to confront them.

I turned, felt another whoosh of air. Then something heavy crashed into me, and I slammed onto the floor.

Chapter Twenty-nine

I tried to jab my elbows backwards, but he'd jammed a knee into my back.

"Get off me, asshole!" I barked.

He or she did, but the cold chill of a gun barrel at the back of my head replaced the weight.

"What do you want?" I hated the tremor in my voice.

"Who are you?" he said. The voice was male and guttural and low.

"I could ask you the same thing."

"But I'm the one holding the weapon," he said. Laughter and a hint of an accent.

"Persuasive. Since you don't appear to want to instantly shoot me. What are you doing here?"

"Never mind that."

"Let me sit up." I could grab his balls and twist. But maybe the gun would go off. *Cripes!*

"Bossy," he said.

His weight lifted off me, and I breathed deeply.

"Go ahead, sit up," he said. "But stay on the floor."

I pushed myself to a sitting position and gingerly danced my fingers across my face. Damn, but it hurt. So did my sprained arm. I wished I could see him. "Now what?"

"I was looking for the Marshes," he said. Definitely an accent.

"Me, too."

"No, you were looking for something in the Marshes' house."

"Well, yes, but ... can I at least light my flashlight?" I didn't sense that he was going to hurt me.

"No, you cannot."

He grew still, and a bead of sweat slid down my face. My eyes finally adjusted, and his silhouette showed his hand with the smallish gun aimed right at me.

I should jump him. I ...

"Hold out your hands!" he said.

Did I dare? Those who went meekly into the night ...

"Do it!"

I was acting like a coward, a fool. I went to shove him, but he grabbed my hands, wrapped something around my wrists and tightened. I bit back an "ouch."

He bent down and hooked his hand through my left arm. He pulled me up, but I refused to help.

"Come on," he said. "You're not so small."

I relented. Standing, I pulled my arm away from him. "I will not be a lamb to slaughter, damn you." His soft chuckle infuriated me. "Stop acting like some histrionic mystery person. Do what you're going to do and leave me alone."

"What a drama queen, curly top."

"Curly top, my ass." I kicked him and ran.

I flew down the stairs with him charging after me, raced down the hall, through the kitchen and mudroom and to the—

My long hair was grabbed and yanked. "Shit!"

I flipped onto my back. I tried to catch my breath, but

couldn't. A booted foot pressed down on my chest. "Screw you!" I screamed. It came out like a whisper.

He dragged me to my feet. "You *are* amusing. Come, curly top, we're going for a road trip."

We bumped along unfamiliar back roads at the speed of a slug, which gave me way too much time to think. I could finally see him, and I was surprised at his age—he might have been in his late sixties or early seventies. Given that, he possessed an unusual strength for a man his age.

His newish flannel shirt was sharply pressed and his chinos seemed, for some indefinable reason, not to fit the man. He was dark-skinned, perhaps Caribbean, but I wasn't sure about that. His iron-gray stubble gave him a scruffy look that was belied by his strong chin and high cheekbones. His longish gray hair was twirled into Rasta locks that poked out from an ill-fitting blue Red Sox cap. He wore tight brown leather gloves that seemed incongruous with his costume. Then I realized it *was* a costume. For whom and why I couldn't imagine.

Even sitting, he appeared to be a large man. Except for the semiautomatic gun resting in his lap, he was quite a character.

Bound as I was, I should have been more afraid. The guy gave off strange vibes that I found confusing.

In Concord, he got on Route 93 north, retracing the path I'd taken earlier that day, but in the opposite direction. He never glanced over, never took his eyes from the road. We were driving through the White Mountains National Forest when he slipped on his Ray Bans.

He sipped constantly from a green plastic travel mug. Coffee? I imagined prying the lid off and flinging the hot liquid in his face. But he wasn't that dumb. Anyway, the liquid would be lukewarm at best, and all I'd do was piss him off.

I tried to read him. The messages were mixed. I didn't

think he'd rape me, although I believed he'd kill me if need be. He was on a mission, and now I was a part of it.

We finally got off 93. The back roads were narrow and curved, and he slowed accordingly. I decided to pull the car door handle and roll out. I could make it. Better than being trapped in a car with a violent stranger.

He appeared focused on the drive. I inched my hands closer to the door handle, while stealing a glance at my kidnapper. He was studying the road, curiously intent, his arms bent, torso leaning forward.

I found the handle and waited. Trees lined the narrow, serpentine road. A curve, all I needed was a curve—he was sure to slow—and I'd roll out, then run into the trees. *Take it easy, girl. Take it easy.*

Up ahead, a bend. I took two slow calming breaths.

One, two, pull ... Crap. The door didn't open.

A slow smile spread across his face. "I do love these childproof locks."

"Bite me." I slumped in the seat and began cooking up a new plan.

I couldn't believe I fell asleep. Riding in a car always did that to me. When I awakened, I was furious at myself. I bet I'd snored, too. How the hell I could sleep in the clutches of a ... what? I still hadn't figured that one out.

"Have a nice *schläfchen,* curly top?"

"You're not American. And how did you know in the dark I had curly hair? So what's the deal? Who are you?"

"Those questions require many answers, ones I'm not prepared to give."

"Where are you from?"

"Well, mon, can't you tell?" he said in a fake Jamaican accent.

"I see." Maybe I could bite off the wrist restraints. These were the kind Kranak used when he needed to subdue a subject. He'd brag how foolproof they were. "A chameleon."

He smiled. All his teeth were capped. Vanity? I didn't think so. More like something had happened to his permanent ones. Hunger? Bad hygiene? Fights?

"You're getting warmer," he said.

I could grab the wheel. But I really didn't want to end up smooshed against a tree. Still, the man made me nervous. More than nervous. Beneath his mellow, near-jocular demeanor, I recognized a killer. But of whom? Of what?

I moved my hands toward the wheel.

He lifted the gun and pointed it straight at me. His eyes never left the road. "Please believe that I would rather not shoot you. But I will, curly top. Put your hands in your lap and leave them there."

I did as told. I believed him. I looked out the window. I needed time to think.

"How about you tell me where we're going," I said.

"Delighted. We're headed for Bethlehem."

Maybe forty minutes later, my kidnapper's posture shifted. His face tightened, and he tilted his head left, then right, as if trying to ease some discomfort. He frowned, and then he removed his gloves.

I gasped. Crisscrossed scars and puckers of skin from severe burns covered his hands. He reached into his shirt pocket and fished out two pills. He downed them with his coffee. Seconds later, I sensed his body relax. He replaced the gloves as he drove.

I started to say something when we passed a sign that read: LITTLETON 16 miles, BETHLEHEM, 10 miles.

His eyes traveled to me. "Do you get it now?"

I paused. I didn't want to blow it. This was a thoughtful, bright man. "Perhaps."

"You do, Tally Whyte. You are simply being a cautious puss."

"And you, Sir No Name, are playing a game with me that I can't say I like. Obviously this has to do with the Marshes or whoever it is that's up here. The people that shot John Noguchi."

"Yes. And no." He pulled the car off the road and parked in a copse of trees.

My nerves came alive. This would be a perfect kill spot. We were in Nowheresville and hadn't seen a house for many minutes. No malls, no people. Just woods. Lots and lots of woods.

He slid the keys out and began to open a small Leatherman.

I again tried the door handle, frantic to escape. "I won't go easily."

"You're not going anywhere." His tone wasn't jocular, but deadly serious.

"Then what the hell …"

He aimed the knife at me, moved it forward, slapped a steadying hand on my shoulder and clipped my restraint.

My hands sprung free. Each was numb, and I flexed them repeatedly to bring back the feeling.

"Why do that here? Now?" I said.

"Because you will be an asset, which is why I bothered to bring you along." He flipped the knife back into its socket, folded the Leatherman, and put the keys back in the ignition.

"You know my name," I said. "I assume you know who I am."

"I do. And I know Veda Barrow from the old country. And Bertha, too. I know you're a homicide counselor and that you are trying to find the person responsible for killing two children. I, too, am here to catch a killer of children. Did you know that he has killed before?"

"No."

"Many times. Many. The *Sins of the Father* … A cliché, but one Veda recognized from something long ago. It was she who called me to this country. And yet I have been unable to talk with her. Sadly, I failed to catch him before he killed Eva Lange."

"He. Who's 'he'?"

"We will see."

I looked at the man—a strong, kind face, aged, but beautiful. A face a person might trust. Yet I realized he could be involved with the attempt on Veda's life. Perhaps he was lying about their friendship. Maybe it was this stranger who'd gone after the children, and now he was hunting Bella. I glanced down at my reddened wrists.

"So tell me, Tally," he said. "What is wrong with Veda? I am perplexed. I have tried to see her, but cannot. Something is going on, and so I've held off contacting you. Does that make sense?"

Perfect, except I didn't trust him. "No, not when I don't even know your name or how you know Veda."

His stare heated my cheeks.

"And ...?" I said.

"I'm trying to decide if I can trust you."

"Well, while you're giving me your stare of death, how about we don't run off the road."

His laugh boomed through the car. "Just as Veda said. My name is Milosh. I am part Romany, what you Americans call Gypsy. Does it make sense now?"

I suspected, but I wanted him to tell me. "Not really. No."

"You're playing me now, curly top. But that's all right, after what I put you through."

A sign for Bethlehem appeared, and he flicked on his turn signal. Minutes later, we turned off 93 for Route 302. It was the same exit I'd taken for Littleton, except I'd turned left and we now took a right.

"Please go on," I said.

"Veda and Bertha and I met as young children in the camps. The Nazis took Romany, too, you know. My father was Moroccan, but my mother was Romany. They killed her, along with so many others."

"The Nazis tortured you, didn't they? Your hands."

They tightened around the steering wheel. "Not as badly

as some others. They gave me my scars, but they also gave me a mission. I do not give up. I am relentless. I am, in more colorful terms, a Nazi hunter. And the Marshes are my prey."

Nazis? The Marshes? They were too young to be Nazis, unless he meant members of Aryan Nation or some other cult. I wasn't getting this at all. Milosh projected a terrible sort of purpose. His body language conveyed his intensity. I believed *he* believed what he'd said. But it made no sense to me.

"Milosh, you've confused me. You mean German Nazis from World War Two?"

"Yes. Those are the only ones I hunt."

"But the Marshes aren't old enough."

"No, they're not." He grinned. "Patience."

Talk about a frustrating conversation.

We drove through the town of Bethlehem, New Hampshire. Sweet shops, smaller than Littleton, slow and sleepy. The town passed in a blink and right outside we turned right on an unmarked road. A tumbledown barn in faded red was followed by an old farmhouse that tilted left, as if it had been pushed over by the wind. Massive boulders poked from the brown earth that was trying desperately to become spring green. But the wind slashed and the temps were still mean this far north in the state. A soft rain began, and soon the wipers beat a rhythm that reminded me of a ticking clock … or a time bomb.

Alongside the road, a new Cape was followed by a double-wide trailer, neither of which fit the landscape half as well as those other old buildings.

"So what are you going to do?" I said. "Kill the Marshes?"

"Not unless that's necessary. I mean to return them to Germany."

"They look English. They sound American. You're telling me they're German?"

"Born and bred. Marsh is a fine old Teutonic name. Of

course they are German. But, curly top, they have been killing little children to wash away the guilt they feel. The fathers of both Marshes had high ranks in the death camps. The fathers took many, many lives. So you see, the Marshes are killing children—German and Japanese and Italian—as sacrificial lambs. You think on that. I must check my GPS."

He pulled a handheld machine from the glove compartment and scanned it. I kept hoping his inattention to the road didn't get us killed.

I processed what he'd said. Certainly it was possible. To wash away guilt, people do all sorts of horrific things. If revulsion with their Nazi heritage was strong enough, I could see them killing. Maybe. Boy, but it was a stretch.

They'd have to sustain a level of passion and delusional thinking over long periods of time.

"I'm having trouble with your theory—"

"It's no theory," he said. He set the machine beside him and, at the next corner, turned left onto a serpentine road set between tall granite walls and slowed down. "We're almost there."

My stomach tightened. "First off, I have to pee. Second, I don't want to be a part of your big scheme. I want to find the Marshes, too, but I'm not at all convinced of your rather grandiose ideas."

"That is your problem, not mine."

"What, the peeing or the convincing?"

"Both."

"There has to be more," I said. "Something is off."

"Veda always said you were a clever one."

He glanced at the GPS, and we soon came to a break in the granite walls darkened by the rain. He made a sharp left, and about a hundred feet down the long dirt driveway, pulled off the road.

"Now what?" I said.

"We walk." He picked up his gun and signaled me to get

out of the car. "Don't run. It's a waste of time. Nothing out here but Nazis. A whole nest of them."

"*What*? A nest?"

"Patience," he said.

"I'm out of it, goddammit." I walked behind a large bush. Nothing like peeing outdoors in the rain.

When I returned to the car, I was shocked at the mini arsenal Milosh had piled on top of the car trunk. He was in the process of strapping a huge knife to his arm. He put his coat over it, but I saw the break in the sleeve, the better to reach inside.

The small, hideous-looking gun was … "That's an *Uzi!*"

He nodded. "In fact, it's called a micro *Uzi*. Quite amazing, isn't it?"

"You said you didn't want to hurt the Marshes!"

He lifted his head. His eyes had grown cold. I felt his utter detachment and shivered.

He picked up a small 9mm. "Here. It's a Glock. Subcompact model. Perfect for you. You'll need something for protection."

I held up my hands. "No way. I don't even know that these people have done what you say they have."

His lips thinned. "Believe me, they have. You should not be so squeamish. Neither Bertha nor Veda were. They'd want you to take the gun."

I took it and sat on a large boulder. Maybe I could diffuse the situation. All I knew was I didn't want to want to walk down that road with Rambo in the lead.

"Let's think about this for a minute," I said. "If they're hunting children as sacrificial lambs, I can understand Rose's death. Her ancestry is half-Japanese, although it's Japanese American. Her 'race' was culpable during World War Two, which is really stupid, I might add. But psychologically it would make a warped sort of sense to people in desperate need of absolution."

He shook his head. "So what are you saying here? C'mon, we've got to go."

"So why Eva?" I said.

He slung the *Uzi* over his shoulder and began to walk down the side of the dirt road. I ran after him.

"Eva?" he said. "The answer is painfully obvious. Eva Lange's ancestry is German, of course."

"No, it's not."

He stopped so abruptly I slammed into his back. He turned, and I saw fury tighten his face. "The child was of German ancestry or, perhaps, Austrian or Polish. 'Lange' is German."

"But Eva was a foster child, and her real name was Zimmerman. She was of Jewish heritage. So where's the absolution in killing her?"

He didn't answer, but tore down the road. I raced after him, imagining him Rambo-ing into the camp, bullets flying. I ran faster.

Chapter Thirty

Bushes slapped my face, and suddenly my ankle twisted. I flew forward, caught a tree branch with my sprained arm. I ran on, my arm throbbing. My panting was loud in my ears, my eyes half-blinded by the rain. The gun I carried must have weighed a hundred pounds. At least it felt like it.

Up ahead, Milosh's Rasta locks streamed behind him, as his body bladed through the rain, his armament slapping his back. Perhaps he *was* a superhero.

All of a sudden we stumbled into a clearing with two small cabins and a tent. Chickens scratched in the dirt, an unlatched door slapped in the breeze, and rain poured into an open window. I saw no one. A feeling of abandonment pervaded the place.

Muddy tire tracks and footprints marked the soil.

"What's going on?" I said.

"They're gone," he said. "Fewer than I thought. Look." He pointed toward something lying in the dirt.

I walked beside Milosh toward the clump. As we neared, I

saw a hand poking from what looked like a pile of clothing near a small puddle of red. "It's a body."

"Two. Or someone waiting for us." He aimed his *Uzi* at the body.

"Don't fire!" I said. "They could be hurt."

He scooched down, and with the end of the gun raised the blue cloth covering the faces. I still couldn't clearly see.

He pressed two fingers to the man's neck. "He's gone. She is, too."

I crouched down and gasped. "It's Charley. One of the techs from the medical examiner's office." I sat back on my heels, stunned.

"Curly top? A friend?"

"I've known him for years. He must have been the one who helped the killer get inside The Grief Shop and leave Rose. And the other?"

He caught some rain in his palm and wiped it across the woman's mud-smeared face. Shock rippled through me again.

"My God. I didn't know her real name. I knew her as Brooke. I met her at the hospital. She tried to warn me about Veda's murder, but then she disappeared. But from what I've learned, she was involved in it. She was young."

"I'm sorry," Milosh said. "Veda is at risk because of me."

He donned gloves, and then rifled thought their clothes. He then went from cabin to cabin. When he exited the tent, his face was even more grim.

"We must hurry," he said. "To see lives wasted like this … But after all, what could I expect? Death is Glaumann's signature."

I stood. "Glaumann? Who the hell is Glaumann?"

I sat beside Milosh as we drove through the New Hampshire woods, only this time my hands weren't bound. We were headed for the Marshes' home, where I'd left my car.

Long minutes of silence passed after we left the dreadful camp. The guns, the rain-soaked bodies, the pool of blood—it all felt surreal.

At a pay phone in Franconia, he alerted the police to the bodies at the camp. He swiftly returned to the car.

"This is worse than you were expecting, isn't it?"

"*Ma-sh-llah!*" he said.

"What?"

"As God wills! I must find the Marshes. With Glaumann on the scene, they will be pressed to kill another child. He is a monster. He lives for these killings. And I fear this time little Bella Marsh will not be so lucky."

I saw Bella and felt a terrible fear. "Please tell me about the Marshes and who this Glaumann is."

Silence again. Our wet clothes steamed up the cab of the car. He flipped on the defroster, and the air slowly cleared.

"The Brotherhood of the Pure," he finally said. "That's what they're called. They formed long after the war. A generation of mostly German offspring and grandchildren of Nazi officers. The children were deeply ashamed of their heritage and what their parents had done during World War Two. They particularly despised the death camps. They would meet and talk and pray. That was all.

"One day, perhaps twenty years ago, a stranger entered their midst, one Herr Hans Glaumann. The group was harmless, until Glaumann fed his theories to them, much like someone would ferment wine, causing an actual chemical reaction. Glaumann knew what to say and how to say it. He insisted that if a child was sacrificed by The Brotherhood, then the children and grandchildren of those Nazi killers would be absolved of their parents' sins."

"One of the oldest myths," I said. "That if we sacrifice that which we love, we will be absolved. I am reminded of Agamemnon's sacrifice of his daughter Iphigenia, and Abraham's sacrifice of Isaac, and of course, Christ is God's sacrificial lamb."

"He died for our sins," Milosh said.

"Wrapped in enough myth and mystery, I can see weak souls buying some crazy absolution through sacrifice. I would bet that Glaumann is quite charismatic."

Milosh smiled. "Indeed, he is. And old, with a long white beard and bushy white eyebrows and startling blue eyes. At least that's how he looked ten years ago, the last time I saw him face to face."

"You sound unfortunately intimate with him."

"I am, curly top. I first knew him in the camps. He was young then, and vigorous in his pursuit of alleged science. He was particularly fond of torturing children like myself for his experiments."

I turned away so Milosh wouldn't see how his words had moved me. I'd seen the photos, heard the words from Veda and Bertha. The searing pain I felt was little compared to the incomprehensible suffering experienced in the camps. I'd swear we would still hear their voices a millennium later.

And then there was little Rose, comforting me with "*Hushhhh. Hushhh.*" I smelled those roses and her face swam before me, flush with life. Warmth suffused my body. It began at my feet and fingers and worked inward to ease the hurt that cramped my soul.

"Tally?" he said.

"Um, sorry. So Glaumann commandeered this cult, which he professed was to heal sins, but was really for the pleasure of killing children again."

"And more. Herr Glaumann has had many agendas over time. Money is not the least of them."

"What about the Marshes?" He turned onto 101. We were nearing Temple.

"The Marshes ... Sad. From what I can tell, they were living a fine life here in the U.S. They had Bella, and all was well. I suspect Andrew Marsh always liked to dress as a woman. But they kept that hidden until Glaumann entered the picture. How he knew them, I have no idea. But he sucked them into The Brotherhood using his usual method of guilt and absolution. He's failed with some, but not, unfortunately, with the Marshes and the two poor souls dead back at the camp."

"Sad and horrible."

"Yes. This is the end of it. Others and I destroyed The Brotherhood's operations in Europe, Glaumann's real base of power. He knows the U.S. is his final act. He's desperate now."

The rain let up, and the sun appeared low on the horizon. The world looked normal, but we were talking insanity.

"Why is Glaumann making the killings so obvious?"

"I don't know. These are showy killings. Especially leaving Rose Noguchi at the medical examiner's office. There is much I don't understand."

"What I don't understand is how Veda got involved in all this."

Milosh nodded. "As I said, Veda brought me into this when she recognized 'Sins of the Father.' She has worked behind the scenes with me for many years. Glaumann found out she was a problem, one he could solve by killing her. I thank God that John Noguchi's loyalty proved true. You have said Veda is safe. Now we must look to the Marshes. They're the key to finding Glaumann. He knows this, and he will try to kill them, too."

Milosh grew silent again. I began to recognize scenery and realized we'd almost arrived in Temple.

"Now what?" I said.

"Now? I ache to wrap my hands around his throat and squeeze. To feel bone and cartilage break beneath fingers that he scarred. To watch him gasp for—"

"Milosh, don't," I said. "I understand. But that would damage you far more than the monster."

His teeth gleamed beneath his broad smile. "Oh, curly top, it would not."

Milosh flexed his hands on the steering wheel. I could almost feel the pain of those scars. We turned into the Marshes' driveway, and Milosh instantly bristled. "Get down!" He raised the Uzi.

"Don't!" I said.

SWAT police carrying guns and wearing helmets surrounded the car. Milosh could fire, but we'd die with a certainty.

A bullhorn demanded we leave the vehicle with our hands in the air. Someone would open our doors for us.

We stepped from the car, Milosh on the driver's side and me from the passenger side. I held my hands high, petrified I'd twitch and that would be it.

A bear of a trooper grabbed me, and I shrieked. He squeezed me so tight I had to fight for a breath.

"Kranak?" I finally wheezed out.

"How the fuck could you get into such a mess?"

Kranak and I sat at the Marshes' kitchen table. A damp chill seeped into the house, a stark contrast to the smoldering heat in Kranak's eyes. He was a large man at all times, but in his body armor, he was immense. He engulfed the room, and if I hadn't known him so well, I would have been terrified. As it was, all I wanted to do was hug him and tell him everything was all right. Which, of course, it wasn't.

A nameless police officer slid a Styrofoam container of tea on the table for Kranak and one for me that held coffee. The officer whispered something in Kranak's ear, then left.

I drank slowly, trying to delay the inevitable and gather wits scattered across all of New Hampshire.

"I've had a long day, Rob," I said. "Let's just forget it."

"Screw forget it. I could strangle you."

Ohhhh boy, this was Kranak at his most angry. "So when did you join the *commandos?*"

He snorted. "Stop with the quips. That Milosh guy has one scary rep. I don't think I've ever been this pissed at you."

"That's your problem."

He pushed himself up from the table and stormed over. I squirmed. I'd never seen Kranak's fury directed at me. Not like this. "Rob, what—"

He pulled me to my feet and kissed me, hard. I grew dizzy with passion. I cupped his face and pulled him closer. God, he felt like home. He tasted sweet and hot, like cloves and warm honey.

I couldn't get enough of him. I desperately wished he'd touch me everywhere, slide inside me, fill me.

"Sarge?"

Kranak pushed me away, but slowly, gently, and I wanted to melt back into him. I ached. His eyes said he did, too.

"Jesus," he whispered.

"Me, too," I said.

I peeked on tiptoe over Kranak's shoulder. A young officer stood in the doorway, all red-cheeked, eyes glued to the floor. "Sarge," he said. "We got a problem out here."

"What is it, Officer Drist?" Kranak said. His hands cradled my cheeks and his eyes seared mine.

"The prisoner wants a phone call," the officer said.

"Give him one."

"Um, we need you to come out and sign."

Kranak gave me a final look, released me, and pounded out the door. I slumped into the chair.

I might have dozed. When the screen door slapped, I bounced up and turned. Not Kranak, but that same fresh-faced officer who'd called to him earlier.

"The sergeant said to make sure you had everything," he

said, still fascinated with his toes. "And then I was to drive you home."

My nails dug into the table. "Where's Sergeant Kranak?"

"He drove into Boston with the prisoner."

"Where, exactly?"

"I don't know, ma'am."

"Did he leave me a message?"

The kid chewed his lip. "I, um, don't think so."

I swiped up my keys and purse and slammed out the door. "I can drive myself."

"The sergeant said if you did that, I'd get no overtime for a month. Ya see, I need that—"

"Never mind." I tossed him the keys.

Ninety minutes later, courtesy of Mr. Slowpoke Officer, night had fallen. We pulled in front of my apartment. I charged inside and was greeted by ... zip. No one. Nada. I stood there damp and smelly and feeling an utter aloneness I despised. Where the ...

Of course, upstairs. Carmen and Jake and Penny were at Jake's place taking care of Veda.

I shucked my coat, flew up the stairs, and pounded on the door. "Hey, Carm! Jake!"

Noises, and then the door opened. "Carmen." I hugged her, and she did the same.

"Heard ya got in a mess," she said.

"Geesh. Did I ever."

Penny's single front paw slammed onto my chest, and I hugged her fiercely. Her gleeful whine made me hug her harder.

"*Lehni*, Penny. Down." I turned back to Carmen. "God, it's good to be home. Where's Jake?"

"The studio."

I headed for his spare bedroom to visit Veda.

"She's not there, Tal," Carmen said.

I was afraid to turn. "She's …"

"In the hospital. It's not good."

"Let's go," I said.

"In the morning." She rested a hand on my shoulder, and her eyes grew serious. "It's too late tonight. There's time in the morning."

Around eight the following morning, we left for Mass General, Carmen, myself and Penny. Carmen talked, but I didn't hear. I felt hollow inside. How ironic that Glaumann, who'd failed in his mission to kill Veda, had done something that was far worse—he'd entombed her mind in a maze.

Apparently the heart medicine Veda had been prescribed had sent her to Mass General with a toxic overload of digoxin. Had Carmen not been a nurse and recognized the symptoms, she would have died. The new doctor properly regulated her digoxin levels, but not before she'd caught another infection in the hospital.

I sipped a cup of Starbucks morning blend. As I drove, I told Carmen what happened.

"Good one, Tal," she said. "You sure landed in it. Again."

"I did, didn't I? If what this Milosh says is true, then the Marshes will kill again and we have a Nazi monster in our midst."

"I've never met a real Gypsy," she said.

"I think they prefer to be called Romany."

"So you think he was for real?"

"Who, the Nazi or Milosh?" I turned onto onto Parkman Street.

"Both, I guess," she said.

"I'm afraid I do. I'm glad you took Veda to Mass General. Does she have a guard?"

"Ayuh." We drove into a parking garage, and around and

around before we found a spot, giving Carmen ample opportunity to swear in kaleidoscope colors.

Minutes later, we were inside the hospital complex. Carmen pressed a button, and we headed up to intensive care.

"You didn't tell me she was in ICU."

"I just assumed you realized, Tal." She lifted a phone on the wall and called inside. Seconds later we were buzzed in. Our feet made squeegee sounds on the linoleum. The central nurses' station was flanked by glass-walled rooms, some of which were curtained. It was a hushed place, where both jokes and tragedies were told in soft voices.

The hiss and pump of machines scattered my thoughts, and I blindly followed Carmen to a curtained room where Veda lay in a bed. Numerous machines hooked to her body transmitted facts on how her body was functioning. Nothing about the mind's wellness. Or the heart's. The soul's.

Veda looked asleep. But her eyelids twitched, as if her dreams had become her reality. She appeared to have lost weight in the twenty-four hours since I'd seen her.

I sat on the chair and took her hand. "If anyone can overcome this, Vede, you can. C'mon. You always joke about your eleven lives."

Her fingers moved, and I'd have sworn she knew it was me.

"Vede?" I said.

Her lips moved, and I bent closer. "Do you hear me, Veda?"

Nothing.

Warm hands squeezed my shoulder. "She might know, Tally. We've got to go now."

"We just got here."

"There's a time limit in ICU. Plus, they want to bathe her. We can come back."

I stood and leaned over Veda's bed. I wrapped my arms

around her frail body, raised her up and hugged her. "Love you so much."

I laid her back down, brushed a stray lock of hair, and ran my fingers across her cheek.

She would leave us. Soon.

Chapter Thirty-one

The buds on the trees had burst into fledgling leaves and the air tasted of spring. The rain was forgotten. The sun glistened. My blood quickened, and I felt the pulse of life rejuvenate me. Carmen and I drove down Storrow along the Charles. Skulls and sailboats dotted the river, and rollerbladers whizzed by on paths along the banks. Joggers, too, and on the greening grass, a kid threw a Frisbee to his Golden Retriever.

God, I wanted Veda to see summer. One more summer. Just one. If she did, I'd … I didn't know what. Say a daily prayer or something? Geesh. Who was I bargaining with?

I was exhibiting classic symptoms of those who experienced impending disaster. Bargaining with Fate or God. If only x, y, z happens, I'll do such-and-such. If only …

"I've got to check in at MGAP, Carm. Shall I drop you off at the apartment?"

"Um, yeah. I'd like to see what flights I can get."

"Home. I understand, hon." I hated it, but it was time for

Carmen to leave. What a trooper she'd been. I squeezed her hand. "You're the best."

"So, what'll you do now?" she said.

"Look for the Marshes. Bella."

"I meant Veda. Don't you want to talk about her?"

"No."

"So how are you going to find the Marshes and that crazy Nazi?"

"I have some ideas." I pulled to the curb in front of my apartment. "I've got to do something, now that Milosh has been arrested."

"It sounds scary," Carmen said.

"I know." I waved good-bye, and Penny and I drove to OCME.

MGAP was quiet, with few cases on the board. Gert unlocked my office door with the new locks and key sets. She gave me a set and left for lunch. Judy Ethridge hadn't bothered MGAP since the last foray. But for how long, I wondered.

I sat at my desk, but had trouble focusing on the towers of paperwork and pink message slips. Outside my window, the sidewalk bustled with workers and medical personnel and students, many wearing spring jackets and short-sleeved shirts and light suits. In the branches of the maple where I'd seen the robin, she'd apparently built a nest with her mate.

I smiled and wondered when she'd lay her eggs.

I'd called Kranak last night, but had failed to reach him. I tried now, but he wasn't in his office. He didn't answer his cell, either.

I called the toxicology unit at the crime lab in Sudbury and reached Dick Archer. "Hey, Dick, how goes it? It's Tally."

"I'm on my way out, Tal."

"Quick, then. Where are you at with the tests you did on Dr. Barrows's blood?"

"Look, um, I've been told not to talk to you."

"*Pardon?*"

"Yeah. Doc Ethridge said we weren't to say anything about the case. Not to nobody."

"Dick, we've known each other for ten years. You've helped me out a million times."

"Sorry, Tal. Ethridge is chief now. No can do."

"Should I call Kranak?"

"Call the fuckin' Pope, for all I care. Ethridge is one scary dame, and I'm not going against her."

I got down to some serious paperwork whittling, taking breaks to call Kranak twice more. He never got back to me. I packed it in around four, visited Veda again, talked to Bertha, and took Carmen out to dinner.

All pretty normal stuff. Except I felt I was wasting time better spent searching for killers.

The following morning, after I'd gotten MGAP in motion, I returned to the apartment with a plan. I printed out the Photoshopped image of Andrew Marsh as a woman and headed over to the Tall Girls Shop for Clothing.

I walked to the shop, which was in Back Bay on Berkeley. I hoped the exercise might leech out some of my fury at both the stonewalling cops and Ethridge.

As far as I could ascertain, the Tall Girls Shop was the only one of its kind in the Greater Boston area. I hoped that Andrew Marsh's desire to wear women's clothing was real—Milosh thought it was—rather than a disguise. If so, he'd want to try on the clothes he was about to buy.

I didn't know where else to look for the Marshes; hadn't heard from Kranak. It felt like my world had spun out of control.

I longed to talk to Hank, but felt I'd betrayed him with my longing for Kranak.

I stopped amid the crowd bustling down the Boston streets. I had trouble breathing. Headed toward me was a little girl—Rose Noguchi. Our eyes met, and she smiled. That smile warmed me, and a beautiful calm washed over me.

You are almost there, Tally.

The voice was in my head. Had to be. But that sweet smile was real. I saw it. Felt it.

The little girl approached me. "Are you all right?" she said.

I blinked to clear my vision. The face. It wasn't Rose's. She was a brown-haired child holding the hand of her mother, who looked concerned.

"I'm ... fine. Thank you so much."

The shop was pleasant, but undistinguished. It was also one of the few clothiers I've shopped where I actually felt small. Definitely an odd sensation. The saleswoman was pleasant, but neither she nor her boss recognized Marsh's picture. Worse, she told me I should also try the Gap, Banana Republic, J. Crew, Old Navy, and several other stores that carried clothes for tall women.

Oh, hell. Who knew?

I left glum. I'd made no progress. Rose—God, I believed it was Rose—had said I was close. Was it possible? What was I missing? What was I forgetting?

I walked, hands in pockets, head down, trying to think, to piece together something that ...

Then I remembered the Wirth Gallery's guest list. How had I forgotten?

I rifled through my apartment for forty-five minutes, tossing papers and letters and files. Nothing. Where had it gone? I'd had it. For sure. Or had I?

I sat on the sofa and dialed the gallery. Naturally I got voice mail. Didn't *anyone* answer the phone anymore? I left a message asking for another copy of the guest list.

"Screw it!"

Penny's ears perked.

"Come on, Pens. Road trip."

We drove to Newbury Street and double-parked in front of the Wirth Gallery. The windows looked dark, and I couldn't see anyone inside.

I left the car running and raced to the entrance. A CLOSED sign hung inside the door's window. I searched for the gallery's hours, but found none.

I ran back to the car, put it in drive, and headed for the Suffolk County Jail. I hoped to talk to Milosh.

I knew I was on a hamster run—no direction, just zooming around like a crazy woman—but I desperately feared for Bella Marsh's life.

I entered the imposing stone building I'd "visited" way too many times when working with the families of homicide victims. I passed through the screener with no problem and found myself in the cavernous central hall.

The building's presence, its weight, and the prisoners' fear pressed down on me. The jail housed around nine hundred pretrial detainees. At the grilled cubicle, I asked the officer on duty to speak to Milosh.

"Last name?" he said.

"None that I'm aware of."

The officer's bushy eyebrows shot up. "He's got to—"

"I don't think he does. Truly."

"One sec," the officer said. He leaned over an intercom and spoke softly, so I couldn't hear. He finally looked up. "It'll be just a few minutes, ma'am."

While I waited, I tried to patch together the fragments of ideas on how to find the Marshes. I hoped Milosh could offer me some direction. I wasn't even sure the police were still looking for them.

I checked my watch. Fifteen minutes had passed. Officialdom sure worked slowly.

"Ma'am?"

I turned. A second officer appeared beside me. He wore no uniform, and I figured he was a Boston PD detective. Or maybe my escort, if I was in luck.

"Why are you looking for this Milosh?" he said.

This didn't sound good. "Is there a problem? I simply want to speak to him privately."

"And you are ...?"

I handed him my MGAP credentials. "These should do it."

He examined my MGAP ID and my driver's license, as well as my psychologist's license. He passed these on to the officer in the cubicle.

The second officer slid my credentials back to me. "Here you go, Ms. Whyte. Everything looks in order."

Then a lawyerly looking man bustled up to the grilled cubicle. The plainclothesman gestured me to a more private space. "Tell me again, Ms. Whyte, why you want to see this Mr. Milosh."

I smiled. "As I recall, I didn't tell you the first time. I'd rather not share."

"Suit yourself." He snugged his hands into his pockets. "Either way, I'm afraid you won't be seeing him today."

Ah, yanking my chain. A familiar sensation. "Look. I can call several officers in the Boston PD to vouch for me. State police, too. Would that help? I really do need to see the man."

He let out an exaggerated sigh. "Well, you can't. He's no longer here."

Now it was my turn to sigh. "Then where was he taken?"

He shrugged. "No clue. He was released two hours ago. No charges."

"No charges? You're kidding? The man kidnapped me!"

"Well, I don't know about that. Some diplomatic immunity bullshit. All I do know is we opened the door and out he went."

* * *

Outside the jail, I checked the time. Damn. I had my survivor group in fifteen minutes. I'd make it, with luck.

My luck failed. I entered the group counseling room filled
with eleven homicide survivors, apologies flowing from my
mouth. We quickly got down to the business of digging into
the feeling of having a loved one ripped suddenly and vio-
lently from your life.

I'd been with these folks for a long time. Some for a
dozen years. The "old-timers" were my helpers now, easing
the more recent survivors' pain and guiding them back to
mental health.

I wasn't on my game. I kept thinking about Milosh and
what he must be doing. What immunity, I wondered. From
where? Germany? Israel?

Ninety minutes later, we parted, agreeing to meet the following week. Our ritual.

It was noon, and Kranak should be on. I poked my head
into his office. No Rob. I asked one of the guys about his
whereabouts, and was told he was on "special assignment."

Time seemed to be speeding up, and I wasn't able to
catch it.

At least the wheels of MGAP were turning smoothly.
Donna was getting takeout at the bagel place, and I piggy-
backed with a toasted bagel topped with lox and cream
cheese.

I gave Penny her lunchtime walk outside. Crossing back
through the lobby, I saw Ethridge leaning against the wall,
legs and arms crossed, no longer wearing her ME's white
coat, but rather a blue suit that revealed way too much cleav-
age. She looked like some wiseass school kid faking leisure,
but who was about to pounce.

I nodded, but otherwise ignored her.

As I walked by, her hand snagged me. Her polished nails
dug into my wrist. I winced. Penny growled.

I yanked my arm away. "What is it, Judy?"

She glanced down at Penny. When she looked up at me, her eyes glinted with pleasure. "New rules."

"How exciting. Send me a memo."

"No can do." She smiled. "Animals are now forbidden in the building. No more doggie for you."

My stomach flip-flopped. "Sorry, babe, but you haven't the authority."

"Of course I do."

"Of course, you don't."

A door banged, and Fogarty materialized. Ethridge's ally. Not what I needed.

"Judy!" he said.

"What is it, Tom?"

"You said we'd wait."

Fogarty wouldn't meet my eyes.

"What's going on?" I said.

"C'mon, Judy," he said. "You've got to."

She rounded on him. "I don't *have* to do anything, Tom. As the new chief, I can do anything I want."

He shook his head. "You're a fool." He turned to me. "I apologize, Tally. I've never been fond of you, but I wish you hadn't learned quite this way."

I rested my hand on Penny's head. I felt her tense. "What the hell are you two talking about? I really have no clue."

"See, Tom?" Ethridge said. "She's has *no* idea."

"Of what, dammit!" I said.

Ethridge leaned forward. "They're voting today to make me the new Chief Medical Examiner for Massachusetts."

"You're crazy. Veda—"

"Is *dying*," Ethridge said.

I slapped her cheek. "You have no right. *No right* to talk about Dr. Barrow that way."

Ethridge brushed her fingers across her cheek. "Tomorrow the dog is off limits. Soon you will be, too." She turned and pounded up the stairs.

Fogarty grimaced. "Tally, I never thought I'd say this, but I'm sorry."

I stared at my hand. I couldn't believe I'd slapped her. I looked up at Fogarty. "Is it true, what they're doing?"

He nodded. "I'm afraid so. You know how devoted I am to Veda."

"I do, Tom. That much I know. They're not even going to wait?"

He shook his head. His blue eyes behind his glasses pooled with tears. "No."

I walked back to my office in a fog. They weren't giving Veda a chance. She'd been chief forever. She had a right to get well, to be waited for. She deserved ...

Deserve had nothing to do with reality. Who was I kidding?

"Here's your sandwich, Tal." Donna handed me the bag with the bagel.

"Thanks," I said.

"Anything up?"

I shook my head, walked into my office and closed the door. Screw them about Veda. If she did recover, she'd blister their asses.

And about Penny? What was Ethridge going to do, forcibly evict her? Hell, no cop would do that to Pens. She was a former Canine Corps hero.

I dropped the lunch bag on my desk and sat. I tented my fingers.

Time was running out. For Veda. For our grief assistance program here at OCME. And for me. I felt sick. Hard to erase years of work. Of a life.

I picked up the phone to call Kranak, but he'd vanished into the cop ether. Carmen? Gert? They'd all help, be sympathetic about Veda ... and her death sentence. But that's not what I wanted. Not really.

I wanted it all back like it used to be. I rested my chin on my knees. That wasn't going to happen. Not ever.

If I focused on Rose and Eva, and on who'd tried to kill Veda, I could live with things. For a while, at least.

I was close.

Earlier, at the jail, I hadn't thought much about Glaumann. "Why not, Pens?"

She poked her head up.

"Right." I smiled. "Milosh had said the girls' killings were odd in that they were ... What did he call them?" I paused. "Showy." So what had changed? Why were these deaths different from all the killings in Europe?

I popped open a Diet Coke. What if Eva and Rose's deaths weren't the point at all? Maybe the girls were a disguise for Glaumann's real purpose. So what was his real purpose? Maybe Veda knew, which was why he sent the pseudo Brooke after her. But when I visited Veda weeks ago and she asked me about Rose, her query was genuine.

Geesh. I was on another one of my damned hamster runs.

I'd go back. Retrace. Write down events and when they happened. I'd get it then. I had to. Because I believed Bella was about to die.

I pulled out my bagel and lox, suddenly ravenous. I got out a yellow legal pad and a fistful of pencils and began to write.

Chapter Thirty-two

Two hours later I still didn't get it.

I had a sheaf of paper. I'd spent an hour on Rose and Eva's murders—the when, the where, the why. Another forty minutes on Veda. Same elements, but with different results. Veda was mentally damaged, but not dead.

Hard to believe that *nothing* had come to mind.

"Y'know, Pens, I'm not thinking straight. I can't take my emotions out of the equation. It all started in New Hampshire with those little girls. So that's where we're going."

I stopped by the apartment. Carmen was packed and had called a van to drive her to Logan airport.

"I would have taken you," I said.

She hugged me. "I know. You have so much on your plate right now. I wish I didn't have to go."

"I understand. Truly. Give Bob and the kids my love. Thank them for loaning you, eh? And Hank ... um, give Hank a hug from me."

She faced me and held me by the shoulders. "Listen here. You watch your back." A honk from the van. She hugged me again. Then she was gone.

I missed her solid presence instantly.

School was out by the time I drove into the parking lot of the South Meadow Middle School on 202 in Peterborough. I hoped that some of the teachers or administrative staff would still be in the building. I found a secretary in the office, but all the fifth grade teachers had left for the day.

I wasn't sure what I hoped to learn, but I was disappointed that the trip had been an exercise in futility. I drove into Peterborough in search of the tarot reader, Pricilla Magee. She wasn't at The Renaissance Room, and when I called her number, I got her machine.

I visited the Rite Aid, picked up the *Monadnock Ledger* and the *Peterborough Transcript,* and took them to The Toadstool, where I planned to read them and have a bite to eat.

The curried chicken salad was delicious, but I was kidding myself when I tried to remember anything written in either paper. I was just marking time. If I could only connect the dots ...

That night, on my way back from New Hampshire, I stopped at Mass General. Veda appeared to be resting quietly. She hadn't spoken for two days. I drove to the harbor and parked. Penny led the way down the wharf to Kranak's boat.

"Rob!" I said.

No lights inside the cabin. He wasn't there, of course. I scribbled a note and tucked it in the cabin door.

I went home, took a bath, and went to bed.

I opened my eyes. My illuminated clock read two A.M. I slid my feet from beneath Penny's heavy body and walked to the bathroom.

Something I'd read that day in the Peterborough papers had pinged my brain. I sat behind the desk in my living room, fired up my Mac, and hopped onto the Web.

I wished I hadn't left the papers at The Toadstool. But maybe I could recreate them online.

Damn. The local police reports weren't available on the Web. I'd have to wait until morning to call the papers. Why had I left them at the bookstore?

I padded to the kitchen and made some cocoa, then returned to the living room. I piled some logs and kindling on the hearth, crumpled up some old *Boston Globe*s, and lit it.

I dragged the afghan over my bare legs. Penny slipped up on to the couch beside me. I sipped the cocoa. It was three in the morning. Moonlight filtered in from the French doors.

The steaming mug warmed my hands.

What had I read in the police report? A child had pushed a woman with only one leg. The woman toppled and was injured. Not seriously. The child's age was given as eleven. Oddly, the child's parents were being charged along with the child. Huh.

Not an article, but in the police reports of … I couldn't recall the town. That was the problem.

I thought of Bella, and her reaction to Penny. She'd wigged out when she saw that Penny had only three legs. And wheelchair-bound Teresa Noguchi implied that Bella didn't deal well with Teresa's disability. Perhaps Bella *had* reacted the same way to a one-legged woman.

I took another sip. Sure, it was a long shot that Bella Marsh had anonymously appeared in the paper. But it made sense, too.

Why the hell not? My gut said yes.

I'd go back to New Hampshire to see if I could find the child and her parents.

Early that morning, I ran to the office and put everyone in place for the day. Luckily Gert was on, and I had little to worry about. So far, no announcement about Ethridge as the new chief.

I had to get to the Marshes before Milosh. If Glaumann was controlling the couple, perhaps they could be awakened from his terrible spell. The Marshes could also lead me to Glaumann.

I left Kranak a message that I was going in search of the Marshes. He might have vanished, but I'd bet he was still getting his voice mails. He'd never frozen me out before. I didn't understand it, especially after that last kiss at the Marsh house.

I wished he was with me.

I took my pepper spray and Penny. The drive up to New Hampshire was uneventful. I'd packed maps of the area in case I needed to find a particular town or street.

The day was raw, with a mean wind and rain slanting from the west. Spring in New England was often cruel, and Temple Mountain oozed gloom. A brown, plump bird with a small head skittered across the road. I pumped the brakes. Damn, what was that? It sure didn't seem inclined to fly.

My arm ached, and I rubbed it. I come through almost unscathed from the accident, whereas Kathleen ... Lauria would have loved this. She had unerring instincts, and in the most dangerous of situations, told dumb jokes that leavened the atmosphere. I missed her.

I reached for Penny, and scratched her behind her ears.

According to the FBI, they had few leads on who'd run Lauria's SUV off the road. They'd said I was the object of the killer's desire, yet I hadn't felt threatened for weeks. Not since ... when?

Something else to add to the timeline. I wasn't sure it mattered, since so much of what had occurred this past month felt random, at best.

I pushed the gas to sixty. I was eager for a confrontation.

* * *

I ran in and out of the Rite Aid and drove to the Peterborough Diner. I got a seat at a booth where I could keep an eye on the car and Penny. After my coffee and salad arrived, I began to page through the local papers for the police reports.

I found what I was looking for in the *Monadnock Ledger*.

> An 11-year-old cited for knocking down Ms. Thelma Sterling. Ms. Sterling, whose recent leg amputation contributed to her fall, was rushed to Monadnock Community Hospital. She is reported in good condition.

The town was Jaffrey.

Talk about a stretch. But my gut believed … I peered at the 4Runner. Penny's black nose peeked out from the half-open window.

I pulled my maps from my purse and spread them on the tabletop.

Jaffrey wasn't far. Just a town away down Route 202. It had to be Bella and the Marshes. I'd find them. I knew I would.

I drew some cash from my purse, and as I laid it on the table, a large hairy hand wrapped around my wrist.

"Going somewhere, are we?"

I stared up into the cold eyes of Milosh. "That's none of your business," I said. "Now let go of my wrist."

"You're hunting them, aren't you?"

"Not like you are, Milosh."

He released my wrist and slid into the seat across from me.

"You're welcome to stay. I'm leaving." I gathered up the newspapers and my purse.

"Fine," he said. "I'll follow you."

"Then I won't go where I was intending."

His leathery face pleated into a grin. "I will keep on you. I believe you know where the Marshes are hiding. You have marvelous instincts, Ms. Tally."

"Even if I'm right, I won't lead you to them."

"What?" he said. "You think I will just open fire on them?"

"Perhaps, in your fervor. I have no reason to trust you."

He pressed his hands together on the table, as if he were praying. I saw the swollen joints and knew he must be in pain.

"If you do not help me in my quest, they will kill again. Perhaps their own little Bella. Or maybe another child. A foundling, like poor Eva." His face tightened. "I don't know Glaumann's purpose here, but he *has* an agenda. Believe it. We can stop him by finding the Marshes—his soldiers, his pawns. Help me."

I heard truth in his voice, read it in his eyes.

"All right," I said. "But I have one test you must pass."

"Only one?" He looked stern, but his eyes danced with humor.

Outside I led him to my car. I opened the door, and Penny bounded out. I said nothing.

Milosh crouched down. He didn't move his hands to touch her, but rather talked in a soft, smooth voice. "Pretty girl, Penny. Good girl. *Hodny,* Penny. *Hodny.*"

"Do you know everything?" I said.

"Because I know that your Penny is Czech?"

Penny sniffed him. Then she butted her head against his chest, and he began to pet her.

"You're an impossible man," I said. "That's obvious. Please don't think I've underestimated you."

"I'm in?"

"All right. Yes. For now."

* * *

We drove down Route 202 toward Jaffrey, past bucolic farms and a ball bearing plant and a pretty lake where high on a hill sat a majestic brick colonial home. On a more leisurely mission, I'd have driven to see the house up close.

On the outskirts of the town, I pulled into a strip mall and called Gert. The day was sailing along at MGAP, mostly because Ethridge was out of the office. Gert looked up the Marshes in Jaffrey, and, as expected, they had no Jaffrey listing.

When we hung up, I turned to Milosh. "We're going to have to figure a way to get the police to give us their address. Small New Hampshire town, they'll be reluctant."

He pressed his index finger to his pursed lips. "You are sure it's them?"

I squeezed the wheel. "No, I'm not. It was just a report about a child of Bella's age knocking over a disabled woman. I don't even know if it was a boy or girl. But I remember Bella's reaction to Penny. Most kids adore her. Bella was revolted by her, *and* her disability. Teresa Noguchi, who's in a wheelchair, told me Bella didn't do well with her disability, either. It's a long shot, I know."

He narrowed his eyes. "You Americans are precipitous. But I trust your instincts, curly top."

"Damn, why do you keep calling me that when you know it just ticks me off?"

His eyes grew soft and distant; his face, slack. His smile was wistful, like a remembered bird in flight. "She was sweet, my sister." He laughed. "I'm swarthy and dark, with Romany eyes. My hair was black as night. *My* curly top was so different. Her hair was curly blonde and her eyes … oh, they were a breathtaking alpine blue. You could swim in her eyes. But it was her sweet, sweet smile that captured hearts. She was all gentleness and joy."

He looked straight ahead and grew silent.

"Milosh?" I said.

He slapped the dashboard. "That's all! Let's find the coppers and get that address. We are running out of time."

I found the municipal police station and was about to go in when Milosh held me back. "I'll go. *You* ... stay here."

"So they're going to tell you and not me," I said.

He grinned. "Of course, curly top. Of course."

Five minutes passed, then ten. I was about to go get him when my cell rang. Caller ID said it was Gert.

"What's up?" I said.

A Bazooka bubble popped in my ear, then Gert stuttered out a string of vicious swear words.

"Gert?"

"Movas."

"What?" I said, not quite getting her Brooklynese. "You mean, moving men?"

"Yeah. They're takin' out all the files and computers, all our stuff."

"Those bastards. Ethridge and Fogarty. Screw them."

"You comin' back? We needja."

Just then, Milosh slid into the passenger seat. He gave me a thumbs up. "Hold on, Gertie."

"I have the address of the child," Milosh said. "A boy named Smith. Or maybe it's really Bella Marsh dressed up as a boy. Let's go see."

"Gert, listen. Call Sal, our lawyer, then lock the doors on the central office and mine, and don't let the movers back in."

"Got it, Tal!"

I turned to Milosh. "Let's go. And let's hurry."

We drove for ten minutes and parked down the street from a beautifully preserved colonial built in the 1700s. While the town of Jaffrey had a bit of an industrial flavor, this section, called Jaffrey Center, looked like something out of the history books—quaint and charming with stately greens and majestic trees.

We got out, and I leashed Penny. *"K noze,"* I said. "Heel." I hooked my arm through Milosh's, and we strolled up and down the street. A green sedan sat in the driveway, but we detected no movement inside the house.

"Wait," Milosh said. He pulled a Sig-Sauer 9mm from his armpit holster, checked the clip, slammed it back in. "Now, we go inside."

"We are not Rambo, Milosh."

He looked toward the house. "No. But we are not fools, either."

"I don't want to scare Bella."

"If we must, we must. We have a job to do, Tally."

His eyes said I should trust him. I nodded, and we walked down the driveway. I patted my pocket, checking for my pepper spray. Penny hugged my side. She knew.

"Why don't you go around back, and I'll go to the door and—"

"No!" he hissed. "These people would not hesitate to kill you or hold you as a hostage."

"But I can—"

"Not an option." He tightened his grip on my arm.

A few leaves blew across the granite path and steps. Milosh rang the bell.

I wasn't sure …

The door yawned open. A grey-haired woman holding a broom peered out. "Can I help you?"

This was not Marlene Marsh.

"Hello." I smiled. "We're looking for the—"

"Smiths," Milosh said. "My grandson is a friend of their child. We hoped to set up a playdate."

The woman nodded. "I just clean here once a week. The Smiths said they were going hiking on the mountain today.

They haven't been gone long. I'd say thirty minutes. They hike every day I clean. Strange people."

"Well," I said. "Another time."

The woman's blue-veined hand shook as she stretched it out and smoothed it over Penny's head. "What a pretty dog. I like dogs. I'd best get back to it. I'll tell the Smiths you were here."

"Oh, don't bother," I said. "I'm sure we'll hook up with them sooner or later."

Chapter Thirty-three

I slid behind the wheel and got out the maps. "Here, you read them."

"Mountain?" Milosh said.

"Must be Mount Monadnock. It's the most climbed mountain in the world. It's near here. Let's go." I gunned it, and Milosh barely had time to snap his seat belt before we raced toward the mountain. I talked as I drove, suddenly sensing an incredible urgency.

"Something's wrong," I said. "I can't explain it."

"Ah, so you feel it, too. You'd make a good hunter, Tally Whyte. What is this mountain?"

"Monadnock. It's not a bad climb, more like a vertical hike, and the top offers incredible vistas of the area. The local Indians believed it sacred."

"Just drive." His words were clipped, his tone terse.

As I drove the narrow backroads of Jaffrey, I felt a growing sense of dread.

"The woman," I said. "Maybe we should go back."

"No. We must find them. Now."

Penny whined.

I drove back down 124, but away from the town of Jaffrey.

"How far is it?" I asked.

Milosh had the road map open in his lap. "I cannot tell from the map. Not far, I think. Turn right at Dublin Road."

I did, and we traveled yet another back road. I wondered how anyone found the damned mountain. Something so big shouldn't be hiding.

"Now what?"

"Go left on Poole Road."

"Poole?"

"Yes."

I pressed on the gas, came to Poole, turned left, and drove up a narrow road flanked by majestic maples and oaks and pines. We finally saw the entrance to the park, guarded by a small hut.

I paid and received a trail map in return. Then we turned left into the parking lot half-full of cars.

"It's quite civilized," he said.

"I wonder if the woman warned them," I said.

"I hope we didn't misread her," he said.

We parked in front of the headquarters, a small campy-looking building with a welcome flag luffing in the breeze. The sky had turned an ugly lead, and the air felt heavy with the promise of rain.

I opened the trail map. "Look." I pointed. "The White Dot Trail, the White Cross Trail, the Cascade Link and on and on. I don't know what I was expecting, but it wasn't half-a-dozen trails. How will we find these people?"

We walked around the parking lot looking at cars. I'd put on my running shoes, but changed back to my Merrells for better traction.

"Boat shoes?" I said to Milosh.

He shrugged. "They're comfortable."

"Geesh. They have no traction except on boats! Okay, the last time I saw the Marshes in a car, Andrew was driving a Volkswagen SUV."

He raised his hands. "Hooray for the Fatherland."

"Let's see if we can find it."

We searched the lot, but neither of us saw the car I'd followed from Peterborough.

"The cleaning lady could be wrong," I said. "They might not be climbing."

"Or," he said, "they could be in another car."

"Be right back." I ran back to the 4Runner and exchanged my sweater for a jacket. I spotted a park ranger, and it dawned on me they must keep some count of the climbers on the mountain. It wasn't Everest, but I suspected they would track hikers, since one could be injured or worse.

I signaled Milosh to come over, and then I approached the black-bearded ranger. "Excuse me, sir, my father and I are looking for some friends who are hiking."

He grinned. " 'Course you are. We've got forty miles of maintained foot trail and hundred-mile views to points in all six New England states. We're good place to hike."

"Well, um, yes. That's why we were meeting them here. To hike the mountain. But I don't see them."

He looked us up and down and frowned. "We're a real mountain, ma'am. You two aren't exactly dressed for hiking."

"Right. Yes. This was sort of a last-minute thing. See, I'm wearing my Merrells. Like I said, we're meeting friends."

"Not many on the mountain today. Maybe a hundred, since the weather looks to turn nasty."

"Right," I said.

He frowned down at Penny. "Pets aren't allowed anywhere on the mountain, ma'am."

"She's not a pet. She's a ..." I clamped my mouth tight.

"A what, ma'am? You're not going to give me trouble here, now are you?"

I'd seen that look before, but I gave it one more shot. "She's a working dog, sir."

He hooked his fingers around his belt. "What kind of working dog, ma'am?"

That I didn't want to tell him. "Is it okay if I leave her in the car?"

"Fine by me, as long as you don't bring her out again."

"Nope, I won't." I walked back to Milosh and told him about Penny. When I opened the door, she climbed into the truck with great reluctance.

"We should return to the house," Milosh said. "We stand a better chance of trapping them there then on this mountain."

"They're here. Now. I'm afraid if we leave, we'll lose them again. And they are our only real link to Glaumann. We've got to find him."

He leaned against the truck, oblivious to the weather. "What I do not understand is Glaumann's strange behavior. I do not see why he isn't cutting his losses and running. That's what he *does*."

"Maybe he's made a life here. Maybe he wants to stay."

"If that's so," he said, "then why is this different from all the other places he's been? What is making it different? I am not seeing it."

"I'm not, either. But for now, I just want to find the Marshes. I'm afraid for that little girl." I spread the trail map on the hood of a nearby sedan. "We're here." I pointed to the parking lot. "Four trails on this side. We've got to start somewhere. We can both start at the White Dot trail. Then you can take the White Cross, and I can stay on the White Dot. We can agree to meet at the top. I'm betting that as we climb up the mountain, we'll meet up with them as they make their way down."

He shook his head. "The rain is coming. That's bad for footing, for apprehending those who wish to escape. I don't like the uncertainty of it all. What if they are using a different trail?"

I leaned against the truck. He was right, of course. But this might be our one chance to find the Marshes. We could guard Bella, even learn the location of Glaumann.

I watched a man and woman arrive in the parking lot. They looked scruffy, beat. The woman was limping.

"One sec," I said to Milosh. I walked to the couple. "Hi. I'm looking for some friends. A couple and a child around eleven-years-old. Did you happen to pass anyone like that on the trail?"

"Sue?" the man said.

"No. Today was mostly guys. Not many kids. After all, it's a school day."

"Right." I smiled. "Thanks."

I trotted back to Milosh. "That's how we'll do it. We'll ask everyone coming off the mountain if they've seen a couple and an eleven-year-old. No genders. With Andrew Marsh, who knows?"

"Brilliant, curly top. Let's go."

We stood by the trailhead as the rain picked up. The wind snatched at my jacket and almost blew off my pink Red Sox cap. Milosh, bareheaded, hands in pockets, didn't seem to mind. He smiled at each returning hiker and listened attentively as to whether they'd seen the Marshes.

I needed a bathroom break. I signaled Milosh, and headed for the ladies room. When I came out, the sky had darkened even more. Milosh was talking to a clump of young men when I saw an older couple arrive at the base of the trail.

I trotted over and asked the question.

The woman nodded. "Yes, we did, in fact. Coming down White Cross. They were coming down, too, but because of the child, they went much more slowly."

The man frowned. "Isn't it a little late to meet up with friends for hiking?"

"Oh, we *were* going hiking, but now I think we'll just meet for dinner. Thanks. White Cross, you said?"

The woman nodded, and a gust of wind sent them scurrying to their car.

I ran over to Milosh and told him the news. "Let's go," I said.

"We wait here for them."

I shook my head. "No. I can't, Milosh. I can't do anymore waiting. I've got to get to them."

He shrugged. "I hoped ... ah, well, let us go. But you be careful. They may have guns. They may use their child as a weapon. Do not underestimate them."

"I don't plan to."

We began to climb White Cross as light grew dim, and the moon slipped into the sky. The sun was still up, but barely.

The trail essentially went straight up the mountain. I wish I'd asked the climbers how high up they'd seen the family. A half hour later, we came to a place called Falcon Spring. I could see how in good weather, the climb would be glorious.

After Falcon Spring the trail was unrelenting in its ascent of the mountain. The path was strewn with rocks and roots, and I found the way tough going.

"You hanging in there?" I hollered back.

"I am!"

Race. Race!

I heard the voice, and knew it was Rose's, or mine. It didn't matter. I believed her now, and so I moved faster, my feet finding purchase where I hadn't expected any.

I looked back. Milosh was climbing slowly, but steadily.

Up ahead, a shout that sounded like "No!" Then a woman's shriek.

I kicked into high gear, not running, but pulling myself up with my hands as well as my feet as fast as possible.

A bang. Thunder? It sounded close by.

"Haaaaaaaa!" Milosh yelled something. I couldn't tell what. The wind swallowed his voice.

Two more claps of thunder, which weren't thunder at all, and I moved faster still, turned a corner, and gasped.

I flattened myself on the path just as another shot boomed.

"Milosh, get down!" I screamed. I looked back, but the curve in the path hid him from sight.

Up ahead, three bodies lay across the trail, blood streaming from their faces. Dear God.

I inched forward.

The boom of gunfire, then more cracks, as if from a different gun. Milosh.

I moved, a boom, and something scalded my arm.

"Shit!" I pressed my hand to the pain and came away with a bloodied palm.

More cracks of a gun, then silence. A dreadful silence. Too much silence.

I continued to inch up the path on my belly. I had to reach them. Had to.

"Bella!" I called. "Andrew! Marlene!"

They didn't move. One hand, nails painted red, flopped up and down. Maybe someone *was* alive.

I reached the child first, and pressed my fingers to her neck. No pulse. My tears mixed with the rain. The drizzle of rain moved her blonde bangs and I saw the hole in her forehead. It was so small. Really nothing. A blemish. That's all. But I knew what the bullet had done to the back of her head.

Empty blue eyes stared at the sky that rained upon her. *I'm so sorry, Bella.*

I only needed to push up another couple of inches to reach Marlene. The woman's exquisite face was frozen in a mask of fury. She knew. I pressed my fingers to her throat. Gone. I turned to Andrew, who lay beneath his wife. He was smiling, and I suspect his was the first shot we heard. He had no idea his family was about to be erased.

His pulse was silent, too. All gone.

I returned to Bella and pressed her hand against my cheek. The rain pounded harder, and the chill seeped deep into my bones.

Had to be Glaumann protecting himself. But why the child? Why Bella? What harm could she possibly do to him?

I slid my hand into the lining of my jacket and felt for my cell phone. The sky was weeping in sheets now, pounding the earth, the stone, the lifeless flesh of the Marsh family.

I felt rather than saw a presence above me. I turned my head. A form in a black slicker that brushed the ground. A large-brimmed hat shadowed the face. Black-gloved hand raised, ready to fire.

Bam!

A gunshot, but I was still breathing. It was from a distance. *Milosh!*

Bam!

The shooter turned and ran, limping, as he traversed the mountain.

A third shot rang out, then silence but for the roar of the rain.

Milosh suddenly appeared. Shoulder bloody, he trudged after the man in the slicker. I sprang up and raced after him.

I stumbled, crashed on my knees, rocked by pain. I watched the killer melt into the woods. Milosh slogged after him.

"Milosh, don't! Milosh!"

He turned. "I must."

"No," I hollered. "He's too fast. You won't catch him. Let me call."

He shook his head and kept going.

I flipped open my phone and punched out 911. I told them where I was and about the bodies and the killer and Milosh. My arm ached, but I thought I could get off the mountain myself.

I said I'd wait until someone came for the bodies.

I stumbled back to the path and the Marshes.

She was a lovely lady, Mount Monadnock. A grand lady. But not for the Marshes. Not for little Bella.

I sat beside the bodies and watched the rain stream the path red.

Chapter Thirty-four

I remained at Monadnock's base camp for hours. The small lodge was a warm and cozy 1930s building cluttered with marvelous artifacts of an earlier era, tons of fun souvenirs, drinks and energy bars, and almost the kitchen sink. The pretty gal ranger wrapped me in a blanket and sat me in front of the crackling wood stove. Soon an EMT was cleaning and bandaging my surface wound, which turned out, not surprisingly, to be a gunshot. I was lucky.

"Milosh?" I said to the state trooper.

He shook his head.

I stood on wobbly legs. "My dog can find him."

"You're in no shape," he said. "Will she go with me?"

"If I tell her to."

Outside, the parking lot swarmed with police and medics and a New Hampshire Medical Examiner's van.

I got Penny out, leashed her up, and had her smell the coat Milosh had left in the truck.

"Pens, go with this man." I handed her leash to the trooper, and I explained she understood Czech and English and that her three legs would do just fine. I handed him a list of commands in Czech, with English translations. "You probably won't need this, but it's a good idea to have it."

He crouched down and patted her. She licked his cheek, and I relaxed.

I had her smell the coat again and said, "Go with this man, Penny. Find Milosh. *Stopa*, Penny. Track. *Stopa!*"

Off she went, up the White Dot trail, just as we'd done.

I slumped in the truck, beat. A plainclothesman with the DA's office arrived and had me tell my tale yet again.

When they released me, I went into in the public bathroom and changed into the spare clothes I always carried. I splashed some water on my face and scrubbed my hands, and I felt nearly human as I got back into the truck. No sign of Penny yet. No word on Milosh or Glaumann.

I dozed.

I see the Twins. They're dancing, each with hands in the air. Mirror dancing. One moves left, the other right. Their gypsy skirts swirl about their bare brown legs. Rings encircle their toes and fingers.

They clasp hands and dance faster, kicking feet into the air, but never letting go.

Red skirt skips a beat!

But yellow skirt catches it.

They dance, faster, faster. A jig!

They stop, collapse on the floor, heads bowed, black hair streaming like a canopy around their heads, brushing the floor, hiding faces.

"Tally!"

I jerked awake, fists up, ready to punch.

"Ho-oh!!! Ho-oh!!!!" came the call from a distance.

Penny reappeared, and I flew from the car to the officer. Behind him, two rangers carried a large red basket.

Whoever it was—Milosh? Glaumann?—was cocooned

in a blanket. I couldn't even tell if he was alive. I reached Penny first.

"She found him," the officer said as he handed me her leash.

I hugged her and slipped her some treats. "*Hodny*, Penny. What a good girl."

I ran to the basket. *Milosh*. *Alive*. "Thank God."

His brown eyes smiled up at me, but he remained silent.

"Are you all right?" I said.

He nodded.

"Ma'am?" said one of the rangers. "We've got to get him to a hospital."

"Oh, sorry." I brushed my hand across Milosh's cheek. "I'll go with you."

He shook his head. "Your office. Glaumann. Veda. Go. Go!"

I kissed his cheek. "I'll see you soon."

"Soon."

I drove off, and as soon as I had cell reception, I called Mass General. A nurse told me that Veda was resting quietly. Bertha was with her.

My heart tightened. Bertha believed this was the final stage before Veda left us. I hoped she was wrong.

I careened into OCME and slammed on the brakes. In an instant, Penny and I were through the lobby and striding down the hall to the MGAP suite of offices.

I jerked to a stop. "My God."

The doors to the central office and my office had been hacked through. The broken doors lay on the floor.

"Gert!" I yelled.

"In here!"

Papers piled the central office's floor, and coffee cups and wastebaskets and pads and other office detritus lay scattered about, as if some whirling dervish had taken the place apart.

Gert stood on a chair and was unscrewing what we called the Daily Board, a large white board with the day's schedule.

"Erase it and leave it."

"But …"

Her pale face was even whiter than usual, her lips chapped, her eyes red.

"Get down, Gertie," I said. "You don't look so hot. Please."

I sensed a presence behind me. Ethridge, I'd bet. I rounded on her. "Why you little shit."

Kranak's eyes widened. "No one's ever called me little before."

I sagged, overwhelmed at the destruction of something I'd built over a dozen years. "I thought you were Ethridge."

"Not today," he said.

"How about you go away and leave me alone, huh? I've been trying to get in touch with you for days. All I got was silence."

"Don't be such a ballbuster, Tal."

I could have shot him at that moment. "Just leave me be." I walked past him into what remained of my office. I couldn't even slam the door. Damn. I began gathering the papers scattered by the movers.

"Let me help," Gert said.

"With what?" I put the papers in a pile and stood. "I thought the new locks would hold them at bay."

"Ethridge, she's crazy," he said.

I lifted my picture board from the wall. It wasn't much, just a bunch of photos and notes and memories that I cherished. I clamped it to my breast and felt the heat of tears.

Good God. The last thing Gert needed was to see me cry. I drew in a breath, scooped up the papers, gave my office a final glance, and walked out.

Gert came over to my apartment, and she fixed us some drinks while I showered off the day's blood and misery.

While scrubbing my hair, I thought of places we could set up MGAP.

None felt right.

I decided to table any conclusions until the following day.

"Cheers, Gertie," I said as we clinked glasses in front of the fireplace.

"Cheers," she said.

"We can pay you and the part-timers through the end of the month, no matter what happens. We have all our case lists on our computers."

"You're gonna reopen, right?"

"I'll let you know. Right now? I need to sort through these." I pointed to the stack of papers on my coffee table. "I need food, I need to see Veda, and I need to chill."

"Have I gotta deal fa you?" she said in her best Streisand imitation. She grinned. "See that pile of papers?"

We ate Chinese, and then I left Gert at the apartment to go through my office papers while I visited Veda.

Veda had been moved to a regular room, and I had left instructions that if that happened, we would pay for round-the-clock nursing care. Her state police watcher remained at the door.

When I arrived, I kissed her and pulled up a chair beside Bertha, who was knitting. Bertha and I had a big reunion, with many hugs and kisses. Little had changed with Veda, although now and then she would talk or even yell something, most often in German. Her sister would always answer. And Veda would grow silent again.

"She's leaving us," Bertha said.

"Maybe," I said.

"She is, *liebchen*. You must accept it."

"I can't."

"You must. She's going so slowly because of you. She doesn't want you to suffer."

"Why can't she come back?" I said like a plaintive child.

Bertha took both my hands in hers. Her eyes bored into mine. "Because our beloved Veda, the one we knew best, is gone. The quick, witty, brilliant woman we knew and loved is not with us. Only her sweet soul remains, trying to ease you, Tally, into acceptance."

"Well, I can't. Not yet. I can't."

"You will. You must."

Bertha kissed both my cheeks and went back to her knitting.

By the time I returned home, Gert had gone. She'd left me a note that she'd finish going through the papers.

Penny and I sat on the couch. I felt utterly alone. I called two hospitals and checked on Milosh and John Noguchi. Milosh was good, Noguchi not so hot. He had yet to regain consciousness. He'd taken a great risk for Veda, and I owed him and his wife and his son.

I lit a fire. The cause of this terrible sense of aloneness made perfect sense. Each day that passed, my beloved Veda was drifting farther and farther away. Somehow, knowing the "why" didn't help.

I wanted to call Hank so much, but I had hurt him too badly to dump a whiny phone call on him. I didn't want to think about Kranak. Carmen was just back with her family and Gert was overcome with the devastating loss of MGAP.

I had other wonderful friends, but no one like Veda.

She was the only mother I'd ever known.

I poured another bourbon and allowed myself a second drink in lieu of a self-pity party.

Tonight, I'd just chill. Tomorrow I'd sort out the mess with MGAP and move forward in accepting Veda's imminent passing. Most important, I'd try to imagine Glaumann's next move. He'd disposed of his faithful followers—Charley, Brooke, the Marshes.

Hard not to think about the monster. I stared into the fire and shivered.

Glaumann stares down at me, rain dripping off his wide-brimmed hat. I sense elation. A feeling of great purpose. He aims the gun at my face. I picture what I will look like, missing half my face, with brains and blood and splinters of bone sticking out.

I am frozen. Unable to move.

And then he was gone, running, shot, limping, but running still.

I sat my drink on the table.

I had become so obsessed with Glaumann that my brain had snapped into a pointless loop. The Marshes' killer, the man who'd pointed the gun at me, couldn't possibly be Glaumann. The speed at which he ran, the grace of his movements, the killer had to be much younger than a Nazi who'd worked the death camps.

So who was he, and why had he erased the Marshes from this world? Was he following Glaumann's orders or flying solo?

I must have awakened ten times in the night. I saw a fuzzy-faced Glaumann, the dead Rose, Marlene's red-painted nails, the day we opened the doors at MGAP, Veda comforting me in the hospital after my father's murder. The parade of images went on and on, spinning fast like some out-of-control carousel. They took on a fantastical quality as they all blended together into a kaleidoscope of color and sound and smell.

The following morning, my head felt cottony from lack of sleep. Nonetheless, I climbed out of bed, dressed, and hopped into the 4Runner with Penny. I drove north yet again to Monadnock Community Hospital.

I hoped Milosh had answers that I didn't see.

On the way, I slipped my headphone on my ear and called Gert, Donna, and the other MGAP staffers. All marvelous people. I told them that we were going on hiatus and that all would be paid through the end of the month. I asked them to call our counselees and tell them not to worry about this brief hiatus.

I dialed Veda's room at the hospital, and Bertha said nothing had changed. Finally, I got connected to Fogarty.

"Why, Tom?" I said. "Why destroy MGAP?"

"It wasn't me."

"Oh, come on now. We've been at odds for years. You've threatened MGAP and me numerous times. You pushed Ethridge to do this."

"You've got it backwards. That's all they were—threats. I confess I got a kick out of baiting you. Believe it or not, I love Veda. And she loves MGAP. I'd never destroy it. But because of this thing with that hood Pisarro hanging over me, I'm not in control. Judy is."

"I assumed that you and she ..."

"We were a couple. But once she became acting chief, and had the power, we were all over. She's ... she's gone over the edge. They haven't made her chief yet. But even though I'm almost out of hot water with the cops, Judy is remaining acting head."

"I'm sorry, then," I said. "I've misjudged you."

He laughed. "No, you really haven't. I'm a bastard. I truly love tormenting you. But I wouldn't do what she's done. Not in a million years. It's really quite a stupid move, politically speaking. She's going to end up with fried ass."

We signed off, and I wondered yet again about Judy Ethridge and her motives. Maybe Glaumann's Brooke had started to harm Veda, but it was Ethridge who'd given her the heparin.

Ethridge was a doctor, had access to meds, wouldn't alarm Veda as a visitor. They didn't keep visitor records in hospitals anymore. But Fogarty might know.

I called him back and asked him to find out if Judy Ethridge had ever visited Veda in the hospital. His eager agreement made me wonder if Ethridge shouldn't watch out for her former lover.

Whether Glaumann or Ethridge or someone else, whomever had attacked Veda must know that I would never give up on finding them. *Never.*

Milosh slept through my visit. I wanted to stay later, but I'd promised Bertha I'd be at the hospital by one so she could run some errands. According to the nurse, Milosh's rapid improvement meant he might be released the following day. I left a note saying he could recuperate at my apartment, if he'd like.

I realized I didn't even know the man's last name or where he lived.

When I walked into Veda's hospital room, I found her screaming, two hospital nurses trying to tie her wrists to the bed, and Bertha bellowing at the nurses to stop.

I would have laughed if it wasn't all so horrible. "Stop it!" I stamped my foot.

The room instantly quieted, which surprised the hell out of me.

I brushed past a nurse and stood by Veda's head. "Hey Veda, Vede. Ssshhh. What's wrong? Can I help?"

"Nein." She compressed her lips and crossed her arms.

I brushed her arm with my hand, back and forth, in a soothing motion. I turned to the nurses. "Dr. Barrow is never, *never* to be tied down. If I hear that ever happens, I will remove her from this hospital so fast, you'll be dizzy. Understood?"

The nurses nodded. "I hate it, too," said the one in the striped top. "But Dr. Barrow gets out of control. She screams, tries to get out of bed. We're afraid she'll hurt herself."

I shook my head. "I understand how challenging that behavior is. But she cannot be tied. As a child, she was a prisoner at Auschwitz. They tied her down and ... Please do not do that."

"We'll do our best," she said. "We'll be back to give her meds in thirty minutes."

I slumped in the chair beside the bed. "Bertha, I've had a hellacious day. Where is Veda's private nurse?"

"You? Ha! I've had to contend with those people. *Ach.* Horrible. And I sent that other awful nurse away."

Swell. "Sit beside me?" I patted the other chair. Veda's eyes never left us.

"Fine idea," Bertha said.

Veda smiled, and it was horrible in its vapidness. "You look pretty, Emma."

Oh, no. We were back twenty years. "Thank you, Veda. I will be right back. I'm going to bring you a surprise."

I went to get Penny.

Chapter Thirty-five

Sometimes Penny's three-leggedness comes in handy. We walked down the hospital halls, and I kept mouthing "working dog" to one and all. No one challenged me.

When Veda spotted Penny coming through the door, she beamed. After a momentary look of confusion, she said "Purtzel! Dear one."

Penny trotted over to the bed and slapped her front paw on Veda's lap. Veda laughed, and I was happier than I'd been in weeks.

She rested her cheek on Penny's large head and stroked her fur.

Bertha leaned toward me. "We had a German shepherd as children. Your Penny has the look of her. Her name was Purtzel. It means 'tumble,' because she was always tumbling down as a little pup. The Nazi's…. you know."

I knew.

We sat in a comfortable silence. I replayed the day on the mountain and tried to imagine how I could have saved the Marshes. Futile, of course, as there were no alternate scenarios. The parents had committed heinous acts, but Bella ... She was let down by the system and by her parents and by my inability to find her sooner.

There must be a clue to Glaumann somewhere. Had to be. The police had torn apart the rental home in Jaffrey, but found no reference to Glaumann. The person I believed to be Glaumann's minion had been injured. Would the monster kill him, too?

Suddenly Veda said, *"Ich habe geseh'n wie sie getötet hat, unsere liebe Purtzel. Die Leute sind böse und werden auch uns umbringen."*

I sat up. "Aunt Bertha, those are the words she said days ago. I tried to write them down but ..."

Bertha's lined face slackened. "She says, 'I saw them kill her, our dear Purtzel. They are evil and they will kill us, too.' Why is she talking about this now, Tally?"

"I guess she's back there," I said, "back in Germany with the Nazis. But something has to have triggered these memories." I pulled a pen and pad from my purse and wrote what Bertha had just translated.

Bertha nodded. "Yes. But sister isn't one to live in the past. Not like me."

"Sie haben alles mitgenommen," Veda said. *"Unser Spielzeug. Muttis Silber."*

"It's similar," I said to Bertha. "Similar to what she said days ago."

"She says, 'They've taken it all. Our toys. Mama's silver.' " Bertha took her sister's hand and held it to her breast. "Sister?"

Veda looked at her sister. *"Sie werden uns umbringen, Bertha. Ja, bestimmt. Bestimmt."*

"She says, 'They will kill us, Bertha. Yes, They will. They will.' "

I scribbled the words.

"They will not kill us, sister," Bertha said. "We are safe. All safe."

"*Nein!*" Veda said. "*Die Mädchen! Wo sind die Mädchen am Meer? Wo?*"

"What is she saying, Bertha?" I asked.

"She's talking about our trips to the seashore. I don't understand."

I rested a hand on her arm. "Please give me the exact translation."

"*Ach.* She says 'The girls! Where are the girls by the sea?' "

I tapped my finger to my lips. Why would that particular phrase agitate Veda so, especially now? Why even more than seeing her dog killed? "Bertha, could Veda mean something different than just a trip to the seashore? Is there anything else that—"

"*Ja!*" Bertha said. She turned back to her sister. "*Veda. Unser Ausflug an's Meer? Oder das Bild vom Papa*"

"*Ja! Das Bild, blöde Schwester! Die Mädchen am Ufer! Ich hab' es geseh'n. Die haben es.*"

Bertha chuckled, then sighed. "Just like my old Veda. She called me 'stupid sister.' Shame on her! But ... here is what else. I said, our trip to the seashore or the picture of Papa's. She says 'the picture, the girls by the seashore.' She's saying that she saw it and that 'they' have it. The picture is something the Nazis took. She's back reliving the Nazis invading our home."

"Oh my god," I said. "The girls by the seashore. A painting. That's what triggered this intense memory." Had I seen that same painting? At the Wirth Gallery? Was it possible?

Rivers of tears coursed down Bertha's cheeks. "Who is 'they,' sister? Who do you mean?"

Veda closed her eyes, and when she opened them they were filled with tears. "I can't remember. It was Papa's picture. I can't remember who. Why can't I remember?" She sobbed and Bertha slid onto the bed and held her sister, as I imagined they'd done as children in the camps, where their parents and all they loved had been ripped from them.

* * *

Veda drifted off to sleep in Bertha's arms. Bertha laid her back on the pillows and tucked the blanket up to her chin. She pressed a finger to her pursed lips, took my hand, and led me from the room. I signaled for Penny to follow us.

"We must talk, but not in there." Bertha's body shook with tension or fear, I couldn't tell which.

"I should leave, Aunt Bertha. I've got to—"

"Wait. *Wait!*"

I asked Veda's state police guard to keep an eye on her, and Bertha pulled me down the hall to the visitors lounge.

We both sat, but she couldn't keep still. I'd never seen her like this, her blue-veined hands a-flutter, her lips mouthing words I couldn't discern.

I was terrified.

"Don't look like that, *liebchen,*" Bertha said. "I'll be all right, once I tell. I think I understand. Now here is a strange story. My father had a painting. Long ago." She wiped her hands across her hair. "It's been years since ... As sister said, the Nazi's took it, along with everything else."

I held her hands in mine. Hers were cold, and I tried to warm them. "That's what Veda was talking about, you think? That painting?"

"I think so. Oh, I have to go back to the beginning. Veda said, 'They are evil and they will kill us. They have taken everything.' That day, when the Nazis came, she was home. Sister had a constitution of steel, but that one day, she was home, sick in bed. I went to school. I didn't see."

Bertha sighed and closed her eyes. "When I arrived home, Mama and Papa weren't there. Our home was horrible, horrible." Tears squeezed from her eyes. "Clothing scattered everywhere. Food. China gone. Paintings. Silver. All gone. Our light, our menorah, smashed. Our dear, sweet Purtzel dead, her throat slit. Much more."

I had to think. So many years had gone by. "It's been years, Bertha. Veda is ill. She was so young. How could she remember a single painting among all the others?"

A smile twitched the corners of Bertha's lips. "Ah, *of course* she remembers. Sick … well … long ago … now, it doesn't matter. Because the painting was *speziell*. Special. Oh, yes, very special. It was an awful painting. Two little girls with horrid expressions. Frowning like crab apples. Papa loved that painting. He brought it home one day, all puffed up with excitement. Oh, I can see his face! I *hated* that painting from the moment he hung it on our living room wall. Mama couldn't stand it, either. *Ach*, but Veda loved it. It was a painting of us, you see. Of Papa's two girls. And sister adored it. We would fight for hours over that awful thing. So you see, Tally love, she could not forget."

"No, she wouldn't forget that. Not our Veda." We paused at the memory of the Veda we remembered. My chest tightened with grief. That woman was gone forever.

I kissed Bertha's cheek. "You go back with her. I want to think. I'll be there in a sec."

"I love you, Tally." She hugged me.

"Love you, too," I said. "So much."

I literally shook trying to contain my anger until Bertha had left the waiting room. Once she was gone, I began to pace. I kicked a chair that screeched across the floor. "Damn you, bastard!"

I had seen that painting, all right. Oh, yes. It hung proudly, *arrogantly* at the Wirth Gallery, the property of Nick Wirth himself. Not for sale. Nope suh.

The gall! I kicked another chair.

"Ouch! Dammit." I sat on the sofa and rubbed my foot. I was an idiot.

A nurse popped her head in. "Everything okay in here?"

I smiled. "Oh, sure. Sorry about that."

"Just try to keep it down."

I waved. "Will do!"

Carmen had seen the painting, too. I flipped open my phone, then remembered I shouldn't call from inside the hospital.

I told Bertha I'd be right back, and then I walked outside.

Nick had been so kind, so sympathetic about the Holocaust victims, about wanting to help. But Nick was no Jew. He was pure German, born during Hitler's reign, one of the favored ones.

I dialed Carmen at her restaurant. While I waited for her to come on the line, I paced back and forth beneath the hospital canopy. And then she was there. We said our hellos, and I brought her up to speed.

"Bastards!" she said.

"It's unbelievable. Nick acted innocent as pie. He'd told me all the Holocaust art that hung at the gallery had provenance. He had papers, signed affidavits, from the families of Holocaust victims who wanted to now sell or display the art taken by the Nazis. Provenance, my ass."

A string of epithets burst from Carmen's mouth. "What crap. I wonder how many pieces hanging at that dump are dripping with the blood of Holocaust victims."

"Oh, I'm sure quite a few. But not all. He's not that dumb." I chuckled. "He must have had a fit when Veda recognized the Gauguin of the two girls at the seashore, when she said it had belonged to her father."

"You think?"

I paced. "You know, maybe she wasn't that clumsy. Maybe she simply asked a few questions about it. She said nothing to me about it. Perhaps she wanted to check, verify."

"So maybe she wasn't sure," Carmen said. "Maybe she didn't trust her memory, but planned to investigate. Hang on. I've got to help one of the girls."

While I waited, I sat on the bench beside a doctor who was smoking a cigarette. I inhaled, and felt the visceral twinge familiar to all former smokers. I still longed to light up.

I imagined Veda at the gallery, flirting with Nick. Thinking he might be a part of her future. Then seeing the painting and *knowing* it had once hung in her house in Germany.

Yet questioning it. Because she was cautious and reasonable. A scientist who wanted all the facts before rushing to judgment.

Veda was also crappy at dissembling.

"I'm back," Carmen said.

"He knew."

"Huh?" she said.

"Nick Wirth knew something was up with that painting. Veda really stinks at playing a role. He did this to her. I don't know how, but he did it."

She whistled. "That sure is a leap, Tal. From gallery director to murderer."

"Oh, Carm. People have killed for so much less. The painting is worth millions. I've got to go. To think. You've been fabulous, as always. Thanks and—"

"Hold it! I know you. Don't go charging off half-cocked."

That was the only way I knew to charge off. "No, of course not. I'll be cautious."

"You are *such* a liar!"

"Think about it, Carm. Really. I'm not going to do anything stupid."

"Don't. Just don't."

"Roger! Ten-four … or something. Bye!"

I clicked off before she could go on another rant.

I sat back on the bench and stroked Penny's fur. I tried to be calm. I took a couple deep breaths to cool down. I smiled at the current bench smoker, a nurse. I said a few "ohms" to myself.

I dialed upstairs to Veda's room, got Bertha, and told her I had to check on something at the Wirth Gallery, but that I'd be back soon. That she should give Veda a kiss from me.

Then I stormed off. I could be at the gallery in fifteen minutes.

*   *   *

I found a great parking spot on Newbury Street, just down from the gallery, and sat there for a moment. First, I wanted to see the painting again. Second ... no, no second. But if Nick Wirth was the one who'd tried to kill my Veda and had instead stolen her mind, I wanted to be a cautious soul. The last thing I needed to do was show him I wanted to strangle him.

I could still hear him say how that painting was a part of *his* collection. Not for sale. And his kindness, his thoughtfulness for the Holocaust victims. How he'd brought Veda that wonderful art book in the hospital. How he was going to propose marriage and *give* her the painting.

I boiled.

I slipped the pepper spray into my pocket and left the car with Penny leashed by my side.

I entered the gallery, and, as always, was stunned by the beauty of the art. Several patrons gave Penny long looks, and one asked if he could pet her, which of course he could.

I viewed the Japanese gallery first. Of the items for sale, all had red dots. Amazing and wonderful. Maybe it would help mellow me out. But I was in a space and a place I no longer trusted.

Then I entered the Holocaust gallery, the one Veda had helped assemble, with paintings and sketches by the titans of the art world. The gallery projected a soothing quietness designed to enhance the illusion of fabulous wealth. Of course, if you looked closer, you'd see the photographs that hung beside the art. Thinking of those images, my stomach cramped. I curled my fingers into fists.

I stroked Penny. Her fur was soft as silk. Better.

I saw Nick talking with a woman in front of the Rubens. A murderer? The man who stole my Veda? I turned away, pretending to look at the Picasso.

"Tally Ho!"

I whirled around. "Nick." I went for innocuous with my smile.

"Good to see you, my dear," he said. I got my typical Nick hug, and maybe I held on longer than usual, still hoping that Nick was innocent.

But he wasn't.

Electricity flowed between Nick and myself.

"Do you know why I'm here?" I asked.

He took my hand and folded it through his, so it rested on his forearm. "My dear Tally Ho, no matter why you are here, I am just glad that you are."

"Thanks, Nick. I'd like to look at some of the paintings again." I looked at the Picasso and then the Monet. Finally, I walked to the Gauguin with the two girls by the seashore. I studied it for long minutes. *That* was what had taken Veda. A painting. In trade for my beloved foster mother. All that Bertha had said avalanched into my head.

I thought I would explode.

"How's Veda?" he said. "I've been to see her again and ..." His eyes moistened.

I wanted to kill him. I'd set Penny on him to rip out his throat; I was so tempted. I looked into his face, eyebrows raised with his question about Veda.

It would be so easy. *"Dog Gone Wild,"* the headlines would read. And Veda would be avenged.

Except I couldn't do that to Penny, nor could I live with myself. He wasn't worth it. I had to get out of there. Had to. "Um, Veda is doing okay. I've got to go."

I fast-walked through the Holocaust room toward the arch. I literally was seeing red. I blinked, and when my eyes cleared, I saw a man standing beneath the arch at the entrance to the Holocaust room. He was backlit from the window, turning him into a silhouette. With his left hand, he leaned on a cane. His right hand rested in his pocket. I couldn't see his face.

Glaumann? Yes! No, *not* Glaumann. But the killer on the mountain.

Chapter Thirty-six

I stopped. Was I crazy? I didn't think so. I'd first seen the killer the same way, in silhouette, as he'd stood over me pointing a gun at my face. This man's shape echoed that of the killer's.

I shook my head to clear the cobwebs and the fury and the imaginings.

I turned back to Nick, who was waving at me to stop. But, no, not at me. He was waving at the man standing beneath the arch.

"Alex!" Nick said. "Over here! It's Tally!"

Alex limped toward me. Milosh had shot the killer in the leg. That fit, too.

And it all came together—Nick wasn't merely an art thief and destroyer of Veda. He was Glaumann, the Nazi who'd murdered countless children and who'd scarred Milosh and done horrific things in the camps.

Penny growled as Alex neared us. Of course. She'd smelled his scent on the mountain while searching for Milosh.

This was crazy. I didn't know what the hell was going on, but I had to get out of there.

I pasted on a smile. "Hi, Alex. Good to see you. I'm sorry about your leg. What happened?"

"No biggie. Little accident. I'm glad you're here." He pulled his right hand from his jacket pocket. It held a gun.

I kicked him in his injured thigh and ran.

Nick shouted "No!"

A gun boomed. "Halt! Or the dog dies!"

I froze.

That voice, behind me. But not Nick's. Or Alex's. Not at all. I turned, slowly, trying to buy time for who-knew-what.

Good God! Stan Wirth stood before me in all his black-T-shirted, gold-chained, black-booted worst. His left hand held his semiautomatic, aimed right at Penny's head.

"Stan?" I whispered. Small, trendy Stan, always over-shadowed by Nick, his elegant younger brother. Synapses fired and in an instant, the world assumed a profound clarity.

Stan Wirth was Glaumann. He'd shaved his Glaumann beard and head. It was he who controlled the Marshes. It was he who killed Charley and the fake Brooke, he who had Rose and Eva and Bella murdered. Simply as a smoke-screen to mask his attacks on Veda? No. Ridiculous.

But as Milosh had said, the murders were showy.

But I looked into Stan Wirth's face and it glowed with joy and triumph and power. I stuttered in a breath. I saw his greed and treachery with the Holocaust paintings. I saw his joy at poisoning Veda. I saw his lust for power.

Fury erupted inside me, and I exploded toward him. "You shit!"

A searing pain in my shoulder knocked me backwards. I stumbled, fell sideways.

Penny growled.

"*Fuj!*" I screamed. "No! *Zustan!* Stay!" I lurched to my knees, hand clamped to my upper arm. "You bastard. Monster."

Stan smiled, and I felt his horrific joy. "I thought you'd get it first, Tally Ho."

"Shut up." The pain in my arm seared my whole left side.

He grinned. "Nick, we have customers. See to them."

"Stanley?" Nick said, his voice threaded with fear and confusion.

"Quiet, brother. All will soon be explained. She's our enemy."

"Enemy?" I laughed. "Of course I'm your enemy."

"Nick, look what she did to Alex."

Alex cradled his injured leg as he rocked on the floor. Blood seeped through his fingers. His face was a mask of fury as Nick helped his son to his feet.

"I'm not your enemy, Nick," I said. "You don't understand."

Stan walked toward me. Penny growled, and he halted. "Nicholas. See to the customers in the shop. Tell them we're reviewing some performance art, hence the noise, and that we are about to close."

Nick walked past me and soon returned, shutting the door to the Holocaust room behind him. "They're in the Japanese room. I told them what you said. They asked for a few more minutes."

Stan smiled. He was somehow taller, his back sharply rigid, his shoulders thrown back. A stance of power, so unlike the Stan Wirth I'd always known.

"Good, brother," Stan said. "Yes, performance art. One of my great performances, don't you think Tally Ho?"

He intended his mockery to infuriate me. I'd lost it once. I mustn't again.

"Do you know what your big brother did to Veda?" I said to Nick. "To little Rose and Bella and Eva? He killed the children. He poisoned Veda. He did it all for greed and power and money."

Stan sighed. "I did nothing of the sort, especially to Dr.

Barrow. It's simple. Sadly, Tally wishes to make a profit from the art. She's the one who wants the money."

"What money?" Nick said. "What are you talking about, Stan. Please put the gun down. You, too, Alex."

Alex looked at Stan, who shook his head.

"Nick," I said, words racing out of my mouth. "When you were a child in Germany, your name was Glaumann, yes? Stan took care of you, but he went away and joined the SS. He murdered thousands of Jews and Romany and Catholics and—"

"She's crazy, Dad," Alex said.

"Am I, Alex?" I took a step forward. "Nick, did you realize most of these paintings were not legally obtained from the families of Holocaust victims?"

"Is *that* what this is all about?" He casually walked toward me. "Each has its own papers and provenance."

Penny felt my fear and growled. Stan aimed his gun, and I moved in front of her. I couldn't bear to have her shot. I didn't think he'd kill me, not yet.

"The papers are forged," I said. "All of them. These are the original pieces stolen by the Nazis. Not given back to the real owners."

"Hush, now," Stan said. "Or you die."

I rushed on. "The Gauguin belonged to Veda's father. The Nazis took it. When you were organizing the exhibit with Veda, she recognized the painting. That's why your brother tried to kill her, to silence her. You say the painting is yours, Nick? Who gave it to you?"

Nick pivoted. "Stanley? Brother?"

Stan shook his head. "I'll explain all. Later. All will be clear. You'll see that none of what she says is true."

"But that was our father's last name before you changed ours. Glaumann. I remember."

"You were young!" Stan said. "A child. You don't remember."

"I do," Nick said.

"Alex, tie her up," Stan said.

Alex snorted. "How the fuck am I supposed to do that with this gimp leg?"

"*Must* I do everything?" Stan said. His sigh was exaggerated as he slipped his hand into his pocket. He pulled out a metal tube and began screwing it to the barrel of the gun.

A moist silence darkened the room. All eyes watched Glaumann, and I knew what Stan would do. I glanced at Nick, whose face was a mask of confusion. Alex glowed with triumph, and thoughts ping-ponged around my head as to how to escape.

A soft knock at the door jerked me to life.

"Did you lock them?" Stan barked.

"No, I …," Nick said.

Stan waved the gun at me. "Into to the back room."

"No way," I said. "Not a chance." Maybe it was Milosh or Kranak or …

He aimed the gun at Penny's head. I leapt in front of her. Pain seared my thigh, but I was able to keep standing.

"The door!" Stan shouted at Alex.

But it was too late. The double doors swung open, and … Dear God. "Bertha?"

Stan's laugh ricocheted around the room. "This is rich!"

My foster aunt stood before the monster, her face folded in consternation. She wore her black coat and blue wool beret and sensible black shoes.

"Leave, Aunt Bertha! Get out."

She smiled. "What's going on, Tally?"

"Bertha, please."

"I can only leave sister for a little while now." She smiled at me again, and then she turned to Stanley Wirth. "Even after all these years, I recognized you, Herr Glaumann. Do you recognize me?"

"You? Of course not."

"*Ach*, this charming man raped me when I was ten. *Achtung!*"

Stan straightened, but couldn't keep the laughter from his voice. *"Ich würde dich jetzt nicht ficken, altes Weib."*

She shrugged as her smile widened. Her coat pocket exploded, and Stan blasted backwards into the gallery wall. His face rictused in shock, and he slid down to the floor, leaving a bloody trail on the white wall.

"Dein Verlust," Bertha said. *"Nazischwein."*

He blinked once, and then the life force faded from his blue eyes.

Alex raised his pistol, and Bertha shot him, too. He landed hard on the floor, moaning in pain.

"Not Nick, Aunt Bertha!" I screamed. "He wasn't involved."

She compressed her lips and nodded. "I know, *liebchen.* I know. Remember, I told you Papa taught us how to shoot. You should learn."

Chapter Thirty-seven

Two weeks later, I sat by Veda's bedside, Penny at my feet. We were home, at Veda and Bertha's house in Lincoln, Massachusetts, where they had lived forever. The large room, with an ancient Oriental carpet and mahogany four-poster, had a window seat on the south side. During the day, sun had streamed in from a cloudless blue sky. But now it was night. I'd closed the maroon tapestried drapes to keep in the warmth. I'd also lit a fire in the fireplace that had been built in the eighteenth century.

The clock read two A.M. I'd been asleep on the cot in the room. The fire had died to a soft glow, but the room remained warm.

My bandaged thigh and arm ached. The pain awakened me, and I reached for a Percoset. I changed my mind, and instead downed three ibuprofen with some warmish Diet Coke.

I sat up and listened. Penny snored beside me on the floor. Even so, I heard Veda's labored breaths. In ... wait ... then out.

Ten days earlier, we'd taken Veda out of the hospital and brought her home. Bertha was a hero, and the Suffolk County's district attorney had told me there would be no charges.

I could not bear to think that Veda would leave us soon. But I knew it to be true. Each minute that passed, she slipped further away from us. Per instructions, Bertha and I gave her morphine to ease her passing, and the hospice nurse slept downstairs, ready if we called.

I got up to see how she was doing. Bertha was asleep in the chair on the other side of the bed. I let her be.

I rubbed Veda's lips with a pink sponge "lollypop" dipped in cool water.

Her gray roots showed more than an inch beneath her black hair. Her sunken cheeks flapped as she breathed through her mouth.

She had said nothing for two days. The hospice nurse said she would be gone soon. She'd seen it many times.

I took Veda's hand in mine. No reaction. I pressed my cheek to her hand. "Love you, Vede."

My heart swelled. I saw her, twenty-some years earlier, when she'd met me in that hospital where I'd gone after my father was murdered. "You saved me, you know. Remember Pal, and what a sweet dog she was? She was the best gift ever."

Her eyes moved beneath her closed lids. Maybe she was hearing me.

"Remember the day we brought the trunk down from the attic? And how we got to giggling on the staircase? I was sure the trunk was going to go flying."

I lifted her, fluffed her pillow, and lay her down again. She was bones and heart and soul and not much else.

"Remember how Rand Brink broke up with me for that cheerleader? And when you dated that French chef and I found you and he in bed, and he ran out of the house bare-assed in embarrassment? Remember? And when I graduated from Cornell, how for the first time you suggested I start MGAP? You were so damned proud and excited and ..."

I rested my cheek on her hand and wept.

"I have so much to tell you. I don't know what to do about Kranak and Hank. Is it possible to love two men at the same time? I'm surprised they're both still speaking to me, but they are. They've grown distant, and I hate that. I've got to choose, but I don't know how. I could use your advice, Vede. I really could."

A knock and the door opened. The nurse stood there, hands folded.

"She's fine, Janie," I said.

"I heard noises. I thought maybe ..."

"No. I couldn't sleep. I thought I'd talk to her for a while."

The hospice nurse squeezed my shoulder. "Call me if you need me."

I nodded.

When I again looked down at Veda, Penny's head rested in her lap. Amazing, but Veda's hand lay on top of Penny's head. Had she put it there or had Penny slipped her head beneath the hand?

It didn't matter.

I began to talk again. I told Veda that evidence gathered by Fogarty got Ethridge canned from OCME.

"Fogarty's back, Vede. He's in charge, just as you wanted." Pain though he was, Ethridge was a thousand times worse. "Fogarty wants MGAP back, and Gert's going to run the program. She will do an amazing job."

I couldn't go back to The Grief Shop. Not ever.

I went to the bathroom and then resumed my vigil by Veda's side. I wanted to tell her Nick was overseeing the return of the Holocaust paintings to their rightful owners, and how Alex was in jail, charged by a grand jury with the murders of Marlene, Andrew, and Bella Marsh.

But I couldn't get the words out.

I looked at the wall across from Veda's bed. Bertha had hung the Gauguin of the girls by the seashore there.

"Milosh has been by. He sends you his love."

In ... pause ... out ... pause ... in.

After Milosh's visit to Veda, he'd disappeared back into the ether. He did promise to write. I wondered if he would.

"What am I going to do without you, Vede? I love you so much it hurts. No one else gets my lame jokes or remembers how I failed bio or how that silly rock singer I dated snorted when he laughed. God, I'm being selfish. I'm sorry. But I don't want you to leave."

She inhaled a rattled breath, and I held mine. Long seconds passed, and I waited. She finally exhaled. So did I.

"Now here's the corker," I said. "And I need your help with this. I have this great offer from Maine's chief medical examiner to begin a homicide grief assistance program up there. I'd told you about that. I was pumped, just about to say yes, when I got a call from New Mexico's chief. New Mexico's offer was even better. So now what do I do?

"I'll take Bertha with me or she can go live with your niece. It's really up to her. But where do I go? What do you think?"

She began to breathe through her mouth, great heaving breaths, and then the stillness for even longer seconds, and finally, the exhale.

The air became charged with a tension I couldn't explain. I'd swear I heard little Rose's voice saying *Wake your auntie. Wake her now.*

I walked around the bed, rubbed Bertha's shoulder and whispered in her ear. "Bertha? Auntie?"

She sprang to her feet. "Sister?"

I looked down into her soft grey eyes. "I think she's going now." The last word caught in my throat.

She pressed her finger to her pursed lips and listened.

In ... pause, pause ... out ... pause, pause ... in.

"*Ja*," she said. She took her sister's left hand in both of hers, and I walked around the bed and slid onto it. I cradled Veda in my arms.

Penny, front paw on the bed, nuzzled Veda's lap.

"We're here, Vede," I said. "We love you."

In ... pause, pause ... out.

Bertha smiled at her sister. "We've had a long road, my darling. You will see Mama and Papa and Purtzel. Kiss them for me, eh. I'll be along soon."

In ... pause, pause ... out ... pause, pause ... in.

"You changed my life, Veda. You gave it back to me." I rested my cheek on her head. "Love you, dear Mother. Love you so much."

Penny whined.

In ... pause, pause ... out ... pause....

VICKI STIEFEL

THE DEAD STONE

It starts with a mysterious phone call, summoning homicide counselor Tally Whyte back to the hometown she thought she'd left far behind her. Almost as soon as she arrives, Tally hears that a young woman she knew as a child has been found ritualistically murdered and mutilated.

The deeper Tally probes into the bizarre murder, the more chilling it becomes. Each glimpse into the killer's dark mind only unnerves Tally more. Despite frustrating secrets and silences, Tally suspects she's getting close to the truth, but perhaps she's getting too close for her own good. As each new body is found, Tally has to wonder…will she be next?

BODY PARTS
VICKI STIEFEL

They call it the Grief Shop. It's the Office of the Chief Medical Examiner for Massachusetts, and Tally Whyte is the director of its Grief Assistance Program. She lives with death every day, counseling families of homicide victims. But now death is striking close to home. In fact, the next death Tally deals with may be her own.

Boston is in the grip of a serial killer known as the Harvester, due to his fondness for keeping bloody souvenirs of his victims. But many of those victims are people that Tally knew, through her work or as friends. Tally realizes there's a connection, a link that only she can find. But she'd better find it fast. The Harvester is getting closer.

WHEN THE DEAD CRY OUT

HILARY BONNER

Twenty-seven years ago, Clara Marshall and her two young children simply disappeared. Her husband claimed that she was having an affair and had taken the kids and left him. *Everyone* seemed to suspect him of murder. But without a body or any hard evidence, he could never be formally charged....

But now that might change. Parts of an unidentified skeleton have been fished out of the sea, and Detective Inspector Karen Meadows believes this may finally be the break they need to reopen the cold case. Would justice be done at long last? Would there be enough evidence to prove the case? And where are the children?